D0975602

THE SHIBBOLETH

THE
SHIBBOLETH

BOOK TWO IN THE TWELVE-FINGERED BOY TRILOGY

JOHN
HORNOR
JACOBS

Carolrhoda LAB
MINNERPOLIS

Carolrhoda Lab™
An imprint of Carolrhoda Books
A division of Lerner Publishing Group, Inc.
241 First Avenue North
Minneapolis, MN 55401 U.S.A.

For reading levels and more information, look up this
title at www.lernerbooks.com

Main body text set in Janson Text Lt Std 11/15.
Typeface provided by Linotype AG.

Library of Congress Cataloging-in-Publication Data

Jacobs, John Hornor.
The Shibboleth / by John Hornor Jacobs.
pages   cm. — (The twelve-fingered boy trilogy)
Summary: As Shreve Cannon's ability to absorb the memories of others has
him teetering on the edge of insanity, he returns to the custody of the state of
Arkansas, this time in a mental institution, but he must collect himself and find
Jack, the Twelve-Fingered Boy, if he is to stop an unspeakable evil that is stirring
in Baltimore.
ISBN 978-0-7613-9008-4 (trade hard cover : alk. paper)
ISBN 978-1-4677-2405-0 (eBook)
[1. Psychiatric hospitals—Fiction. 2. Supernatural—Fiction. 3. Ability—Fiction.
4. Memory—Fiction. 5. Bullies—Fiction.] I. Title.
PZ7.J152427Shi 2014
[Fic]—dc23   2013009535

Manufactured in the United States of America
1 – BP – 12/31/13

FOR LISA, MY SISTER
WHO HAS YET TO READ ANY OF
MY NOVELS WHICH EXPLAINS
WHY SHE CONTINUES TO ACT LIKE
I'M NOT TOTALLY AWESOME

"We are all one consciousness
experiencing itself subjectively . . ."
—Bill Hicks

"I am large, I contain multitudes."
—Walt Whitman, "Song of Myself"

PART ONE:
THIEVERY

—into the brilliant sun-wrecked air and the parking lot between the cars of teachers and the older students, the world stinking of diesel and the fumes of buses where my moms waits in our smoldering station wagon, cigarette smoke curling around her perm and looking at me sadly, still in her uniform, name tag, and apron as coach williams places me like some block of wood or dumb inert thing in the backseat where it is warm and the vibrations of the car soothe me even though she's talking

—shit I can't be taking off work every time you got yourself a goddamned sniffle she says but her tone's not angry just tired and weary and bloodshot as her eyes

she leans into the backseat as she drives and touches my cheek, my forehead, with a terribly cold hand as I watch the trees pass overhead in the sliver of sky visible from where I lie and says my lord I could feel your fever before I even touched you, shree, turning back to the wheel and ashing her smoke out the cracked window

I can hear it, feel it, without even opening my burning eyelids when the car enters the holly pines trailer park and the sensation of pulling into our trailer hits home like a dropped piece of bologna slapping on the floor. I let myself spill out of the car and walk like an untethered balloon into the trailer and back to my room and onto the bed into darkness where I shiver and pass in and out of consciousness like some sort of ghost until her cold hands return, pulling off my shoes, tugging off my jeans, holding a cup of water to my mouth

—my sick little man she says, cold hand on my cheek, as she lies down, arm thrown wide over me and snuggling down into my comforter, closing her eyes, facing me, and I raise one trembling and hot feverish hand looking into her white face, lined with care and eroded by the tides of alcohol and place my palm on her cheek, feather-light. I stay still—so still—so she'll stay here with me, sleeping, sleeping and quiet, moms and her sick little man who'll never ever let her go, never let this moment end never let it—

• • •

Once upon a time Casimir was safe, part of an everyday rhythm to a song I knew by heart, every phrase familiar, every verse comforting. But that's all gone. The world spun into uncertainty.

Jack is with Quincrux now, and I'm stuck here, alone. Waiting. Wondering.

Watching for Riders.

• • •

The television displays thirty frames of video in a single second. Each image hits your eyes in a wave of light, incredibly fast, like breakers scraping at a rocky shore, and your brain cannot interpret the light as a still image before the next wave crashes on the beach and the next, giving you the illusion of motion. This is called the persistence of vision.

What Warden Kay Anderson is concerned with is just five frames. Just a fraction of a second, a part that your brain would barely even notice.

She turns in her chair and fiddles with the controls of the VCR on the pushcart. On the outside, there are HD TVs and this lopsided look like a water balloon warping in flight, and my mouth is open as if I was caught midsentence, saying something really stupid. Which I was.

"Oh, I love this one," she says and taps the screen with a long, lacquered fingernail. "I've asked the guys in AV to enhance this image so I can print it out and get it framed, but they say you can't do that. Enhancing images from television. That's only on TV shows."

"You probably can't take pictures of us for your own pleasure, either. That's kinda creepy, honestly. There's got to be some law against that. But I'm glad to see you're still *so* concerned about the welfare of us prisoners."

Without turning to look at me, Booth says, "Wards." For some reason, they don't like calling us "prisoners." No mention of "cells" or "lockup." Technically—because we're minors—we can't be prisoners. We are wards of the great state of Arkansas.

The warden looks like she's been stung by a bee. "Yes," she spits. "Not prisoners. Wards." She frowns and runs her tongue across her teeth, like she's trying to clean them of lipstick.

"Have you been sleeping?" Booth asks, apropos of nothing.

"What do you think?" she says and throws her bony hands into the air, exasperated.

"Folks aren't sleeping. It's happening." Booth isn't selling his words, though. He sounds washed-out and distracted. Like he's not getting any sleep, either.

"Um, I'm right here, guys. Prisoner, front and center!"

They ignore me.

"The wards in the D Wing are seriously getting restless. Up all night, howling at the ceiling. Spitting. Cursing." Warden

Anderson clears her throat uncomfortably. "Masturbating frequently. And publicly."

"Damn," I say.

Booth says, "Obviously, we're swamped here. Crime rate in juveniles is up a thousand percent in the last month, and the judges, because it's an election year, are taking the hard line." He shakes his head. "I've ordered all guards on watch with Tasers. Any incident of public masturbation will be dealt with extreme—"

"Creepiness?"

"Shut up, Shreve," Booth says, not even glancing at me. "With extreme prejudice."

The warden looks exhausted. But she sets her shoulders and straightens the jacket of her sharp-cut suit, remembering why she's in a room with Booth and me. "However delightful this part is," she gestures again at the screen, "it isn't what we're here to discuss, is it?"

We've done this before. Many times before. But she wants to go over it again. She lets the video play at full speed. I carom across the room headfirst into a tangle of desks with my arms crossed in front of my face.

Ox comes to lurk above me. One of the other punks says something, moves closer to the smaller kid.

To Jack. My roommate. My friend. My brother in all but name.

The warden's claw of a fingernail jabs forward and pauses the video.

"Here we are." She nudges the scene forward a frame. "Here it comes."

One of the punks steps forward, raising his arms. Jack moves, raising his own in response.

He puts out his hands, and even through the fuzziness of the security footage, you can make out that there are too many fingers for his hands.

His body goes rigid.

The warden nudges the video forward. "Here."

First frame, the boy approaching Jack begins to fly backward, and Ox teeters over me.

Second frame, Jack seems to compress. The punks are off the floor now, lifted right off their feet, and one of the kids who had been approaching Jack, his shoes sit on the ground. Knocked right out of his shoes.

"That."

Third frame, Ox is down and on top of me, and the desks are totally destroyed.

Fourth frame, the punks are vertical and windmilling arms and the desks behind them are beginning to move backward, but it's very blurry.

Fifth frame, the camera shows a blurry image of the wall, the camera knocked loose in its mounting.

Next frame? Static.

"Tell me again what happened here."

"Right here? Nothing happened here." I look around the office like I'm seeing it for the first time.

She puts her hand on the Taser at her waist.

I could pop in, look around and see if she was truly going to Tase me or if it's just a habit. I could go in, maybe tinker with some things, make her forget all this. Maybe make her not *want* to know what happened.

She jabs a button and stabs the remote at the TV screen like she's stabbing someone with a knife. The screen flickers, and she's back to where Jack's hands are up.

"Right *there*," she says. "Something happened. You were there."

"Knocked on my ass."

Booth says, "Language, boy."

"I didn't see nothing."

Booth's not looking at me; he's staring out the Admin window at the light streaming in, a slanted pillar teeming with dust particles like silt in a glass of river water. There's gray at his temples, lightening his Afro and creeping around the crown of his head. He has his big hands clasped in his lap, staring with this faraway look in his eyes like he can't be bothered with all the grit of administration, interrogation, and audio *slash* visual fun and games. He's gone beyond all that now. He can't be bothered to make his pencil-thin bristle into an angry caterpillar. He can't be bothered to press his slacks. He can't be bothered to wake up and assemble the parts that in total become Booth.

Warden Anderson snaps her fingers and glares at me. "Shreve, let me explain something. There are liars in this world. There are good liars. Liars like politicians and priests and murderers."

And wardens, I think.

She leans forward. "You are not a good liar. You're just a petty thief and candy dealer who got lucky once and was in the right place at the wrong time or the wrong place at the right time—"

"I wouldn't call it getting lucky. I spent a month in the hospital crapping in a bag." I peer at her bloodless face. The makeup and lipstick do the exact opposite of their intended

8

purpose. She's rapacious, all jagged bone and sinew held together by Revlon. Maybe she's not Warden Anderson at all. Maybe she's got Quincrux in her right now. Or worse. The Witch. Ilsa Moteff.

Crap.

It's like I always come to this place. They say that just because you're paranoid doesn't mean they're not out to get you.

I have to know.

Before I make my run at her, I look at Booth. He's still staring at the light pouring through the window. I wonder if he'll be able to sense what I'm about to do. Possessing someone has to cause ripples, at least.

I look at the warden, and she's looking back at me, beady eyes steady and dully reflective.

It's like this, but it's not *always* like this: You hold a snake in your hand, a tiny infant thing, wet and new. It squirms and writhes and wants to get free as if your hand is an egg. The snake is you; your body is the hand. And it thrashes and writhes and forces its snout into the crack of flesh, the space between fingers, and with a great wrench, it slips through. It's free. To fall. To find *another* cupped hand to enter.

I close my eyes. Somewhere, I hear a voice saying, "Shreve, you can shut your eyes, but you can't shut me out . . . Answer me! Tell me what happened—"

I can shut you out just fine, Warden Anderson. But can you shut me out?

No longer incarcerado, I find her and look at her defenses. I don't want to push her out and take over her body. I just want to get in. I just want to get in enough to rummage around in her closets, look in her medicine cabinet. Peek under the bed. And that, sometimes, is harder than just kicking in the front door and evicting the tenant.

I'm lucky. Getting in is easy. I'm in and there's a moment of dislocation as I look upon my body—feeling such anger at me—and I see how thin I've become. Back when I was dealing candy, I wasn't fat, but there was meat on those bones. Now I look like some emo rocker, rail-thin, with a shaggy mop of brown hair and a sneer. I really sneer like that? All the time?

No wonder adults are always so cranky.

In and down.

It can be a mansion of the mind; it can be a motel. Some people's noggins are like a photo album; some are like a movie. Some are like *being* in a movie. Others are like panning for gold. And some are like jumping into deep waters with fast currents. Warden Anderson's head is full of echoes. She's focused, so very focused on the present and the future that it brings her awareness to a point, like some fire-hardened stake, and the rest of her memory and consciousness is like a long hall filled with wraiths and ghosts and collapsed into a single dimension, as flat as a razor. There is no physical space in someone's head, but it's easier to think of it that way, even for me.

I race down hallways, if there were hallways. Back and back and down and through, and dammit, she was really considering using the Taser on me, and only Booth's presence stopped her. Farther back and down, past the recent memories and down into the basement where she keeps her older ones, there's a moment that's ringing like a bell, sending out a tone—a *frequency* I seem attuned to. I'm being washed with the vibrations and images and feelings. Not long ago and in this same office, a nice, bland man in a black hat and severe suit crosses his legs and sits delicately across the desk from her and says, "I'm from Health and Human Services and would like to interview—" He shifts and pulls some papers from his briefcase. Riffles the papers. "A Mr. Jack Graves, aged thirteen."

His sound, his scent—the *feel* of the man—is all over her. If I was incarcerado, I would shiver. His passage inside her rings, echoing, like the moments after a gigantic bell tolls, the air still vibrating. He got in her head. He came in and did exactly what I'm doing now.

She thinks about this incident more often than she'd like, and she can't remember why. It puzzles her. It's sent tendrils out into her awareness, this memory. It's such an invasion, what Quincrux and I do.

God help us, we're monsters.

I almost pull out of her then. But she *wanted* to Tase me. Like a fat kid wants a slice of chocolate cake.

I move on, back and back, running through her mind. She's done the usual evils—cheated on her husband, on her taxes, on tests. She shot a man who broke into her house, killing him, and instead of remorse, she felt a great joy at her accomplishment and bragged about it to her friends. She boxed in college and *oh* . . . here's something interesting, another woman she loved with all her heart. A fellow student. And they screwed like rabbits for a month until they fought, over money of all things, and Kay struck her lover in the face. And that's the image burned into Kay's memory of her Jill. They're in a bedroom somewhere in Chicago, and the sounds of the city hum and rattle and clank and honk through the open window while Jill, naked, sits heavily on the bed and stares wide-eyed at Kay. Jill's mouth is open, and her hand's at her cheek.

Kay knew in that moment that she'd destroyed something wonderful in a fit of rage. But she hardened and resolved to live with it. To *use* it. Just like that. With her knuckles still stinging from the blow—just seconds after—Kay's righteousness solidified in her at that moment, like a hand covered in Krazy Glue strangling a human heart.

I go beyond that, further into her history, when she was a girl and, strangely, she wasn't such a tremendous bitch. The time before the blow that sent Jill reeling, she was different. She was sweet and insecure and confused at her attraction to both men and women, and maybe that point when she struck Jill changed her life forever in a direction she never wanted to go.

There's one last ringing moment, and I enter it. It's bright like an overexposed photograph, fuzzy around the edges, and the light is hazy and she's on the beach, suffused with joy. Just a girl. Waves fall sluggishly on the shore and the sun is bright but not too hot and her father is holding her in his brown arms and tossing her *high* in the air, so high she feels like she's flying but not scared, not scared at all, because her father would *never* drop her. Never ever. She's laughing and giggling and he's throwing her high and that memory is so bright and full of love and pain and joy it's almost impossible to bear. He would be dead in months, her father. But she has this memory.

Something in me twists and suddenly her joy is mine and washing over me, and it feels so good, like cool water on a brutally hot day. Like the morphine drip they had me on in the hospital. I never want it to end, this memory of Warden Kay Anderson's. I want it to go on forever.

I live in it and have no awareness of time, because I could stay here until the world ends. Beyond the end of all things.

"What the hell are you doing?"

It's like being yanked out of a wonderful dream, or splashed with water. It's like being Tased.

Booth stands over me, furious. I glance at the warden, and her eyes are open; she's got the thousand-yard stare. Her hands twitch. Her lips are parted, mouth open, facial muscles slack.

He grabs my arm and yanks me up. My body is loose and uncoordinated, and I'm having a hard time getting it under control. There's part of me, a very important part of me, that still hasn't figured out where I am. And Booth is unimaginably strong, it seems. He sets me on my feet and roughly shoves me toward the door, but I manage to stop the movement and watch him.

He approaches the warden, checks her pulse. Then he rushes out of the room, knocking me to the side of the door with his passage. In a moment, he's back, holding a first-aid kit. He breaks the packet of smelling salts under her nose. She twitches, starts, and then shudders awake. She sits upright, blinks heavily. Glares about the room until her gaze settles on me. She looks as though her mouth has flooded with lemon juice.

"Get off me, Horace," she says to Booth, pushing him away. "I must've nodded off."

"I hardly think—"

"You're not paid to think," she says. "You're not good at it, anyway. But if you must know, I've been sleeping poorly, like everyone else in this damned country. The insomnia epidemic. So. I must've—" She looks at me, eyes narrowing. "I must've nodded off."

Something is different about her now. She looks . . . older? Meaner? She's all teeth and tits and gristle.

"You." She jabs a clawed finger at me. "Saturday privileges revoked until further notice. Computer privileges suspended." She looks at her desk calendar. "July tenth is the next family visitation day. If you have not spilled everything you know about the incidents on that video by then, you can tell your mother and brother not to bother showing up."

"Warden," Booth says. "I don't know if that's—"

She shifts her gaze to him and then runs her tongue over her teeth in an unconscious gesture. "Zip it," she says, very distinctly. He does.

"You are trouble, Shreve. You have always been trouble." Kicking her feet, she rolls her chair away from the TV and back to her desk. "Take this cart back to AV."

She straightens her papers on her desk as I unplug the cart and Booth helps me to move it into the hall. I can feel the pressure of her gaze on my back.

I push the cart into the hall and let the door swing shut behind me.

"What have you done?" Booth asks, his voice empty. It's beyond disappointed. It's almost as if he expected it.

What have I done?

I don't know.

Something horrible.

TWO

—flooding my mouth with saliva at the sight of mince pie with ice cream and mounds of peanut brittle——food covers the table while the Christmas tree flashes blue and white and red in circuits and patterns as momma pulls one beautifully wrapped present from beneath the tree and smiling hands it to me saying "only one present on Christmas Eve, honey" and I unwrap it with trembling hands and inside there's the dolly we saw at the five-and-dime, rosy-cheeked and unwinking, and I love her love her love her love love

daddy takes my hand and we go out into the hard-frozen night and look at the nativity, the baby Jesus nestled so snug in his cradle, the dead grass crackling under my feet and a familiar smell in the air and I can feel the rough texture of daddy's hand from planing boards all day at the mill but so gentle and kind and he looks up and I follow his gaze to the heavens and something soft and cold lands on my cheek and I realize it's snowing, fat snowflakes and then the air turns white in a million flakes like a storm of blessings in the mind of God and daddy whispers, "A white Christmas. O, lord, what majesty, a white Christmas," and holding me up in his arms and his breath on my face like peppermint and tobacco and I can only breathe and cry and wish this feeling could go on forever, forever and ever go on—

...

We pass through Administration, and the kid sits there next to a desk where a fat woman in a floral-print dress asks him questions in a soft, cloying voice. Her name is Mildred Clovis; she's fifty-three years old and loves the baby Jesus with all her heart. She's never left Arkansas in her whole life. She adores fried chicken and church and the two get kind of mixed up in her mind. She's never eaten a salad and thinks Muslims are devils placed on Earth to torment the living and execute Satan's evil plan to win human souls. She has a penchant for angel figurines. She weighs 215 pounds and stands five foot three. She has sex twice a year with her husband—once on his birthday and once on their anniversary. More would be ungodly. She fantasizes about chocolate when he's on top of her.

Today, she's very, very concerned with a particular boy's welfare; you can just hear it drip from her voice.

"Honey, you ever had the measles? No? TB?"

—oh lord this poor boy, Jesus save him—

He shakes his head but turns to watch Booth and me walk by. No expression touches his face. He just watches, implacably, holding his hands loosely in his lap, looking like a boxer resting in the corner of the ring.

He's older than me, but not by much, and he's got the lean and wary look of the abandoned. I don't even have to peep him to know that he's had a hard life, but I go in to peep him anyway. You can't ever be too sure that Quincrux, or the Witch, isn't staring out of those eyes.

It's like hitting a brick wall. There's no way in because something is already there.

A Rider.

...

As long as Booth is with me, I'm safe from the general pop.

I get a lot of hard stares walking through the Commons. Kids haven't been sleeping well, and that's made the general pop turn mean. Who knew not getting enough sleep would make kids so damned ornery? Couple of boys caught me at the pisser two days ago and decided to practice drumming. On my face.

All the crap that happened last year pissed off a lot of people. Ox and Fishkill got tickets to the Farm. Sloe-Eyed Norman got hurt beyond repair—he's now got a new tenant upstairs: the Witch. Police and feds came in and turned Casimir upside down.

No one has forgiven me for *not* getting in trouble. The TV called me a hero, and no one forgets that. Everyone here knows I'm not.

You can do anything in juvie, but the minute they think you're getting special treatment? You're meat.

We pass through security into B Wing, where I still live in the cell that Jack and I shared. They replaced the crumpled toilet at the taxpayer's expense but had maintenance unbend the mangle of my stool and bed, pulling the metal back into place. Everything wobbles a little.

Booth nods at the security guard,

—goddamn woman didn't even say thanks when I opened the—

who presses the appropriate button and the door to my cell swings open and we enter.

Booth doesn't dick around, hemming and hawing. "What in the Sam Hill was going on back there?" he asks. "What did you do to her?"

"Who says I did anything?" I used to deny everything on

17

principle, back when I was dealing the sweet stuff. Now I want to draw him out.

"Don't play titty-baby, Shreve. We both know you're so beyond that."

Never been a titty-baby. "And you? I wish you'd stop playing ignorant. You see the kid in Admin?"

"Yeah?" Booth's smooth face hitches, his eyes narrowing, lips drawing down into a line. "What about him?"

I sit at my wobbly stool and straighten the few comic books, sketch pads, and novels I have on my desk.

"You didn't notice?"

Booth gives me this dumbfounded look, mouth slightly open.

"Last year? Quincrux? The Witch? Oh, sorry, her name was Isla Moteff. Remember them?"

He shakes his head as if trying to clear it but pulls his hands in tight to his thighs in balled fists. Not a good sign.

"You remember them taking us in the yard? Quincrux took me and you. *He got inside!* You remember?" I'm surprised to find myself yelling, spit flying everywhere. "Remember? Huh? When the Witch took Jack? Remember that? You remember drooling and walking around like a zombie when he was *in you?*"

"I—" Booth is getting pissed. "What does this nonsense have to do with the boy in Admin?"

I look at Booth—really look at him—and consider *making* him understand. I did that once to Jack. I huffed and I puffed and blew down the doors of his mind and went inside and showed him what I needed him to see. Booth is strong. But I am stronger. I don't even need to have the contest to know that I could rip down his defenses and go on some crazy redecorating spree inside his noggin.

But I won't. Not that.

Except he has to look that in the face before he can even begin to understand the Riders.

I start again. "I don't know how to explain it, Booth. But you have to believe me. Quincrux and the Witch are . . . mind readers. Telepaths, maybe. But worse than that. They're demons. They can possess you."

"Shreve, you sound insane—"

"It's true. Think about it. Jesus Christ, Booth, a year ago you looked totally different. Look at you. Look!" I point to the dimpled mirror in the bathroom. "You use to give a shit about your appearance. Hell, you were sparkly."

His eyes crinkle, and he puts his hands on his hips. "No, I wasn't. That's a damn-fool thing to say, boy."

"Your hair was all slick and your nails were shiny like a woman's and for chrissake you used to tuck in your shirt, at least."

His hands involuntarily go to his waist, begin shoving his shirttail into his pants, stop.

"We've been through the same thing, you and me," I say, softer now. I try to make sure there's no sneer on my face, but crap, I can't ever be sure. It's like it lives there. "They got in our heads and possessed us. Made us do what they wanted. But when they do that, it leaves something behind. It's like it can infect you."

"This is all just crazy talk. No one can possess someone else like a demon—"

"I can." I say it loud enough to stop him. He'd been raising his hand to make his point, the soft pink of his palms contrasting with the deep brown of his skin. His hand remains there, tenuous, like some bird caught in flight, and his eyes widen as he looks at me not because I'm doing anything—I'm still firmly incarcerado—but because I'm going to and some part of him knows it.

I go in, not full strength, but enough to give his whole chassis a good rattle. He's got his defenses up, but I am to Booth as Quincrux is to me, a dragon dwarfing his little castle. I breathe fire and screech and crap in the moat before tearing at the wall, just to let him know I'm serious.

For an instant, I see the image of a fish swallowing a smaller fish swallowing a smaller fish, and I laugh.

He's got some defenses, Booth does.

—he's more than gristle, Ilsa. But no matter. Round one is over, Mr. Cannon. And round two will tell all—

Maybe Booth senses my moment of doubt—he's like me, right? Just not as strong—and he steps toward me where I stand in front of the door to the cell's bathroom. He's fast, despite the fact he's gone all slovenly. So it's there that we have the battle.

I blow out the windows of his mind, and he rocks back on his feet as if he's been hit by an invisible shock wave. I've knocked him totally senseless, so it's easy now to slip behind his eyes and start working the levers and walk his body past mine, into the bathroom, and to the mirror.

His face is wearing *my* sneer when it says, "I can do this to you. You can do this to others. But Quincrux is still out there. And worse. The Riders. They're coming here."

Booth has sprung a leak. Blood pours from his nose in great gouts, discoloring his once-thin mustache.

He recovers quickly, and he pushes my mind out, hard.

Before I know what's going on, before I've recovered from that moment of dislocation that comes with being put back in the box everyone comes shipped in, Booth has me by the neck in one big hand. The other's moving too fast to see until it comes to a dramatic stop in my stomach and I fall to my knees. All I can do is gape in wonder at the stars zigzagging at the edges of my vision and work my mouth open and shut to try to say something. But of course, I can't because sound needs air to vibrate through to be heard and Booth took all the air in the world with him after he punched me in the gut, turned on his heel, and left my cell.

And I didn't even get to tell him about the Rider.

···

It's night, after lights-out, and Kenny in 16 is screaming again in his cell, crying and screaming, and the rest of the wards begin hollering too, moaning. No one sleeps in Casimir anymore. No one closes his eyes. There's just the watchful, sleeplessness night after night.

They're pumping our food full of saltpeter now, but the boys still masturbate furiously in the dark, and occasionally you'll hear a cellmate yell, "Souza's rubbing one out, *again!*" and then a rough, desperate laughter followed by more howling. Screaming. Gibbering.

There is no sleep. No rest. Not for the wicked.

THREE

I miss Jack. There's no getting around it. I miss Vig and Coco and freedom, but I miss Jack.

Especially times like now, morning, when the cell doors swing open and the cry and clatter of a thousand delinquents rises to fill these gray cinder-block walls and the whole world stinks of Pine-Sol and mold and cheap laundry soap, the heavy breath of a penitentiary.

Sometimes I feel like my head is too full, my heart too empty. I have no one to watch for. And this terrible gift has given me knowledge of things that no kid from the trailer park perched on the big piney woods should ever know. It's a burden I used to share.

...

In general pop, we assemble for mail call. There's a new bull today, one I've never seen before. He shuffles through a stack of letters, calling out names. *Brendan, Buxton, Cacciatori*, and then, surprisingly, *Cannon*.

A letter.

I snatch the proffered envelope and dash to the table nearest the wall. Its return address is in Washington, DC.

Shreve,

Sorry I haven't written you more often. There's been a ███████ so we've been busy. It's kinda weird here. We go to class in the morning, but we're taught by what they call "employees" and there are ██████████ all over the place. I don't feel totally safe just because the "employees" don't truly seem to care if we learn or not. We're tested regularly, but it's never about the school assignments. They're more ████████. The food is okay and some of the other kids are great — I gotta tell you something. I've got a girlfriend! She's so incredible, but I don't want to say too much because I think they're reading my letters to you. But yeah, man. A GIRLFRIEND.

In the last year, I've grown a lot! I bet I'm a foot taller than you now. For a while, at night, I couldn't sleep either (they say there's some sort of insomnia problem out there now, but we don't get much news here—they *say it's because it's like camp). The nurse said it was because my legs were always aching and finally she gave me my own bottle of ibuprofen. "Here, kid, don't take 'em all at once or you'll never wake up." Said it was growing pains.*

Anyway, I wish you were here too. I train every afternoon using my ███████████████████ ██████ ███████████████ *and that is hard and I don't seem to be getting any better. Occasionally kids don't do well here and they "wash out" and disappear from the general pop, stuff gone from their dorm rooms in the middle of the night and I'm scared that I might wash out. I need you to come coach me. I always got better* ████████████ *when you worked with me on it.*

How's all the folks at Casimir? Still buying candy? I can't say I miss the place, wasn't there long enough. But I never was anywhere long enough to call it home. And that's why I really need you to come. This place is becoming home to me and I want you to share it. (And I don't want to WASH OUT!)

Mr. Quincrux—they call him the director here—told me to give you this number. All you have to do is call and someone will extract you from Casimir. I don't know why all this spy stuff is necessary except that he said there are other "interested parties" and they are watching you. "So we must be circumspect," he said. What's circumspect? There's not a dictionary in this whole freakin' place and only employees have computer privileges.

Anyway, please call the number. You'll love it here.

Your friend,

Jack

This is the third letter he's sent asking me to come. I want to, I do. But something inside me balks at the idea of living all cozy and comfy with Quincrux. The man is a murderer and a monster and made me into this. I would rather kill them and die myself than join them. And Jack always mentions other "interested parties," but I can't sense them watching.

Except for the Rider. The new Rider in the general pop.

■■■

The bull in Commons looks tired—insomnia, likely—when I ask him why Booth isn't on duty.

"Called in sick."

"Sick? Booth has never called in sick."

He turns a yellow eye toward me and hitches a finger in his belt, near the pepper spray and the Taser. "Hell do you care, kid?" He looks me over

—freakin' smart-ass punk kid needs a foot in his ass—

and turns back to scanning the boys in general pop, who're making a thunderous noise moving toward the cafeteria and the classrooms.

I think about his question. *Why the hell* do *I care?* This asswipe is new and hasn't even learned our names, not to mention learned that playing the dozens with me is a losing proposition. I sniff. "Just used to seeing bulls around here, instead of steers."

Takes a while for it to sink in, but eventually, the word *steer* percolates down through the muddy water of his awareness. When the realization hits bottom . . .

—oh no he did not just say what I think he—

he snaps me up in his big meaty paws—bounces me like a red rubber dodge ball against the wall, and when I hit the ground, he easily wrenches my arms behind my back. Then he places his shiny, black, patented-leather shoe in the small of my back. Not hard, not vicious, simply officious and firm. I should just blow out the candles in this guy's head, go in and start pulling his strings. But my face is turned toward the boys passing through the Commons like cattle in a chute and they're so damned happy at my predicament. Laughing now, giving this bull—and I have to admit now that he *is* a bull—smiles and salutes. Except one.

The kid in Admin. The one with rangy arms who never

had tuberculosis.

The boy with the Rider.

He watches me half in disgust and half in fascination. He's got his orange jumpsuit unzipped and the arms of it tied around his waist—an old campaigner, an old-school resident of other juvie halls in other days. He's got that mean streak written all over him, bred in the bone, heavy scars on his knuckles and his ears already flowering. He's a bruiser, born to violence. And savage.

He stands there, watching me with a curl to his lip, and it's either a sneer or a rictus of fear, some abject animal misery. Maybe he knows more about me than I'd like him knowing. Instead of toying with the bull's mind, I blink and make another assault on the Rider. I go at him. I harden. I sharpen myself like a toothbrush whittled down to a shiv, the fire of my outrage at having this asswipe's foot on my back but not at the asswipe himself, *at the audience*, the hundreds of smiles and laughs at me

—oh he gots the narc's ass pinned!—

—cut off his damned hands, the thief—

—trick ass little bitch gonna get stomped by that bull! hells yeah—

being flopped belly-down on the Commons tiles by this bastard of a guard. For an instant, in my rage, I feel this pressure at the back of my head, like some ball of incandescent fire, pulsing, threatening to overthrow all reason and escape, to run rampant in the minds of all these foul-mouthed children like a forest fire leaping from treetop to treetop—these poor hateful boys, sneering and dismissive, but boys all the same, despite their do-rags and their muscles and scars—boys one and all. I couldn't make them jump and march about like Quincrux, but I could burn up their minds in an instant if I let myself.

But the Rider is there. And instead of blowing out this multitude of candles, I focus everything down to that single piercing point and make the hard run at his mind.

It's worse than running at a cinder-block wall. His mind is impervious, and whatever the amount of scratching and scrambling, I find no purchase on its hard, smooth surface. But he smiles a little, either the Rider or the boy, I can't tell.

The boy blinks, looks about the Commons as if discovering himself, turns, and joins the rest of the boys heading to the cafeteria and class. The guard grinds his foot on my back enough to let me know my place before he grabs my wrists and yanks me up, nearly popping my arms from the sockets.

"A little lesson for you. Keep that goddamned tongue civil, boy, or next time you'll have a little surprise."

"Taking the Lord's name in vain? That's—"

He rolls his eyes and places his hand on my chest.

I stop. Maybe I went a tad too far.

He cranes his head to look at the faded numbers on my coverall.

"Okay, ward number three thousand, four hundred and ninety-eight. You get what you want. You have my full attention." He takes out a small notebook from his back pocket and the well-chewed nub of a pencil and writes something down. I can only assume it is my serial. "Go on, you're free to run your mouth. Go ahead."

That doesn't sound so good now, come to think of it.

I take a step back, until his hand leaves my chest. I'm raw from the run at the boy and his Rider, the constant hate-spawned

—this kid doesn't know who he's dealing with as god as my witness

28

i will go nuclear on his sorry ass and not give one damn he was on tv. i'll go pure frankenstein—

thoughts I'm constantly receiving now. They say the center cannot hold. I'd say it's totally crumbled and lying in ruin around us.

I'm scared. I'm tired. There's just so much hate and bad intentions behind people's eyes, and it's like a radioactive leak, the constant chattering noise of their minds. I turn as slow as possible, with my mouth shut, and walk to class.

—it's not just the grass and the wide expanse of field or the lights and the crowd roaring or the faces of the opposing team looking at me; it's not the way the air smells or the heat making my jersey dampen with sweat and my shoulder pads slip some with each footfall; the breathless air full of noise and the clatter and ooofs of linemen crashing together; not the way the pigskin smacks into my palm with such authority and tucks tight like some precious infant waiting to be born on the finish line or how the opposition falls away with each stride; no none of that at all. it's that he's watching and i'm putting all of their defenses behind me, i'm boundless and wild and leaping, trailing players like a comet dragging a rocky tail through the vast emptiness of the end field——he is watching, father——and will be proud and will love me and realize that I do it all for him and we can reset all the past and he'll love me again and it will never end, never hit me again, he'll love me—

■■■

I kinda bypass classes at this point. It's weird—I'm expected to attend, but I've tested out of everything, English, math, algebra, trig. Humanity is my classroom now, and I have a desk, front row, center.

Eventually the people that you inhabit, they inhabit you. I have their memories, and maybe they have some of mine. And with that comes knowledge. Of quadratic equations, network routers, tantric sex positions, the novels of Dickens and the poetry of John Donne, the pathology of lymphoma, and the intricacies of love, which no one really understands. But I've bedded women (and men) and been to college fifteen times. I've killed everything that's walked the earth, fought in Afghanistan, in Vietnam, in Korea. It's a terrible weight, the murders, and at night, when I'm lulled into the pillow, it all comes back in a bilious rush. The edges get blurred, and the memories of flesh fuse into one being.

I have bad dreams, and I don't even know whose they are. They could be anyone's. I'm just sixteen but have lived whole lives in other people's heads. But I still must sit in class and listen to Mr. Allenby

—so live that when thy summons comes to pass that innumerable caravan—

lecture on the three-point enumeration. Say what you're gonna say, say it in three points, and say what you said. Big fun.

He drones on, and I watch the kids and think about the video. There's thirty frames a second, every second. And it was right there, in front of me, that Ox gave me the beatdown and Jack did his thing.

■■■

I reach out, lightly touching the flames of the other students' minds, burning bright, each at a desk. It's like running imaginary fingers through a candle flame. It's better when they aren't considering me. Their minds are calm and less full of hate. Then I go a little beyond, in the next classroom and the next until I'm out and high above the plane of earth, soaring disembodied over the land and heading east, looking for one particular brightness on the face of the moving waters and mountains and flowing field. And there's a pull from the east, like a personal gravity that tugs at the invisible connective tissues that run from me to every other living, breathing creature.

I could unlatch the parking brake and just roll on, toward the eastern seaboard and to my end.

My doom.

It would be easy. Because I'd end up in Maryland, where the Riders come from. It would be a release, falling into that well.

When the class ends, it takes me a little while to get back fully incarcerado. I sit there until everyone is gone

—the skinny freak-show thief can only stare and drool but we'll show him—

and make my body rise. It's the first movements after going in the great blue yonder that remind you who and where you are. I grab my notebook, stand, nod at Mr. Allenby—George—who, it turns out, is a good guy, forty-two, popular with the ladies in high school, minor football star in college but discovered he enjoyed the rigors of composition far more than the gridiron; who ran some touchdowns because he was fast and dogged and feared his father, who'd beat him with a razor strop, hard, but never enough to injure him beyond bruises. Strange, the controlled, measured beatings, delivered with a steady hand by a blank-faced man who'd always utter, "This will hurt me more than it hurts you," a bit of reasoning George had heard in television and movies but never expected to appear in the story that was his life. No, it was the fear George's father wielded, not pain from the strop's impact on his innocent flesh. The fear in so many ways was worse.

I know George. I know him.

Into the hall, there are no other wards around, except for a couple of titty-babies trying to cozen Mr. Mailer

—grieving still for mother, grieving forever at her loss—

into giving them better grades on their algebra quiz or to make a recommendation to the state shrink that they're model wards of the state and ready to regain their place among the un-suspecting public.

I hang back to let the boys vacate the classroom before I leave. It's easier when they're not swarming. Fewer covert punches to my back, fewer shoves. Fewer murderous thoughts like ringing bells sounding in the hollows of my mind.

In the hall. Like a statue. The boy with the Rider stands waiting, like he knew I was coming.

"Boy," he says in a hoarse voice.

Don't know how to respond to that. He says it like he's my grandfather or something.

"I'm not your *boy*."

He raises his hand in a strange gesture, like he's a priest giving a benediction. Then a confused expression passes over his features, like he's had some hard thought or bad memory.

"Boy," he says, almost croaking. "Leave." He takes two steps forward, bringing his body very close. "The elder will awaken. You must—"

"The elder?"

"*Leave.*"

"I don't get wha—"

"*Be ready. Be prepared. You must leave!*"

Something sparks there, in his expression, and the distance it seems to travel is terrifying.

A long pause while he gives me the stink-eye.

I say, "That's what I was trying to do, man. And you were blocking the way." I try to slide past him, but he sidesteps and stands in front of me again.

Screw this noise. I start to turn when his arm reaches out and plants one right on my ear, a real ringer of a knock, and I can't tell if it was with a fist or openhanded because my head's vibrating like a bell and my ear feels like it's on fire.

With the pain, instincts whirl my body around to meet the larger boy, and my fists go up, not in some boxer's pose. That is all too graceful for me, head ringing. I bring my fists up just to get something between him and me.

Lower and slower, he says, "Leave, boy. There's nothing for you here now. You must *leave!*"

"Damn it, stop calling me boy." I do stupid things sometimes. I fight. I fight what's inevitable.

I throw a punch.

And it lands. The boy's head rocks back, his mouth pops open. When he brings his head back forward, he blinks a few times in quick succession like he's waking up. He raises his hand to his nose to wipe the blood welling from nostrils and dripping over his lip and patting on his white T-shirt.

I drop my hands in surprise.

"What the—" he says, staring at me hard. "Why the hell'd you do that, slim?" He glances around the hallway as if he's surprised to be there. "What the hell?"

His voice is different. Higher, more vibrant, more . . . *present.* But smooth and mellow, like he's from some southern Louisiana parish swarming with mosquitoes, stinking of blood and barbeque.

He doesn't waste much time breaking me down into

component parts, a big knobby fist whipping into my left side, and—*again*—the air whooshing out of me while his other paw clips me on the jaw as I'm falling, sending the world tilting out of control. The lime-green tile flooring rushes up and smacks me in the face.

"Punk," he says, wiping at his nose with his bare hand and leaving long red streaks up his forearm. "Why the hell'd you—" He stops, probably coming to the same conclusion I'm reaching

—people are seriously messed up—

and because of his Rider, I know that's my thought and not his. The Rider's lurking there, like some bouncer at a club, just waiting for me to try to get past the velvet rope.

Yeah, people are seriously messed up.

He looks about, scanning for witnesses, and then, with one more scowling look, skulks off toward the Commons.

###

When I can get up, I follow the boy down the hall and into the Commons, where there's a constant, roiling commotion, the boys hooting, hollering, slap-fighting, singing, rapping, cursing, preening, posturing. Some look at me, recognize my distress, and smile. There's a maelstrom of noise in the air and in the dim ether that I'm so attuned to, the mental frequencies. And in some ways, it's easier in the Commons. There are so many thoughts flying about, I can't focus on any single one.

In the bathroom, I run in to two titty-babies, talking in hushed voices

—him the snitch, the narc, oh shit be quiet jorge don't say anything and just walk out—

but they shut up when I enter and watch me with large, wary eyes. They scuttle out like cockroaches when I go to the mirror and inspect my face.

My cheek's swelling pretty good. I hope his nose is broken.

Nothing for it except to go to the infirmary.

Out of the bathroom, through the Commons, where the voices quiet as I pass, and I can feel their gazes on

—little bastard thieving sonofa—

—looks like someone gave him what he deserved for—

—new fish ain't no fish judging by the narc's face, fugly motherfu—

my back, as unwelcome as I am among them now, friendless, alone. But I'll be damned if I bow to them, look scared or hunch my shoulders. They can hate me, but I can bear it and not let the pain show.

—over there over there over there get him—

—aw shit darrel—

Someone yells, "Narc!" and I turn in time to see a boy's body twist sideways in the air, hurtling toward me, elbows tucked tight in some imitation of a wrestling move. He smacks into my chest, his shoulder and elbow hitting sore ribs, and I pitch backward, but there's something—*someone*—there behind my knees, kneeling, and I fall backward with my arms out. Falling, *falling* until my head meets the floor with a *crack* and the world flashes white then black and red, and I'm being cocooned by the howls of laughter and debris being tossed on me, bits of trash, wrappers, empty water bottles. Someone spits, and I feel it warm on my skin, on my neck, my nose, my face. Tracers push into the edges of my vision, but I'm not losing consciousness, just blinking rapidly and thinking, *I've had worse.* The Dubrovniks rearranging my guts, the memories of poor Elissa, who bore the torture of years in a pit—part of her I carry with me always and will never be free of—and the trials and invasion of Quincrux into my mind. My mother, her anger and grief and spite and neglect. My brother, Vig, lost to me.

—This is just physical pain and cannot touch me, inside. Inside I am impenetrable and—

"What's this?" The boys around me scatter, dissipate like smoke. It's my buddy, the new bull. The thick one, the steer.

He looks down at me, prone on the floor in outraged pain and silence, and smiles. "Ah, ward three thousand, four hundred and ninety-eight. Shreve Cannon, also known as 'the Narc,' 'Moleman,' 'Hollywood,' and 'Candyass.'"

Since it's obvious he's not there to assist, I lever myself off the tiles and stand upright, swaying, panting into the close air of the Commons as the hushed crowd of boys watch. I feel something warm on my back, and my hand comes away bloody when I touch the back of my skull. Split scalp, maybe fractured rib, possible concussion. I remember the mechanics of diagnosis like a dream, someone else's memories, someone else's pains and woes. *Dr. Stevens.* From North Carolina. I was him; he was me.

"Read my file, did you?" I say, but my voice doesn't sound right and I'm swaying more and then a great wave of dizziness washes over me and I sit back down, hard, my legs crumpling underneath me to keep me from falling over.

The raw cacophony of mental noise pulsing in the air, and

—oh no this little shit might really be hurt last thing i need is hours of paperwork but i wouldn't piss on this piece of crap if he was on fire—

—messed him up, man, messed him up good—

—badass darrel's the man, damn, that was sweet taking that thief out—

—should put two in his head, goddamn I'd do it, just walk right up and blam blam and watch him fall—

the images of me—*me!*—being wounded, killed, destroyed, stabbed by this maddened and intense crowd of kids, it's

—thief—

—thieving piece of—

—trick-ass bitch ho—

—THIEF! THIEF!—

I feel like a car-struck dog hiding under a porch. No more. I teeter, pitch over, and the world turns to black.

FIVE

—like all the world is new, shy, and coy, a doctor and his nurse between the dispensary and he stops in the hall as if we never kissed that night after the movie and spent that glorious moment, holding me, me holding him, exploring his body with my hands and he mine, he takes me away from that little hospital, holding my hand walking to his car, opens the door for me and when i slide over next to him he pulls me in tight and kisses me, tasting of listerine and the cigarette he had on break and the fecund bitterness of coffee, opaline and somewhat dank, but i couldn't care less because his hands are sweet and he starts his plymouth with a roar, wagging his eyebrows at me in an exaggerated caricature of haste——lust——and to his house even though the radio interrupts the beatles "love me do" by blaring the news about korea and the battle at osan. But the world outside the car, the lobby, his kitchen, his bedroom doesn't exist anymore despite whatever may come later because he's a doctor and i'm just a nurse and there's no balance there. and afterward, staring at the ceiling, smoking like in the movies and ashing into the tray he perches on his belly, it's too warm and too sticky, both our bodies covered in sweat, so we wander about his house, naked as babes, both unrepentant and scandalized by our own nudity. finally we settle on the couch and when we're spent, he turns on the television, a big one, we watch the news and dean martin's variety show and then the midnight movie, dracula, the old one with the frog-featured romanian in formal wear, so dramatic, and he's got his arms around me, slipping into a light slumber, exhausted from our earlier vigors, while the overdressed vampire rises from his stagecraft coffin, moving eerily through the play-act castle to proclaim, "listen to them! the children of the night" in a great bit of cinema histrionics but it's not the movie or the day or the frisson of our sex or the sheen of sweat or the scent of his breath it's just that burning circle of his arms holding me tight and for that one moment i know i'm worthy of love and able to give it in return something i feared had been burnt to a cinder within me. no, it sparks and kindles and i never want the sensation to end, never end the circle never broken stay like this forev—

...

Ceiling tiles and fluorescent lights passing above me, through swinging doors and down hallways

—remember what she did to you, Jack! Remember what she did!—

in the bull's big rough arms. He smells of sweat and the gym and gun oil and for a second I'm reminded of Booth, when he hugged me and told me not to get in trouble, so long ago. Everything is lost now, everything is gone, the lights, the stink of disinfectant on the dull Casimir tiles, everything, just this loathed swaying motion of the bull's body as he carries me down the hall where once Jack and I fled from Quincrux and the Witch.

In the infirmary, he makes me stand, and I can manage it long enough for Mrs. Cheeves to toddle around her desk, a startled expression chasing one of worry across her face until

—oh, this one. the taker. back again and again and someday it'll be with a broken neck and who would blame the boys? after what he did last year, what he does at night, stealing—

she looks somewhat frightened, as if dealing with a small, personal apocalypse. A realization. She's puzzled by her thoughts. And the word *stealing stealing stealing* echoes in her mind as she looks at me and wonders what I have stolen even though she knows with absolute certainty that I am a thief. I have taken something from her. Eventually she shrugs and her face solidifies.

"Put him there," she says, pointing at a bed in the small ward at the back of the infirmary. The bull puts me on the bed, and the nurse peels back my eyelids, shining a penlight into each. When the light migrates back and forth, she stands and retrieves cotton swabs, rubbing alcohol. A vial of something and a needle.

The bull says, "This one's got a mouth on him."

"I know. We're old acquaintances. He turns up in here every couple of weeks. Black eye, broken nose. Seems he's not very popular, despite his little brush with celebrity."

I want to say something barbed and witty, but she jabs at me with the needle and pumps my arm full of something, something full of sleep and the absence of pain. And I hope, forgetfulness.

"You putting him under? He might be concussed."

"No," she says, looking at me with a frown. "His eyes are responding and the rest of his vitals are fine and, honestly, I don't want to hear him squawk when I sew up his scalp." The frown disappears and her face calcifies into indifference now, just as much a sham as her medical professionalism. "Rotten right through, this one. A thief."

Everything's blurry, but I can still see her lips purse, slack flesh working around her dentures. Oh, she really dislikes me.

The bull says, "I read his public file. Remanded to Casimir for auto theft."

"More than that."

"More than what?"

"Stealing a car. This little—" She pauses. Thinks a moment. "Word on the ward is that no one trusts him, and he takes for his own whatever isn't bolted to the floor." If everything wasn't like molasses, I'd snort at that one.

The bull says, "They toss his cell?"

She nods. "Booth does, regularly. Never finds anything. They think he has a cache, somewhere on grounds. He used to deal candy—he's got to have a few stashes around the building."

One in the yard, the foundation stone. One at the back of the gym locker. One in Allenby's classroom, in the air duct behind the periodical case. All are empty. I haven't stashed anything in over a year. I try to muster some feeling of outrage, but I can't.

The bull looks at me, eyes narrowed. He's all puffed full of protein and arrogance, and I'd take a run at his noggin if I wasn't so sleepy. I don't even know his name.

"He's slight as a bird, though," Mrs. Cheeves says as she rolls my body over to get at the back of my head.

I close my eyes.

■■■

I wake from a dream of smoke and war and the wreckage of men from a time before I was born. Not all bad, but blood-spiked and desperate with the fear of death. We were brought in by the Hueys to Kham Duc to relieve the special forces encamped there as the Viet Cong pushed a full regiment toward us. Millar took one in the gut, and his intestines pooled in the open cavity of his body as he called for his mother in a voice terrible and sad and urgent, eyes wide as he pawed at my chest and gave one last heave before his body grew still.

A blue torrent of moonlight spills into the infirmary from the barred, high windows like water from a busted pipe cascading upon the floor and casting the whole ward in a cyan-colored benthic haze. Late and quiet and I can't sense Mrs. Cheeves anywhere about.

I rise.

Shrouded in darkness, it's easier. Without a body, I can't see my reflection in glass, and that's a blessing. I look back at my carcass, lying there, disheveled and gray and lifeless. I move like a specter through the old beast of a building. I pass out of the room, into wild blue yonder, through the door, and into the hall and down to the Commons and its guard station where the bull whose name I don't know sits, feet kicked up on the desk and rows of video monitors pulsing with monochromatic light, reading a copy of *Men's Fitness* and the recent issue of *Ducks Unlimited Magazine*. He sees me approach and half rises, his hand going to his waist and the Taser there, but then he shakes his head as if he's been drugged and turns back to his magazines. He looks up for only a moment but doesn't flinch when I invade his mind.

■■■

—now that I have your attention, Mr. Schneider, I would ask to say a few words and you won't be able to recall them, not immediately, for they will live under the surface of your awareness until you are with their proper audience. Merely stones at the bottom of the stream of your consciousness, if you'll permit me a moment of indulgence into metaphor.

No, do not struggle, I shall not hurt you.

My name is Hiram Quincrux, and I am now speaking to Shreveport Justice Cannon, inmate three thousand, four hundred and ninety-eight and ward of the Casimir Pulaski Juvenile Detention Center for Boys.

The recalcitrant boy, I've come to think of you. Names are important.

Mr. Cannon, by now you've expanded enough to test the limits of the cage in which I—and the very pliant state of Arkansas—have placed you. I imagine that there's a large possibility that you've discovered some of the pleasures available to men of our stripe, and now you might be learning some of the dangers of an unguided person of extranatural ability.

For example, you cannot speak in any meaningful way about your abilities, can you? Not due to some mental block, but due to your overwhelming isolation, true?

No, I do not even need to be with you to know your answer. There are certain shibboleths to our condition—

I'm shocked, and that's not easy.

Out. Out of the bull, disembodied, looking down at him, his body now a loose, ungainly collection of bones and muscles. His expression is vacant, abject, absent. Quincrux has infested this man with his memory. The bull—his name is Alex Schneider—is just a letter, a message, a package wrapped in a uniform and addressed to me.

And when I hear the word *shibboleth*, something shifts in me, a sudden understanding uncurling. Shibboleth.

I know what the word means in a way deeper and rawer and more penetrating than how he just tossed it off. It has such weight in his mind, I can tell by the trill in his voice, how his mouth moves around the word, even in the bull's secondhand memory. It's what we share, this thing, the shibboleth, between him and me beyond that, between me and the rest of mankind—the common utterance, the universality of mankind's thoughts.

This ability I have is the shibboleth.

The bull—Mr. Alex Schneider—stirs, opens his eyes long enough to see me standing here, above him, in my phantom disembodied form—my shibboleth form—and I go back in to finish reliving the memory of Quincrux. His message for me.

a certain gravity that draws us to others of the same ability. That you are not gibbering madly in an asylum, frankly, astonishes me. And piques my interest again in you . . .

And so.

And so that is why I have come to you again to say that we would have you here with us. Jack would have you here with us. There are events and forces moving in the world that will soon become evident, and we need all of the strength we can muster to harness these events to our advantage.

You venture forth at night into the void. I do not need to be told this; I have felt your passing, sensed you moving upon the etheric heights toward your friends, your family. Searching for us. For Jack.

Things happen in patterns, child. The patterns reveal us.

You won't find us. I'm old, Shreve, and have remained concealed for more years than you can imagine.

And because we share this . . . the shibboleth . . . you know what I hide from. The impenetrables. The entity. Whatever lies there slumbering in Maryland. It becomes more active. The sleeper stirs and the impenetrables are moving, and I will not allow you to fall into their hands because I do not know their purpose and cannot risk them collecting you.

You must make a choice now. Come to us, or we will take you. I cannot have you out there as a loose cannon, if you'll pardon the pun. I will give you a very short time to decide.

All right, Mr. Schneider. I will release you now. You will remember nothing of this conversation . . .

In and down I go, into Schneider's brainmeat, into his unconscious, like some psychic cliff diver in a Speedo.

I'm drawn to one bright memory, pinging like sonar from one of the old movies, *bing, bing, bing.* I dive and snatch it up, not so much swallowing it—*but I am*—as immersing myself in it and there's this flash of white light and—

—squalling again, the little brat, snot flying and bellowing from his crib. mom doesn't even stir her fat ass from the sofa and dad is gone, again, again, and again, as always. the brat's really getting the volume up into eardrum-piercing registers, so I put down the controller to the nintendo, stand, and walk to the crib, where he's looking at me and bawling, hands on the bars, like a cellmate in the pen, mouth wide in an O, howling now, his cheeks streaming with tears and his face crusty with snot and I look over at mom but she's blubbering, a box of wine perched on the couch end table.

"come on, buddy, shut the fuck up——" it's all I manage in the blast of noise coming from his mouth. It hurts my ears.

i just wish he'd shut up. be quiet. be silent.

standing in front of him, his mouth is like a foghorn blasting me, and I wince and don't even think when I grab the curtains behind him and wrap his head in the fabric, to shut him up, the little punk, and hold him like that until he quiets. he stills in his crib.

he is quiet.

he is still and mom never even stirs.

but i'm not quiet, i'm not still, there's this rushing feeling throughout my body as the knowledge seeps into me and it feels so good and I unwrap his head from where he lies, blue-lipped and faceup. it surges through me, the power. i feel dirty and strong and terrifying and powerful and electric all at once and the silence is clear and I want the silence to go on forever like that, never interrupted. i gave it to him, the silence. and now it will never be broken—

It's like blood, the memory, blood from a broken nose flooding the back of my throat, repellent and delicious. Taking it into myself is like drinking poison, and at that moment, I don't care.

When I'm done, my whole shibboleth self wavers. Alex Schneider lies splayed before me like a sacrificial offering, and his mind, that massive field of coral that I floated over before, shimmers and blooms, colors deepening, life returning. We are what we do. And I just undid something that has diseased his whole life.

I ate the cancer that has been killing him.

And now it's in me.

Something inside me snaps, like a slingshot, and I'm reeled back into my body, the meatsuit, incarcerado.

The sensation of Schneider's memory curdles in my stomach, and I sit up on the infirmary's cot, sweating and stark. The room is washed in the blue light from behind the bars, and I can see Nurse Cheeves standing above me, her face stern and unforgiving.

"I don't know what you are or how you do it, but your *thievery* disgusts me. You took something beautiful, and now I can't even remember what it was—"

She stops as she sees the expression on my face.

Something's rotten in me now, and I feel like I'm about to slide into the abyss.

—cheeves schneider graves booth dubrovnik stevens masters wilbourne erikson desalle—

Faces and other lives flashing before my eyes, like cruel waves, washing me away. I open my mouth to speak, but something is so very wrong and all I can manage is, "*Je ne peux pas arrêter. Je ne peux pas m'en empêcher. Je ne peux pas arrêter. Aidez-moi. Je peux lire dans vos pensées. Je suis désolé. Donc désolé,*" and each word rings clear as a bell, the tolling of some great bell, shaking me to my foundations.

"Stop this, Shreve. Stop!"

"*Pardonnez-moi. Je suis tellement désolé pour avoir volé de vous.*" It's stuck inside of me, the French—*Desalle* and I can't even remember when I read his mind, but his name is Peter Desalle—and the words bubble out of my mouth, fluid and glossy, the language of love and madness, and I can feel my shibboleth self still juddering and shaking inside of me, full of cancer.

There are no walls now, and everything comes crashing in.

PART TWO:
BEDLAM

I wake up slow, caught in the sluggish tide between knowing nothing and wakefulness. I had no dreams, neither mine nor someone else's.

So I've got that going for me.

On the other hand, I do have a vague recollection of motion, of bouncing. Ambulance, I suspect. And of Schneider leaning over me as my eyelids fluttered. "She said you were a thief," he said, the words thick and hesitant. "I didn't know what she meant. *She* didn't know what she meant. But I saw you, last night—something is different now, and I should want to kill you—" He had a deep, barreled voice. "But I don't. I feel—I feel lighter. I remember what I did, and all the things that came after, but it's like it all happened to someone else. I'm calmer than I have been in . . ." He looked at my face for a long time. "Something's seriously wrong with you, kid—though we knew that already. But I think you stole something from me that I *needed* stolen."

Still, no dream. That's something.

...

It's a hallway I'm in, a long one, full of cots under fluorescent lights. Green tile. The stink of urine and chemicals. It takes a moment for the sounds to percolate through my consciousness.

Painful laughing, sobbing, screeches, hoots and catcalls, cursing. Steady cursing. Boys in blue hospital gowns lie in their beds, read, gibber to themselves. Make strange geometrical symbols with their hands.

I've woken to a nightmare. I put my head in my hands, crush my eyes shut, and rub, hoping when I'm through, this will all have been a dream and I'm back on my bunk in Casimir, safely incarcerado.

Down the hall, one boy masturbates furiously, his head tilted back, saying, "I just want to sleep. *I just want to sleep!*" There's no pleasure in it, and the other boys move away from him. One kid makes a weird ululation deep in his throat as he watches. Another kid trots over to the bulls. He says something I can't hear and points. The bulls hop up and immediately approach the boy with their Tasers out. His body contorts when they zap him, and I can't help but wonder if he came at the moment of electrification. When they're done giving him the charge—*click, click, click, click*—his body relaxes, and he slumps back on his cot. "Pull up your damned pants," the bull says, reluctant to touch the boy. "Or you'll go into solitary. No more beating off, you hear?"

The bulls are both good old American football players. Their biceps strain at their nurse uniforms.

The other one says, "No more room in solitary. Doc Sinequa says we'll have to rotate some out and ship off the others to the Fort Smith psych ward, if things don't change."

The first bull shrugs. "Not my problem. I need to get a damned night's sleep myself."

"I heard that loud and clear," the other says. He looks at the boy, who's crying now and trying to pull up his pants. "Try to sleep, kid. Okay? It'll get better."

The first bull shakes his head as he walks back to the plexi-glass nurse's station by the doors.

My head is full of cotton, and my eyes feel gummy and slow to respond. I look at my hands for a long while, tracing the lines on my palm, and I'm surprised at how interesting my own flesh has become. I want to focus on anything other than the hell I'm in. I try to leave the meatsuit, to cast out my awareness beyond myself. I try to exert my shibboleth self.

Nothing. I look at my hands. No more Ghost Dance. No more shibboleth.

There's a chart at the end of my cot. I pick it up, look at it, but the small type and black scribbles swim before my eyes. Sore all over. Head, back, ass, legs, shoulders. Every muscle aches— but dully. I'm aware of the pain, but it's far away and muffled. It takes a while to realize my bladder is full. I stand, shuffle down the hall. At some point, maybe they'll assign me a room.

Screaming in one of the cells, and a boy sits on his cot and watches me blankly, saying over and over, "The best they is, the best they is," as I walk down the hall to where the two bulls sit at the entrance to the male ward. They've taken my shoes but given me these nice slippers.

At the Berlin Wall checkpoint, they scan my wrist and wave me through. The men's restroom has no door, just a curved glass block wall. And inside, there are no partitions between urinals and no doors on the johns. A fat kid in glasses blinks owlishly at me from one of the toilets. I do my business as quickly as I can. And leave.

A short, dumpy lady bull stops me coming out. She's holding a clipboard, and her gaze bounces between it and me. "Been told to find you. Shreve? That your name?"

"Yes."

"You're to have breakfast. The cafeteria is there." She points a nubby finger toward another set of double doors, these standing open. "Then please report there." Her blunt finger jabs out at an area beside the main nurse's station. Another sliding expanse of Plexiglas, a counter. A small sign says DISPENSARY, and a sour-faced man sits framed in the open window, glaring into the glow of a computer monitor. Behind him, white shelves and racks full of white bottles and bins and cabinets. The drug slinger.

I guess I'm standing there, looking about dully with my jaw hanging, because the nurse touches my shoulder and says, "Earth to Shreve. Earth to Shreve. You hear me?"

"Sure."

"So, go eat breakfast. You can't take your medicine on an empty stomach."

That sounds reasonable, but I don't know if I *want* to take the medicine.

I shuffle off. In the cafeteria there's the normal clang and crash and clamor of trays, but this cafeteria feels more like a cheap hotel buffet than the cafeteria at Casimir. There's a toaster with bread and bagels (but no cream cheese), a hot plate with biscuits and gravy and powdered eggs. A big tub of ice with milk and tiny bottles of juice. Poor, cheap fare. But I am hungry. It takes a long while to get the bread sack untied and two pieces in the toaster.

There's a bank of windows on the far side of the room, high up in the wall. Some kind of plastic. Crazy people and glass windows go together like infants and razor blades. It's cloudy out there, the sky's ashtray gray, washing the dull interior of the cafeteria in dirty light. Rows of long tables sit crookedly, and many of the tables are full. But where the Casimir cafeteria would be roaring with noise and laughter, the air full of tossed napkins and scraps of food, *this* cafeteria is quiet, hushed, waiting for something. The patients move from cafeteria line to table, bearing trays, slowly.

I have no idea how long I've stood there, blinking in the light and watching the glowing mouths of the toaster, when I hear a voice say, "So, what're you in for?"

I'm surprised to find a girl standing next to me. I've been so long in juvie, surrounded only by boys, it's jarring to find myself rubbing elbows with the other half.

This girl, thin as a guitar string and as tightly strung, has a buzz cut and gigantic, luminous eyes. Her eyes are so large, they make her look like an anime doll come to life, but without the boobs. Or maybe it's the drugs surging through my bloodstream. She moves forward, taking my wrist in cold, papery hands. She turns it over, looking at the light blue hospital bracelet complete with bar code. "Mr. Cannon comma Shreve."

"Grand theft auto."

"I don't think that one's in the DSM."

"DSM?"

"Wow, they've really got you lubed to the gills, don't they? Diagnostic and Statistical Manual. Stats for mental disorders. You know, looneyville? The hatch?"

"I'm not crazy."

She laughs and it transforms her face, but not in a good way. There's a twisted, hurt sound in it, and her eyes go mean. But for all that—beyond the cotton in my head and heart—I feel sorry for her. She looks frail.

"Sure you're not crazy. None of us in here are." She pauses. "I'm Rollie."

"Shreve," I say. "So, uh, what are *you* in here for?"

"Anorexia nervosa. Depression. Cutting. You name it. But mostly, the same as everyone else. I haven't slept for more than a few minutes in a week."

I understand but don't at the same time—even before they pumped me full of juice, I was sleeping like a baby back in Casimir.

"Cutting?"

"You really are a fish out of water, aren't you?" She glances around the cafeteria as if checking for observers and then leans toward me. Her breath smells of ammonia. She pulls up her robe, showing me skinny, knobby knees. The gesture is slow and—I've lived enough lives to know this—provocative, like she's unveiling something that will give me an immediate boner.

But her leg is scrawny and asexual and, as the hem of her robe rises enough for me to see her thigh, crisscrossed with half-healed scratches and cuts. She smiles at me, lowering her eyes.

"It lets the pain out, you know?"

I don't, but I nod. By habit, I try to make a run at her, to get inside her mind and see if I can help her. But I can't muster the shibboleth with all the Haldol swimming in my bloodstream. Seems I'm grounded for the time being.

And for a moment, I'm relieved. It's a strange, muffled feeling. The wet blanket of whatever they gave me evens out the seesaw of emotions. I'm just plain ole Shreve again. And that's a relief. I feel weightless and untethered for a moment, free from the responsibility of saving this scrawny girl. Or Jack. Or myself.

We shamble over to the tables, carrying our trays, and I eat the toast and drink boxed apple juice while Rollie watches me. She rips the rind from an orange and separates each section. She arranges the pieces in a pinwheel on her plate.

Eventually, she starts talking again, watching my reaction.

"That guy over there is named Digger. See him? The tall kid."

"Yeah, I see him."

"They call him Digger because they can't call him Corpsebanger."

I don't know if I like the direction this conversation has turned, so I focus on the toast for a while.

When I'm done, I notice that Rollie's right beside me, dumping her tray as well. She hasn't eaten a single wedge of her orange.

In the hall by the dispensary, a big male nurse waddles down the hall, his muscles making his walk bowlegged and his arms hard to hang straight at his sides. He's got the gait of a morbidly obese person, but he's got zero fat. His feet squeak on the tiles and echo off the bare green walls.

"Rollie, you making friends with the new . . ." —he's going to say fish, he's going to say fish, and if he does I might scream if I can even muster the energy to do it, I'm so tired— "patient?"

"You know it, Buster." Bringing her hands to her face, she begins nibbling at her cuticles—probably the only meal she'll have all day.

He looks at me and raises a clipboard that looks toylike in his massive hands. "Shreve J. Cannon, ward of the state, placed here at the Tulaville Psychiatric Ward until deemed fit to be released back into custody of the state's duly appointed representative. That you?" He reads this formally, bored of the routine. I don't have to peep inside his head to know he's sore from lifting weights and, judging by how his breath comes heavy through his horselike nostrils, exhausted from not getting enough sleep. A snorer, this one. Apnea, most likely. Didn't get much sleep even before the insomnia epidemic.

"My name's Sylvester, but everyone around here calls me Buster. Follow me."

It takes me a bit to catch up with Buster. When I do, he cocks an eye at me and says, "Chart says you had a schizophrenic break and you were violent to an old lady."

"I—"

"Hey, kid, don't make excuses. All you got to hear is this: I can rip your arm out of its socket like I was pulling a wing from a roasted chicken. You know?" Matter of fact.

"That right, hoss? I can go in your head and blow out all your lights and then work you like a meat puppet."

He lifts the chart, peers at it awhile, pulls out the pencil and scratches at the paper, and then looks at me again. Slow. Deliberate. Then he begins walking. "Right. Come on."

We bank around the back of the nurse's station—a couple of massive orderlies eyeball me—and approach a small window at the back of the building. At least Rollie isn't following anymore.

"Not gonna repeat myself, right, kid? This here's where you come every morning, right after breakfast—all meals in are in there—or we'll find you. You won't like it if we have to hunt you down. There's the male ward; there's the female ward. Do not try to enter the female ward. Fraternizing with our female guests is fine, but no sex. No mutual masturbation. No nothing.

Got me? You start messing with one of the young ladies here, you'll find yourself in isolation so fast your head will spin. Got me?"

"You said 'got me' twice."

He ignores that. "I'm gonna make Rollie your tour guide for the common areas, since she's obviously sweet on you. You've got an evaluation in that office there—"

"You think that's a good idea? Putting me with a girl?"

"No one else seems interested in you. Might as well be her." He jabs a thick finger at a frosted glass door. "You've got an appointment with Dr. Sinequa immediately following lunch." He steps up to the window and pats the lime-green counter. The sour man glaring at the computer monitor is framed in the window and surrounded by shelves full of drugs. He's got a Taser at his waist.

Buster says, "I need Shreve Cannon's morning candy, if you please, Steve-O."

Steve-O turns to the nearby computer and clacks on the keyboard for a few moments and then disappears back among the shelves of drugs.

"You noticed the Taser, right? Don't know what your problem is, kid, but if any patient is found behind this counter, Steve-O is allowed to put you down."

"What's with the *sturm und drang* routine, hoss?"

He turns to me and snatches my wrist and gives a little jerk.

"Don't call me 'hoss,' kid. Look around this place." He stops, puts his massive hands on his waist, and looks at me. "Seriously, take a good look."

I look. Robed zombies wander the hall, passing in and out of the cafeteria, the recreation rooms, the reading area.

They murmur, mutter, moan, rock. Buster's radio squelches and hisses, and a strange garbled noise comes from the tinny speaker. The air stinks of disinfectant and a whiff of raw sewage. The nurses, men and women alike, keep to the nurse station or move very fast toward their destination, as if the toddling shamblers were real zombies instead of medicated ones.

I try, for an instant, to get out of my skin and go behind Buster's eyes—not to do what I said, but just to understand. Time becomes elastic for that moment, and I'm out and looking from behind his eyes at me, but then the moment is up and the elastic tether that keeps me associated with my meatsuit snaps me back.

Almost had it.

Buster says, "This locked-down psychiatric ward has a forty-eight-patient capacity. You wanna know how many patients we have in here?"

No, not really, but I can tell he's going to tell me anyway. "More?"

"One hundred and twenty. You're Mister One Hundred and Twenty-One."

"That's crazy."

"You hit the nail on the head." He stops, and then something about his expression clouds. "The whole world is going batty at the same time. It wasn't like this a year ago."

"The insomnia?"

He looks at me like I'm a moron. "Bingo, kid. And these poor souls—" He taps me on the shoulder. "Including your little ass—are the first ones to stampede off the cliff."

Steve-O returns with a small tray holding two small paper cups.

"There's your candy, Shreve. Take it."

I pick up the cups. There are two large capsules in one and a few ounces of water in the other. The pills most assuredly do not have the look of candy, and I would know.

"What is this?"

He bristles. "The red-and-blue one makes you smaller; the yellow one makes you larger. Ain't got time for twenty questions. Take them."

"What if I don't?"

"I hold you down and make you take them." He looks around for support. "Steve-O, this one's gonna be trouble. Come out here."

Steve-O moves away from the computer station, puts his hand on his Taser, and exits the dispensary through a nearby door.

"You have three seconds to eat that candy, kid."

It's all happening too fast, and I can't tell if it's because of the gauze of the drugs swaddling my brain and preventing me from touching the shibboleth or if it's really just happening too fast.

"Three, two . . ."

Everything locks. My whole body goes rigid and there's an electric crackling sound—*pop pop pop pop pop*—and I have no control over anything because every muscle is tight and contracted and I teeter and hit the ground.

I try to do the Ghost Dance like so long ago, back in Casimir, when the admin bull ordered me to stay behind the line, but the candy swims through my bloodstream, full bore, and I'm locked incarcerado. Blocked from the shibboleth.

Buster fills my vision, a half-sad, half-determined look

on his face, saying to Steve-O, "Get the pills. One went over there!" He forces open my mouth with his big paws—there's no resisting him—and after a moment of scrabbling and muttered profanity, Steve-O roughly shoves them in.

Buster covers everything that can take in air on my face and says, "Swallow or you'll suffocate. More paperwork for us, but no one's gonna bat an eye at some punk kid who asphyxiates. You got me?"

With his face in mine, I make one more attempt to get behind his eyes. There's the faintest scent of flame, and for a moment, I think I'm about to fly into the wild blue yonder, to touch the shibboleth, but the spark dies and I'm still firmly seated in good ole Shreve.

"You got me?"

The air in my lungs is exhausted of oxygen, and black is pushing around at the edges, but, *yeah*, I get him.

I swallow and the pills, without the sluice of water, feel like stones traveling down my throat, rough and gigantic and full of sleep.

He pats me on my cheek and says, "Good boy," and lifts me off the floor and places me on my feet once again. Turning his head, he nods at Steve-O, saying, "Okay, he'll be good from here on out." He looks back to me. "I'm watching you, kid. There's no fun and games in here. Next time you don't want to eat your candy, Steve-O will pop you in the ass with a syringe full of juice. Understand?"

"Oui, oui."

"What?"

I can't understand why my tongue said that so I just nod and duck my head.

"All right, be a good boy and don't cause any trouble." He pats my head.

I toddle off. My body is sore all over from the electrical charge and my shoulder hurts where Buster almost pulled out my arm and my back stings where the Taser's prongs pricked my skin.

Not my favorite morning ever, that's for sure.

...

Rollie catches up with me as I shamble over to the reading room.

"Hey, beautiful," she says, putting a bony hand on my shoulder—the smarting one—and stopping my forward movement. "When Buster gives an order, you *gotta* do it." Her ammonia breath washes over my face. "*He doesn't play, you know?*"

"Yeah, I kinda figured that out."

"Makes you all jumpy, don't it? The zapping?"

She's looking at me with those big liquid eyes and a grin on her face. She's too happy for a prisoner in a mental ward.

"Don't you ever want to bust out of this place?"

"You mean, escape?" Rollie grimaces and looks at me as if I am insane. More insane. Whatever.

"Yeah, escape. You know—" I wave my hand at the green walls and unbreakable plastic windows. "The wild blue yonder? Baseball fields? Children of the corn?"

She shudders. Her emotions seesaw across her face. Her bony shoulders hunch up into a tight knot. Her hands jitter. "No. It's terrible out there. That's why I'm here. Safe." Her face clears. She tries her smile back on.

"Safe? I just had a gorilla electrocute me. It's not safe in here," I say.

Her newfound smile withers and dies. She whispers, "It's terrible out there. Something's coming. Some cancer is growing, and I can feel it."

"Have you slept recently?"

She ignores that, closing her big peepers and touching her eyelids with her two tremulous index fingers. "Sometimes I can feel it growing behind here. My eyes. Growing. Passing into the world."

I'm cold for a moment, colder than normal, colder than the air of the ward, colder than the tiles of the building.

"What is it?" I whisper back.

Eyes open now, Rollie's giving me the lip-nibbling look of worry, like she's said too much. So I give her the old salesman grin, my tool of the trade back before Jack and the shibboleth busted up the party. When she smiled mean—that hurt and desperate smile—it didn't do much for her appearance. But now, this vulnerability softens her and for a moment I feel like I can see her how she should be: whole, 11 percent body fat, olive-skinned, and smiling wholeheartedly on a softball field with other girls, her hair pulled back and threaded through the rear of her cap. Not this rattled bundle of nerves, fingernails eroded to nubs, hair as short as a prisoner's, breathing out the ammoniac poisons her body generates as it devours itself.

No, for an instant, I can see her beauty.

And maybe that's what the shibboleth is. It's the commonality of human existence. It lets me get in their heads because we're the same, all of us, this human utterance.

She blinks and says, "I don't know," shaking her head. And the moment evaporates.

We've been standing right outside the open double doorway, yet no one seems to notice two patients in gowns furiously whispering in their midst. A big bull-nurse sits on a stool by the door as zombies shamble in and out, humming, using their fingertips to trace invisible patterns in the air.

We enter the reading room. There are magazines and *National Geographics* and books for teens, Judy Blume and Madeleine L'Engle. There's a full set of smudged and threadbare Harry Potters and the requisite Tolkien. Fantasy is the preferred literature of the psych ward, it seems.

I find a book of poetry called *The Sorrow of Architecture* by Liam Rector and paw through it. Rollie picks up a *Glamour* magazine. She's silent now, and I have much to think about, but it's hard keeping a single idea in my head with the medication thrumming and shivering in my system. It's as if I cannot concentrate on anything for more than an instant, but each instant is an eternity. But Rollie stays close, occasionally glancing at me as if making sure I haven't gone too far away.

I can't say how long I've stared at the same poem before moving on to a copy of *Songs of Innocence and Experience* and then, because the words begin to swim on the page, onto an issue of *People*, where everyone is beautiful and smiling. Flipping through the pages, I realize that in Hollywood, everyone gets a good night's sleep.

"Aren't you supposed to be showing me around?" I ask when I can't look at any more magazines.

"You've seen the cafeteria. This is the reading room. That leaves the Wreck Room. Wreck with a *W*."

"Gotcha. Because it's a wreck."

"No, because we are." She tosses her *Glamour* onto the pile on the table and stands. "Come on, we can go play Chutes and Ladders. That's not a euphemism for anything." She winks at me. "Unless you want it to be."

In the Wreck Room, there's a smattering of zombies pushing plastic figures around on printed cardboard. There's one table of boys and girls seriously engaged in a card game. One of the boys is just bawling his head off, tears streaming down his face and snot running from his nose, and none of them seem to notice. In the corner, a very tall, very fat girl sings a song and tosses brightly colored Uno cards into a box, one by one.

I am you, and you are me, though we always disagree . . . It's a strange little song, yet she's got a wonderful voice, a choir voice. Rich timbre, throaty. She's found a melody, minor, lilting. *Me is you and you am he, one and two and one make three.* I feel like I've heard the song before, somewhere.

"How 'bout some Scrabble?" Rollie asks. I'd been staring at the singing girl, and the question jars me a little.

"Nah."

"It's getting close to lunchtime anyway. Let's go."

She should be hungry now, since she didn't eat anything this morning.

Back in the cafeteria, we join the line as Rollie again has an appetizer of fingernails and cuticles. She grabs a tray and motions me to do the same.

The big bull-nurse stationed near the door watches closely. My back and knees ache where I fell to the ground when the electricity pushed into me, like Quincrux. My muscles feel achy and sore like in the onset of flu. My eyes won't open fully, and there's a thrumming in my ears and surging in my blood.

"Hey, you don't look so good," Rollie says. "You should eat something. Try the rectangular pizza."

The conversation slips away. We approach the stainless steel line where the food is served. There's some sort of meat patty swimming in brown gravy, mashed potatoes, evil-looking green beans swimming in grease, and, sure enough, a tray of rectangular pizza. Rollie takes some green beans and Jell-O and a milk. I get cranberry juice.

We sit in one of the less densely populated tables, Rollie facing me, her big eyes still watching my every move.

I take a bite of the rectangular pizza. Industrialized food, made with government cheese. I can taste it, and for a moment, I'm reminded of Moms and Holly Pines Trailer Park, out on the edge of the piney woods, out beyond everything I now know. Every month a packet filled with info would arrive at the trailer, pamphlets leading us toward job fairs and alcohol rehabilitation centers. But nestled amidst all the junk mail was an electronic benefits transfer card. Food stamps for the new millennium. Getting food for the family, for Vig and Moms. This was my job.

The memory floods me, like the taste of the cheese and the sugary-sweet tomato sauce and the cheap over-leavened pizza dough. Cheap food for disposable people.

I swallow and quietly, very quietly, I ask, "You said it was coming, from behind your eyes. What does that mean?"

Rollie takes a bite of the green beans and grimaces, putting down her fork. "These beans are too squeaky," she says, looking away. "I hate squeaky beans."

"Rollie. This is important." I don't know any way to make

her understand. "I believe you. I just need to know what you mean."

Rollie does everything but look at me now. Confronted with what she said, she clams.

I sigh, spread my hands. They already think I'm crazy. What does it matter?

"Rollie, I'm going to tell you a secret. Okay?"

Finally she looks back at me, but reluctantly. She suspects a trick. And I don't blame her. I'm sure she's been tricked before.

"You won't believe me. You'll think I'm—" I make loony circles around my ear with an index finger and whistle tunelessly. Rollie giggles. "I'm here because I can read minds. I can get inside folks' heads. Or I could, until they drugged me."

I let it sink in.

Her gaze does this little dance across my features. She frowns, and when I don't react, Rollie smiles a little shyly, batting her eyes and nibbling on her lower lip. With some weight on her, she could be cute. Pretty, even.

And those eyes. Like swimming pools you'd like to dive into.

"You're cute. You don't have to make any of that stuff up just to get with me."

"No, I'm serious. There are things happening out in the world, and what you said—"

"I didn't say anything."

"About the thing that's coming. Coming through your eyes. I need to know what you're talking about."

She shivers and says, "This Jell-O is terrible. Black cherry? Who likes black cherry?"

"I do. Black cherry is awesome with Cool Whip."

"Cool Whip? That stuff is crap. If you get Reddi-wip and you don't shake it, you can huff the nitrous out of the can. It's totally awesome."

"Nitrous?"

She looks at me, curious. "What're you in here for again? You don't know whippets?"

"I read too many minds, and my head got all jumbled. I was incarcerado at Casimir Pulaski—"

"Incarcerado?"

"Oh, yeah. Incarcerated. On lockdown. Caged." It's hard to track a conversation when lubed on antipsychotic medications.

She nibbles her lip some more, processing. I can see the ole noggin at work behind those big eyes.

"Go ahead and ask, if you have questions," I say.

"What's it like? Surrounded by boys all the time."

"Not my favorite thing in the world. You'd probably like it less than I do."

She snorts and blushes. "Not hardly. The median weight of guys in here is like two-fifty or something."

"To answer your question, it's hard, really. I was . . . I am—" I don't know any way to say it. "I'm not much liked there. I'm hated, really."

She snorts again. "Bull crap."

"No. It's true. You might not believe me—about the mind stuff or anything—but it's true. They hate me there. Everyone. Bulls, admin. Inmates."

She looks at my scalp again, the bandage there. My left peeper, yellowed from the last black eye. "They do that to you?"

"Yeah."

"Why?"

"I stole something from them."

"From all of them?"

"Pretty much."

"What?"

"Memories." I don't know how to say it, really. "Not the bad ones. I took the good ones and it was like—"

Her eyes go dreamy for a second, and she smiles beatifically, a genuine smile. "Honey in the vein? Like cumming your britches and realizing you've found something you'd forgotten you'd lost and losing everything all at once and not even caring?"

I wonder for a moment if she has the shibboleth and has been rummaging around in my attic. "Yeah. Kinda like that."

"You're just like me."

Normally I might snort or laugh or smirk—always smirking, always sneering—but there's this wet blanket on me, and all spark of life gets smothered as soon as it lights in the heart, in the mind.

I've got to get out of here.

But I say, "Just like you?"

"Yeah. A junkie."

I shake my head. That's all I can manage in my defense.

"Bullshit, honey. I can see right through you. You got the jones just like me. Something to take away the hurt, to smooth out the edges."

My head stills. Everything's soft around the edges now, fuzzy, and part of me swoons while my physical body is steady, motionless except for the thrum of my heart and the tides of my tainted blood, teeming with foreign, lethargic molecules.

It becomes still and quiet in the cafeteria as Rollie regards me, unblinking, and down the table a weak-chinned boy holds up a clawed hand to the handsome girl sitting opposite him and I hear his voice now, still talking, and he's saying, "My soul grew stronger; hesitating then no longer, 'Sir,' said I, 'or Madam, truly your forgiveness I implore; But the fact is I was napping, and so gently you came rapping, and so faintly you came tapping, tapping at my chamber door—'"

He stops, looking at me, a strange glint in his eye. The girl's gaze joins his, and they stare at me, hard, unsmiling, like two crumbled bits of statuary glaring into the gray light of the cafeteria. I can't help but shiver and wonder if there are Riders behind their eyes. And what was that he was saying? It sounds so familiar.

"Hey, zomboids. He's new," Rollie says.

"I don't fancy the stares, Miss Rollie," says the chinless wonder.

"What was that you were saying?" I ask.

He points a long, gnarly fingernail at my face and says, "Miss Rollie, I do not like this one. This one has no respect for the masters."

That sounds too suspiciously close to Riders for my taste. I pop up, standing as if some elephantine invisible hand has marionetted me erect on wobbly feet. I'd not care for the company of the Rider.

I snatch up my tray and turn, but my brain jerks the old meatsuit clumsily, doped and sluggish and muddied like river water, and I nearly lose my balance reaching for the tray and then overcorrect my movements, clutching it slowly and straightening my back.

"Seriously, Shreve. They're just cocoa puffs; they're not real zombies. Don't get all feelings."

Feelings is definitely what I am. But I force myself to sit, replacing my tray.

The rectangular pizza isn't too bad.

SEVEN

I don't know what textbook or medical journal he's read it in, but Dr. Sinequa seems dead set on using my name every single time he speaks to me.

"So, Shreve, can you tell me about the events leading up to the incident with—" He flips open the manila folder and adjusts the bifocals on his long, very white and very thin patrician nose. "Nurse Cheeves?"

It's a large office, one with a big bay window framing the nicely manicured grounds of the Tulaville mental hospital. I can hear lawn mowers buzzing out beyond the glass, the high-pitched whine of a blower, the angry growl of a WeedWhacker, and I imagine a team of soiled khaki-clad groundskeepers swarming over the morning-dewed lawns and clacking away with clippers at dense privet hedges, scrabbling and resistant, and scratching at their sweat-cooled brown skin. In my mind, one is trimming a hedge into topiary. A trumpeting elephant.

There are big, dark, heavy bookcases lining the room and the faint whiff of tobacco, though the smell might be hallucinatory—shit, I don't know. A wood-paneled wall is dedicated to diplomas, and I can't help but wonder if any of them are from Bethesda Medical Center or Johns Hopkins or the University of Maryland. But they're too far from my seat to read, and it's hard to focus my eyes for long, anyway.

Even if you are paranoid, that doesn't mean they're not out to get you.

"Couple of bully boys in the general pop jumped me. Cracked my head on the ground."

His head bobs in acknowledgment, and he purses his lips. The little hair he's got ringing his speckled cranium he lets run wild like a withered clown in a doctor's smock. A humorless clown, for certain.

"Shreve, have you been having trouble sleeping?"

"No."

He raises his eyebrows. "Really?"

"Yes. Sleeping fine."

He scratches at the paper with a tooth-worn pencil. "Appetite? You look underfed."

"Used to be a slave to the sweet stuff. Then a woman stuck a knife into my guts and ever since then . . . *meh.*" I try to sneer, and I can't be sure if my face is really doing what I'm asking of it. "I eat enough. Just don't get into it like a lot of the other boys in lockup. *Dans la chair, mais pas du corps.*"

Dr. Sinequa raises his eyebrows and adjusts himself in his seat in a way that lets me think his balls are pinched or he's got a terribly itchy hemorrhoid. I would take a run at him to get inside and see what he was writing but . . . yeah, the drugs. The doped sluggish tides of my blood.

"So, you speak French, do you?"

Honestly, that just slipped out there. I know it and I don't know it. "A little. I knew a guy."

He notates that.

"When you assaulted Nurse Cheeves, what were you feeling?"

I don't like the way these questions are going. So I remain silent and look at the spots on his dome. I can imagine a crack opening on his cranium and a little bird's beak peeking out. I smile.

"Shreve, did you intend her bodily harm?"

"No."

"So, Shreve, would you say you were not in control at the time of the assault, then?"

"I don't know."

"Are you in the habit of doing drugs, Shreve?"

"Hard to say. I'm pretty lubed right now."

"Have you used drugs before?"

"No."

"Truly?"

"Yes."

He rifles through more papers. "Ahh. The mother. That makes sense."

If there are tricks he misses, I'd find it hard to believe. His sense of cold and detached competency reminds me a bit of the way Quincrux might look at you, head cocked and inquisitive and calculating.

"Tell me about the Dubrovniks. How do you feel when you think back to when you escaped and ran amuck last year?"

I think of *Duck Amuck*—one of Vig's favorite cartoons he'd watch over and over on weary and threadbare VHS—that terrifying old cartoon in which Donald battles his sadistic animator overlord who keeps shifting the background and situation for the poor feathered idiot. Is that what's happening here? Who's the bird and who's the fish?

"It kinda sucked, honestly."

"How so?" After a long moment of silence, he says, "Shreve, you dislike the memory? On a scale of one to ten, with ten being intense dislike and one being fondness, how would you rate your feelings for your time spent on the run?"

"Five."

He takes off his glasses and rubs his eyes, and for a moment looks truly weary. "Shreve. Let me tell you a little bit about the history of modern psychiatry to put this conversation into perspective, shall we?"

He waits until I nod. When I do, he raises his knobbed hand and points an accusatory finger at the ceiling. "You, a ward of the state, have assaulted an employee of the state and, apparently, had a psychotic break after receiving a head injury. With me so far?"

"I'm with you."

"So, in the years past, a century or more ago, we'd probably lock you up in the darkest padded room or cut little pieces from your brain to calm you down and ensure you wouldn't be attacking little old ladies or raping little girls. Right?"

"I've seen the History Channel."

His black and inscrutable vulture eyes go narrow, and he says, "Or neuter you."

I try to smirk, to sneer, but instead, my anus tightens.

Maybe he senses my reaction. He says, "In the sixties and seventies, when I was just an intern, we'd put you through a treatment of electroshock therapy in hopes of resetting your brain's chemistry—we still do this in dire cases—but the likelihood of lawsuits has caused it to fall out of fashion in most psychiatric wards. Hmmmm. You are a ward of the state with an alcoholic for a mother . . ." He's musing, daydreaming. I half expect him to begin waxing rhapsodic about the "chokey." "If electroshock failed, you'd be isolated and kept under guard. Given what drugs could be given to ease the real physical symptoms of your condition."

"All this is real nice, the history lesson, Doc."

He ignores it. "But now policy has changed. For the worse, maybe. It is now the policy of the Tulaville Psychiatric Hospital and Mental Institution to enforce a regimen of what the critics call 'chemical straightjackets' to those patients who are nonresponsive to psychotherapeutic treatment—like us talking right now." He taps the table with his long finger. Once. Twice. Calling attention to his next words. "Me? I'd have you gelded."

He presses a button on his intercom. "This session is over. Nurse Philmon? Please escort Mr. Cannon out."

A tight, athletic woman pops in and stands behind my chair before I know what's going on. Dr. Sinequa says, "To get better, first, the patient must choose to start on the road to health, and I'm afraid you haven't, Shreve. We'll meet again in a week to see if your attitude toward chatting with me has changed. In the interim, Nurse, we should titrate until he's stiff, if not drooling."

I have no idea what that even means, but I seriously don't like the sound of it. Not one bit.

•••

I don't see Rollie again until late afternoon. She's different now, slower, and she wants only to play Scrabble in the Wreck Room. They give us apple juice and everything's quiet—no screaming, very little muttering, no whistling or tuneless singing. There's just the low, white noise of two massive midcentury air conditioners struggling to push air through the behemoth of a building.

Despite the chemical straitjacket, she's hell on wheels when it comes to Scrabble. Rollie plays the word *SLEEPING*, using the *S* to change my last play of *FIRE* to *FIRES* and going horizontally across to hit the triple word score, netting her—sheesh—more than thirty points. She smiles, but wanly.

"Don't seem too happy about the play," I say.

"Yeah. I used to love winning but now—" Rollie looks up at the fading light coming in from the windows. "I'm not looking forward to night."

"Why?"

She pauses for a moment and crinkles her eyes. "The last time I slept was four days ago, and Buster had to tranq me. Before that it was five days."

No one sleeps anymore. Things move in the ether; something sleeps in Maryland, but no one else does.

"I think I know what might be causing the insomnia."

She slowly pushes her tray of letters away from her and stands up. "Now you're just messing with me. Uncool." She turns and walks away, out of the Wreck Room. The bull-nurse looks at me from his stool by the door, but his attention soon moves to the girl who's feeling the walls, as if probing for a secret door. She places her ear against drywall, listens, then whispers something.

As I put away the Scrabble game, it's hard not to notice the letters on Rollie's tray read *NIHTMAR*.

EIGHT

The sun goes down. I can feel it. I have dinner alone in the cafeteria. Rollie is gone—disappeared into the female ward—and there's this stretched-out anxiety rippling through the zomboids shuffling about in the gathering gloom.

Buster waddles up to me and says, "Hit your cot, Shreve. It's time to take a seat for the night. You might want to grab some magazines or books from the Wreck Room first."

"Take a seat?"

He laughs. "Yeah. It's gonna be another long one."

"Why?" At his look, I hold up my hands. "I'm not trying to be difficult. I'm just trying to understand."

"Come here." He turns and walks out, back down the hall toward the Wreck Room.

The room is deserted now. Most of the patients are on their cots in either the boys' or girls' wards, the lucky ones in their cells, on beds instead of cots. The hoots and strange noises pass through the walls and echo down the corridors and bounce in weird recursive waves off the grimed tiles of the old building. We pass the neckless wonder from lunch with the long fingernails, who's muttering something to himself as he draws on a white legal pad with a dark crayon. I catch a glimpse of black angular animals, birds maybe, or rats. There's another bull-nurse—this one with a Taser at his side—standing watch down the length of the hall, staring over the cots lining the walls. Another nurse walks down the row of patients, handing out small yellow things that look like oversized pills, and it's only as I pass him that I realize that he's distributing earplugs.

I follow Buster into the Wreck Room. He approaches the television, retrieves the remote, and turns on the set. Scrolls through channels until he hits the group of channels with tickers and rictus smiles and perfect hair, stopping on one with a flawless beauty in a business suit saying, "In other news, a lone gunman entered a senior center today in York, Pennsylvania, and opened fire, killing five nurses and nearly all of the elderly in their care, bringing the death toll to thirty-seven, as far as we know. When police arrived, he submitted to custody without a shot, reportedly saying over and over, 'Kill me so I can sleep.'" A series of images washes over me. An aerial view of the senior center, clustered with flashing lights and vehicles, a terrifyingly ordinary man with a streaming face being led away in handcuffs. "Joining us now is Stephen Ballis, author of *Sleepless in America*. Stephen, how do you think this relates to yesterday's mass suicide in Spain or last week's riots in Beijing?" Cut to a thick man, crew cut and horn-rimmed, who begins to speak. But Buster cuts him off by mashing the mute button.

"It's all over, kid, not just here. The crazy. And it's spreading." He thumbs our way through more news channels, and a couple have maps with red spots like fungus. "Moving through the population."

"What is?"

"Insomnia."

"You're saying that sleeplessness is catching?"

"Looks like it."

"But I thought insomnia was, I don't know, mental? How can it be contagious?"

"I don't know." Buster looks defeated, shoulders slumped. "I haven't had a wink of sleep in three days. Before that, four."

Buster waves a big, meaty hand at the hallway beyond us, toward the patients gibbering and moaning and barking and coughing but not sleeping. "You seem like you've got at least one marble rolling around in your skull, so I'm doing my duty to help you make it through the night." His face is strained, like this conversation is taxing his neurons too much. "Stay on your cot. Use your earplugs. Sleep if you can. No one else here will." He turns off the television and trudges to the door. I follow him into the hall and to the boys' ward.

Walking back to my cot, I notice all the wide eyes, staring like those of frightened animals. One kid with fingers like tree branches tugs at my sleeve and says, "My brother, my brother . . ."

But as we pass the chinless kid with fingernails, I notice he's got his drawing pad clutched to his chest as he snores away into the dimness of the hall.

There's one guy here who isn't afflicted.

■■■

Turns out there's two.

■■■

It's morning and I'm sitting in the reading room, peering at a magazine. Too early for breakfast and the "candy," and I'm doing whatever I can to postpone it.

When I look up, Rollie stands above me.

"I'm sorry," I say. "I didn't mean to upset you."

She sits next to me, slippered feet next to my flappers.

"It's just all hard to get used to, you know?"

She remains silent, head down, looking at her feet, her hands clasped lightly together.

"I need your help." She doesn't move. "I need a distraction."

Rollie glances at me. She looks terrible, pallid skin and sunken eyes with deep, sleepless bruises underneath.

"For what?"

"To distract Buster."

"When?"

"Candy time."

"Why don't you just boost a name badge?"

My tongue is tacky in my mouth, and I could use some water. But getting water involves swallowing two stones. And I don't want that.

"Because, if I can stay off the candy long enough, I'll get back the—" It's on the tip of my tongue, shibboleth. But she won't understand that. "My ability. I'll be able to just walk out, if I can get off the candy."

"Kiss me."

"Rollie . . ."

"I just want to know what it's like, you ass. And you're the only game in town."

If that's the price for her help, it's very small. I check the room. The bull is reading, and for the moment, we're alone except for a girl copying a picture in a sketchbook.

Rollie's lips are dry, papery. Her teeth separate, and her tongue probes at my lips, but I don't open mine. I don't let that snake in, and eventually she stops trying.

She pulls away, staring at me, eyes huge. No love or kindness or sadness churns at her features. She's blank now, impenetrable.

But she says, "Okay."

"You will?"

"Yes."

"Let's go to breakfast. Afterward, they'll expect me at the dispensary, right?"

"That's the deal."

"Can you fake a seizure?"

"Yes."

"You sure?"

"Pretty sure."

"Great."

The streamers of sleep and the tides of drugs lighten. I feel almost normal, if you can call reading people's minds and eating their memories normal. But whatevs.

pupils in a paper eye. I crumple the cup in my hand as Steve-O mutters, "Oh, shit," and hustles around to the locked door, throwing it open.

I have to see. I turn. Rollie's standing there, looking directly at Buster with a furious expression like oil spreading across her features, legs spread in a wide stance. Near her foot is a growing pool of urine, and the sharp smell of it stings my nostrils as she launches herself at Buster with a growl and quick—*scary quick*—she snatches at his arm, his clothes, and scurries up his body to scratch like a madwoman at his eyes and lurch forward with teeth wide and gnashing to bite at his nose, his cheek. She's devolved into some furious primate, and Buster's overmuscled arms flail for seconds before he can get one of his ham-hands on her writhing form. When he does, the fat fingers bunch in her robes, and with a great tearing motion, he tosses her away.

Rollie smacks the tiles of the floor at the center of the *X* that marks the cross of ward wings, right in front of the plexiglass nurse station. Two women I don't recognize stand, alarmed, as Rollie slides across the floor and bumps the wall, where she begins to seize, like an unoiled engine catching and burning out. She jitters, she spasms. Her mouth froths and it's flecked with blood and I don't even know if it's her blood or Buster's from where she bit his cheek, which now streams crimson down the curve of his neck and discolors his uniform.

She shudders and bows her back, only her feet and head touching the floor.

Buster falls to his knees at Rollie's side while the two female nurses and Steve-O rush forward to help.

Holy crap.

Now's my time to skedaddle. I knock back the water, turn to hot-step away while their attention is fully on Rollie.

And run smack-dab into Dr. Sinequa.

...

He holds out his hand, obvious.

I don't hold out mine, keeping it bunched tight at my side. The nurses have sedated Rollie now and call for a stretcher. She must've cracked something good in her fit. Buster rises from his hams, and Steve-O is already taking his place back behind the dispensary door.

"This one," says Dr. Sinequa, "plans on skipping his medication today. Mr. Smith, please ensure this does not happen. Actually, let's move him to injections rather than oral dosage. We don't want any more"—he smiles—"distractions."

Uncanny how he picked that word out. Almost as if he'd been listening to us. I'm paranoid, but I can't get that paranoid. Can I?

Buster puts his hands on my shoulders, keeping me still. Dr. Sinequa says, "I'm thinking another hundred milligrams of Haldol. Let's settle this one down. He's got the candy in his right hand."

Buster yanks up my arm and begins digging at my closed hand, and I push away from the warm trunk of his body, flailing at his bulk. He barks out a short laugh as my free hand claws at his chest and then my trapped hand is pried open and the candy falls, with the crumpled paper cup, to the floor with two bright little pings and silence.

They're moving Rollie out of the ward now in a bustle, and I hear a volley of acronyms being spouted: EKG, MRI, ASAP and the good old favorite, STAT. But the word I hear most is *ISOLATION*.

Rollie, that was one helluva performance. Now they're putting you in a closet.

Steve-O makes the long pilgrimage back out of the dispensary, hefting a syringe in his mitt. He eyes me warily. I feel Buster's hands clamp down hard on both my arms, and his buddy darts in and jabs me in the gluteus maximus.

The drugs hit me like a tidal wave, and I swoon, a tsunami of drugs flooding my system. I feel tremors building in my limbs, like some itch I can't scratch, but that itch breeds in the muscles of my arm, my biceps and triceps, my quads and laterals. My body quakes and my heart staggers into a sitting position. Temples pound. Hands numb as my tongue. As my soul.

How much has the wild blue yonder affected me? Those etheric heights that Quincrux spoke of—now I miss them terribly, even with the responsibility and weight that accompanied the shibboleth. I miss it.

I am become small now, inconsequential. I was before infinitesimal, but like a spark, active and shimmer-bright. Now I'm a piece of ash falling from dead skies, carried along by the soft eddies of wind and the suck of gravity.

Dr. Sinequa says, "Yes, I think that will do. Notate his chart that he's due for another dose in eight hours." He brushes his hands together, sweeps back his doctor's coat, and puts his hands in his pockets. He whistles tunelessly as he strides off.

Stuck in the meatsuit for the duration.

We're gonna have to do this the hard way.

It's a good thing I'm a thief.

Eventually, Buster stops glaring at me and tromps away, and the nurses return to their stations. All of them shoot me varying degrees of stink-eye as I stand there, swooning in the tide. There's a moon in the same sky as the sun, today.

I make my way back to my cot. I try to keep the dull smile from creeping across my face. The flesh of my cheeks, my lips, feels numb, masklike.

When I'm at my cot, I carefully place the key card I've held so tightly in my left hand underneath my cot's sheets. Clipped while he was yanking me around and I scrabbled at his chest. It reads *Sylvester Smith, RN, PMHN*.

Time to blow this dump.

TEN

It's night now, or what passes for night in this echo chamber of a building. It's not quiet; the patients are restless and muttering, barking, making birdcalls and strange ululations.

I didn't see Rollie for the rest of the day, and I looked for her as they gave me my second dose of Haldol—a sharp pinprick in my ass and then the sucking tide of numbness as Dr. Sinequa and two frowning nurses watched. The juice almost blotted out my feelings of remorse; with Rollie gone, I was left to imagine the horrors she'd be exposed to by the staff here. All because she helped me.

Sometimes I'm such a selfish prick. I'll set the world on fire and burn everything down to get exactly what I want. The terrible realization of my selfishness is muted and dull in the vast cathedral of antipsychotics. I got what I wanted. But Rollie paid the price.

I wish I could tell her I'm sorry.

One of the nurses has walked down the hall, spraying air freshener, so now the hallway stinks of mold, feces, urine, vermin, sweat, and Ocean Fresh Scent with Oxidizer.

Two cots down from me a boy is singing, softly, over and over, *I am you and you are me, though we always disagree, me is you and you is she, two makes one and one makes three.* The same song the girl was singing. It reminds me of the old poem, "Yesterday, upon the stair, I met a man who wasn't there, he wasn't there again today, I wish, I wish he'd go away . . ." Something about the verse tugs at me, reminds me of the shibboleth.

It's a long hall—dimly lit now to promote sleep for those who can get it—and I'm two-thirds of it away from the entrance to the main psych ward and nurse station. Those patients in the mental ward that actually do have rooms, tonight they're on lockdown, incarcerado. One big bull-nurse sits in a chair at the far end of the boy's ward, face illuminated by his smartphone—he's obviously playing some game, the way his torso occasionally twitches. He's at the farthest point away from the entrance, watching the zomboids and shamblers as they don't sleep. The door to the stairwell is beyond him, with the key card system.

I am you and you are me, though we always disagree, me is you and you is she . . .

At this point, I can't feel anything except the dull tug of flesh and my personal need for sleep. Yet the tension in the hall seems palpable. The temperature has risen, and the air is so muggy it feels like we're submerged in some sluggish underwater seascape. I move slowly, shifting in the cot, watching, sheened in sweat.

It's time to go.

The boy stops singing as a thin young man approaches and stands over him, saying something under his breath that I can't make out.

"*I am you and you is she—*" the boy says, loud enough for me to hear.

I glance at the bull, who's lifted his face away from his phone, squinting past me down the length of the hall.

The standing boy raises his hands, and I can see now that

he's got a pillow clutched in them. His silhouette is almost the caricature of a murderer, a logo for the Smotherers Association.

But the boy pops up, off the cot, faster than you can imagine, screeching, "*THOUGH WE ALWAYS DISAGREE—*" and barrels into the other one, their faces coming together with a thud and twisting into something looking like a manic homecoming kiss. He's pushing him back against the far wall, hands drawing him tight into an embrace, pushing his face into the boy's, mouth to mouth. The lanky boy makes a muffled bellow, falling backward, and I realize it's not a kiss. But I guess the bull realizes the same thing and he barrels past me, hand going to his Taser, bellowing himself.

I don't wait to see if he's bitten the poor fucker's tongue completely off. I fumble under my cot's covers until I have the card in my hand, and I move as quickly as I can, a slow sluggish shamble, toward the exit.

There's yelling now behind me, and I feel like I should look, see what's happening, if there are any bulls coming after me. I reach the door—feeling like I've just swum through fifteen feet of molasses—raise my fist, clutching the key card, and swipe it. It's an eternity before the little light at the top of the keypad turns green. I pull the door open and step through.

•••

I haven't really thought this out.

Once the door shuts behind me, sending echoes up and down the stairwell, I realize I have no idea where these steps lead and no time to figure out where I'll exit. But I head down the steps—I can only hope that there are windows I can peek through so I don't have to open doors blindly.

The clack and swoosh of a door opening below me and the sound of the footfalls and heavy breath that comes with climbing steps reaches my ears. I retreat, heading back up. Who the hell would take the stairs when there are elevators?

I keep following the stairs up, making left turn after left turn, trying to stay quiet and get a glimpse of the person below me in the gap between flights. But I can't see anything except a white hand on the balustrade and a flash of nurse's blues. Can't tell if it's a man or woman. But it doesn't matter anyway.

I remember, once, another chase in a stairwell, with Quincrux and his multitude of slaves streaming blood from their noses, marching after me with limps, and that gives me a little tremor. *Things happen in patterns, child*, Quincrux said.

I've had to use people—I've taken and used them just like Quincrux to *escape Quincrux*. But this time the shibboleth is locked away, and I'm tired and underfed. This time I just have to sack up and get out, alone.

I rise, taking steps two by two. It's amazing what your body can do, even on drugs. My blue-slippered feet make padding sounds as I ascend. Looking up in the space between flights, I can see we're coming to the end of the line. Taking a left and another, I end up at a blank door with a bar release.

I stop, listen again, blood surging in my temples, hot breath blasting from my open mouth.

The sound of feet and wind being pumped in and out of lungs. Maybe some exasperation in there as well.

I press the bar as slowly as I can. It's a heavy, thick metal door. Industrial strength.

Below me, the footfalls continue.

When the gray door opens, there's a hot wind matching my breath, whipping inside the building due to some pressure differential I can only imagine, and I see an expanse of black and then white gravel and then black once more. I slip outside, onto the roof, as gracefully as I can manage, some drug-addled reflection of it. I'm out and moving away from the door before I realize that it might shut with a loud clang and alert the nurse.

Turning, I see the door swinging shut.

In movies, I'd make some dramatic leap, some superhuman dash, and stop it before it closes. But I'm still swimming in molasses, and an ungainly lurch is about all I can manage.

The door slows its movement at the very end, when it's about to close and latch, but I'm still too slow and now I see there's no handle to grab onto anyway, just a deadbolt. I fumble at it, hands numb, but the damned thing clangs shut.

The wind whips over the roof, making any other noise small and indistinct. But I heard the *clang* of the door shutting, and if I did, I have to assume whoever was ascending the stairs did as well.

I whirl about, my hospital gown giving a little flourish, and scope out my surroundings. Big metal boxes, gray-green, and some galvanized tin pipeworks. There's a wall of what looks like stone to my right, and capping the stone are little ornamental teeth, like the jagged skyline of a castle. It's an old building, the Tulaville Psychiatric Hospital.

I shuffle across what I realize now is black tar roofing. I hit a sticky spot, and it pulls the slippers from my feet. I take four steps before I realize the slippers are gone. I turn back to get them, stop, and then turn back again to the gray-green shapes I was heading for. Some sort of electrical or air-conditioning units like gargantuan building blocks. As quickly as possible, I hide behind the bulkiest of them.

It's dark now, and the meager lights of Tulaville wink and tremble in the steamy night air. It's humid and loud with the roar of some ventilation machinery, and the spray of stars above is lost in the high, wispy cirrus clouds whipping by on hot winds.

I peek around the corner at the door. There's a single wire-framed bulb above it, swarmed with insects battering themselves against the glass. The door remains closed.

Breathless, I wait long enough to know that whoever was in the stairwell doesn't have an inquisitive bone in his body. Either that, or he's deaf.

Five minutes? Ten? I can't tell. My breath has slowed, and I'm not panting anymore. Sweating, though.

Eventually, I stand and shuffle back to the door and see if I can open it.

No dice.

I look around, wandering to the edge of the roof, the toothed—*no, crenellated*—wall surrounding me. Not much up here except splatters of bird shit and tar roofing and patches and puddles of water. There's some metal sheeting stacked in a corner, behind the stairwell hutch.

I can see most of Tulaville from the vantage, and beyond that, the phosphorescent lights marking the trestle bridge over the Arkansas River. Below me, the soft, manicured lawns. A parking lot, dimly lit. The building is old and over six stories tall. And judging by the crumbling mortar along the crenellations, falling into serious disrepair. But I guess I already knew that from my stint downstairs.

In the dark, I can make out a sub-roof below me, over the wings of the fourth floor and what looks like another stairwell hutch or some sort of rooftop storage shed, but it's a drop of twenty-five feet. Tulaville Psychiatric Hospital is an absolute beast of a building.

I don't know what to do. I can bang on the door and hope someone hears. But then it'll be more doses of candy and the wet blanket getting wetter. Or I can try to climb down with a high probability of falling to my death.

I have visions of groundskeepers driving trucks with beds full of bags of mown grass and leaves and me just jumping off the side of the building and landing amidst the soft, fluffy lawn detritus like a stuntman from a movie. But to get to where I can jump down over the parking lot—all of the eighty- or ninety-foot drop—I'll have to jump down the first twenty-five to the sub-roof.

They don't do lawn care at night, anyway.

I sit down under the single-wired bulb, arms on my knees and back to the door, and rest my head on my forearms.

After a long while, exhaustion and the seep of drugs wash over me. And I find sleep.

...

Sometime in the night, a furious explosion of black wings awakens me. I lift my head and try to stand but discover that my ass and most of my legs are numb.

It takes a long while for the pins and needles to subside. Finally, I rise, creaky, to look at the now clear sky, brilliant with a million stars. The air has cooled as the hours ticked by, and my skin ripples with goose bumps as I look up into the indifferent heavens. I can see the arm of the galaxy whirling around us, the milky wash of light arcing across the sky.

A raven stands on one of the teeth of the crenellations, in profile. I feel like it's watching me, but it's hard to tell in the dark. Its caw sounds more like the bray of a donkey when it comes, and I jump in my skin. The raven leaps upward, spreading its wings, wheeling out of sight. And then, as I turn my eyes back toward the heavens, the bird crosses my vision, flying overhead, a patch of absolute dark obscuring the spill of stars.

After that, I'm alone. The world settles and dims. All is quiet.

I'm a sentry in the castle, watching for the dragon. Waiting for the attack.

I am the eye of the world.

···

Later, I lie on the roof bone-weary, cradling my head in my arms. Thoughts bubble up in my frazzled brainpan, unbidden.

Rollie.

There's so many I should have helped, if I only wasn't so selfish—Vig, Moms, Coco, even Ox, Warden Anderson. Booth.

Where has that raven gone, and why was it here?

I am pinioned by stars until I cannot take any more of it.

I close my eyes.

···

It's hot already, and the sky is streaked with rosy streamers in the east when I wake. The air-conditioning units roar white noise and cacophonous fury, and I roll to my hands and knees and pant into the morning air like a damned dog, tailless and without a master.

My mouth is dry, and there's a pressure behind my eyes.

I stand, look out upon the world. I see the tops of the trees, the shadows below them shifting, shortening. The black tar road from the highway, lined with Bradford pears, lies straight, an arrow toward the highway. And as I watch, a state trooper turns down the lane, approaching the building.

They've figured out I've escaped. Well, almost escaped.

I could jump. If I lived, I could see what's below. Maybe there's a drainpipe I could shimmy down. Maybe there's a window or a door I could get in through.

I can jump. I can do it. And who cares even if I die?

Jack.

Jack cares. Vig, maybe. Booth.

And I'm a coward. And selfish. I don't want to die yet. Hell, I don't even want a twisted ankle.

And it's already hot again. Sweat trickles from my temples and prickles my back. I haven't had anything to drink since a slurp at one of the water fountains on the ward yesterday afternoon.

The sun's over the tree line now. An ambulance, sirens silent and lights unlit, turns off the highway, following the trooper's route to ye olde Tulaville Psychiatric Hospital.

It passes out of my sight, beyond the lip of the roof.

I wait.

Damn, I'm thirsty. But even so, I've got to relieve myself, and I'm half ashamed that I've been eyeing the corner of the roof where the stairwell hutch meets one of the old stone walls.

There's no atheists in foxholes. There's no modesty on the roof.

And no toilet paper.

On my way around the hutch, I pick up the tar-grimed, blue-green slippers that came with my induction into the Lethargic Boys' Choir.

I take care of the paperwork, holding onto the inner bicuspid of the roof's jaw, not having to strain too hard, and feel miserable afterward, leaving my scat there to petrify in the summer sun.

I've never felt more rooted in my body, more prone to the effects of gravity.

My stomach rumbles. My mouth is dry and my tongue like sandpaper. There's a five-foot pool of standing rainwater near the eastern edge of the roof, black and evil-looking.

I wait, watching the grounds. The air conditioners continue to howl—it's amazing, all this sound and fury just to keep a bunch of crazy folks cool.

I watch for the ambulance or the trooper. Maybe someone else got into an altercation, driven to violence by lack of z's and, well, being batshit crazy. Mr. Fingernails, maybe.

More cars turn down the drive. SUVs and sedans. A white city van pulling a trailer full of lawn equipment. It stops near the western edge of the grounds, and they begin unloading lawnmowers and Weed Eaters and other instruments of destruction and begin work, the buzz of their two-stroke engines inaudible above the steady roar of the air conditioner.

"Hey, guys!" I yell, top of my lungs, like I'm at a football game. I wave my arms. Nothing. They don't turn, but continue to weed-whack and trim and edge.

My mouth feels like I've been gnawing on chalk.

I walk to the eastern side of the roof. Already I'm getting comfortable here, the expanse of black tar. Where's that damned raven?

On my knees, I drink the standing water, trying not to think about how much birdshit I'm ingesting.

It tastes like fresh-squeezed juice from a burning-tire tree. My mouth rebels at the noxious taste—my lips burn, and the soft inner flesh of my cheeks feels hellish as I probe at them with my outraged tongue.

"Good times, Jack," I say and vomit it all up in a rush.

■ ■ ■

Weaker now, watching the grounds. The ambulance leaves. After I watch it go, I sit in the meager shade offered by the hutch, letting my headache blossom and grow to cancerous proportions.

There's a pressure growing behind my eyes. My eyeballs feel like thumbs holding back the water in a hose.

Water.

I could jump.

I stand, go to the edge of the roof over the lower sub-roof. Sun's high and bright and beating down. Twenty-five feet? Maybe. If I hang by my hands and then drop, I might not die.

Or just go to the door. Go back to the ward and take the candy like a good boy and shut out the shibboleth forever. I could *become* the cage, instead of living inside of it.

Become the cage.

I bang on the door and yell at the top of my lungs. Long minutes banging until my throat is raw and my hands are sore.

Nobody comes.

Over at the gigantic air-conditioning units now. I can sabotage them. Once the air-conditioning units go out, they'll send up maintenance men to repair them, right? That's what they'll do.

Standing near the AC units is like standing in the noise of a tornado. I find an access panel, but it has a padlock on it. I check the other units. The same.

I run my fingers around the edges of the panel door, find a grip, and pull as hard as I can, hoping to bend the metal door back. It's not that thick, more like tin than steel.

There's pain, there's always pain. It's our constant companion through life. This time in my hands.

Fingers gushing blood, bright. Dripping. Blood dripping from my hand.

I strip off my hospital shirt and wrap my hand with it, cursing into the steaming summer air, in French, German, Latin, and other languages I didn't even know I knew.

I go back to the hutch and bang on it with everything I've got, leaving blood streaks that dry into brown smears right before my eyes on the sun-seared door. I scream until my larynx rebels and goes scratchy, sweat stinging my eyes and pouring off my body, down my naked torso and discoloring these absurd hospital pajama pants.

Chest heaving, I wait. Hoping someone—Sinequa, Buster, *anyone*—opens the door and takes me back downstairs and gives me water. A bandage for my hands.

No one comes.

I walk back to the edge and stare out at the grounds. Look again at the sub-roof, the howl and rush of the air-conditioning units deafening.

I'm too much a coward to jump, goddamn me.

Eventually, I slump down in the slowly moving patch of shade offered by the hutch. It lengthens to the east, slowly.

My head pounds like double kick drums. The pressure

behind my eyes becomes near intolerable. I unwrap my hand just to peek at the bloody mess. It stings horribly and hurts deeper than just a cut might feel, as if the sharp metal sliced me to the bone.

I hang my head on my knees, panting in the shade, and wait for the sluggish blood to subside.

...

Pressure.

I must have dozed off, because the shadows are longer now and the whole world is wreathed in hazy streamers on this great height and the air roars with the white noise like it will never stop.

It's hard to think now, and it's not even been twenty-four hours since I found myself up here.

I stand, move my body in a creaky jumble of limbs over to the shrinking puddle and fall to my hands and knees. The water, heated by the sun and the semisolid tar of the roof, burns as it touches my lips and scorches my throat. But I drink, forcing my throat to work, up and down, taking the water inside me. As long as I can, I drink.

Pushing up, off my hands and knees, I stumble over to the crenellations above the sub-roof and stand in one of the gaps between teeth and sway there, hands upon the hot stone surface—radiant heat I can feel even through the swaddled mess of my left hand. Looking out at the tops of trees and the manicured grounds with the rush and howl of wind inside my head and pressure behind my eyes, I ready myself for the jump.

It's there, on the ledge, standing between two worlds, one of sky and wind and pain and heat, and the other one, dark and limitless, that I feel the eyes behind my eyes open and I'm out above it all, looking down on the wasted mongrel-ape clutching the stone with one good hand and then falling away, higher and higher until I'm where the raven might fly, far above Tulaville and the Arkansas River winking like hammered silver in the bright light of day and then beyond that, higher and higher, until I can see the curvature of the earth far below me and taste the coldness of the silent void of space, airless and limitless, the cold silences between the stars. I move as thought does, beyond any idea of speed or physics, above the wheeling center of the galaxy where there slumbers some massive black hole devouring all, yet keeping all of creation held in orbit.

I'm transparent. I see all.

Something snaps. The moment of wild blue yonder is over, and my awareness is booted back into the meatsuit.

Dislocation. Confusion. Heart hammering, I tense my legs and feel my stomach burbling with the birdshit-tar water. I cramp, bend over, and send the liquid pouring out of me in a thunderous *wrolf* to the sub-roof.

My head spins and I think I'm going to fall forward, but I push away in the last instant and I truly fall—and it seems farther a journey than the last, flying back from the galactic center—but falling backward to the roof. My head bounces off the roof, hard, filling my vision with bright swarming motes and a matching bright pain in my mouth that fills with blood. Bit my tongue.

The outraged flesh.

On my back, staring up into the hard sky and brutal sun for a long, long while, waiting for the raven to cross the sky above me, waiting for a cloud to pass across the face of the sun, waiting for some indication that there's life in this world other than the living pain wracking my incarcerado flesh.

When nothing happens, I close my eyes to shut it all out. The heat, the taste of my rancid burning mouth, the bile, the empty sky, the rush of incessant white noise.

I hold them closed until I know no more.

...

Night now, and I awake from a dream of vineyards and a girl in the moonlight and the taste of wine and her sweet mouth on mine.

The pressure is gone. The world below is filled with people, and I can sense them like a fish, swimming in coral, senses his own kind through silent vibrations. Through sworls and eddies of water. Through chemical trails and the scent of blood in the water.

I sense them.

Each one moves through his or her evening like upright unlit matches—this is how I see them. Each person a body wearing an unlit match head for a noggin. My brain conjuring images from each. A hurt, a love, a wedding, a funeral. A broken heart. The avalanche of memory crashes in on me in a mad tsunamic rush. But that part of me, the part that would erode and wash away—that part of me that was soft and unyielding—has become stone.

The memories wash over me and recede.

The stars wheel, and I reach out with the burning ember of my mind and light the matchsticks, all of them, flaring up in the darkness of the night. It's like cobwebs burning away.

I look out from a thousand eyes. Listen with a thousand ears.

As one, they turn and look toward the ceiling, to the thing upon the roof.

It's only moments before the hutch door opens and Buster comes through, followed by others. I see my wasted body lying there in the starlight from multiple perspectives at once, yet it makes perfect sense to me now, how I can inhabit a town, a Rider behind their eyes. Pulling levers. Working their legs. Arms.

Buster scoops up my prone form like holding a baby, and we descend through the innards of the building. On the first floor, he places me on a gurney and another nurse—her name is Becky Caldwell—gives me water and puts me on a saline drip and slathers some sort of unguent on my third-degree sunburns. Cleans and wraps my hand. I lie there as wasted as a mummy.

I am a dream to them, behind their eyes. I've learned kindness on the mountaintop. I pass from mind to mind like a daydream or an errant thought.

Buster doesn't realize I'm with him or even that *here is the boy who escaped*. No, I am just a series of tasks that needed to be done, and now that they are, Buster is free to return to the fourth-floor ward.

I move through the minds like a wind over wheat, fast and leaving behind nothing.

In the patients, I cool them. I calm them. I settle upon them like some ghostly Haldol but softer and more beneficent. I race down their hallways and through their attics. There are terrible things there—countless horrors—stored away in cabinets and cubbyholes and hidden in trunks and stashed away in closets. Fathers, mothers, brothers, sisters. War, sex, famine, abuse. Violence. Rape. Revenge.

The ones we love destroy us. The ones we love make us strong.

All of it I eat. I ingest the cancers because I can take it all now and not be hurt.

I am no longer human.

And the pressure never was behind my eyes. It was without. I feel it now like radiant heat from a stone or feverish boy—I can feel it emanating from the outside world. And with just a *twist*, I wall off these people—*my people*—like a levee protects its city from a storm.

Whatever's there in Maryland, waiting, sending out its poison into the ether, it *will not* have these poor lost souls.

Before Buster wheels me into the private room where I will withdraw from the multitude, I wipe any memory of my passing from them all and make sure that they are lying down before I put them into a soft, restful sleep.

ELEVEN

Morning, and I can stand again. Move my body. Piss and breathe and walk.

But I can't find Rollie in the multitude. The shibboleth has returned to me—it has changed and grown, or maybe I have—but Rollie is hidden from my sight.

I shuffle through the memories of the patients and hospital employees searching for her. It comes in fragments. Jumbled images. Poached memories. Stolen scenes.

Rollie shuffling out of isolation, her face numb, seen by Betsy Russell, the scrappy nurse with the muscles. Rollie looked wasted and zombielike, Betsy noted, but Betsy felt very much the same way, not having slept at all the night before.

From Buster—who had managed to sleep two hours the night before—she seemed muted but said, "Sorry about the other day," as he pricked her with a syringe brimming with Haldol. She followed it up with, "Where's the new kid?" Buster was gracious enough to give a grunt. There was no change in her face as the drugs began to swim upstream.

Steve-O answered her. "Busted loose. Escaped. That punk kid." Steve-O noted that Rollie's expression curdled at the news.

From twenty different eyes a glimpse of her shuffling the halls, as if looking for a lost pet, muttering. As she passed

Jacey Krews—the lean boy who so assiduously listened to Mr. Fingernails as he said such strange things—Rollie was saying, "Kissed me. Kissed me," and scratching her wrists over and over.

After that she passed out of everyone's sight for a long while except for a glimpse—from Jordan Stephens, a bipolar gay kid originally from New Jersey and voluntarily committed due to lack of sleep and suicidal tendencies—of her testing the doorknob of a supply closet, opening it, and peering inside.

When she did not turn up for her afternoon medication, Dr. Sinequa rousted the nurses on duty and had them search every nook and cranny of the ward.

It was Christina Fletcher, a plump country girl with a rich voice and a constant tune whirring and circling in her head—*I am you and you are me though we always disagree*—who discovered Rollie's wasted corpse hanging from an exposed pipe in the janitors' closet from a noose made of shop towels. Christina's first thought was that she was surprised Rollie weighed enough to suffocate from hanging.

...

I am a ghost now to the nurses, doctors, and patients. I sense a few Riders, yet the staff makes no fuss or squawk as I walk among them, their gazes sliding over me like a snake slipping over a rock into a stream to disappear. The eyes I see from, they do not see me. The eyes the Rider inhabits . . . I do not know. But it told me to leave back at Casimir and now that I have, it seems content not to impede my departure.

Before the elder awakens.

On the ground floor, North Wing, I find an employee's

locker room and a nurse changing into his blue duds and squeaky shoes. I wait, sitting on the benches, as he changes.

It's not that I'm invisible now. It's that I'm the blind spot in their mirror. I'm a wee little adjustment in the ledger. But still, it's weird to see a guy changing out of his street clothes, down to his tighty-whities, not five feet away from me.

When he finishes, I give a little *twist*, and he conveniently leaves his locker open on his way out.

He's a little thicker around the middle than me, and a good three inches taller, so I have to roll the cuffs and put on two pairs of his socks even to think about getting the guy's big black harness boots to stay on my feet. His short-sleeve shirt swallows my torso in a gulp. And though it's not the most sanitary, I use his toothbrush and toothpaste to scrub the funk from my teeth. Focus on the tongue.

The reflection of myself in the mirror is gaunt, peeling. And sad. I look like a withered old man wearing the clothes of his youth.

I've grown old.

Sixteen and I've grown old. Deep lines shooting away from my eyes. Lean and angular and hungry. I don't like the dead glint to my expression, but I can't seem to wipe if from my face. It's the dull gaze of a predator, the lifeless eye of a shark—cold, implacable. I try to sneer.

I can't.

I'm not really me anymore.

...

Of all the souls in Tulaville Psych, Dr. Billy Grainger—and more specifically his 1970 Plymouth GTX—has my attention this morning. I want to burn the memory of Rollie and Tulaville out on the blacktop, but that particular bit of muscle car seems too suspicious and identifiable.

Given those I might not be able to sway or adjust with the shibboleth—and because I'd rather not be constantly adjusting the general pop—I go with Rusty Greewell's Honda Accord, as bland as cafeteria food and just as safe.

In Dr. Sinequa's office, I stand before his desk as he types a report on his laptop and sips coffee. He does not glance at me.

He looks good, rested. He woke this morning in his office, wondering how he'd fallen asleep and slept the night through. His phone showed multiple messages from his wife. His personal trainer.

But he had slept the night through in this chair and felt wonderful when he awoke. Surprised to find all his staff had the same experience. A blessing and a miracle, the more religious-minded of them had said, smiling.

That helps ease the pain of Rollie, some.

I watch Dr. Sinequa.

I could make him dance, make him give himself a dose of Haldol, enough to float an elephant in a canoe all the way downstream to zombietown.

I don't. I just hold up a finger like a gun, point it at his egg-shell cranium as he continues to type, and say, "Gimme all your money."

He withdraws his wallet, places it on the desk. On a piece of paper, he writes, BANK OF THE OZARKS - PIN: 1947. FIRST SECURITY - PIN: 0531.

"Danke schoen, Herr Doktor," I say.

···

I stop at the highway, look back at the brooding old hulk of Tulaville Psych. The roof looks so remote, half-obscured by the trees lining the drive.

Good-bye, Rollie.

Good-bye, Shreve.

···

Easy enough to look up her address on the computers at the John Gould Fletcher Library. I watch her house until she leaves, gets in her little sedan, and putters off to the local grocery store. A Kroger. Moms used to pronounce it "Kay Roger," which was stupid but still made me laugh when I was a boy.

I follow, easing the Accord behind her.

Driving. I have no license. Just the memories of hundreds of people. I've flown airplanes, manned .50-cal chain guns on Hueys, and dived the Great Barrier Reef. Stolen memories. Tailing a septuagenarian in a Honda Accord is a cakewalk in the park, sniffing daisies.

She takes a long-ass time shopping. I twist and turn the dial on the radio and wait for her to come out. When she does, holding two small plastic bags, I put the car in gear, exit my parking spot, and pull up, blocking her car.

Window down. My arm draped outside. Casual. Like I'm supposed to be here.

"Hey, Nurse Cheeves!" I say. This gets her attention. "It's nice to see you again. I'm not here to hurt you. Actually, I'm very sorry for what happened. I made mistakes. Nobody is going to get hurt this time. I'm taking care of things." If that's not enough, I say, "I promise."

She nods, almost imperceptibly. I can tell she's terrified, little tremors in the flesh of her cheek, a quaver in her hands.

She's standing by her car, holding her shopping bags and goggling at me through the window of the Accord. "I have a little favor to ask. There's a photo that was in my cell at Casimir. I need you to get it for me. It's a picture of Jack Graves and a girl."

"Why, I—"

"If they haven't tossed and cleaned my cell, it'll be in the top drawer of the dresser. If they *have* tossed it, it'll be in Administration. Sorry for the way this sounds but . . . *I command you to get that photo for me.* Understand?"

"Yes. I—"

"You will find that photo and mail it here." I hand her a slip of paper on which I've written an address. The address of Jerome Abraham Aaronson. My old buddy from another hospital, another time.

I'm through with hospitals. I'm through with cages.

"Thank you. What I'm going to say now is not for your ears, and you will not remember it. It is for a man named Quincrux."

She wavers, standing poleaxed. I wonder if she will fall. I open the door, leave the Accord idling in the parking lot, and escort her to her car.

Once her bags are in the trunk, she turns to me, her old rheumy eyes watering. I say, "Quincrux, I am coming for you."

She blinks. Tears pool and make little paths across her wrinkled yellow skin. So small, this woman. I must be gentle.

"Nurse Cheeves? I know I've already done too much. To you. To everyone at Casimir. I'm so sorry. But I have one more thing to say. I *command you* to forget me and go be happy. Can you do that?"

She nods, pouring tears but smiling now. I spark inside her mind, for just an instant. Her match head ignites. Shines bright.

She will sleep well tonight.

■■■

Driving now, and every time I glance at the passenger seat, I feel its emptiness. I drive east, on 40, toward Memphis, Nashville. Beyond that, the East Coast.

To find Jack.

Quincrux.

PART THREE:
THOSE ETHERIC HEIGHTS

TWELVE

Riders. Everywhere. Seems that a large cross-section of folks on the East Coast have visited Maryland at one time or another.

On the drive up, the farther east I move, the more Riders I encounter. I buy new clothes at a Target outside of Nashville, spotting Riders and spending the whole shopping spree worrying about money and feeling guilty about the expense. Used to be, at the old Holly Pines Trailer Park, occasionally a cardboard box of hand-me-down clothes would appear at our front door, enough for Vig and me to get by. Never shopped for myself before. Thinking about Vig hurts some.

Getting a little worried about the ruse. Teenager, driving alone cross-country. But I'm sixteen now, and even though I don't have a license, I could. There's a little stubble on my jaw. And there's the fact that I look like a withered old man.

Strange, I've got a bellyful of memories not my own, but this is the first time I've been alone and in control of my life since, like, ever. Or maybe I've always been holding the wheel: raising my brother, wiping up Moms's spills and lighting her smokes, dealing candy to the general pop back at Casimir.

I feel lost and centered, all at once. Driving is such a hypnotic thing, or maybe that's the aftermath of the Haldol and the return of the shib.

...

Rolling fast on 70 out of Ohio into Pennsylvania. I pull the car into a Chevron, put forty bucks in the tank courtesy of Dr. Sinequa. Nab a Red Bull and some beef jerky and chips. Stand for a long time in front of the candy rack, thinking about all the sugar I've slung. Pocket the change.

Once past the Pittsburgh exits and signage, I catch the sparkle of flashing blue from the rearview.

Moment of panic. All my experience, even my time on the run with Jack, makes me want to bolt, to jam down the accelerator and flee.

But I don't. I wait, heart hammering, and slow the car, pull it over on the shoulder.

The trooper lumbers over, and it isn't until he's approaching that I even think of peeping his noggin.

Damn. Rider.

I make a hard, sharp run at his mind anyway, looking for a crack to slip through, but it's like attacking the hull of a battleship with an icepick. And the Rider doesn't stir behind the trooper's mirrored sunglasses.

He's tall and rangy, this trooper. Looks like a basketball player.

I'm learning that there are bulls everywhere you go. The Casimir bull isn't really any different from the Tulaville bull, who ain't too different from the Pennsylvania State Trooper bull.

When he gets to the window, I roll it down. He says, "License? Registration and proof of insurance?"

Mind racing. Cars and semis whip by in a mad cacophony of wind and the constant howl of wheels on pavement.

Only one thing to do.

At the limits of my range, I cast out my awareness. Everything slows the moment I go into the ether, out of myself, as if it's the flesh that slows down thought and, once free of the synapses and the electrochemical intelligence machine that is Shreveport Justice Cannon, my awareness becomes turbocharged, hopped up on meth and racing far faster than the sluggish normal world.

Back along 70 a quarter of a mile, I see the spark of a woman, the candle flame of a soul burning, cocooned in her own little world, gnawing her lower lip as she listens to an audiobook. I slip in as easy and smooth as I can. Cheryl Greene, CPA, music aficionado and vinyl collector, driving to York, Pennsylvania, to help her grandmother move into a smaller condo (and possibly peruse her ancient jazz and big band platters), doesn't even feel it as I take control of her hands.

It's easy enough to sideswipe the trooper's cruiser, making a thunderous *crunch* that nearly kicks me out of the lovely Cheryl. I get her car under control and, once Cheryl is far enough down the highway, release her and pop back home to the Ponderosa to watch as the trooper hustles back to his now-dented cruiser and speeds off to ticket the only slightly worse-for-wear Miss Green.

I grip the steering wheel hard, panting into the interior of the car.

I put the car back in gear and pass the trooper as fast as I can without speeding. Holding my breath as the flashing lights pass to my right. I catch a glimpse of Cheryl's pretty face twisted into distress.

Sorry, Cheryl. I have this thing, the shibboleth, and I'm going to use it.

That's what I think about. The shibboleth. Used to be, I worried about the morality of using people. Controlling them. The conflicted power of the shibboleth. The common utterance. The password phrase. The metric shitload of filched history I have in my belly. Quincrux. What lies sleeping in Maryland. The Riders. Rollie.

But most of all, where is Jack?

The radio holds nothing for me. I scan the dial, back and forth, looking for something to distract me from my rear window. The music is vapid. Two days locked on a roof burned away my capacity to enjoy music.

Or maybe radio has always sucked this hard.

■■■

It's easy getting the hotel clerk at the Days Inn outside of Brookville to comp me a room, and I spend the night eating pizza and watching skin flicks on the pay adult channels. The women are tanned silicone bags with too much makeup and gigantic hair. The men, all dick and gym-bred muscles. I'd probably rub one out to their shenanigans, but the gyrations and histrionic orgasms seem like tantrums. My dick won't stay hard. Maybe I could spank it if it wasn't for their dead-doll eyes.

Eventually, I find a news station.

The insomnia epidemic has grown.

State and federal police, fire, and medical teams are overtaxed and exhausted, and the US National Guard has been activated to help with overcrowding in Pennsylvania state hospitals. There are parking-lot tent cities being set up to accommodate those suffering from the worst of the insomnia.

Local crime is up 3,000 percent. National car accidents up 7,200 percent.

Two nuclear reactor meltdowns. One in Tennessee caused by negligence and poor safety standards. The one in Arizona, the anchor announces with feigned solemnity, domestic terrorism. Cut to video footage of a dumpy man with glasses walking through industrial hallways with an automatic rifle in his hands, shooting people.

Cut to a mass suicide in the Pacific Northwest in a small Pentecostal church. One hundred and thirty-six dead due to the "sleeping potion" their pastor promised them came to him in a dream. Funny how the God-given sleeping potion looked exactly like poisoned Kool-Aid.

Four different sets of parents murdering their children and then themselves.

Two plane crashes just during the time it took for me to drive through Illinois. United Flight 571 from Chicago to San Francisco went down in an Iowa cornfield, responders too sluggish to save anyone. And American Flight 1114 from Miami to New York crashed on landing at LaGuardia. Dramatic footage of the plane's wings yawing unexpectedly, nipping the ground, and ripping off abruptly in an explosion of fire as the rest of the plane rolls over and breaks in half, pouring smoke. No word yet on survivors.

Cut to the president declaring a state of emergency.

I flip the channel. SpongeBob and Patrick fight, laugh, blow bubbles, hunt jellyfish. I wonder if Vig still loves SpongeBob, or if he's hardened so much now that he can't laugh at Mr. Krabs.

Jack never much liked SpongeBob either.

I don't feel guilty as I fall asleep, the world out there burning.

THIRTEEN

Midday, the skyline of New York becomes visible, beyond the smoke and traffic of the I-78 into Manhattan, but I'm too focused on driving to do anything more than note its presence. All my memories, stolen and native, didn't prepare me for driving into New York. It seems that's something you just have to do for yourself.

I've passed more than thirty overturned cars, some smoking husks. Cops, ambulances. I'm sure the tanks will be there soon. That's the way it works on television, anyway.

Hours later, I'm in the city and parking's a total bitch. I circle two blocks for an hour before cashing out and whipping the ride into a nearby garage. The attendant, a mangy-looking greaser with a ponytail and a bad complexion, has a Rider peeking from behind the iron curtains. For a moment, as I fork over the money, he looks like he's got something on the tip of his tongue.

Or maybe he's just doing his job best he can.

I know I'm long gone from Tulaville Psych, but damn, the paranoia is catching.

I park the car, walk down the stairwell stinking of urine, into the gray streets.

The weather is gorgeous, mid-eighties, the sun is out and there's a breeze, but the people on the streets look hollow and worn-out. Wary.

I head up a couple of blocks to Twentieth, near a park. Gramercy. That name seems familiar.

There are bearded men on boxes on the sidewalk, screaming warnings to passersby. One loon with a blow horn is ripe for Tulaville, trumpeting outraged verse.

I think about Jerry while I try to find his building. It's been a year. He was with me when I recovered from the knife wound the Dubrovnik woman gave me. Sometimes I have trouble even remembering what he looks like, other than the white hair and bushy eyebrows. It's as though I've stolen so many other people's memories, it's ruined my own. But Jerry was funny and asked too many questions. Bright eyes, but full of pain from the gallstones. Loved board games.

And here's the building. A nice one. I manage to catch the door before it closes as a harried-looking woman, cradling a squalling, florid child, exits. The boy's face is furious, screaming. Hands balled into tiny fists. I don't even have to go inside her head to know that she's thought about muffling the infant. And that's the difference between her and Schneider the bull. She doesn't act on the impulse. I am you and you are me though we always disagree.

I go inside the boy's mind like entering a maelstrom of emotion and desire. It's like a sea of water floating in outer space, wracked by millions of gravitational forces. There's no frame of reference. No up or down. None of the mental and emotional order that comes with adulthood.

I spark the matchstick of his mind, and his little head bursts into flames visible only to me. He shuts his mouth. Looks at me. It's strange when our eyes meet, the infant's and mine.

He'll sleep well tonight. And maybe so will his mother.

I move inside the old tiled foyer, pass the doorman who, luckily, has never been to Baltimore. Skim across his awareness and keep his eyes focused on everything but me. I'm invisible as I take the elevator.

The doors hiss open on the sixth floor, and I step out into the hallway.

Jerry's holding the photo when he answers the door. White-haired, eyebrows bristling, he wears a chambray shirt, khakis. White, comfortable tennis shoes and no socks. He's got skinny ankles, a thin chest. Large, liver-spotted hands. He's got the hard, knobby aspect of a withered boxer. He's dressed in a fashion that makes me think, *This is how rich folks dress down.* No sweatpants and flip-flops for the upper crust. Jerry's nicely tanned, making his white hair all the whiter. His craggy face splits into a great smile when he sees me.

"Ay, yay! Shreve!" He looks up and down the hall, bewildered. Then laughs and hugs me. Holding my arms, he leans back, gaze searching my face. "Somehow, I knew you would be visiting. But you look terrible."

"Thanks, Jerry. How's things?"

"Fair. Passing fair, my boy."

I look around his apartment. Nice digs. It's got two big bay windows looking out over the trees of the park. If you opened them, you could hear the bellows of the crazies on the sidewalk, clear as a bell.

I can hear the blow horn from the park crazy even with the window closed. Jerry says, "It is disturbing, these maniacs. Gramercy isn't a public park, and we never have people like this in our neighborhood."

"Looks pretty posh, this area."

He nods, a little sheepish. "It's mostly professional. Or monied. An old neighborhood."

I look about some more.

Big painting of red circles on a black field. Architectural magazines on a blocky, stylish coffee table. Nice comfy sofa. Spare decor except for a few frilly touches and pictures of young adults with children.

He watches me nosing about. Puts his hands on his hips, arms akimbo, and grins at me.

"First time in the city?" he says.

I say, "Ran a record store on the Lower East Side in the seventies." It was too hot in the summer and drafty in the winter and the rats had a field day in the remaindered pile in the basement. But I smoked a lot of weed. Or Wilson Welles did, and I have his memories.

He laughs like it's the best thing he's heard all year. "Always the joker, eh, Shreve?"

I've been here before, or some part of me has. But I just nod and look about. I say, "How you sleeping, Jerry? You're lookin' pretty good."

"The insomnia? Terrifying, no? Strangely, I am not affected. The wife is a different matter."

Figures.

Jerry's one of those knuckleheads, like Jack. A person with mental defenses so tough, getting in will hurt them. Maybe break their mind.

Whatever wavelength the sleeping thing in Maryland broadcasts on, casting its sleeplessness into the world, me, Jack, and Quincrux (I'm betting) are immune. Now we add Jerome Aaronson to those ranks. Not carrying a Rider, but mentally as impenetrable as a steel blast door. You get them sometimes, the stubborn ones. With my new strength—the new and improved shibboleth—I could make a run at him, try to get in. Maybe even do it. I got in once with Jack, made him see what I wanted him to see. It was brutal.

But I won't. In some ways, I like having someone, someone *unaffiliated*, impervious to mind tinkering. It means we can just be friends.

I peek at a picture of a brunette woman, easily fifteen years Jerry's junior, smiling and holding a tennis racket, gripping Jerry's arm.

"How 'bout something to drink?" Jerry says, still holding the picture.

"Go ahead and ask."

"Ask what?"

"What you've been waiting to ask since I knocked."

Jerry's smile falters, and he runs a mottled-brown hand through his white, curly hair. He sits in a chair, tugging up his pants like old folks do when they sit. He tosses the picture on the glass coffee table.

"Honestly, Shreve, I don't know where to start. How did you get here?"

"I drove."

"You have a car?"

"Stole it."

He stares at me for a long while. "I can't tell if you're lying to me or not."

"Jerry, I've never lied to you. Not once. You're the only person I can say that of."

"So you stole a car? Just stole it?"

"I had to escape."

"From juvie?"

"No. Psych ward in Arkansas."

He stands, totters off to a dry bar by the kitchen. Hardwood floors, glowing in the light. Recessed lighting. More modern art. Jerry's got a sweet pad for an old dude.

He says, "I think I'll have a drink."

"It's five o'clock somewhere."

Glass tumbler in hand, he pours dark amber liquid from a bottle, sips. "You sure you don't want anything?"

"Water?"

He disappears into the kitchen for a moment and returns with a bottle of fancy water. Four-dollar water. Nothing but the best for Jerry and the missus.

I twist off the top and take a big gulp.

He regains his seat and looks at me again. "So, you stole a car?" He perks up a tad. "From a psych ward? Why were you in a psychiatric ward?"

"Psychotic break."

He downs his drink in a gulp. Stands, gets another. Returns and sits, tugging up his pants legs at the crotch.

"Are you going to . . . I don't know. Do something crazy to me?"

"I don't think so. Little hurt you even asked that."

"I don't know, Shreve. You stole a car from an asylum? After escaping? And I'm not supposed to worry you're going to stab me or something?"

I sigh and sit opposite from him. The chair is comfy, plush. I sink in. Tired of running. Tired of driving. Tired of being on my own. Being alone. I need to rest. Regroup. And find Jack.

He points a finger at the photo. "They both have six fingers to a hand."

"Yeah. Jack and his girlfriend."

"Jack is the boy you were always looking for when we were in the hospital together in North Carolina?"

"I didn't tell you about him."

He puts his finger against his nose and winks. "I am not so old as to be blind, my friend. I see. He was with you at the Dubrovniks'?"

"Yes."

"Ah. Then why did you have this sent here?"

"Because I couldn't get back into Casimir to get it."

He puts his glass on the table with a heavy *clink*! and frowns at me. "I think, Shreve, I should ask you to leave if you are not going to give me more answers."

I sigh. Roll my eyes. I realize it's the action of a punk kid, but I do it anyway. Maybe to remind myself who I am. Maybe because after everything, I *am* still a punk kid.

I've got to spill.

●●●

I leave nothing out. He stops me when I get to Quincrux at the motel, when Quincrux took control of the clerk and shot the trucker.

"Shreve, I can check this easily online. Where did you say you were?"

"Chattahoochee."

"Is that a real place?"

"Yeah. We were at the Stay Inn! Motel. Quincrux took the clerk and killed the trucker."

He's silent for a while. I remember the big man's surprised expression as Jack and I blew past him. And his big silver belt buckle with a bucking bronco. And the million particles of his blood hung like baubles in the air.

"Okay, boychick. Let me get my computer."

"Hey, can I have a drink? You know, a real one?"

He purses his lips and shakes his head like it's the dumbest thing he's ever heard.

■ ■ ■

I might've fallen asleep sprawled out there in the chair as Jerry researched what I told him. When I open my eyes, I hear him murmuring in the kitchen to someone. Either the house is haunted, or he's made a call.

Later, I open my eyes as he sits across from me, a silver laptop with a glowing apple in his lap, clicking away.

"His name was Jason Crenshaw. The trucker. The clerk, Herschel Tidwell, died later from a massive stroke."

The weight of that sinks me farther in the chair, gravity growing stronger. But I push myself up. I'm so tired, but I need to go. I don't want Jerry to end up like the trucker.

He had a name. Jason.

I move forward and reach for the photo. He places a liver-marked hand on it before I can.

"This stays with me until you tell me it all."

"So you believe me?"

"I didn't say that, did I, Shreve?"

"You always answer a question with a question?"

"You always run from your problems?"

Screw this guy. He's prodding me now. Jabbing a stick

wherever he thinks I'm vulnerable. And I'm vulnerable *everywhere*.

"People get hurt when I'm around, Jer. I just need the photo."

He ignores that like I never even said it. Instead, he says, "So you're telling me you can read minds. Can you read mine?"

I shake my head.

"Why not? Should be easy, no? Old man sitting here asking for it?"

"It's not like that." I sit back down. "Most folks, getting in their head is as easy as sticking a knife in an open jelly jar. But other folks, it's harder. Sometimes because they're disturbed. Sometimes because they've had hard things happen to them and lived with it."

"You're talking abuse. Sexual?"

"Use your imagination. Humans are bizarre and terrible things."

"You say that like you're not one."

I don't reply.

Jerry shuts his laptop, places it on the coffee table.

"Will you finish your story, Shreve?"

I only hesitate a moment and then begin talking once more.

■■■

When I come to the end, he sucks his teeth. Shakes his head. His brow furrows, crags and crevices and crevasses.

I've told him everything. All of it. The theft of memories, the possessions. Rollie. I held nothing back. It felt like a confession.

"You stole those poor souls' happy memories? Like some

junkie?" He points to the window. "We have junkies here. More every day with the insomnia. Pitiful creatures."

"So you believe me?"

"I don't yet know. But if what you say is true and you've done these things . . . these things have been done to you. This man, this Quincrux . . ."

"Do I need to prove it to you?"

"I think that might be necessary."

"Okay."

"We'll need to go out. I'm hungry anyway."

Even though it's gorgeous outside, sun lowering into the golden hour, Jerry puts on a light tan jacket and a white straw hat. Very slowly, he changes his shoes, from the comfy running shoes to leather loafers. From a closet at the front door he gets a cane. Wooden, with a simple metal knob.

"Aren't you the clotheshorse?"

Jerry raises his considerably furry eyebrows. Possibly in amusement. Maybe outrage.

"I prefer 'clothes thoroughbred.'"

He does look quite dapper. We leave the apartment, taking the stairs instead of the elevator. Despite the cane, Jerry moves pretty well for an old dude.

On the street, he says, "You like pizza? We'll get you a New York slice."

The air smells of sewage and smoke and is filled with the sound of furious honking and the scream of sirens in the air. Men and women hustle past us, heads down. The crazies at the park have gone, maybe moved on to some more populous area. Multiple sirens. An NYPD cruiser whizzes by us as we walk south on Irving a couple of blocks away.

"Oh, no," Jerry says. He's limping a little, just a touch, and using his cane—*clack clack clack*—but he picks up the pace.

Pizza D'Resistance has been husked out by some sort of fire, and recently, judging by the char and melted-plastic smell, along with the two stores nearby, one selling shoes and the other a nail and pedi spa. The upper floors of the building have broken windows, tarred black by smoke.

"It's like a war zone or something," I say as another NYPD cruiser blasts past, sirens blazing. Despite the noise and confusion, there aren't many cars on the streets. Maybe it's too dangerous to drive now that everyone is working on zero hours' sleep.

Jerry's cane pops across my chest. Not hard. It's like he's getting my attention, stopping my forward movement, both physically and conversationally.

"Shreve. There are places in the world that this—" He pulls the cane away from my chest and jabs it at the burnt husk of a building. "This is far better than their everyday life. And war? What do you know of it?"

The smell of burning human waste and the percussive chuffing of the helicopter rotors as we unloaded the body bags to the LZ in the middle of the moisture-drenched Cambodian air. The chatter of rifle fire in the bush.

But I say, "Nothing. Living off the fat of the land, Jer-bear."

He frowns, either at the nickname or the pained expression on my face as I say it. "I do not like that."

"Sir, yes, sir."

"Always with the mocking." He sighs. "Maybe you can't help yourself. And maybe you know more of war than I might have thought. Come on, I see Herschel's is still open."

The door chimes as we enter, and at the deli counter Jerry orders a "half-and-half" sandwich with extra rye and two bags of chips and two sodas.

"Just one sandwich?"

"Just you wait."

At the register, I whip out my wallet, since I'm flush and don't want Jerry to think that I'm a mooch to top it all off, but he looks at me so furiously, furry eyebrows waggling like out-raged caterpillars, that I relent. He pays.

"Jerome!" The cashier's name tag reads DEBBI. "Such a shame about the fire, yes? Things getting terrible. No sleep and people getting careless," she says, almost gleefully. Some people thrive on tragedy.

Jerry nods his head sagely and tsks. "A terrible thing. No one was hurt, I gather?"

"In that, they were lucky. Everyone was awake when the fire started," Debbi says, taking Jerry's money and giving him a numbered ticket. "This your nephew?"

Jerry's old enough to be my grandfather, but I don't correct her.

Jerry says, "No. An old friend."

We take our chips and drinks and find a table in the near-empty deli. There's a couple eating furtively in the rear, heads close together. A tremendously fat man drinking coffee near the front window. And us.

By the time we've sat and I've opened my soda, Debbi calls out, "Fifty-three!" and I go back to the counter and take up the tray with what can only be described as a small mountain of meat with a single piece of rye bread perched on top. I assume the other piece is buried underneath the three hundred pounds of pastrami and corned beef. A massive plate with extra bread and pickles around the edges. I return to our seat carrying it.

For a while, all we do is eat, using our forks to make small sandwiches from the pile. Mustard. Pickles. It's very good. I didn't realize how hungry I was.

Afterward, Jerry says, "So."

"So?"

"How should we proceed?"

"You need proof."

"Yes."

"All right." I reach out, touching the flames of the nearest minds. No Riders in the building. No knuckleheads, either.

I close my eyes. Out in the ether—*those etheric heights*—and into the fat man at the front of the deli. His name is Massey D'Lainge, born in Podgorica, Montenegro, on New Year's Day, 1960, immigrated to America with his parents at the tender age of six. New York is all he's ever known. Never left the city. It's world enough for him. He weighs in at 337 pounds. Hasn't slept for a couple of days, and his heart hammers away in his chest furiously. In his considerable meatsuit, I stand, painfully—three-hundred-plus pounds is hell on the knees and ankles—and waddle back to where Jerry and the now vacated Shreve meatsuit sit.

I take a chair from a nearby table and sit. Jerry watches MeMassey closely.

"I can tell you anything you want to know about him, Jerry."

Gotta hand it to him. Jerry doesn't gape or go all agog at the parlor tricks. He says, "What was the game we played in that hospital in South Carolina?"

I laugh. It's a thick sound coming from this guy's meaty throat. "It wasn't South Carolina. It was North Carolina, Jer-bear. And the game was Double Shutter. You kept trying to tell me that your 'people' invented it."

"So, you're in there, Shreve? You didn't pay this man to say these things?"

"No." I say this simultaneously from both MeShreve and MeMassey. This time, Jerry jumps a little at the echo.

"Will he remember this?" he asks, raising a trembling hand.

"Maybe. Some do, some don't. The shibboleth works differently with different people. Some folks I can leave with a 'suggestion,' and they will forget. Or do what I ask of them if their will isn't too strong, and it's not anything they wouldn't do in normal life. I couldn't, say, tell him to kill the president, and he'd go buy a gun."

Jerry's eyebrows continue their thoughtful dance. "Let him go."

I do, diving back in the good old Shreve chassis. I open my eyes. Massey's looking somewhat startled.

"Massey," I say and bridge the gap between our minds. "I command you to forget this conversation. Also, I command you to go immediately to your doctor and have your heart checked out, and then I want you to go home and sleep. You will have no more trouble sleeping. Also, this isn't an order, more along the lines of a suggestion—lay off the doughnuts. Okay?"

The man nods his head, chins wobbling. He stands and lumbers out the front door.

I turn back to Jerry.

"Oy, vey. It is true."

"I've never lied to you, Jerry. Well, okay. Maybe a couple of times. But not about anything that really matters."

"You called it a shibboleth."

"*The* shibboleth. Quincrux said that to me once. He planted a message in one of the Casimir bulls' memories."

Jerry rubs his face. Looks out the window onto the street. Before he seemed pretty spry, but now he looks tired.

"You know what it means?"

"I think so."

"In Hebrew, *shibboleth* literally means 'grain.' Or sometimes 'stream' or 'fluid.' Or 'torrent.' And it was used as a password by the Gilead men after a battle. It has interesting connotations the way you use it."

"It just struck me when Quincrux said it. Sort of the phrase I hung all the weirdness on, if that makes sense."

He nods, and he's about to say something when his phone begins chirping. He holds up a finger and answers the phone, saying, "Ahuvi! Hold on one moment." He stands and walks away a few paces. After a few moments, he returns and says, "That was my wife. She hasn't been sleeping well lately—like everyone I know—and went down to a spa with some of her friends for the evening in hopes of relaxing. She won't be back tonight, which is good, I think. Because we have many things to discuss, do we not?"

"You tell her about me?"

"I mentioned I was having lunch with a friend, Shreve." He says this like he's squeezed the last bit of patience out of the tube he bought at the local bodega. "I did not tell her with whom."

"That's good."

"You are a wary young man."

"Being a fugitive with psychopathic telepaths on your ass tends to do that to you."

"Point taken. For the moment, it is just you and me. But Miriam will return tomorrow, midmorning, and before then we must figure out your final disposition."

A couple thousand different ways to tell him that I'll be captaining this vessel pop into my mind, none of them as snarky as I'd like.

So I nod like an idiot and say, "You got it."

"Let's get back to my apartment. We have much to discuss."

"You'll give me the photo then? I need it to find Jack."

"We shall see."

FOURTEEN

Sitting at his kitchen island, Jerry makes me start again from the beginning. Somewhere in North Carolina, after the Dubrovnik episode, when I was in the hospital. Hearing about my conversation with Quincrux, he exclaims, "That maintenance man was Quincrux? Very polite, yet I sensed something wrong with him. He kept coming in to change lightbulbs or take out the trash or check pipework—even though no pipework was in evidence. Limping, no?"

"Yeah." A permanent limp, I hope.

A look of creeping horror spreads across Jerry's face. He passes a hand over his eyes.

"You all right, Jer?"

"When I was a boy, a friend of mine went for a vacation in Florida and captured a snake. He would carry it around and feed it mice he bought at the local pet store. All the boys in the neighborhood were wild about that snake, and we'd congregate on Richard's stoop on Saturday morning in hopes of him letting us hold it."

"I've heard this one before. But it was a coral snake, right? And eventually it bit the boy and killed him."

"No, this is a true story, though your expression makes me think you do not believe me. Trust me, this is the story that *created* your story."

"Okay. So, what happened?"

"You said you know the story."

"I've heard it. He's showing off the snake, but then someone who knows something about snakes realizes, as he sees the boy handling it, that it's not a milk snake, it's a coral snake. And as the boy freaks, the snake bites him and he dies."

Jerry shakes his head. "Unfortunately, no. He was showing the snake off at the local park—it *was* a gorgeous creature. And some herpetologist happened to spy it and 'freaked out,' as you say. But it was not the boy who died. It was the snake. They snatched up sticks and killed it right then and there on the spot, even with a herpetologist present. Poor, beautiful creature."

"No way."

"I was there."

"I don't believe you."

"I have never lied to you, Shreve. Well, except for a couple times." He winks at me.

"Jerry, sometimes you really surprise me."

Jerry raises his eyebrows. "I do not celebrate death, nor should you."

Good point. "But why'd you bring it up?"

"Eh? Oh." He stands, not looking at me, as if he's ruminating on something, and toddles over to a cabinet and withdraws a plate. He uncaps a cookie jar and places some cookies on a plate. Jerry's got his own speed.

He sets the plate down, and I take one of the wonderful little vanilla cookies and pop it in my mouth. He picks one up and chews very thoughtfully, very slowly. Finally, he says, "Sometimes, learning one little thing can change your whole view of the world."

"Like learning that a snake is poisonous."

"No. Like the world suddenly changing its whole opinion about *you*."

"I don't get it."

He looks at me. "You will, someday, Shreve. You might have lived a hundred lives, yet you are still a boy. It's all about sweat equity."

There's a thundering boom that shakes the building, and the lights flicker off and on. We move to the bay windows and look out at New York's nighttime skyline, close-up, over Gramercy Park. A car has exploded, as far as I can tell, down the block. Trash fires spew living embers that make intertwined patterns as they rise. Shadowy figures rush along the streets, casting long shadows like wolves skirting the edges of campfires. Jerry pushes open the windows.

The smell of burning rubber on the wind and the scream of sirens reach us.

Jerry says, "This is not good."

No shit, Sherlock.

"Come, there's no need to stare out at the signs of our time. We are on the brink. But you must finish the story."

...

We return to the kitchen. The electricity remains on, though the lights flicker. The clock on the microwave blinks 12:00, over and over.

I take up the thread of the story. The cookies are gone, and I've reached my stint in the Tulaville Psychiatric Hospital and the sad end of Rollie. It's hard to talk about, her inglorious end.

"You liked this girl, did you?"

"In what way? I thought she was smart, I guess. But I didn't know her very well. I wasn't even attracted to her."

"Then why did you kiss her, like you said?"

Dammit. Why can't he just shut up?

"Because she asked me to."

"That's not a reason."

I probe the hard, steely surface of his mind. Still like a ball bearing. *He gets right to the heart of it.* But I say, "Because I needed her help."

"So you used her. Is that right?"

I can just stand up and walk out the door. I can do it right now.

Jerry frowns. "You just looked twice at the door. You are going to leave?"

"Hey, what is this, psychoanalysis?"

He waves a hand at the door to his apartment. "Go ahead. Leave. Run away. It is what you do, is it not?"

"You don't really know anything about me."

"I know more than most. It's okay to feel bad about the way you treated this poor girl."

"It wasn't my fault."

He remains silent for a long while, looking at me.

"No. Her death is not *on* you, I don't think. But you should have treated her as a human. Not as some . . ." His eyebrows do more interesting things. "As some *pawn* in a game. Do you understand?"

"I don't need this, Jer-bear."

"You obviously wanted it." He sighs and looks ineffably tired. "I worry about you. And I thank the Creator that you cannot get inside me. Not with your mind. Not with your words.

You are a problem, a cipher."

"Don't worry about me," I say. "I'll be just fine."

"Oh, Shreve. This ability will separate you from the rest of humanity. We will all become pawns to you. Tools for you to use. Like your Rollie. Despite her obvious imbalances. Her— how do you say? —'iffy' state. No, you are not to blame for her death. But you were a factor. A catalyst. In that sense, you bear some responsibility."

"I—" I have nothing to say for myself.

I think of the roof again, the burning sun and the taste of birdshit-tar soup and the countless little match heads beneath me waiting to be lit as I sat upon that great height. I think about the shibboleth and my power now. About Quincrux and Ilsa Moteff and their ability to play people on the board. And Rollie. The ammonia taste of her mouth and how her tongue wormed against my teeth, trying to enter, desperate and lonely.

My heart expands in my chest. It's the burn in the back of the throat that hurts, trying to keep the sobs from coming. Jerry watches me, placid and calm. If I can just choke it back and forget about everything, I'll keep control. I need to keep control.

It's like a flood. And when the sobs hit, I double over on the kitchen seat. And weep. For Rollie. For myself. For Jack and Vig and Booth and Moms. For us all.

You're born into pain. Never a moment free of it.

Jerry watches. He doesn't pat me on the back or coo comforting words to me. He doesn't offer sympathy. He just watches.

Finally, when I'm done, he snatches a paper towel off the roll by the sink and hands it to me. It's rough against my face.

He walks to the bar, takes out a bottle of wine, pops the cork, and then surprises me when he pours me a glass. I wipe my streaming eyes, my running nose. I feel husked out by the crying jag. And I hate that he saw.

"Growing up, my parents always served the older children wine at dinner. It was a symbol of our increasing maturity."

The glass stands before me. I pick it up. Smell it. It holds spices and the fragrance of smoke. And it smells like Moms. I put it down.

"I thought you wanted a 'real' drink?"

"Now that I think about it, no. There'll be time enough for that, I guess, later."

Jerry takes his glass, tilts it back, and pours half of it down his throat. "I do not have your mental abilities." He pauses, thinking. He drinks some more wine, sipping this time. "However, I knew you would decline. Which is why I offered it."

Some people know things just by intelligence and wisdom. Not by mind reading and psychic whizbangery. They kind of suck, the smart ones. My cheeks burn with embarrassment of it all—the titty-baby behavior, the predictability of my not drinking the wine. My damned situation.

"The way I see this is—" He counts his points off on his fingers. "One, you have to learn the nature of this thing in Maryland and stop whatever it's doing. The insomnia. The craziness that's taking over the world."

I say, "The Riders."

He nods. "Ahh. Yes. The Riders. I can't help but think their role in this will be revealed soon." He raises another finger. "Two, you must confront this Quincrux, or you'll never be able to have a life for yourself."

He drinks more wine and thinks for a long while without saying anything. His eyebrows make interesting shapes.

"Three, you must use this ability of yours to help people as you can. If not, you'll become less and less human, Shreve. This is important. We will all become pawns to you."

"That won't happen. The shibboleth—" I don't know how to say it. "It's like I'm more connected to everyone and everything. Not distant."

"Be that as it may, you must do this thing that you did to the people of the Tulaville Hospital. You must do this thing wherever you go."

"It's my job to save the world?"

"No, it's your job to save yourself. Doing this will help with your grooming."

"What?"

"You'll be able to look at yourself in a mirror."

"Ha. So funny. You import that stuff?"

He waves his hand, shooing my comeback away like a fly. "And finally, you must free your friend. Jack. You and he are bound up in this business. Quincrux too. But Jack is the thread that strings the pearls. He will be your partner in this great work." He sighs, pulls out the photo from his pocket, and tosses it on the island counter. "It is yours, Shreve. In the morning, I will have some money for you."

"For what?"

"So you do not have to steal."

"Nah. You don't have to do that."

Jerry sighs and then finishes his wine. He looks at me gravely. "Stealing is the most callous of crimes. It assumes that you are above the needs and rights of your victim. It dehumanizes you. And we need you to stay human, Shreve."

"Why do this?"

"I like you, you stubborn fool. And I do not have your gift. Or the will and youth to use it. I am old."

"Yeah, but all this . . ."

"My wife. My son and daughters. My grandchildren. None of them can sleep. You must help them." As he said it, the sound of glass shattering somewhere on a floor above us comes, bright and cacophonous. Bellows and thumps through the floor, as if men are fighting. Jerry stared at me like it was some sign.

"I hear you, Jer-bear."

"You will accept the money?"

"Yes."

"And commit no more thefts?"

"I can't swear to never steal again. Necessity, you know, is a real bitch."

"No, necessity is the mother of invention."

He looks tired now. And I feel it as well. The long-ass day grinding to its end. The weight of the conversation. The rawness of my throat from the crying jag. Being a titty-baby can take a lot out of a boy.

The responsibility of what he laid on me.

"I have a sofa for you, Shreve. We used to have another bedroom, but Miriam converted it to her office once our boy left home. You will stay here tonight?"

I'm yawning as he says it. I can sleep in the car. I'd rather sleep in the car, really; I've already made a nest in the back-seat of new, scratchy clothing stinking of the factory they came from and dangling price tags that I bought with money I stole.

But that's too much like some animal. Like the shadows that move beyond the firelight illuminating the wild New York night.

So I say, "Okay. You got an alarm clock?"

Jerry tries to grin, but it sort of dies on his face.

"You are a wary young man. I wish you could relent."

"Just love the early morning sunshine, Jer-bear."

His face clouds. "Please explain this name to me. 'Jer-bear'?"

"Well, there's this cartoon and there are these bears, right?"

"Okay. That explains part of it."

"And they *care*. They're *care bears*."

"What do they care about?"

"Hell if I know. Kids, I guess."

He nods. Puts his hands on his waist, arms akimbo. "Then this is okay. You may continue to call me this."

Well, that takes the fun out of it, I think, but he's already heading to the hall to get blankets and a pillow.

···

Before sleep my mind unspools into nighttime air and I send my awareness out, through the building, lighting fires in the minds of everyone in it, flames jumping from match head to match head. Then farther out, to the next building, and the next.

So many people. Thousands and thousands within a few feet, a few yards, from me. Pacing, cursing, screwing. Hating and hurting their loved ones. Crying and moaning and gibbering into the sleepless night.

I touch their minds. I set their heads on fire, and they burn down the matchstick and fade into slumber, sigh into sleep. Into death maybe, when someone wants to die. To sleep. To dream.

Turning on lights and turning them out.

Farther and farther afield I fly, dashing like a forest fire from treetop to treetop, leaping from mind to mind until I can touch no more. For a moment, hovering and intractable above the city's multitudes, I have an instant of vertigo, a yawing, teetering sensation, as if I'm going to have all the memories come crashing back in and begin babbling in French once more. But the memory of sun and the rooftop and the taste of tar on my tongue and the flapping and clatter of raven wings comes to me and I steady. Become myself again. Or less of myself.

It takes a while to find my poor lost body, lying in Jerry's posh apartment on Twentieth and Irving, New York City, New York State.

Thousands will sleep tonight.

But I don't know if I will.

FIFTEEN

I hear his phone start buzzing and rattling on the granite counter before I realize Jerry's been puttering around in the kitchen for a while now. I haven't slept, but I did enter a trancelike state where images and memories flickered across the dark cinema of my eyelids, fleeting. Not asleep enough to dream, but asleep enough to have strange catfish from the murky depths of my subconscious come up and slap at the surface of my awareness.

Jerry says, quietly into his phone, "Ahuvi! I've missed you. Yes, I'm fine. I have a guest here now—yes, this early. I understand that it is strange. Yes, dear." He pauses and remains quiet for a long while. "It would be best if I explain it to you when you get home and have an opportunity to meet him."

Another silence, longer.

"Yes. Mir, we have been married a long time now and you can trust me, no? I have not brought home some mongrel stray—" He catches himself. "Or maybe I have, at that. But mongrels are always the best dogs, are they not? We can talk about this when you get home."

After a bout of protestations of love he hangs up. I stay where I am, lying on his couch, listening to the building. It's quiet except for some creaking, the normal expansion and contraction of wood and stone and steel. The chuff of the air-conditioning and the ticking of a thousand clocks.

Finally, I rise, creaky in places, just like the building.

"Ah, you are up!" Jerry grins at me from the kitchen. "Are you hungry?"

"I could eat." I could eat a whole loaf of bread and a package of bacon. But I imagine there'll be no bacon here.

"Wonderful! Come! I will make you my specialty."

I slip on my shoes and make sure the photo is in my left pocket, the Accord's keys in my right.

Turns out Jerry's specialty is toast and eggs. He fries them up nice while I slurp at a glass of orange juice.

"There is an envelope for you, there."

I pick up the envelope and peek inside.

Cashola. Green. Lots of it.

"Jerry . . ."

"No, no more discussion on this matter. You have a hard path to hold to."

I take it, stuff it in my pocket. It doesn't feel right, this massive gift, but nothing feels right. And where did he get all that money this early in the morning?

"And you earned it, I think," Jerry says, smiling.

"What're you talking about?"

"I walk every morning with Al Rosen—" He points to the ceiling. "On the tenth floor."

"So?"

"He texted me this morning, telling me he was going to go back to sleep."

Ah.

"And judging by the lack of explosions or ambulance sirens, the whole neighborhood slept."

I go to the bay windows. It's early, but everything seems

calm. No trash fires. No crazy preachers around Gramercy. Some cars move through the streets, but not a lot, especially for a city with so many people jammed together so tightly.

Jerry, who's standing behind me, says, "You did a good thing, I think."

"Well, I didn't want the building to catch fire while we slept."

"Strange, but you don't look as if you have."

I don't say anything but go back to my plate and eat the eggs and toast, finish my juice.

"You will set out today?"

"I guess so."

Jerry places a set of keys on the counter. The BMW logo is very conspicuous on the large black key.

"You've got to be crazy."

"At some point, whatever car you've stolen will be reported, if it hasn't already."

"It's not that. I just can't . . ."

"I, however, will not report my car missing. So you'll be safe."

I remain quiet. The money? Okay, because I need it and Jerry obviously has quite a bit of green fluttering around his private stash. But the car? It's too much. He'll never get it back.

"I can't. I can switch out cars easy. But taking this one . . ."

There comes a jangle of keys and the sound of the front door opening, not visible from the kitchen. A woman's voice rings as clear as a bell, "Dearest, I'm home early!" Another jangle as keys are plopped down in the bowl on the table by the front door. "I couldn't sleep, and your mysterious guest made me want to get home . . ."

She walks into the doorway, smiling, looking from Jerry and then to me. She's a looker, decked out in tight, hip-hugging capris with cute little tennis shoes and a white button-down shirt. Expensive sunglasses perched on top of her head. Nice leather purse in her hand. Silver jewelry at her wrists, throat, ears. She's tanned and exuding the look and scent of money.

"Ah, ahuvi, let me introduce you to Shreve Cannon. I told you about him. We met when I had the gallstone attack in North Carolina . . ."

Her face goes blank. The purse falls to the floor. She turns, not quickly, toward the small desk nook where the calendar hangs over a pile of paperwork and a telephone. Turns like a robot, picking up the receiver and beginning to dial.

"Ahuvi . . ."

I snatch the envelope and jump from the stool. "Jerry, she's been—"

But Jerry's moving toward her, looking worried.

I slam into him, knocking him sideways. He claws at the counter and drawers to slow himself as he begins to fall, an expression of surprise and outrage crossing his features.

"She's been touched by Quincrux!" I'm yelling, but I can't help it. "You have to get away from her or she'll—"

Into the phone, she says, "He is here. Visual confirmation."

She turns to us, phone still to her ear. Jerry's saying, "Ahuvi! Miri! What is going on?"

I grab Jerry's hand, pulling him up and away from her. Keeping the island between us.

She judders. She shakes. And then she smiles.

"Mr. Cannon. So good to see you again."

"Ahuvi." Jerry's voice sounds terrible. Forlorn and broken. I grab his arm and turn him to me.

"Jerry, it's Quincrux. I've got to run. Once I'm gone they'll let her go."

"No, you must stay—"

In the corner of my eye, I can see her moving. She opens a drawer and sticks a hand inside.

Throwing myself over the island, I slam my foot against the drawer, pinning her hand inside. Her eyes go wild and she begins to judder once more, howling and crying in pain, crying for Jerry.

"Shreve, what are you doing?"

I keep my body pressed against the drawer, keeping her hand inside. She hasn't lowered the phone.

"It's Quincrux. He's got her. Programmed and now he's *in her*. Don't you understand? I told you about this!"

"But how . . . why would he?"

"Because he wants me." I try to calm myself, but my voice still sounds high-pitched and terrified. Deep breaths. Miriam— Quincrux, really—squirms against me, trying to withdraw her hand. "Jerry, what's in this drawer? Knives?"

She's still moaning, but the sounds are quieting now. I can tell by his expression that, yes, this drawer is full of slicers and dicers.

"Quincrux wants me. And he'll hurt you to get to me. So, go to your room or the bathroom and lock the door."

"I can't. Not with her like that."

Miriam says, "Yes, Mr. Cannon. Not with her like this. Did I ever tell you that I can stop my vessel's heart?"

I don't believe it for a second. *Because I can't and I should know.* But the demon inside her is a damned good liar.

I say, "Jerry, he lies. He can't. And she can't drop the phone or he'll lose the connection with her. So go lock yourself up, and I will yank the cord from the phone before she can go all stabby on you. Okay?"

He's shaking his head. So I really put my back into it and grind her wrist in the drawer. Miriam screams. Her nicely tanned wrist has some breaks now, and for that I'm truly sorry. But damn. She's possessed. There's gotta be some dispensation for those of us just doing what we have to do, right?

Miriam doesn't drop the phone.

"Okay, Jerry?"

He nods and takes a step backward, toward the living room and the hallway to the bedrooms. And another. Another until he's out of sight.

When he's gone, Quincrux says, "Nicely done, Mr. Cannon. You have removed a pawn from the board. But I am still in possession of this one."

"Yeah, well, don't get too comfortable, boss. Did you get my message?"

Her face clouds a bit. Then brightens. "'I am coming for you'? Of course I did. But, my dear boy, I *want* you to come to me. It is time you join our ranks. We will welcome you."

"You know what?"

She cocks her head slightly, phone cradled in hand. "I do not 'know what.'"

"I just don't like how you asked, asshole."

It's stupid. It's risky. But I'm always stupid and risky.

I shoot forward out of the meatsuit. I go in fast, not trying to drive him out. Not trying to hurt him. I'm trying to catch his scent. Catch his trail. To snatch up the invisible tether.

And maybe that's the trick. Not to go in to destroy, but to suss out. To trace. He can't stop me, and I feel his mental fingers scratching at my ethereal body. I feel his mind trying to grapple with the greased pig of my psyche.

He's my truffle.

It's a golden filament I see, stretching off out of the kitchen, into the west wall of the apartment. And right then, I'm gone, off into the wild blue yonder, into the etheric heights, following it home. The earth, the ground, the sky, the water. All a blur. Racing home.

A flash of light and the jolt of breath. The weight of arms and legs and balls and the scent of tobacco on my breath and the tang of addiction. There I am in a small, bare office, sitting at a desk with a phone pressed to my ear. An open laptop flickering and displaying data. There's a green blotter in front of me on the desk, papers stacked to the right. A coffee cup full of pens.

My leg aches. My heart hammers in my chest.

Quincrux's chest.

Across the desk, set at an angle and illuminated by a computer screen, is a woman in a business suit that isn't a uniform but could easily pass for one if you squint. She has short-cropped, almost white hair and glasses. Bluetooth headphone set. Nose ring, eyebrow ring. Tattoo on her neck. She's thickset but not fat. From where I sit in Quincrux's carcass, I can see that she's almost half tits.

Quincrux, you dog.

Face intense and staring into the monitor, she says, "Red Team is en route to Gramercy location. Orange Team on standby with stasis bomb, should things go pear-shaped. Give the order to intercept?"

Stasis bomb?

I try to sit forward, but my damned leg doesn't move like it should, and it is seriously making it hard to think. I have a choice, dive into Quincrux's memories and take everything he's got but—

Something rattles the psychic chassis. Quincrux. It's like the Hulk and Mr. Hyde have been snorting crank for a week and decided they want inside Quincrux's skin. Except it's already got a squatter. Me.

He's too strong for me to keep out of his own meatsuit. But I can hold on for a moment.

Leaning forward, I shuffle through the papers on his desk, until I find an envelope.

"Director? Is there a problem?" The white-headed woman asks, index finger on her Bluetooth headset.

I try to remember all the ways military people in movies sound when asked similar questions and can't think of one way, for the life of me. Maybe because I'm not in my body and I can't make the connection to those far-off chemical memory banks, or maybe because I'm under pressure. So I just say, "No."

"You sure?"

"One moment." I hold up Quincrux's finger in a shushing motion.

There's another shuddering jar in the ether, and the crushing pressure in my head almost snuffs my consciousness like wind extinguishing a candle. But I have time enough to pick up an envelope and read what the front of it says. #15, Old US Highway 10, Montana, 59759.

Another huge push against my—or Quincrux's—cranium, like water building behind a dam, and I have time only to snatch up a pencil and scrawl across the papers lying there—

You don't have to be such a tremendous DICK

—before I'm kicked out.

It's only moments of dislocation and bodilessness and the rush of travel before I'm back in good old Shreve, still holding Miriam's hand hostage in the drawer. She's howling and obviously not chock-full o' Quincrux, so I let her go, grab the phone she's still holding at her ear, and toss it away.

"Jerry!"

I move Miriam, cradling her arm, to a stool. Jerry pops into the kitchen as if he's been waiting, moving quickly. I can't imagine how hard it was for him to back out.

I let Jerry take over, helping Miriam, who's stopped howling and begun to ask over and over, "Why? Why?"

The weight of that question tears at me.

I know. Why?

I put my hand on Jerry's shoulder. Squeeze. Try to put what I'm feeling into it. "Jer, I'm so sorry. So very sorry. And I have to go. *Now*."

He looks away from Miriam, to me, his face streaming. "But, wait, you must—"

"I'm gone," I say after one last squeeze. I run out of the kitchen and into the living room. I hurdle the sofa, and at the front door, crack it open and peer down the hallway toward the elevators and the other way to the stairwell.

No one. Yet.

Whatever I do, I sure as hell ain't going up to the roof.

I can't imagine what the "capture team" might be holding—guns? Brainiacs? Knuckleheads?

A bunch of explodey people?

The Witch?

Oh no. It'll be the Witch.

I run back to the kitchen, where Jerry looks surprised to see me again so soon. Some guests just never take a hint, I figure. Miriam's face is contorted in pain, and she's cradling her mangled hand.

"Jerry, where's your car?"

"In the building garage." His mouth stays open. Stupefied, really. I can see this whole morning has been too much for him.

"I didn't want to, Jer-bear, but I gotta take it," I say, grabbing the keys from where they still sit on the counter. "Go ahead and call 911 for her. She's gonna need it."

He blinks. Digs in his pocket for his mobile as I race back to the door and burst into the hall. For a moment I consider taking the stairs, but it seems like that's what everyone does when trying to escape, so I run down to the double elevator bays and press both the up and down buttons.

My heart is like two jackrabbits humping away in my chest. It's hard to wait and watch the LED number indicators count up from 1 and down from 13, but I manage to do it without my brain exploding.

There's a *ding!* and one of the steel elevator doors slides open. Nobody's home. I jump in, press all the buttons above my current floor—six—and then jump out just in time to hear another *ding!* as the opposing elevator opens. There's a young bearded man in it, dressed in what looks like black military garb, lots of doohickeys at his waist. He's thick around the middle, and he's got a small Bluetooth headset on, like the white-haired woman in Quincrux's office. He looks surprised to see me.

He looks even more surprised when I kick him in the nuts with everything I've got. His body reacts to the blow, dropping to the floor, curling up. I press the button marked G—I have to assume that's the garage—and then reach down and snatch his headset from his ear, drop it to the floor, and stomp on it.

"What the hell?" he says, miserable. "Why'd you have to—"

There's a Taser right next to the handcuffs. I slide that away from its holster with my foot before kicking him in the head. Once, twice, three times. Until he stops moving.

I check his breath. His pulse. It'll be a toss-up if he'll need more ice on his balls or his brains.

On the second floor, the elevator shudders to a stop. The doors slide open to reveal a young woman—apparently well rested, thank you very much—in expensive jogging clothes, holding a lapdog in her arms. They both look from the un-conscious guy on the floor to me and back to the guy with the same alarmed and rather goofy expression. I don't say anything. What's there to say?

The moment hangs until the doors slide shut. They do not get on the elevator.

The elevator passes the lobby without its doors opening. The only thing that could make this ride worse would be some light jazz, but there's no Kenny G on the way to G.

The garage is very small, damp, dimly lit. It smells of mildew and concrete, the exhaust and fluid leaks from cars. There's a steep ramp leading out to the street. At the top of the ramp is a closed metal garage door. I can only hope there's a radio-controlled trigger for it in Jerry's ride.

I leap from the elevator carriage, pulling the keys from my

pocket, mashing the unlock button. I hear a chirp.

It's a sweet chariot, this BMW. The leather seats kissing my ass are totally cherry. Jerry likes nice things, that's for damn sure.

The car roars to life and thrums underneath my hands. I whip it out of its parking space and up the ramp, stopping at the garage door, which begins to open without any help from me. The light brightens as the door opens and reveals a black van half blocking the drive and exit to the street.

The driver—another Bluetooth-wearing young man—glances at me, surprised. He's got partially hydrogenated corn syrup for blood and was born and bred on the backs of Oklahoma football players. I slip from behind my eyes and take a short, sharp stab at his head. He's walled up tight, but I'm desperate and I blow past his defenses in a heartbeat. My nose begins to trickle blood.

Solomon Blackwell, this is your life.

I can't banish him totally from his consciousness—he's that gristly and strong—but I can get enough of a hold to make him shift the van into gear and mash down the accelerator. The van careens forward, banging into a sedan parked in front of it with a massive *crunch* that sounds like the rending of the world. The steering wheel explodes into silvery white air bag goodness, smacking his face so hard it knocks him unconscious and knocks me all the way back out of his head and into the BMW. Which I now gun out onto the street and down the block.

Only to be stopped at the traffic light.

There are a lot of folks out this morning, most looking happy. Apparently, when people sleep well, they want to get out and drive around.

It's hard to stay calm waiting for the pedestrians to pass and the light to change. When it does, it's not like I can race forward, seeing as there's some sort of small delivery truck in front of me.

It's the slowest chase scene I've ever witnessed.

In the rearview, I can see the van behind me. A couple of black-clad people are pulling Mr. Blackwell from the wreckage and pointing in my direction.

Oh no. One of them—a girl—takes a few steps in my direction and jumps. It's like she's disappeared. But it doesn't take a mind reader to guess she's got twelve fingers. She's somewhere above me now. Flying. Glommed onto a building maybe.

Torpedoes be damned, I whip the Beemer out and around the delivery truck and almost run smack dab into a Yellow Cab that veers to the right just in time for me to pass between and shoot in front of the truck. Then down two blocks at a fast clip until I hit a large avenue. I can't get any idea of where I am and the traffic is crowded around me, so I cast out my awareness and snag a police officer and go behind his eyes.

Bruno Conti, you aren't the nicest guy in New York, that's for sure.

I shuffle through the memory banks, trying to avoid the lawsuits and alimony payments and the pulsing urge for a drink and/or sex and dredge up the info I need.

First Avenue. Take a left, then a right, and head to the FDR on-ramp going south toward the Williamsburg Bridge. Which will, eventually, take me east onto Long Island through Brooklyn-Queens Expressway unless I head north through construction.

Being stuck on an island is like being back on the roof again.

Bruno, despite being a brute and as corrupt as they come, has 20/20 eyesight, so it's no problem picking out the black SUV muscling its way down Twentieth Street toward me. Bruno also spends time in the gym, when he's not drinking and hound-dogging underage girls, so I set him off jogging back the way from which I came in the BMW.

Bruno approaches the van. The driver—a middle-aged woman with short-cropped gray hair and a Bluetooth headset—ignores him. But the passenger has a familiar face, one I remember from the old days at Casimir Pulaski Juvenile Detention Center for Boys. Good old Sloe-Eyed Norman.

That means the Witch, Ilsa Moteff.

Bruno's heart and mine jump as one at the sight of him. Jack killed her. Broke her neck in a fierce explosion of desperation and force, but she took over poor, hapless Norman's body and never gave it up.

When Bruno raises his sidearm, both Ilsa and the driver show puzzlement ratcheting up into alarm. He empties the clip into the engine block.

I'd wanted to have him shoot her with all my heart, but it seems Bruno is not a totally bad guy, after all. Part of him struggles with me enough to change the aim. Good for you, Bruno Conti. Now you've let a monster live.

What feels like the mental version of a charging rhino caroms into Bruno's brainmeat, and I'm booted out of his head. If you can mentally reel, I'm reeling like a steer with a sledgehammer blow between the horns.

The Witch. Damn, she's strong. The pressure ebbs as I gain distance. But my brain feels slimy, filmy, like she's left a residue all over it. There's really no words for how bad she is.

Her mind is a wormhole to hell.

There's honking behind me. The light is green. I gun the Beemer onto First Avenue, whipping by people and cars and cabs. I'm nabbing directions from pedestrians' brains as I drive—*steve michonne ahmad tony jennifer another jennifer ANOTHER JENNIFER dj willum joe helen johan eduardo petrova chanda bobbi weston liz jim.* Like the car I'm in, I can feel the shibboleth shuddering around me as I play mental ping-pong, bouncing from head to Shreve from head to Shreve again while barreling down the road.

I've got to get off the island.

Hands at twelve and two, just like I learned in one of my many teenage memories. Up the on-ramp and onto the FDR and into traffic. Heading south and upping the speed now into the fifties, low sixties. That's as fast as the traffic will allow.

Approaching the bridge, the cars bog down, slowing. I adjust the mirrors to point up into the sky as best as I can. For an instant, I catch a glimpse of black wings, or the raven's flutter of the jumping girl. Like Jack. Tailing me from on high.

The cars grind to a halt, and I feel the mental pressure building again—the Witch is back in range. I crane my head, looking for the van, but can't see it. And she's strong. Unimaginably strong.

Once, when I was in junior high, I smarted off to the wrong guy—Barry Levitt—and when he came after me, I tried to fight him off, grabbing his arms, his wrists. But he was enraged and fueled by whatever hatred or desire propelled him and his arms were like pneumatic pumps pushing toward me. I remember being surprised, thinking, *He's not supposed to do that!* That's what she feels like. The Witch. She's like a boa constrictor choking out my air. Tightening. The pressure of her mind is a house collapsed on top of me, lumber and stone too heavy to lift. But in the end, no metaphors can match her.

Blood pours from my nose, and I taste the warm, salty flow of it. My head feels like a watermelon with an unpinned grenade inside.

The Beemer slams into the car in front of me—making another terrible crunching sound. It's my turn to have an air bag explode in my face.

The pain drives off the Witch for a moment.

I feel stupid and clumsy. I've left a nice blood spatter across the silver material of the air bag. Opening the door, I lurch out into stalled traffic and stumble between the cars to the median and pull myself over into the northbound lane, where the cars are whizzing past. A fat man from the car I hit stands by the driver's door and screams profanities and shakes his fist at me. I ignore him. Look to the skies, buster. You see anything?

It's like a game, trying to judge the speed of the oncoming cars, except, *unlike a game*, if I screw up I'll be splattered across the pavement. So screw that. Again I employ the psychic whiz-bangery and hop into the head of the nearest oncoming car—hello, Mrs. Schulte!—and make her slow her car and slew it at an angle, blocking most of the lanes.

I stumble across the road and climb the fence into what Mrs. Schulte's brain tells me is the East River Park.

It's not even eight in the morning, and it's already been a long day.

SIXTEEN

I run. Not movie-star fast. Not fancy.

My breath comes in great painful heaves and my side is in stitches and the pressure of the Witch is back in my head. Through the canopy of trees shading the promenade, I can make out the dash and flutter of black clothes high above. They're following me. Many of them.

I'm not going to make it. The cover of foliage will give out in just a few paces, and I'll be exposed to them. No telling what they'll do to me. What she'll do to me.

I slow. Stop running. There's a water fountain. I drink. Let my heart slow and my breath come more slowly. I let my body calm. Joggers and folks with dogs stare at me uneasily. I wipe my nose, leaving a long red streak up my forearm.

There's a thick-bearded jogger staring at me intensely, and I don't even have to peep him to know he's got a Rider straddling him.

"Before the elder awakens!" he says.

"Yeah, I heard you the first time."

"These . . ." He pauses as if searching for words. Distant. "Embers, they will take you away. Away from the elder."

"They'll try."

"You cannot hope to resist. And you must away to Maryland."

"Damn, man, why you have to talk like that?"

"If the elder wakens, all will be lost. You cannot hope to resist!"

"Resist?" Screw this guy right in the eyehole. "Watch me."

I turn and walk to where the trees give way to sky. There's a short wall with steps down to a lower level—closer to the water—full of planters. Some of the park denizens seem demented and sleepless—there are two hobo preachers, a couple of junkies, some human bits of flotsam and jetsam. Other people in the park seem rested. Some scowl at me and look murderous. None of them seem happy to see me. None of them seem to see the flying people in the sky.

Maybe I'm shithouse rat insane and gibbering in the Tulaville Psych Ward.

But they look so normal. No capes or spandex costumes. They look like a floating SWAT team.

There are six of them out there, hanging above the sluggish gray waters of the East River like ungainly, spastic blackbirds. Two seem to be orbiting each other, as if each one has a personal gravitational field that constantly asserts its power over the other. Two just float like they're standing on an invisible platform, holding long, slender tools that look too much like hunting rifles.

There's the brunette jumping girl hopping back and forth.

And then there's Sloe-Eye Norman, current home of the Witch. Floating calmly in the air.

When she—he?—sees me, she holds up her very male hand and points. She says something to her cohorts that the river wind whips away.

The cyclists, joggers, miscreants, derelicts, and hoboes of the East River Park stop, keel over, and fall to the ground.

That's a neat trick.

I trot over to the nearest. Check his pulse. Still living and breathing. Just asleep. He probably will appreciate it when he wakes up.

When I look back, the Witch wearing Norman's body floats closer, hanging fifteen feet in the air and within a stone's throw of me. She's waving her hand like someone directing a friend into a narrow parking spot. Eventually, she bunches her hand into a fist and comes to a stop.

She's not flying under her own power.

"Delicious boy, so nice to see you."

"Looks like you've lost some weight."

S/he laughs. Not a man's rich, bellowing laugh. Not a woman's high, bell-pitched cascade. Both and neither, all at once. "How droll. I might say the same for your appearance. You look positively *famished*."

I don't like where she's going with this, and I wish we could just get to the main wrestling match, but I'm scared. Okay? I'm scared. I've got balls big enough to admit it.

"Yes, it's been a while since you've indulged yourself, has it not?"

"I don't know what you're talking about."

"Of course you do, my little *greedy guts*." Wearing poor Norman's face, she licks her lips. She waggles her hand behind her, telling her handlers to bring her closer, and she floats near, not ten feet away. I get the impression of some ancient potentate waggling his glistening, fat, and beringed fingers to his couch bearers and porters, too large to move on his own.

The ground beneath the Witch is lower than where I stand, sloping down to the river, and we look at each other eye to eye.

"You and I contain multitudes, do we not? We can remain immortal as long as we have the sustenance we need."

"I don't . . ."

"Nonsense. I know this is true. I've inhabited some of your victims, the poor unhappy souls of Casimir Pulaski Juvenile Detention Center. Those boys, those men and women you cannibalized."

She tosses the word out there like a grenade. And she's right. I did feed from them. Their happiness, I siphoned it away to ease my own existence.

You're born into pain, your constant companion through life. How could I have forgotten that?

But never again.

"All that's over now."

"It doesn't have to be. You come with us. You join your friend Jack, and you will have all the sustenance you require." S/he chuckles, and it's the same piggy throat sound I remember from so long ago.

I try to remember the light and the heat on the roof where much of me burned away, sublimed into the air. I remember the clatter of raven wings and the feel of the thousands of people I've been and who live inside me. I let my heart expand and the shibboleth swell.

Because I'm gonna fight the Witch.

Before, in the BMW, I was on the run, driving, snatching directions out of drivers and pedestrians. But now . . . *I'm here.* I'm centered.

And I'm not just some crappy punk kid she can push around.

I'm the original crappy punk kid.

"I'm stronger than you," I say. And I believe it.

This makes her laugh and laugh more.

So I prove it.

It comes from somewhere beyond me, from the black unlimited spaces between atoms or the empty spaces between the stars or the finite space between my molecules. It comes from the blood surging in my veins, pulsing, driving forward, the unspent semen in my testicles. The saliva swelling in my mouth and the tears at the corners of my eyes.

It comes from my youth, the pure tenacity of the young. It comes from my age, having lived countless lives. It comes from guilt, from those I've hurt, I've stolen from. It comes from the leathery beef jerky of my soul. It comes from the million times I've wiped my brother's ass and dressed him for school and fed him breakfast and fed Moms dinner and served her drinks. It comes from scarcity and a life of discomfort and hunger and want.

It comes from the pain. It comes from love. The love I bear Coco and Vig, Jack and Rollie. Booth and poor, doomed Sloe-Eyed Norman.

It comes from the multitudes that infest me and the multitudes I infested.

I am Legion, for we are many.

No dicking around now. No fancy footwork or strange visualizations.

I am the sharpened stake. I am the bullet in the brain.

And I am stronger than her.

Her eyes widen in alarm, terrified, but I'm already past. I'm inside her. I'm inside him.

I am you and you are he, two makes one and one makes three.

SEVENTEEN

She was born in 1824 in Switzerland with a caul over her oblong, glistening head. Her father, on spying her, wanted to snatch up the bundled infant, take her into the snow, and dash her brains out on the cobblestones leading to their small house, down the lane from the mill. But her mother, fat-chested and full of love and the milk of human kindness, clutched the newborn to her breast and cooed over and over again, *"Ilsa. Mein liebes kind. Mein geliebtes kind, Ilsa. Ilsa,"* leaving Herman, her father, to look on in shame and disgust and question how he could hate something that was so new to the world.

One thing is clear: they should have walked the child into the frigid waters of Lake Brienz and drowned the damned squalling thing.

···

It's a foul place, the vaulted chambers of her mind. Filled with thousands of moments ringing like a chorus of bells swelling into some hideous chord. It mocks the idea of music and happiness. Each memory is a moment of cruelty, a moment of hunger.

It is almost too much for me to bear. But I am stronger than her.

All those moments of cruelty. Three lifetimes' worth.

I eat every one.

I am you and you are me.

••••

When I'm done, what's left of Norman/Ilsa collapses and hangs motionless in the air with a gasp.

I thought I knew pain. Disgust. Hatred.

I ate her cancer. I ate her past. She's in me now. Forever.

••••

Her black-clad minions, the Flying Burrito Brothers, give a collective floating lurch at her fall, and before I know it, there's a red flower blossoming from my shoulder and a dramatic sharp pain.

I seriously hope that dart doesn't have any Haldol in it, I think before staggering, taking two steps, and face-planting on the ground.

••••

I awake from a dream of eating children in Munich, devouring their minds in mad, gluttonous abandon. Frau Rhinehart hired me as their maid with a letter of recommendation from Hans Trienne, the Brientz constable whom I had seduced into submission, and now their incessant bawling and demands drove me into a frenzy. Each mind with its memories, its raw untapped emotions, was like warm *schokoladenpudding*. They huddled together and cried in the nursery, but that didn't last long as their minds evaporated like water on the hot skillet of my appetite.

I'm strapped to a gurney now, a saline drip—or something eviler—in my arm. I can tell by the rumble and whine and the curved ceiling that we're in a plane. I can turn my head just enough to see the husk of Norman lying near me, eyes open, mouthing unheard and unfathomable words.

"He will recover, I think," Quincrux says from a seat nearby. His legs are crossed, and he seems relaxed. The space we're in looks like a hospital room schtupped an office building and the resulting mongrel was born with wings. Despite being on a plane, Quincrux withdraws a pack of Peter Stuyvesants, removes a cigarette, and delicately tamps the loose tobacco on his wrist before he lights it. "He will be reborn into the world new, pink and squalling. His past lives almost all forgotten."

"Ding, dong, the Witch is dead."

"Quite. A very impressive feat, Mr. Cannon. She was one of the strongest of us."

"Us?"

"We . . ." He inhales deeply and then expels the smoke into a cloud at the cabin's ceiling. He points with the glowing cherry of the cigarette at me. "We are members of a very old society."

"Like the Shriners?"

He ignores that. "And now you are also a member, *will ye or nil ye*."

"I don't want to be in any club that would want me as a member."

Quincrux sighs, puts down his smoke in a crystal ashtray on the desk. He uncrosses his legs and adjusts his chair to where he's facing me. He opens the laptop on the desk and turns it to where I can see the screen.

"Ah, Mr. Cannon. The difference between you and me is—"

"Good looks and morals?"

He smiles at that. It was a weak one, I agree. I don't have any morals. And my looks are gone. "The difference is, I actually *respect* your abilities. You do not."

Not much to say to that. He likes who he is. I don't like who I am.

"Well," I say, doing my best to let the good old sneer creep back in, "aren't we getting chummy, now?"

He doesn't respond except to turn back to the laptop and tap the touch pad, bringing the screen to life. He types in a password, waits, types in another, waits. I figure now's as good a time as any to make my move. I've got the Witch in my belly. Why not snack on one more monster?

"Before you get too belligerent, Mr. Cannon," he says, swiping the touch pad with his fingers, "I'd advise you to watch this."

He taps again, opening some sort of video file, and the screen fills with a flickering moving image. It's a living room in what could be any home in America: couch, two comfy-looking chairs, drapes, a pile of toys peeking from the open lid of a wooden box in the corner. A flat-screen television with game console. Books and board games on shelves.

My heart skips a few beats when Vig barrels into the room. Looks like he's had a snootful of sugar. And he's grown some since I've last seen him. He's with an older boy, shaggy-haired, and they look comfortable together; Vig is smiling, talking to the other boy, who laughs a little. They don't look at the camera, like they don't know it's there.

A gray-haired man wearing a tank top, with thin arms corded with muscle, comes on-screen and says something to Vig and his companion, and they turn to look at him, talk back, but it's hard to make out what is being discussed. Eventually, the boys turn back to the television, flip it on, and begin playing some sort of video game that involves shooting things.

The man, with the boys' attention on the television, turns to the camera and gives a single, unsmiling nod.

"Cat got your tongue, Mr. Cannon?"

"If you hurt him—"

"That is entirely up to you." He shifts in his chair. Unblinking. "I require your cooperation." He cocks his head in the inquisitive, birdlike manner I remember so well. The plane rumbles, and I feel the lightness in my stomach that accompanies altitude change. "No. Let's phrase it like this: I require your services, and in this, you haven't a choice if you wish no harm to come to your brother, Vigor, who—" He gestures at the computer screen, where Vig leaps up, controller in hand, saying something to the older boy. Excited. Triumphant. Happy. "—is apparently thriving at his new foster home. Indeed, he seems very well. His grades are up, his school outbursts have ceased, and the state-appointed psychologist says that he is acclimating very well."

"You'll regret this."

"That remains within the realm of the possible. But it all depends on you," Quincrux says. I think he's talking about something different than I am. "You were stronger than Ilsa, this is true. Will you risk your brother just to find out if you can best me? I am old, boy, and know all the wiles of mankind."

I remain silent for a while. Ilsa was nearly two hundred years old, hopping from body to body. Who knows how old Quincrux is?

It's not a hard decision to make.

"What do you want me to do?"

I'll give him this: if he's gloating, he doesn't let it show on his face.

"I require you to obey me, first and foremost. There are strange forces moving in the ether..." His eyes narrow, gauging my reaction. "Surely you're aware of the entity?"

"In Maryland?"

"Of all the people in the world—even those of our society—only a handful are aware of its presence. You and I seem attuned to it more than other people." For a moment, he looks as if he is woolgathering. "When *our* game first began, it was solely Mr. Graves I was interested in, and you were merely a by-blow of that acquisition. However, now you are one of my main concerns, equal to, if not more than, Mr. Graves. Possibly because of the entity's interest in *you*." He smoothes out his slacks in a finicky little gesture. "And your besting of Ilsa. In all honesty, you have done me a favor there. She was . . ." He thinks for a moment. "She was unruly and hard to control."

"Not shedding any tears for the Witch, then, are you?"

"And should I? You know her now as well as anyone. Do you feel remorse for her?"

"Not one damned bit."

"Why would you assume that I would be any different?"

"Go figure."

"'Go figure' indeed. And the impenetrables?"

It takes me a moment to figure out what he means. "You talking about knuckleheads? Or the Riders?" Being able to talk with him about them somehow makes it all worse. It's like the opposite of unspooling my story to Jerry. It's like gravity has increased, pushing me down into the gurney. Or maybe the plane is gaining altitude once more.

"Always glib, Mr. Cannon. But apt. I am referring to the 'Riders,' as you call them. As you probably have surmised, no one is totally impenetrable to people of our abilities. It is just a matter of will."

That makes sense. My will had grown, or the Witch's had weakened. Or both. "So, the knuckleheads . . ."

"They are just normal people with extraordinarily strong will. Sometimes survivors of great trauma. Often, it can be the love of the invader himself that puts up the walls—"

"You mean, those people I can't get into, it's because . . ."

"You don't want to." He smiles as that sinks in. "But the 'Riders' are many orders of magnitude beyond that—"

"They're something else."

"Indeed." The silence that falls is like the awkward ones at a funeral. But Quincrux is thinking, eyes narrowed, watching me. "Tell me of your contact with the Riders."

"Just banging my head against the walls."

Before the elder awakens, it said.

I can't tell him about the message. Not yet. Not until I get some idea of what he's planning. "What about the thing in Maryland? The insomnia? What are we going to do about it?"

"'We'? Is it 'we' now?"

"You *do* know that whatever it is in Maryland is causing the insomnia?"

He chortles. It's a dry, humorless sound. He picks up his cigarette and puffs on it. "Of course I know."

"Well, what are we going to do about it?"

"That is not your concern. Your concern, for now, is to

obey. He closes his eyes, apparently to think for a moment. Maybe he's tired. "Now, with what you've done to Ilsa, and your knowledge of the entity, I must consider your position most closely. Should you pass the testing, I will set you to training Mr. Graves."

"The testing?"

He nods, a slight smile curling at the edges of his mouth. "Yes, Mr. Cannon. The testing. We shall see how strong you have become."

That doesn't sound good. A thought occurs to me. "Jack, he pass this test?"

"It is not a pass-fail equation. However, Mr. Graves is not progressing as he did when you two were on your own, trying to evade me. It seems—" he shifts in his seat and holds his cigarette in a kind of effeminate, European manner, palm halfway pointing at the ceiling. "It seems your natural abrasiveness was the perfect goad. You were the electric rod, and he the cattle's rump."

I think about all the times I pissed Jack off. Pushing. Making him do what he didn't want. And before that, Vig. Pushing, punishing, manipulating, just to get him to brush his teeth and eat something other than chips. Turns out I'm the obnoxious big sister. That might have bothered me before . . . but now it's just another day in the salt mines.

"So you're not going to do anything about the insomnia?"

"Oh, efforts are in place. Those suffering from sleeplessness will soon pass into slumber." He looks at his watch as if he's dosed the general public with a massive horse tranq and now he's just waiting for it to keel over so he can have his way with it.

"People are dying, man."

"That isn't my concern, Mr. Cannon. And there's more at stake than a few people's lives."

"A few? We're talking hundreds of thousands. There's been plane crashes, nuclear meltdowns!"

He stands. "This has been quite entertaining, Mr. Cannon. Yet I have much larger matters to attend to and cannot spend the rest of my day answering the questions and demands of a mere inductee."

"An inductee? More like prisoner."

"Hang whatever name you want upon your condition, it matters not to me."

A change of tack might be required. "Hey, dickweed. The girl with the tattoo on her neck—what's her name?"

His eyes go even narrower, his gaze boring into me.

"She's kinda cute, in a supernerd kinda way." I do my best to sit up. "You are old, hoss, but that don't mean you know everything. And remember, you might have peeked from behind my eyes before, but I've taken you out for a test drive too. And I didn't need a phone connection to do it."

He says nothing. He stands stiffly, and it doesn't take a mind reader to know his leg is hurting. I make no effort to hide my amusement as he limps past me, toward the forward cabin. He leaves the stink of cigarettes behind him.

When he's gone, I say, "You don't have to be such a tremendous dick."

PART FOUR:
THE SOCIETY OF EXTRANATURALS

EIGHTEEN

They call it Big Sky Country.

We fly over countless mountains blanketed in trees, over landscapes that look dry and lush by turns, over swirls of mineral deposits in flatlands and the bizarre fractal patterns of hot springs viewed from a great height. Very few roads and even fewer buildings.

The pilot is a military knucklehead, Captain Steve Lawson. Now that I know from Quincrux that the knuckleheads aren't truly impenetrable, just stubborn bastards, worming my way inside his noggin is easy. Okay, not that easy. Blood trickles from my nostrils, just a little, and my eyes water by the time I'm done. But by then I'm watching from behind his eyes as my abandoned body rocks and shudders on the gurney in the back of the plane. I wonder why an air force pilot would be chauffeuring Quincrux around and do some pearl diving in the brainmeat, but he doesn't know himself. He's got his orders, and the check clears every week.

Tip o' the hat to you, Mr. Quincrux, for telling me something I didn't already know. I'll use it for my ends. Not yours.

When we land, one of the bully boys from the Flying Burrito Brothers pops my saline drip, shoves a wad of cotton in the crook of my arm, and tells me, "Hold it or you'll bleed everywhere," and escorts me out of the plane and onto the tarmac. It's bright and blustery outside. Big mountains, wreathed in pine trees. There's a Quonset hut hangar and a couple of other military-looking vehicles parked in the lee of the building. An evil-looking box sits on top of a building, looking suspiciously like a ground-to-air missile launcher.

I feel like I should have a bag, but all I've got are the clothes on my back. I'm sorry now I made a nest of all the clothes I bought at Target. I guess they'll give me some threads. I don't know.

I check my pockets. Wallet still there, chock-full of Jerry's cash. Keys to the Accord still there too.

The rest of the Flying Burritos saunter onto the tarmac from the rear of the plane, bags in hand. They're silent, looking grim. They've lost one of their own today, and even though they didn't like her (or him, this I know from her own memories squirming within me), it's a shock when a team member goes down. Because if it can happen to one, it can happen to any of them.

There's a definite lack of good vibrations coming from them toward me.

A faint tickling sensation feathers my mind. The tadpole in the palm. But this time I'm not the tadpole. I'm the palm.

It's the girl. She's standing on the tarmac, a black nylon duffel bag hanging from one inert hand. She stares at me. The thousand-yard stare.

She's trying to get in.

I saw her jump. She leaped up and flew. But now she's trying to get in my head? I thought you either had the telepathic abilities or you had the explodey, physical abilities. Quincrux never levitated. Neither did the Witch. Not under her own power.

Seems I have some things to learn. But for right now, I have some things to teach.

I face the girl. She's pretty, brunette. Slight build with her female parts hidden behind the black military fatigues. No insignia or badge. Not real military, but she shops at the same stores.

I swat the niggling doubt of her mind away like a fly. Not too harshly, because there's something hungry inside her. Something that calls to my own hunger. But the pressure isn't that great. She's not nearly as strong as me.

She takes a step backward, unsteady on her feet. Her nose begins pouring blood. I cast out my mind, dig my claws into her consciousness. Not too deep, but deep enough to leave a thought in her head. *Naughty girl.*

Surprised, she wipes at her nose and waves off the attention of her team members. They give me black looks and bundle her off to a waiting troop transport. It roars to life and clatters away, down into the valley.

Soldiers wait for me. No red-carpet chauffeur like the girl and her pals.

Two of them approach me, rifles at the ready. They frogmarch me over to a drab green troop transport, seat me in the back, and sit down opposite me, holding their rifles loosely. The barrels seem huge.

"You got that thing on safety?" I ask the nearest man.

He ignores me and bangs on the partition between us and the driver, hollering for the driver to haul ass. The motor ratchets up, and we're off, trundling down a gravel mountain path, away from the airfield. I grip the transport's rough bench. It seems like we drive for miles, but all I can see is the drab olive tarpaulin that covers the bed of the transport. The soldiers sway and watch me. When the transport stops, they muscle me out. The transport sits in front of a massive, dull gray blast door seated in the raw stone of a mountainside. It's framed in six-foot-thick concrete. It's the kind of door that's intended solely to keep the zombies/nuclear explosion/mutants *out* or the zombies/nuclear explosion/mutants *in*. The sinking sensation in my stomach indicates the latter.

With a squeal and flashing yellow light, the door slides open, revealing a tidy motor pool where a woman stands, hands on her hips, scowling at me.

The soldier grabs my shoulder and yanks me forward to stand in front of her. It's the blonde, tattooed woman I saw when I inhabited Quincrux and checked out his office. She takes three steps forward, like a drill sergeant approaching to inspect a recruit. Her lip curls into a sneer.

It's like she's trying to walk straight, military, but her body betrays her. Her hips sway, and her boobs jiggle. She keeps her hair shorn tomboy short and dyed white while the twining, dancing black tribal tattoos wind up her neck and peek out from her up-rolled sleeves onto her forearms, which are knotted with thick twists of muscle and end in flat, brutal, square hands that look like they could crush rock. Or heads.

Mixed feelings and desires burn through my body like a forest fire. On the one hand, she's got gargantuan boobs. On the other, she could rip me in half.

I've got the memories of so many people. Screwing men and women. And that sometimes twists and squirms inside me, and I can't look at it too closely. What does that make me? Bisexual? I wouldn't have eaten those memories if it hadn't felt good, warm, suffused with light.

This woman confuses me.

I cast out my mind, surrounding hers. She's a knucklehead, definitely. And there's something else—a tremulous, thick vibration to the ether. It's sluggish. Cloying. And that presents a mystery. I can tell when the drugs hit me and the wet blanket falls, but this is different. It's external. It niggles. It wouldn't stop me from going behind her eyes and working her over.

But right now, it's a fight I don't want.

I'm tired, honestly. It's not the drugs they hit me with or my drive to New York or my stint high on the roof where the shibboleth burned away all the dross of my existence. I'm just tired. Tired of being alone. Tired of always fretting and struggling against the bars of my cage. Tired of the shame and outrage of moving from cage to cage. Tired of fighting being incarcerado.

She hoists a clipboard in one powerful mitt and glares at me. "Cannon, Shreve?"

"That's me."

She sniffs and looks me over, her buttons straining as her chest rises and falls. She doesn't like what she sees. "You're scrawnier than I would have thought."

"What, you don't remember when we first met?" I say it lightly. I don't know if she knows I inhabited Quincrux for that short time earlier ... today? Was it yesterday? The drugs the Flying Burrito Brothers hit me with have left me missing some hours.

Her face clouds, and she narrows her eyes. "We've exhausted too many resources—including one of our team members—nabbing your sorry ass, Cannon, but now we have you, and the director tells me that we're going to salvage the losses out of your hide—"

"The director?"

"Hiram Quincrux. The director of the Society." She clears her throat. Probably not used to being questioned or interrupted. "As our director has already told you, the Extranatural Society is a federally funded project that was created in the sixties to harness, control, and develop the post-humans that present themselves within the American populace—"

"Wait. What?" I ask.

I didn't think it was possible for her to sneer *more*, but her upper lip contorts itself into disgust. It's like a double sneer. "The American people. Though, we do also operate in Central and South America."

"No, the 'post-human' thing."

She looks at me. "With your abilities, surely you can't consider yourself still human?" She laughs, but it is not kind. "We've moved on, Cannon. We've outgrown the human race."

And I had felt it before, on the roof. That all my humanity had been burned away, sublimed into the quivering air, pregnant with a million possibilities and supercharged with the shibboleth. But her stating it now, so blandly, tagged with its own catchall moniker—*post-human*—that jars me. That this society can take something so extraordinary and rare and reduce it to a hyphenated word terrifies me.

"Welcome to your new home. In the morning, we'll start the testing. I recommend you give one hundred and ten percent. Otherwise . . ." She dusts her hands like a farmer might his hat. "Wash out."

"Wash out?"

"You don't want to discover what that involves, Cannon."

She obviously hasn't read my psychiatric report, then.

"No extranatural abilities will be used except during testing or training or at the command of an administrator. My name is Ruark, and I am the chief executive officer of this organization." Strange. Is that a first name or last? "You will not address soldiers unless given explicit permission. If you disobey any of these directives, you will be punished. And believe me, Shreve, you've never been punished in your life like you get punished here." She gives me a meaningful stare and walks over to stand near a black box protruding from the concrete wall by the blast door. It has a flashing yellow light, some galvanized metal electrical tubing racing away from it, and a small sign with a lightning bolt visible.

One soldier moves to stand by her; another flanks me.

She glances at the first soldier. "Go ahead and crank up the Helmholtz a couple notches."

The soldier jabs at the keypad with his finger.

The vibrations in the ether increase. It's like a mental earthquake making it impossible to concentrate.

"That is called a Helmholtz field. Pentagon developed it. It limits telekinetic and telepathic powers. This is just an in situ Helmholtz. There's a giant Helmholtz generator on top of the mountain that can blanket this area with a massive pulse. For miles and miles around, there are these little babies—" She pats the box. "Some hidden, some in the open. They fire randomly and at different strengths. So if you can fly, like many of our inductees, and you try to leave without permission, you *will* encounter one of these fields before you can escape. And very few live through the altitude drop."

"So, it's not really a *society*, then, is it?" I say.

"What?"

"It's a prison if you have to use those things to keep us here."

"Call it what you want. If you find yourself in one of these fields, whatever tricks you might have up your sleeves, you won't be able to play them. So don't get any ideas, got me? We can take away everything about you that you think is special." She becomes still, arms by her sides. "Go ahead and try."

It's rigged, a trick. But whatevs. I am about to find out.

The ether thrums and shivers, and I'm in the vast spaces between stars and the short jump between minds. After all, we're all the same. Star stuff and hairless apes. It's hard to concentrate with the etheric vibrations, like trying to do long division while a car alarm sounds, but I'm able to find her.

I go in, with brutal and ferocious force, choking her off and out. She fights me, hard. She's tenacious and fierce, but I am the stronger. Part of me—a part that I don't like to think about—comes alive with the struggle. It's the Witch inside me, gleeful and hungry, oh so hungry, and her hunger drives me on, past the poisoned heights of the ether, past Ruark's defenses.

The ravenous wolf inside me raises its snout and howls in triumph when I'm inside. I feel expansive and contracted and savage all at once as I look out from behind her eyes and banish Ruark, boot her out.

In and down, past whorls of memories and great shelves of events ringing like bells—a smorgasbord of memories I could eat until I died, but somehow, they don't look so good to me now. The part of me that lusted, that hungered for the easy and the anodyne—the *escape* of pleasure—it's gone. Lost to me.

I shuffle through her memories enough to discover her particular talent. She's a telepath like me—they call us *bugfucks* here—and borderline insane OCD. Mostly in regards to clothing, but it's also her hair and the accoutrements of life that need to be ordered and collated. Counted, labeled, numbered. Folded lovingly. And money. She's a regular Ebenezer Scrooge, she is. Counting pennies makes her happy.

But her ability? Her talent? It's so normal, it's hard to discern it's even telepathic.

She's a truth machine. If you lie, she knows it.

I can taste blood. Her nose must be streaming. From her viewpoint, I look over at my empty meatsuit. I look husked and hollow, hair a clotted mess in the failing light of the Montana mountains.

Sometimes I worry that when I'm not home, when I've busted loose of the cage, what happens if someone else like me comes along and walks right in and takes over? Possesses my skinsuit?

It's a harrowing thought. And this is a society of bugfucks and mentalists. Who knows how many kids will be here who can do the same things I do? I'll have to be very careful.

I go back home, and I've never felt more relieved to be back within my body, the light weight of my limbs and my bony chest and my dick and nuts all in their proper positions.

Mine. All mine.

Ruark coughs, splutters. Turns to the soldier and yells, "I told you to turn that field *up*!"

He looks bewildered in the face of her rage. Her nose pumps blood over her lips and down her chin into the neck of her uniform, discoloring it.

"What was the setting?" She is furious, and I understand why. It's a violation when someone takes over. And she felt safe. It's like Jerry's story of the snake. She thought one thing, and then the world turned, pivoted, and became different.

"Ma'am, it was on 6.5. That's the recommended setting you sent in your last memo."

She glances at me, eyes blazing. "Crank it up to 8.5," she says.

"But, ma'am, at that level, it will put a strain on the bunker's electrical grid—"

"Did I ask you to discuss power reserves? Turn it up, you moron."

He cranks a dial, looking uncomfortable.

But I can feel it. It skitters and howls. It thrums. The ether is poisonous now, like an acid eating away at the membranes of the mind. It's hard to think at all with that part of my awareness being scoured. I can feel the shibboleth withdrawing, retreating inside of me like sap sinking into a tree with the coming winter.

Ruark looks at me, defiant. I rouse the shibboleth. I find it in me to go up and out into the space/not space. It's painful, the juddering, shivering mindscapes between lit match heads. But I can do it. It hurts not like calcium-brittle bones, nor the deep-seated rot of cancer, but like a fever of the spirit—as if at any moment the cohesion of my being, my thoughts and hopes and emotions, will just erode away and dissolve into nothingness forever.

For now, I can manage it. I can make another assault, make her dance to my fiddle. The shibboleth heeds my call, and the pain is bearable.

I am stronger than this.

That frightens me, more than I can say. I've unseated Quincrux. Instead of the Witch eating me, I ate her. Where does it all stop? After I've unseated God himself? When I've supplanted the thing in Maryland? Where does my appetite end?

I *am* stronger than her Helmholtz field, for now. But it might be better if I don't let her know that.

So I go back home. I let my shoulders slump. I hope she won't notice that my nose isn't bleeding.

Ruark's expression turns hard and gleeful all at once. A cruel smile thins her lips, already coated in gore.

"Good," she says. "Very good. New operating procedures will be put into effect immediately." Only now does she wipe her nose, but delicately, as if determining the extent of the mess.

"You asked for it," I say.

The sun has passed over the rim of the world, and the open door of the motor pool looking out among the pines has been cast into gloom. A door slides open in the far wall, and two more soldiers exit, holding guns and looking at me without much warmth. Fluorescent lights tick, flicker, and illuminate the area in a blue, artificial glow. The air stinks of gasoline, exhaust, and oil.

"You're strong, kid. Good for you." There's blood in her teeth as she says this. Her tattoos look like intricate bruising in the failing light. "But you're just a flea compared to the director. And we have your little brother, understand?"

I feel small now. Beaten flat.

"We can always arrange a little attitude adjustment for you. At first, we'll only break his arms."

I've killed people before. Stolen memories of men in battle dying in the sights of my gun, choking the life from a Viet Cong soldier with my bare hands in the mud, his bayonet piercing my thigh. And more recently, taking everything that was Ilsa Moteff into myself. I can do it, let her loose to run rampant, like some tiger in a movie, burning bright, hungry and terrible. The beast in me, free to stalk on vaporous feet.

I could so easily wring Ruark as dry as a sponge.

I don't.

"Indicate in the affirmative if you understand your—and his—situation."

"I understand."

One of the soldiers hands Ruark a handkerchief. "You should clean yourself up, ma'am. Getting dark now, and the mountain lions will come down from the heights if they smell blood." He moves to the opposite side of the blast door from the Helmholtz box and waits, looking at Ruark. Near him is a control panel that features a keypad and a large red button.

Ruark steps over the bunker's threshold and moves to stand by the transport we arrived in.

She scrubs her face with the handkerchief. When she's through, holding the bloody rag, Ruark nods at the soldier, and he enters numbers into a keypad and then depresses the button. A yellow light flashes into action, and the air is sundered by a short siren. The blast door squeals and shrieks and then begins to close with a rumble. The view of the pines narrows.

"You break the rules, you go feral or try to escape—and we know you like to bust out of every place you've been stuck—we'll make sure that the rest of your short, sorry life, and your brother's, is full of pain. Got me?"

"Got you."

"Good. These gentlemen will escort you to your home for the immediate future."

She's smiling as the door obscures her from view.

It closes with a clang.

NINETEEN

The elevator is a big metal box, remarkable only because of the extensive security and a ring of metal benches. One of the soldiers—the bunker bull—places his hand on the biometric scanner and then taps a series of numbers into the keypad.

I really shouldn't, but I go in and snatch the number from his mind. The Helmholtz shivers the ether, but I get it. Fifteen numerals: 384623829317293. The length of the key code is unfortunate—I'll never be able to remember it all—as is the fact that they change it every day. So, to escape, I'll have to chop off his hand, place it on the scanner before it cools, *and* remember the code. I guess I could take over his body, pull his gun, and kill all these guys. Then find Jack. So close.

Craptacular.

"What's with the benches?" I say.

"You'll see. Sit down."

Once I sit, the soldiers follow suit. The elevator shudders into movement. Descent.

"Fifteen up and fifteen down. How much of my freakin' life is spent in this damned box?" one of the soldiers says. "Be glad when I'm back on perimeter or guard duty."

"Shut up, Markos. We've got a package." This from Sergeant Davies, the man with the passcode.

"Figure, up and down with every escort, that's five, six times a day. That's three hours, seven days a week, twenty-one hours a week."

"Boo-fucking-hoo. I said shut it, soldier."

"Least they could put some Muzak on in here."

Another one of the guards snorts, shifts in his seat.

Boredom is part of the job of a soldier. Long periods of nothing punctuated by intense episodes of violence and terror. I remember. But these boys are edgy, trying to break the stress with humor. I scratch at the surface of Markos's mind. He's seriously freaked by his assignment. One image is clear: kids flying in formation in a clear blue sky over a mountaintop. The idea of it corrodes his mind. He can't explain it, and that challenges him, wears him thin. Everything here—in this bunker, on this mountainside—is wrong, and with each descent, it's like being swallowed by strangeness. He's overcome with panic.

I soothe him, calm his mind. He relaxes and leans back into the bench. Davies, watching him, grips his M14 a little less tightly. When he's satisfied Markos is cool, he shifts his gaze to me, notices me watching him.

Most folks avert their gaze when challenged with another unvarnished stare. Not Davies. He just looks at me, indifferent and efficient, holding his rifle lightly, swaying with the movement of the elevator car.

What seems like ages later, it shudders to a stop. The door slides open, and cold air seeps into the elevator car. There's a short hall leading to a dark stone wall with a single door. There's a Helmholtz box next to the door. Everything is rough; I can see the crags and fractures in the face of the stone, made prominent by the single fluorescent light. It buzzes and flickers.

"And here we are." Davies unlimbers his rifle and uses the barrel to indicate I should disembark. "Men, stay here."

He walks me down the hall, presses the code again at the keypad, and the simple metal door swings open, revealing a quite large room, a single bed, a toilet and sink. A stool. The Helmholtz pulses the ether, rising and falling, stronger than I've ever felt it. Around me, all around, is rock. The only sparks of life are Davies, Markos, and the other soldiers in the lift.

Davies gestures for me to enter the room.

"Can I get room service?"

Davies grunts. I can imagine him with a cigar in his mouth. "I'll have the concierge bring your bags." He puts his hand on my shoulder and gently shoves me into the room. He pushes the door, and it swings shut with a click.

It's cold here, almost cold enough that I can see my breath.

There's a crackle, and I see a speaker hung high up on the rock wall of my room. There's a small cluster of devices nearby, most likely a camera and a microphone.

The speaker squelches, crackles, and then I hear a voice, a familiar voice say, "You're a half a mile underground. The bunker's on lockdown. Once the soldiers exit, no one will be able to enter or leave until I release the new access codes. So even if you've tried any of your little mental . . . tricks, you're here for the duration." She chuckles. It's a *look-at-how-powerful-I-am* chuckle. "Consider this a little tenderization. Nighty-night, Mr. Cannon."

The lights flicker and go out.

Absolute darkness.

"You guys forget to pay the electrical bill?"

Silence.

Darkness.

"Really?" It comes out more like a scream than the snarky way I'd heard it in my head. "Leave me in the dark? *Really?*"

I wait for a response. Nothing.

Reality stretches. For ages I wait, panting in the cold darkness, waiting for them to turn the lights back on. I have the car keys, and my wallet, loaded with the cash Jerry gave me, fat lot of good that does me now.

Eventually, I fall on my hands and knees and crawl forward until I find the bed. The thick wool military blanket is rough on my skin as I wrap it around me and begin shivering in the dark.

The ether pulses with poison. The cold seeps into my bones. The darkness is complete.

And sleep won't take me.

I am alone.

...

I cast out my mind, but the ether thrums with the corrosive effects of the Helmholtz and I am tired and the darkness is complete. I cannot fathom where I end and the night begins or the rock or the cold. I am misery bound tight in a woolen blanket. Muffled and buried underground.

I have my memories.

There was a girl once, buried underground. An evil man and his twin sister held her for their games. Held her secret and near death in the dark. Until two boys rescued her.

Me. Jack.

He's nearby, I know, but farther away than ever. And I am locked here, incarcerado.

Who will save the saviors?

···

Darkness visible. And impenetrable.

I've forgotten light. Colors are merely abstract thoughts, like numbers. I can't remember warmth or sunshine or the sensation of wind. The scent of anything but hard stone beneath the mountain.

It presses down from above. The weight of the earth and the mountain compresses me, like a deep-sea diver in the mounting darkness of the deeps. I am tiny, a particle trapped in a cage.

I am nothing. Nothing except cold and gnawing hunger.

No dragon in the East. No insomnia. No Riders. No Quincrux or Jack or Booth. No light, no love, no friends. Bound in a nutshell and the king of infinite space, left only with stolen memories.

The leg of the bed will not bend. The stool will not break, no matter how many times I hurl it at the stone wall. The sink is metal and indestructible. I plunge my head in the toilet until my lungs strain in my chest and my body rebels, falling slack.

I would end this darkness.

My mind.

Going.

Going.

I am you and you are me, though we always disagree, he is you and you is she, two makes one and one makes three.

Two makes one and one makes three.

···

It is joyous pain when I hear ticking and buzzing and the ceiling explodes in illumination. The creation of the universe, billions and billions of particles like stars.

The speaker crackles.

"Wake up, Mr. Cannon," Ruark says.

I make my body sit upright. The light hurts, and it's hard to see in the brilliance of a thousand suns.

"We've been enjoying the infrared video of your last forty-eight hours. Good stuff." She chuckles. It's a tinny, rough sound. The speaker makes it sound less than human, or maybe that's the cruelty infusing it.

"Let me out." My voice is cracked, raw. I screamed at the darkness for a while, I guess. A few hours, maybe.

"Not just yet, Mr. Cannon. You need to marinate a little more." The door clicks and swings open. Flanked by two soldiers, Davies enters holding something in his hands. A tan packet. He tosses it onto the bed next to me. Black lettering reads MRE. And below that, BEEF STEW.

"You have now cost us seven dollars more. Eat quickly—the lights will be extinguished in ten minutes."

"No! Just—"

"Sergeant? If you would."

Davies looks at me and I scrabble at his mind, but I'm too hungry to concentrate and the Helmholtz thrums away, pulsing.

"Ah, your body temperature has risen a degree in the last fifteen seconds. Please refrain from using your abilities, Mr. Cannon."

"Let me out. You've got Vig. I'll do what you say."

"Yes, you will." The smile is audible in her voice. "But we need to make sure you've been housebroken before we can let you out among the general populace."

Davies steps backward, through the door, and it swings closed once more.

Her voice continues. "I would keep you here in this bunker and dust you off only when we need you, but the director thinks that won't serve us best. He thinks you need someone else to complete you, to make you whole. Your little friend, Mr. Graves. Without him, you are useless. And possibly, without you, he is."

I tear at the MRE, ripping the top of the thick plastic packet off with my teeth. I manage to gnaw a hole in the beef stew packet and squeeze the salty meat-slurry into my mouth like squeezing toothpaste from a tube. It tastes wonderful. A smaller packet reads BROWNIE so I rip it open and stuff it into my craw.

"But remember, should you ever disobey . . . "

The lights go out.

I don't know what I say then; it's lost among the rage and screams. But from the speakers come laughter. Then static.

Then nothing.

■■■

I explore the MRE by touch. A block feels like a granola bar. A thicker, mushy packet feels like congealed ranch dressing. As I shuffle through the contents of the MRE, my hands greet an old friend, known from hundreds of cigarettes lit for Moms. Fancy running into you down here.

A pack of matches.

My hands move of their own accord, by rote. Peel off a match, scratch on the coarse striking strip. A blossom of light in the darkness. The bright smell of sulfur, like a whiff of hell. I hold the match high and can only see a few feet in front of me.

I shuffle through the rest of the MRE. Crackers. Bacon-flavored cheese spread. Chiclets gum. Instant coffee.

The match burns down to my fingertips, and I hiss with the pain. The darkness lasts only a moment before I've lit another. There are eighteen more in the pack.

Thirty seconds of light, this time, before the match light dies.

I light matches one after another. I stare at the flames, thinking.

The last match flame dies. I feel like my own awareness has been snuffed out as the darkness rushes back in.

■■■

I'm sleeping when the lights come on again and Davies is standing over the bed.

"Get up, son. You have an appointment."

I stand. It's not that I'm weak, I'm just not a morning person. And the light hurts my eyes.

"An appointment? With who?" My voice is hoarse. It hurts to talk.

"Whom. And you'll find out."

We ride the elevator up and out. I don't have the energy to make a run at his head, take today's key code from his mind. I barely have the energy to stand.

When the doors slide open, exposing the motor pool, I'm overcome with light.

"Kennel up," Davies says as another army bull muscles me into a waiting windowless van.

TWENTY

"Fire up the Helmholtz. Use the new protocols Ruark gave us," Davies says. The ether thrums, and I don't even care. My throat hurts.

The van rumbles over gravel first and then, judging by the sounds and vibrations, a smooth tarred surface until we hit another gravel road. More turns left and right up another switchback mountain road, I'm guessing. I don't know. Somewhere, somewhere near here, is Jack. I could reach him, hijack the driver, find my way to him. But the thought of Vig presses down upon me, and every time I close my eyes there's darkness. There's always darkness waiting.

Growing up, there were always dogs leashed to the weedridden trash heap trailers in the Holly Pines Trailer Park. They barked at every passing car. Now I know how they feel.

The van slows to a stop. A rumbling sound and then the van moves again. Another rumbling. The doors open, and the soldiers indicate I should get out. A motor pool. Like the last. Ruark stands there, sour-faced, flanked by a lean, silent man.

"Mr. Cannon, I hope you found your lodgings instructional."

When I don't reply, she gestures at the man standing next to her. Her companion is a dark-haired, olive-complexioned man wearing black fatigues. He's one of those guys who in clothes just looks thin, but under the fabric is rippling with lean muscle. He weighs maybe a buck fifty, tops. His dainty waist is encircled by a police belt that holds a pistol, a Taser, handcuffs, and buttoned compartments that could conceal any amount of evil devices. His nearness to her indicates he's protection, and his body language radiates danger.

Ruark laughs. "Shreve, let me introduce you to Mr. Negata, the only person of his kind in the whole world."

"Negata? He, like, from Japan or something?"

"We think so. We don't know, actually."

The man steps forward and extends his hand.

There is no Helmholtz field, the ether is calm, and maybe I can do it before anyone notices. I slip into the wild blue yonder to find the man. I sense Ruark, and he should be right there, in the half-lit world of the space beyond ourselves. Yet, he's not. It's as if he doesn't exist. An inverted ghost, this one existing only in the physical world. The thought chills me. I shoot back to my own meatsuit.

My skin crawls, but I extend my hand to shake. There's a moment just before the flesh of our hands presses together that I think he's a projection, a mental hologram. Then our hands meet. His palm is warm, solid, totally real.

Something about him makes me terribly uneasy, and I let go of his hand after one pump. His gaze never wavers.

"Mr. Negata doesn't exist to you and me, except here in physical space."

"I can see that."

"We don't know why or how, but he was born without whatever it is that lets one of us touch him."

"A soul?"

"Possibly. He's never spoken in my hearing. Maybe his brain has arranged itself completely differently from ours because he's never used language. Language makes certain pathways and patterns in the brain, in the synapses and neural networks, and without language, a person is rendered invisible."

"Really?"

"It's a theory." She shrugs. "No idea. It could just be his power, and he doesn't like to talk. He seems to understand English. But maybe he can decipher the meaning without being sullied by the words. I don't know."

What would life be like without the wonderful clutter of words? Empty and drab, most likely. Like living in the dark. I shudder.

"After you proved stronger than we realized—" She touches her nose with the back of her hand, lightly. It's a subconscious gesture, I think. "We thought it best that we keep him about the place, in case you turn unruly."

I want to say *I'm always unruly*, but I don't want them to put me back in the dark. "I'd think you'd have a team of scientists figuring him out."

She laughs, but it's not a jolly laugh. "You obviously have a mistaken idea about the resources or effectiveness of our government."

"This place seems pretty cush. You've got an airplane."

She harrumphs, which is a feat, really. It sends large sections of her chest moving in alternate directions simultaneously, like tectonic plates shifting. "Are you ready to begin the testing, Mr. Cannon?"

"There's more?"

"Indeed. You're fractious and from all indications don't play well with others. Consider this an object lesson. A *gentling*."

I don't like the sound of that. It reminds me of when

Dr. Sinequa so gleefully mentioned gelding. "I want my brother to be safe. I don't . . ." It's hard to admit the weakness, but screw her. I'm strong enough to say I'm weak. "Don't put me back in the dark." It comes out a whisper.

She smiles in answer. She'll never stop punishing me for taking over her mind.

"And what happens if I fail your test?"

"I suggest you give one hundred and ten percent." She turns and gestures to the guards standing by another elevator. There's a large *B* painted on the concrete wall. "Williams?"

A soldier fiddles at a keypad, and the elevator opens.

"This way, Mr. Cannon."

Negata remains standing to one side, his hands free, legs slightly parted. Ready for action. Ruark saunters off, a little bounce to her step.

Nothing to do but follow. Into the belly of the beast.

■■■

The elevator descent doesn't take as long as the one in my bunker. Five minutes, maybe. Since I've come out of the dark, I have trouble telling time. My mind races.

When the doors open, a bland office environment is revealed. Tile floor, hung ceiling. Many vents pushing conditioned air.

We walk down hallways, past innumerable doors, each one with a key card lock. Some with what looks like fingerprint bioscanners. No pictures. It's an office building, pretty much. I can't help but note the lack of Helmholtz fields. I could jerk Ruark around, if I wanted to. And do something about the dark, silent figure of Negata.

"Here we are," Ruark says, stopping at a door labeled 142a. Looking down the hall, I see a door labeled 142b.

Ruark punches a new series of numbers into a keypad. The door clicks, and she pulls it open. Negata waits and watches from fifteen paces away. He keeps his distance, yet during our walk, I felt like he was tethered to me at all times. I might not be able to sense him in the ether, but in physical space, he's got my attention.

"Okay, kid. *Entre vous.*"

"Uh, you not coming?"

She grins at me, and it does not-so-nice things to her face. "It's all you. Have fun."

...

It's dimly lit, the room, and something about that bothers me. It's like they're reminding me they can take the light away, if they want to. It makes me nervous.

The room's bare. It's got the same antiseptic smell as a hospital, minus the smeared feces and urine splatter. And screaming psychopaths, though my stint at Tulaville Psych might be coloring my memory. There's something utterly impersonal and dehumanizing about the space, but it's hard to pinpoint what. There's a plastic lawn chair and a large mirror covering half a wall. Beside the mirror stands a door, no handle. Below the mirror is a matte-black box bolted to the wall—a Helmholtz field generator. A large plasma screen is mounted on the wall to the left of the mirror opposite the door I entered. A business-card-sized camera sits perched above it. Around the room, in all the corners, I notice other cameras. And some sort of sensor. Heat maybe. Or infrared.

I turn back to the door I entered through and, of course, no knob.

A tinny small voice says, "Mr. Cannon, please direct your attention to the screen." There's a small hiss following the words, and I quickly come to the conclusion that somewhere there's someone peering at me through these cameras and breathing into a microphone. Just like in my other hole.

I don't like this one bit. So I pick up the chair and chuck it at the mirror. It bounces off, skitters across the floor.

The hidden speakers squelch, and the voice—not any voice I recognize—says, "Hardly original, Mr. Cannon. Please take a seat and direct your attention at the screen."

"Had to try," I say, not expecting an answer.

"Obviously. There's a reason why the chair is plastic. This isn't our first rodeo," the voice responds. It's not Ruark. This person sounds young, a woman, maybe, or a man with a decidedly tenor voice. It's weird, but I like the person behind the speaker and the cameras, despite everything. There's a spark of humanity there, and not the shitty arsonist spark either.

The screen flickers to life, showing another room like this one. In the room on the screen, there's another plastic chair. And the plastic chair holds another boy, maybe a little older than me, judging by the scraggly fuzz darkening his chin. He's got a fauxhawk and earrings, some tattoos on his arms.

In the corner of the screen, in the lower third, read the words, *142b - Cameron, Reese - CN: The Liar.*

"Mr. Cameron, you have your instructions. Please begin."

Cameron—*The Liar?*—looks at the ceiling as if trying to discern where the voice is coming from, an annoyed expression on his face.

"Begin, please, Mr. Cameron."

Cameron looks at the screen. It's like he's looking at me, but not quite. The camera isn't squarely in his field of view. He looks at the paper, looks back at me.

"You owe me twenty dollars," he says, looking into the camera.

I check my wallet, just in case. It's still there.

After a moment of silence, the voice says, "Reading complete. Proceed to the next example."

"You've got lung cancer and only have a month to live."

Nah, that's total bullshit. If Moms hasn't gotten lung cancer yet, I sure as hell don't have it.

Again, silence. "Reading complete. Next example."

"Jack Graves is dead."

Huh? Okay, this is getting too weird. They're fucking with me now. And I don't like being fucked with.

"Reading complete, next example."

"Your hair is on fire."

I snort. Yeah, right.

"Reading complete. We will proceed to the next phase of the test."

I don't know what's going on here, but something is definitely weird.

The ether thrums, shivers. The Helmholtz has been triggered.

"Mr. Cameron, please proceed."

Cameron looks at the paper and says, "Hey, man, you owe me twenty dollars."

Nothing.

He runs through the same statements again. After each, the

voice says, "Reading complete. Proceed."

After he tells me my hair is on fire, the thrumming increases, rising to an uncomfortable level. At the voice's prodding, Cameron runs through the bizarre statements once more.

When he's finished, the voice says, "Mr. Cameron, section one of the test is complete. Please join Mr. Cannon in the other room." A buzzing sounds, then a click. The door next to the mirror swings slowly open. On the screen, Cameron stands, still holding the piece of paper.

"He crazy or something?"

"Hey, I can hear you, dude," I say.

He grins, walks into the room. "Listen, man. They're gonna have me say some more stuff, but I promise I won't make you do anything you don't—"

"Mr. Cameron, please refrain from speaking, immediately," the voice says, but it's different now. Another person. Gruffer.

Ruark.

Cameron turns and pops the bird at the nearest camera. Turning back to me, he sticks out his hand to shake, and I take it. "Name's Reese. They call me The Liar. I hate that damned name."

"What does it—"

"Mr. Cameron, start with phase two, immediately."

He looks at me apologetically, shrugging. "You'll see."

"Mr. Cameron, please start phase two, immediately."

"Okay!" He glances around as if looking for a fight, fauxhawk bristling, the paper balled in a fist. He uncrumples it, spreads it in front of his face with two hands. The ether is still and placid.

Cameron looks at me closely and says, "Sorry about this, man, but you owe me twenty dollars."

I reach for my wallet, because I like this guy and I don't want to welsh on him. I can't remember how I borrowed the twenty, but now that he's asking for it and I'm flush, no reason not to pay him back. I whip out the wallet, peel off a twenty, and hand it to him. He smiles, takes it, puts it in his pocket.

"Reading complete. Proceed, Mr. Cameron."

Cameron nods, bows his head, thinking. Then looks to the ceiling again. "Really? I have to do this?"

"Proceed, Mr. Cameron."

"Goddamn you. Goddamn you to hell," he says. His jaw is locked, and his face takes a fierce expression, rapacious, yet full of sorrow. "I'm so sorry for this. They have my parents." He stops, breathing deep, then looks at me. "You've got lung cancer and only have a month to live."

At first the words don't register, but what he says settles in, the horrible truth of it. I touch my chest, staggering back. I can feel the tumors blossoming in my chest like black flowers in the light of some cancerous sun. My mind races back to every cough, every clearing of my throat in the last six months. How could I have not seen it?

I'm going to die. We're all going to die, but I'm going to die soon. In a month. Or less.

Immediately, I think of Vig, the little dude, left to fend for himself. Of Moms drowning herself in a sea of alcohol, broken beyond repair.

I think of Jack, vulnerable yet strong. Booth, kind and full of concern. Jerry, full of wisdom and mirth. I'll never see them again. I'll never be normal. I'll never have a real life, but I guess that was already my fate, and the realization of that hurts more than the harsh reality of my oncoming death. It's the shame and embarrassment I feel, fooling myself that I could somehow cobble together a normal life for myself. God, I'm such a pathetic idiot.

My face streaming, I turn away, toward the far wall, so that Cameron can't see my stunned grief. I can feel coughs building in my chest, like bubbles rising. I can't stop them. They tear at my throat, the coughs, and I can feel bits of my lungs sloughing off and traveling up my windpipe.

It's hard to breathe.

The disembodied voice and Cameron remain quiet, leaving me to my coughing and sobbing and heartache, huddling away from the bland room. I'm there a long time, lost in my own private apocalypse.

"Can we stop this?" Cameron cries. His voice sounds as distressed as my own. "Can we stop this bullshit?"

The voice says, "Reading complete." Not Ruark anymore. It's thick, the voice, as if choking back some emotion. "Proceed."

I can't even turn to look at him, but I hear paper being uncrumpled. I hear his breathing. He says, "Is this necessary? Is it?"

"Proceed, Mr. Cameron."

"No. Let him get up. What's his name? Steve?"

"Mr. Cameron, proceed with the testing. Immediately."

"No, damn you. Give him a second." There's a long silence, and then he says, "Steve, hey, listen, you're not dying. You've been cured, okay? You're going to live."

You can't come out from something like that in a second. My body reacts to this news—there's been a horrible mistake, and I'm going to be all right—but I'm still a wreck. The sobs and coughs have ripped my chest to shreds, it feels like. But there's a small burning ember of hope now.

"Mr. Cameron, proceed."

"Can I say this? Can I say it? You are all evil. You hear me?"

The voice isn't so sure now when it comes through the speakers. It wavers a little. "Please proceed, Mr. Cameron."

"They've got you too, don't they? They've got you. *I can hear it in your voice! They've got you!*"

"Please—" It's almost weeping now, the voice. "Proceed, Mr. Cameron."

The microphone squelches once. A voice returns. "Mr. Cameron, if you do not proceed, Mr. Negata will escort you from the room. You will fail the test." Ruark again. They're fighting over the microphone, it seems.

"I've passed your shitty test already!"

"There are always more tests, Mr. Cameron," Ruark says, her voice smug. "No position or place is assured in the Society."

Who is being tested here? Me or him?

That thought shocks me out of my self-pity for a moment. I always live at the center of all worlds. That's just my due.

"Proceed."

Another long silence. Then Cameron says, "Jack Graves is dead."

The world is ending. We spent so much of our times at odds, Jack and I, but I love him and he's gone now and I'll never get a chance to tell him so. Something here is so wrong, it affects me on a physical level. My heart races; my blood pounds and surges in my temples.

Something here is wrong.

"Reading complete. Proceed, Mr. Cameron."

"Really? This one?" Cameron says. "It's just stupid."

"Proceed," the voice says, implacable.

"Your hair is on fire."

I twist and roll, frantic to extinguish the flames. I can't feel the pain yet, but my body reacts anyway. When you cut your finger to the bone, it takes a while for the body to report. These flames pouring from my head—each person like a match head, unlit, dormant—will at any moment begin to sear my flesh, melt my skin from my skull. I drop to the ground and slap at my cranium, furiously.

Yet it doesn't burn. How can my hair be aflame yet my skin not burn?

Something is not right here.

I stop thrashing. There's a moment when I wait for the searing heat to attack me, ripping across my head and flesh, but it doesn't come.

I stand, look at Cameron.

"Yeah, the last one was a doozy."

Ruark's voice says, "Mr. Cameron, repeat the last example, please."

He looks at the ceiling. "Can't. The circuit's been tripped, can't you see?"

"Mr. Cameron, repeat the last example. Immediately."

"Fine," he says, and looks at me. "Dude, so sorry about all of this. You ready?"

"What just happened?" I ask, though I'm getting an idea.

"You tell a lie too big, and it breaks the trust. Flips the switch. If the lie contradicts what their senses tell them—"

"That's your ability? Telling lies?"

"No. My ability is making people believe my lies."

Ruark's voice sounds from the speakers. "Mr. Cameron, you have three seconds before Mr. Negata will escort you from the testing area."

"*I got it the first time!*" he screams. "Your hair is on fire."

It's most definitely not. I don't have cancer, and Jack isn't dead.

Holy crap, this kid could rule the world.

"Gimme back my twenty."

He grins a little sheepishly, digs in his front pocket. "Hey, I didn't want to. They made me."

"You said they have your parents, is that right?"

He stills, but before he can answer, the outer door opens and Negata stands framed in it, holding something in his hand. A Taser.

Ruark's voice says, "Not another word, Mr. Cameron. Please accompany Mr. Negata out of the testing room."

Cameron looks at me apologetically and heads to the door. Negata steps aside and lets him pass. The door glides shut with a click.

"This concludes phase one of your testing, Mr. Cannon."

TWENTY-ONE

They leave me in the room for a good long while with nothing to do but think about all the implications of the boy named Reese Cameron and his ability. It's funny, but I'd been walking around thinking that I was the baddest mofo in the valley. Part of me is glad I'm not. Part of me is scared.

But he was missing a tooth. Someone did that to him, I wager. I wonder if they keep him deep underground, like me.

The outer door clicks and swings open, and there stand Negata and Ruark. Ruark's expression is blank, yet I can sense some excitement in her. A smile tugging at the edges of her mouth. I'm tempted to go out into the ether and peek, but the Taser in Mr. Negata's hand dissuades me.

"There any need for that?" I ask, nodding at the zapper.

"Both you and Mr. Cameron were quite obstinate during the first phase. A show of force may be necessary."

"Nice. You guys are class, all the way." I shouldn't mouth off, but hell, they're going to stuff me back in my hole anyway.

"Follow me, Mr. Cannon, for phase two of your testing."

She walks away, down the hall. Negata stands waiting for me to move. Which I do.

"Miss Ruark?" I say. "Can I ask a question?" She ignores

me, not even glancing back. "What's the point of all this?"

"The Society of Extranaturals is dedicated to assisting and supporting the American government in its operations at home and abroad."

"Huh? No, I mean here. Right now. This testing."

She's silent for a bit, walking straight ahead. Then she says, "What do you think, kid?"

"Do you really want my answer?"

She shakes her head, sighs, still walking. I glance behind us and there's Negata, holding the Taser and watching me closely. The man just reeks of the possibility of impersonal and unsmiling carnage. Simply with the set of his shoulders, the grace of his stride.

"Isn't it obvious, Cannon?"

Ah. We've moved on from the "misters." We've become chums.

"No, not really."

"All testing is to determine aptitude, of course. Special abilities."

"Of course."

"But this testing also plumbs the depth of your will, your ability to think, to cope in certain situations."

"Is that what all the 'reading' stuff is about?"

"That's classified."

She stops. I stop with her. She turns to me and then, pointing her index finger like it's a gun, she jabs me hard in the nipple. I step back.

"And," she says, her voice hard and low. "The testing is to remind you exactly what your situation is."

"And what is that?" I try to stop myself from asking, but the question just sashays to the tip of my tongue and dives headlong out into the world.

"Dire." She smiles again. "Your situation is dire."

She turns and begins to walk once more.

TWENTY-TWO

The next room is smaller, tighter. No mirror, but the same plastic chair and plasma screen. Once I'm in the room, Negata stands in the doorway, watching me until the door shuts, hands like blades, ready. I spend an interminable amount of time just breathing in the close confines of the room and listening to the air circulate through the vents.

When Ruark's voice squelches the speakers, it's almost a relief.

"Cannon, please direct your attention to the screen and we will begin."

"What happened to the other person, the last person telling us what to do? The nice one?"

"Please direct your attention to the screen."

I sit down and wait for the coming attraction. This time the screen shows me a backyard, somewhere in America, because there's a plywood fence, a swing, the edge of a concrete patio. Trees crowd in close beyond the fencing, and the sky is blue. In the bottom right corner of the screen there's a time code and a date. If it's today's date, they had me down in the hole longer than I thought.

There's no one on-screen, but the way the light moves, the shadows sway, I can tell it's a video, not a still image. A bird flies over the yard to settle on a power line. A figure comes on-screen. He's small, wearing a Spider-Man T-shirt, jeans, tennis shoes.

Vig.

He backs into the yard, into view of the cameras, hands up as if warding off someone. He's not crying, but I can tell from the way his lip is pulled to the side in a grimace that he's seriously distressed. A larger figure appears, and this time I can only see his back. Another boy. An older boy, judging by his muscles, the tightness of his T-shirt across the thick wedge of his back. Vig says something but, thank God, there's no sound, so I don't have to hear the smack of fist on flesh as the older boy hits Vig and he goes tumbling across the patio and into the grass.

But he's tough, my little dude, and pops right back up. He doesn't have his hands up anymore; they're balled into tight little fists even though his mouth is smeared with blood. When the larger boy steps forward, swings his fist again, Vig jukes to the side, scrambles forward, latches onto the larger boy and begins to grapple for his left arm. He clamps on and sinks his teeth into the boy's forearm. He looks wild, my brother, his face smeared with blood and his expression screwed into a paroxysm of animal fury. My skin itches, watching. My heart throbs in my chest.

The larger boy howls soundlessly and slings Vig away, sending him tumbling once more. Vig is slower to rise this time, so the boy's shoe catches him perfectly on the chin before he can stand and flips his body over to fall on the grass, faceup, staring blindly at the sky. The older boy kicks him two more times, once in the head, once in the ribs.

Before he stomps off, he spits on Vig.

It's a long while before Vig moves, rolling over and pushing himself to his knees. A thin dribble of bright red blood spools from his mouth into the grass. He stands unsteadily, looking about the yard. He sits down, hard, on his ass. Blinks a few times. Rolls onto his knees again and pushes himself up.

He slowly walks toward the camera. He's not crying at all. For an eight-year-old, his stare is remarkably cold. He's pissed. I don't know if that older boy knows what he's got coming to him.

Once Vig has passed out of view, the screen flickers and dies.

"Reading complete. This concludes phase two of your testing, Mr. Cannon. Please wait for Mr. Negata to retrieve you."

TWENTY-THREE

It's twilight now as they take me back to the bunker. It's hard to tell how far we travel in the back of the van, without windows.

"Why aren't there any windows back here?"

Davies tugs at his bottom lip, considering, and then says over the growl of the van's engine, "No need for you to get too cozy around here. No idea if you'll make it through the testing."

The van turns, and the driver shifts into a lower gear. I think about what he's said.

"That's crap," I say. Davies's shoulders tighten. "You don't want anyone to see me."

Jack could be out there right now. But the dark. Vig.

"I don't give a damn who sees you. To me, you're *no one.*"

"My name is Shreve Cannon."

"I don't care."

The Helmholtz is running but it's not strong. So I touch his mind and see. He's not lying.

The van stops. There's a rumble. I have to assume that's the blast door opening. They get me out of the back. Two soldiers wait for us with rifles.

They've gotten me out of the van before the blast door has shut. There are shadowy trees and a slight breeze. It smells wonderful. Like freedom. It's dark now, but the stars have begun to scatter across the vault of sky. It will get darker tonight, I'm sure. At least for me.

■ ■ ■

Fifteen minutes riding down. The elevator car shudders silently. I think about Jack. I think about Vig. The minds of these brutes are open to me. I could ride them to freedom.

Vig.

■ ■ ■

When the elevator doors open, the hall doesn't lead to my cell. There's a locker room here stinking of jockstraps and athlete's foot and the cold, clammy smell of wet rock. A quick perusal tells me there are no cameras or sensors in here. Soldiers don't like being filmed while they shower.

"Get the clothes," Davies says, and one of the soldiers tromps over to a locker and removes a folded stack of duds and hands them to me. Black military issue, like the Flying Burrito Brothers wore. White T-shirt. Tighty-whities.

"What's all this?"

"You're starting to stink. Disrobe."

"No."

"Disrobe. That's not a request."

"No."

I can compel you. The memory of Quincrux comes unbidden.

Davies's jaw locks, and I can see he's going to be Mr. Pushy.

"Whitmore. Stevens." Davies chucks his head at me.

The soldiers set down their weapons. Davies unholsters a Taser.

It's easy enough to snatch up their minds and hold them. There are just four. I am not yet whole. If I was, I could make this whole yard of boys kill each other. Gleefully.

For an instant, I have the urge to snuff out the burning matchsticks of their consciousness. To extinguish the light for them as they have done to me. And plan to do again. But it seems I'm haunted by ghosts. Jerry's words echo through me.

They're staring, blank-faced, locked in the stasis of my possession. Turning to Davies, I open both pairs of eyes—mine and his—and allow them to find the other's gaze in an infinite feedback loop. I'm looking at myself looking at this guy looking at myself.

"Everything I say you will remember. Do you understand?"

He nods, caught in my gaze.

"There's a man named Horace Booth. He is—or was— the assistant warden at the Arkansas Pulaski County Juvenile Detention Center. You can find his e-mail on the state website. *I order you to contact him.* You will use whatever resources you need to get this done. Once you find his contact information, deliver this message: 'The man from the Department of Health and Human Services named Quincrux holds Shreve Cannon and Jack Graves prisoner in a military compound in Montana. The address is Number 15, Old US Highway 10, Montana." I pause here because I can't remember the zip code. But what else can I do? "Repeat that back to me."

He does.

"You will tell no one about this. Do you understand?"

There are small tremors running through his frame. His left eyelid twitches. I ride him hard, on the inside. He cannot match me.

"Good. Davies, you will do as I have said. Otherwise, you will feel an unease." Crap. That's no good. An unease? It needs to be worse. It needs to be bad, if he doesn't do what I say. It hits me now. I continue, my fists balling. "You will not be able to sleep. The insomnia will come back to you if you do not do as I say and contact Horace Booth. Do you understand?"

I relinquish enough control to allow him to nod.

"You will recall this exchange only as a punk kid talking smack. Say yes if you understand."

His jaw unhinges like a zombie's, and the single word "yes" falls from his mouth.

That's good enough.

The soldiers turn and face the wall as I peel off my clothes and shower.

...

Davies leads me to my cell. The ether is aswarm with millions of wasps from the hive of the Helmholtz.

Another MRE waits on the bed, this time labeled CHICKEN SPAGHETTI. I eat most of the contents before the lights die and I'm left in total darkness.

I light the matches, one by one, but halfway through the pack, I stop. Knowing I can light them is enough.

I lie down on the bed, and the shibboleth curls and twines within me. The ether thrums and shivers with poison.

I think I sleep. It's too dark to tell, really.

The walls echo.

TWENTY-FOUR

Negata waits, standing in the center of the oil-stained motor pool. There's a Jeep up on a lift, no tires. A large *H* is painted on the motor-pool wall. He makes a strange, soundless welcoming gesture.

The elevator doors slide open, and Ruark appears. Today she's strapped down her prodigious physique with a man's shirt, tie, and vaguely military jacket, all to diminish the lines of her curves. She's at war with her body, truly.

We all are incarcerado. The cages take different forms.

No verbal sparring or banter today. Ruark's all business. "Mr. Negata will be your escort today. Indeed, he will be your shadow."

I can smell a faint whiff of tobacco coming from her as she turns and bounces off. The smoke has nested in her hair and clothes; she's been with Quincrux. He's around here somewhere. I could try to find him, but Negata would quickly reduce me to component parts.

Negata gives another awkward butler gesture, indicating I should come with him. He walks by my side, constantly adjusting his pace to match mine so that he's leading me but not pulling ahead, letting me fall behind him. It's a neat trick, the leading from the side. I'm sure he's full of neat tricks. Deadly neat tricks.

Eventually, we stop at a door in another featureless hallway. He punches in the code and we enter. There's another kid already in the room, watching me closely. She's pretty enough, hair blonde and pulled back in a ponytail. She has the fresh, lightly freckled face of someone who spends a lot of time in the sun, outside, under the sky. She's missing her right arm from the shoulder down.

It's so good to see someone else. Someone who doesn't hold a gun or glare at me. I like her face.

In the center of the room there's a short, glass-encased pedestal. Sitting inside the glass case is an old typewriter with a piece of paper fed into it.

The disembodied voice—the kind one from yesterday, the one I liked—says, "Please type your name on the typewriter. Proceed."

I walk closer to the pedestal. Negata remains watchful and waiting by the door. The girl approaches me.

"Hi," I say, but it comes out as a croak. I guess this is the first time today I've spoken. I try again, my voice dry and painful. "This seems kinda stupid. How're we supposed to type our name on there if we can't reach it?"

She ignores me. Looking at her, I notice her one hand is normal, no extra fingers. After approaching the typewriter, she circles it once, as if taking its full measure, and then places her stump against the glass. The keys depress, and I can hear a muffled clack as the arm of the typewriter darts forward and hits the paper. Again. *Clack, clack. Clack clack clack.*

When she's done, she looks around the room as if waiting.

"Miss Klein, you have completed this portion of the test. Please proceed to the exit. An attendant will escort you from the building."

"Hey! What about me?"

"The test will be complete when your name has been typed on the piece of paper."

"Hey, um—" I look at the paper in the typewriter. "Casey. My name's Shreve. Could you do me a huge favor? My name is Shreve Cannon."

She nods once, meeting my smile with her own. She steps forward, leaning a little. She has no arm, but the gesture is unmistakable—she's reaching out to shake. I raise my own hand in response, and I can feel the warmth and pressure of hers. An invisible hand.

"Nice to meet you, Shreve," she says, and she places her shoulder once more on the glass. "It's spelled . . ."

I spell out my name slowly, and the keys depress again, making the muffled clacking sounds. When she's through, the voice says, "Test complete. Please proceed to the next testing area. Your escorts will show you the way."

● ● ●

Negata takes me to another room. This one with a desk. Upon the desk is a stapled bundle of newsprint with the letters *PSAT/NMSQT* on the cover. There's a pencil, a granola bar, and a bottle of water also on the desk. In the corner is what appears to be a bathroom stall next to a sink, paper towel dispenser, and small trash can. I wander over and peek inside. Sure enough, a toilet.

"Mr. Cannon, please take a seat and prepare for the test."

"Prepare?"

"Examine your pencil. You will have fifteen minutes for the first portion of the test."

I sit down at the desk. Pencil looks sharp.

"Ready? Then begin."

· · ·

Hours later, I've finished the water and the granola bar, pissed twice, and completed the PSAT.

"Please leave your test on the desk." The door hisses, clicks, and swings open, revealing Negata, silent and clad in black. "Mr. Negata will escort you to the next portion of the test."

"Does this mean you guys are gonna send me to college?"

I hear a snort on the microphone, and then the voice says, "Please exit the testing area, Mr. Cannon."

I exit, falling in beside Negata. He walks forward, sees I'm not following, stops. Looks at me, dark eyebrows raised.

"So, what, you're a meat ghost? That it?"

He stares at me.

"Can you understand what I'm saying?"

He nods, once.

I take two steps forward and hold out my hand.

He doesn't take it.

I tap my chest. "This is all you are? Just flesh? Nothing else?"

He remains still. I go into the quiescent ether. He's not there, not there at all. And while the ether isn't quite space and doesn't relate to one's body like real space does, there is a component of location involved. I couldn't suss out some random Chinese person on the far side of the earth. I don't know if that's because of location or the limits location places upon my imagination.

"So, you're their hit man? You kill people? Like Quincrux does?"

He blinks. Frowns. Doesn't indicate a yes or no.

I shake my head. "I feel sorry for you, Negata. Someday I hope you have the balls to take a side. To become a real boy."

He makes the ever-polite gesture to follow/accompany him.

As we walk, I can't help but think that all of that was more for my benefit than his. He'll never be a real boy. And he'll kill me if he's ordered to. It was stupid even thinking otherwise.

I sigh and walk along with him.

TWENTY-FIVE

I think we're back at the room I was in yesterday. The one with The Liar. Reese Cameron.

While we're in the hallway, things look familiar, but all these bunkers look alike. Negata punches a ten-digit key code. The door clicks and I enter, Negata following closely behind.

Inside, there's a chair. It's not plastic. It's like a crash couch in space shuttles or airplanes. It's a semireclining chair with numerous straps. The chair faces the screen but is also in view of the mirrored wall next to the other door. There are thick bolts affixing the chair to the floor. Negata stands near it and gives another one of his gestures.

Welcome to the torture chamber.

The disembodied voice doesn't sound amused now. It says, "Please take a seat in the chair and allow Mr. Negata to strap you in. This is for your own safety."

"I don't like the way that sounds. You guys have never really had my safety in mind before."

The voice repeats its original message.

"What if I say no?"

Maybe it's the way I'm holding my body. Maybe this is old hat. But Negata moves like an oiled piston shuddering home, crossing the room in a black blur, his bladelike hands moving to smack into the small of my back, sending an explosive shock through my system, dropping me to the ground. Before I can recover, Negata has snatched me off the floor, holding me by the wrist and bending my hand in such a way that I can only move where he wants me to or my hand will be irrevocably broken in a colossal explosion of bone and blood. My ass hits the chair. My hands are strapped down on the armrests, and he works on my legs.

Negata walks over to a blank, featureless wall and presses something, and what appears to be an oversized medicine cabinet swings open from the surface of it. A cabinet designed to not be visible when closed. Huh. I look at the rest of the wall, trying to puzzle out what else it could conceal.

From a box he takes two blue latex gloves and puts them on his hands. He approaches me with a semitransparent piece of plastic held up, pushing it toward my face.

A mouth guard.

"Please open your mouth, Mr. Cannon. The dental guard is for your protection," says the disembodied voice.

I open my mouth to say something incredibly barbed and scintillating. Negata, faster than my wit, pushes the dental guard into my mouth and then snatches some kind of head harness and puts it over my face, preventing me from opening my mouth and spitting out the guard.

I could go into the wild blue. At the restraint, the shibboleth bucks and frets within me, looking for somewhere to go. Negata is invisible. Where are the watchers? Can I reach them even with the shib so wound tight within me?

The moment I go still, Negata turns and goes to the door that is already opening for him. When it closes, the lights dim slightly and the screen flickers to life. Where Cameron was yesterday, there's a girl. In the lower third of the screen it says *145b - Montgomery, Sarah - CN: The Bomb.*

She's pretty enough, I guess, though her posture is horrible. She's slumped over on a stool, wearing sunglasses even in the lowered light, with her arms crossed over her breasts as if fending off oglers. She's wearing black fatigues, and they make her look like a rebellious high school freshman experimenting with punk and contemplating her first beer. Her hair is long and unkempt, like she's refused to comb it. Behind her stand two women, two bull soldiers. Drab olive green. Carrying automatic weapons.

The girl, Sarah Montgomery, straightens as if someone is speaking to her, and she says something. To the disembodied voice. She looks pissed, some. She talks for a while—none of it I can hear—and then, in a silent yet obvious huff, she whips off her sunglasses and looks directly into the camera for a long while. Once she looks away, she replaces the glasses on her face. Pissed.

Her hand has the wide, extra-digit girth of someone with more nose pickers than usual. Twelve fingers.

Eventually, one of the female soldiers moves offscreen. I hear another hiss and click, and the door by the mirror swings open, revealing the same soldier. On-screen, Sarah Montgomery, the Bomb, stands, crosses the room, and appears in the doorway.

She moves in front of the chair I'm bolted in and stands, waiting.

At first I thought the soldiers were there with guns to keep Sarah under control—her own version of Mr. Negata—but instead, they flank her to each side and point their weapons at me. Even though I'm totally immobile.

"Mr. Cannon. The Helmholtz field is not engaged, you will notice," Ruark says over the speaker system. Looks like they let her DJ during the fun stuff. "Should you try to flee your body or possess anyone here, you will be shot and killed. Nod your head to indicate that you understand the situation."

I do. I nod.

"Good. We have an understanding. Miss Montgomery, you may remove your glasses now and speak with Mr. Cannon."

Sarah looks at me, still with her glasses on, and says, "He's gonna hurt himself against those restraints, y'all. Why don't you just mark his chart and let me go back to the damned bunker?"

Her skin is pale. She's got a tattoo crawling up one arm—a very nice tattoo of a Chinese dragon. Her fingernails are nubbin short. She's a chewer like Rollie, but she's better fed.

"Please proceed, Miss Montgomery," Ruark says.

Sarah looks at me, still behind sunglasses, and says, "This is gonna hurt you more than it's gonna hurt me, buddy." She takes off her glasses and stares at me. I can see her eyes, one green, one blue. She says, "Hi, little fella."

It's worse than being Tased, really, because looking at her feels so good. My body thrums with excitement, and immediately I have a raging erection that is so painfully hot and inactive that I twist in the chair. *These damned restraints.* If only I could be free of them, I could be joined in the flesh with her. Her body, her eyes, her breasts and hair call for me, like some siren in wine-dark seas, and I will do anything to reach her. I am meant to be hers and she is meant to be mine and my body sings that electric song. I strain against the tethers, twisting, thrashing. My back pops with an audible *crack* and then after a moment *cracks* twice more. Every part of me is alive and thwarted.

"Y'all. He's looking pretty bad here. He's bleeding," she says, and the sound of her voice is the most erotic thing I've ever heard. I would murder a million people to hear it again and not feel a moment's remorse.

These damned straps. I twist and feel a bit of slicked looseness in my right arm. I bend all my energies and strength there at that weakness so that I might be free. To join her.

My hand pops free, slinging a fine arc of blood droplets to spatter on the wall of the room. I scratch and grapple at my other hand, to free it.

"Okay, that's enough," Sarah says, and her voice is like fire. She puts her glasses back on and turns away from the chair, once again with her arms crossed on her chest, her back hunched. "God, you people really suck, you know that?"

It takes a while for my body to stop its thrashing. I can't understand where the woman I wanted so badly has gone. My wrists and carcass howl in outrage.

And I've still got a painfully exquisite boner.

The women soldiers grin at me, looking over my body. Something about the situation seems extraordinarily funny to them.

"Miss Montgomery, please exit the testing area with your escorts. Mr. Cannon, remain still. Mr. Negata will join you once the room is clear."

Sarah glances at me behind her sunglasses as she's walking out. "Sorry, dude. Just FYI, in case you're one of the ones who gets some crazy idea . . . I'm not into guys, okay?" She stops, as if waiting for some acknowledgement from me. "Even without all this," she waves her hands at her face, indicating her glasses or her power or whatever, "you're all too desperate and I'm just not geared that way," she says and walks out of the room, followed by her smiling guards.

In a few moments, when the room is clear and the door where Sarah and her guards exited is firmly shut, Negata reenters. Before he unstraps me, he returns to the oversized medicine cabinet and retrieves some gauze and disinfectant and treats my wrist. It's not too mangled, just scraped bloody across the meat of my thumb and knuckles. It stings as he applies the disinfectant.

Once I'm unstrapped and able to stand, I realize the extent of the damage straining against my tethers did to my body. My back feels ripped and tenderized; my arms and legs feel like I've been fighting an army of ravenous monkeys in a bare-knuckled cage match. My dick is chafed and raw. My jaw aches terribly. I nearly bit the dental guard in half.

"This concludes your testing for today," Ruark says. The speaker goes silent. Mr. Negata gestures to the door.

TWENTY-SIX

In the van again, trundling over the mountain, back to my bunker and the hole in which I sleep. I've made friends with the dark. We're old pals now.

Davies watches me blankly. I rifle through his memory, despite the van's small Helmholtz field. He didn't sleep last night at all. And he's started his search for Booth. Before duty this morning, he used a computer in a command center.

Clacking and typing. Quick and breathless, calling up a browser and searching the Internet. Reading. Remembering. Alone until Ruark and a smaller, mousy woman enters. "We'll need to test the new stasis bomb prototype in Hangar D before the director returns," Ruark says. The smaller woman nods and says something that Davies can't hear. "What are you doing here, soldier?"

He closes the browser's incognito window and stands. "Checking e-mail and waiting for you."

"These computers are off-limits to military. Employees of the Society only."

"Understood, ma'am. It won't happen again."

He wants to tell her something, but his tongue won't work correctly.

"Something to report?"

"The night's sensor readings of the Little Devil have been uploaded to the server, ma'am."

"Is that it?"

"Yes, ma'am."

"Don't you have somewhere to be? Collecting the Little Devil for his testing?"

"Yes, ma'am."

"Then go."

Now he stares at the passing trees and wonders why he can't sleep.

The Little Devil.

Fantastic.

...

No shower tonight. Helmholtz on high, casting silt and poisonous waves into the etheric heights like an erupting volcano.

Davies stares off, woolgathering, in the descent under the mountain to my cell. Gestures with his rifle for me to exit the metal box of the elevator.

Tonight's MRE proclaims it's MEATLOAF WITH GRAVY. It tastes like dog food.

When the darkness falls, I hold the matches in my hand. I feel cut off from myself. Somewhere out there, something stirs in its sleep. The dragon in Maryland.

I am a little devil, and it is the dragon.

For an instant, I feel it tugging at me, beckoning me to come to it. To join it. To be subsumed.

I am you and you are me, though we always disagree . . . disagree . . .

I wonder how Jerry is. Has the world fallen apart yet? Has

the insomnia worn at the fabric of civilization enough for it to fall?

I want to light a match. I want to reach out through the ether to Jack. To Vig. I'm so tired of being alone. To touch some mind other than my own. To feel what it's like to know friendship again.

But I can't. The darkness is complete.

In the end, I light a match. Let it burn down to my fingertips until my flesh bubbles and the fluid from the blister breaks and extinguishes the flame.

That's the only match I'll light tonight.

TWENTY-SEVEN

Ruark isn't with him this time. The van slews to a stop, the blast doors open. The van enters. I can picture it all with my eyes closed. The blast door closes.

They get me out, frog-march me around the vehicle. Bunker H again. Negata's standing there, looking at me with an inscrutable gaze, everything about him dark—his clothes, his hair, his eyes. He raises an olive-toned hand—it's a small hand, the fingernails trimmed down so that each finger looks knobby and blunt—gesturing for me to accompany him. I approach and he steps backward, gracefully, and takes a few paces toward the elevator. Stops, looks toward me, waiting. I join him.

His combat boots, burnished bright, make no noise. We enter the elevator, leaving the soldiers standing in the morning light streaming through the open blast doors. There's just the hush and whisper of air moving through vents, the whisk of clothing rubbing against clothing. Our breath. There's a mild scent in the air, like some organic cleanser infused with herbs, but I can't make out what it is.

We reach our floor and exit. We walk down long corridors. Eventually Negata slows, stops by a door. I'm reminded how big this bunker must be. The hallway we traveled down stretches behind us as straight as an arrow at least fifty yards. What else do they have down here? Lasers and sharks and the

Frankenstein monster and the Ebola virus? What *is* a stasis bomb? Ruark mentioned it when I hijacked Quincrux's body. I don't get any warm fuzzies thinking about it.

But now Mr. Negata stands in front of a door and enters the key code, and the door clicks loudly in the hall and swings open. All this is becoming old hat. The door reads 212a.

I enter the room and sense immediately that it's much bigger than the other rooms for testing. The ceiling is twice as high as the other areas I've been in, maybe twenty, twenty-five feet tall. Up near the ceiling there's a bank of mirrored windows—behind which, I can only assume, are people watching. No tiling in this room, just ductwork bolted into what looks like a painted black concrete or stone ceiling. Below is thin, industrial carpeting. Steel rings are affixed to the walls, and a large wooden contraption is pushed up against an expanse of off-white cinder blocks that looks like a collapsed bleacher. All in all, I'm in some kind of demented gymnasium.

The door swings shut behind me as I'm looking around. In the center of the large space is a huge, bulky, dull metal bell. There's a small ring at the top, and from where I stand I can see no seams or bolts; it's like it was cast from one pour of molten metal into a mold. Beyond the bell are two doors, swinging open simultaneously. Out of one a small boy steps forward, looking about and blinking. An older girl steps out from the second door. She seems a little bemused at first, and then she spies me and frowns.

The small boy walks over. The left side of his face is discolored, and his eye is swollen shut. His lips are fat and split. If we were at Casimir, he'd be titty-baby material, for sure. Slight, with a baby's stomach.

"What happened to you?" I ask.

"Reindeer games," he says, trying to sound tougher than he is. I'm familiar with that particular stripe of reindeer games, I want to tell him, but now doesn't seem to be the time.

"They don't keep you alone? You know, isolated?"

"No. Put me in a dorm with a bunch of other kids," he says.

I think about that for a bit. "You meet a kid named Jack?" I hold my hand up, palm down, to my nose. "Yay high?"

"There's a tall kid named Jack. He's my dorm mate."

"He didn't do that to you, did he?" I point at his face.

The boy shakes his head. "They caught me in the woods."

"Cripes," I say, wincing. I stick out my hand. "I'm Shreve." He looks at it as if it's a mousetrap or something. Eventually he takes it, pumps it once.

Then, slowly, a weak smile tugs at the ruin of his lips. "James Hollis."

"What are you in for?" I ask.

He frowns, face souring. "You asking what I can do? That's not good form."

"Why?"

"Because it's personal, right?"

"Sure, but I figure—"

"You go first."

"I can read folks. Get in their heads."

He blinks. "You're a bugfuck."

"So you know what *I* can do. What can *you* do?"

"I don't know," he says. "My ability deals with perception . . ."

"How so?"

"Sometimes I can stretch time."

"You stretch time?"

The girl walks toward us now, just as the speaker crackles and Ruark's voice booms overhead. "Miss Galine, Mr. Cannon, Mr. Hollis, each of you will go to the yellow markers."

I notice three *X*'s of crossed duct tape. Fluorescent yellow. Set on the carpeting in the rough outline of an equilateral triangle. Hollis takes his position.

It's my natural inclination to balk at stuff like this. I go to the yellow mark and look at the girl. She's quite pretty. Full lips and lustrous dark hair. Bright, piercing eyes.

"What the hell are you looking at, slick?" Disgust crosses her features.

There's no Helmholtz—that would inhibit the testing—so I go into the ether, find her and take note of her defenses. And Miss Cynthia Galine is as defenseless as a babe in the psychic woods.

The shibboleth twists within me. So long in the hole, in the dark. And now another mind. Thing is, this life I lead, this terrible gift, I'm learning to use it. And I'm learning how *not* to use it. The people I tap, I don't want to see all their secrets. I don't want to know if their uncles touched their willies or their mothers abused them. I don't want to know their delicious ringing moments of joy and wonder. I don't want to know what makes them tick. All I want is to use them, to take them over and get what I need and get out. Because I don't want to have any empathy for them. I've got blisters on my fingers, and I can't worry about being a good boy anymore.

I go in, behind her eyes. I seep into her brain stem, shooting through the corpus callosum enough to know her power, to suck from her everything I need to know about what she can do.

It's a shallow, petty gift she has. She can move things, lift them, throw them about.

A poltergeist.

I have her now.

"Beneath that bell," Ruark's voice says, echoing in the large space, bouncing off the stone walls, "is a slip of paper with a key code. That key code will allow the possessor to exit this room. The bell weighs one ton. That is two thousand, two hundred and forty pounds. There are pallets in the large locker near the bleachers on which you may rest." She pauses. "You may not use the restroom, nor may you have food or water, until this test is complete. Do not urinate or defecate in this room or you will fail the test."

Hollis looks at me with a blank expression. "That's no good. Too much coffee in the canteen this morning."

Ruark's voice says, "No talking. You may begin the test."

I close my eyes in my meatsuit and totally invest myself in the stonechucker's. Though I don't want to get to know her that well, I race down her hallways, looking at every way she's used her power. Throwing darts, rocks, garbage cans, sodas, food, bricks, lumber, acorns, dogs, cats, knives, water. There, right there, on the streets of Mumbai, her sister's leg trapped and mangled beneath a motorcycle. She snatches up the bike in a mental hand and tosses it away.

"Stand back," I say to Hollis, who takes a couple of paces backward. "No, no. More than that. I've never done this before."

He walks ten or fifteen feet away. "Here?"

"Perfect."

I am in Galine like a virus, a fever. I spread myself out inside her, testing all the edges, sinking my tentacles and tendrils into her psyche, filling her like a poison, a smoke. I am the Helmholz itself. I can feel her power thrumming instead of the tainted ether. I hold her/my body still, heavy with inaction, every muscle tense as guitar strings, rigid and vibrating like high-tension wires.

The bell reflects the light, dully, an inert yet massive service bell.

I dredge Galine's power up from the murky depths of her frame like I'm gathering myself for the mad leap into the wild blue yonder. I focus the kinesthesia, breathing in and holding the pregnant air inside Galine's chest.

I hold it. And hold it.

And *release*. The bell makes a dull, deep, and hollow sound, like someone striking an anvil with a hammer wrapped in velvet. It tilts some, just a little, enough to see from Galine's eyes a white rectangular object underneath. The slip of paper. But only for a second.

"Can you do that again?" Hollis asks. I can feel the ghost of Galine fluttering at the edges of my vision, trying to get back in. Trying to resume control of her body.

Hollis looks at my vacant body and then back to Galine. An expression of understanding crosses his features. "You weren't kidding about getting inside their heads, were you?"

I look at MeShreve, the original packaging that this bit of psychic leather came in, and his nose streams blood. I can taste it on MeGaline's lips too, bright and meaty, full of salt. Must be a gusher.

"No," I say.

"Why don't you just let her do it?"

"I don't know." There's a velocity to need. There's an

inertia to desperation. And I keep barreling forward even when I don't need to. Jerry said they'd become pawns to me, figures to be pushed around on a board. Quincrux gave me this terrible gift, but I'm reshaping myself in his image. Like father like son. What a horrible thought.

"Can you do it again?"

"I don't know. I've never done it before."

I catch his shocked expression. I've hijacked this girl's ability. Maybe that's rare. Maybe if I knew it was rare, I wouldn't have been able to do it.

"I can shove something underneath right at the moment you tilt it up." He shakes his head.

"That's a good idea." The blood makes my words come with strange plosives, pops and bubbles.

Hollis runs to the edges of the gymnasium, looking for something to jam under the bell if I can raise it again.

I vacate Galine's body for a bit, and she slumps to the floor and begins blubbering and looking at her hands like she's lost something terribly valuable. Which she has, I guess.

I walk over to where she sits on the carpet. She looks up when I approach.

I hold out my hand to pull her up.

"Screw you. Screw you, you *shit*."

The word hits too hard. It's all too much. For an instant, the world teeters and I feel all the people I've been come rushing back once more. I don't care. I don't care.

I do what I have to do.

Somewhere, Jerry's saying, *We will all become pawns to you. Tools for you to use.* And I have nothing to say for myself. Nothing.

The gymnasium yields nothing except an empty trash can, the collapsed wooden bleachers, and the bell.

"What about those?" Hollis asks, pointing at the bracing and metal framework on the ceiling. Above the bell that hides the key code is a matching metal ring, bolted into the living rock of the ceiling.

I jerk a thumb at Galine. "Let her try."

"Look there," Hollis says, pointing at an area of the ceiling we haven't examined as closely. "See that?"

There's some extra wiring coiled and zip-tied against the trussing that holds the lights.

"Yeah." I can see where he's going with it.

"We could use that to lift the bell."

"How?"

"Put it through that ring on the ceiling, tie it off on the bell. Use that as a pulley."

"It literally weighs a ton, Hollis. Two thousand pounds."

"It's worth a try," he says, like he's trying to politely convince his coworkers that the new initiative will increase the bottom line.

"That idea is idiotic," I say. "If I had to try to lift that damned bell, I'd herniate myself."

"Okay, fine. What do you suggest?"

"You could use her power to fly up there . . . "

Galine holds up her hands and says, "No. Don't do that again. Just tell me what to do, and I'll do it."

I glance at Hollis and then back to Galine. "Okay, fly up there and get that cable."

"I—" She stops, looks at the expression on my face, and then starts again. "I can't. I can't fly."

"No time to learn like the present."

"I've tried. I can't."

"You can throw things. Just throw yourself up there."

"I can't."

"Maybe I can."

"No!"

"No what? You just said you can't. So I should give it a whirl. Slide over."

Reluctantly, she stands. She looks terrified and furious all at once. "Okay. Okay!" She holds out her hands like I've got a gun on her. "Don't get any ideas."

"I'm not going to do anything!"

"Let's just keep that straight, then."

Hollis moves to stand by me. "You sound like a hillbilly gangster."

I can't help but laugh.

"Listen," Hollis says. "Maybe it would be easier if she—"

"Shut up for a second."

Wheels moving, gears coming together. Thoughts move like glaciers.

"Jesus Christ on a crutch, this is stupid . . . " It becomes clear to me now. "You know what they did to me in the second test?"

Hollis shakes his head. Despite her disgust, Galine moves to stand by him, watching me.

"They showed me a freakin' video of my little brother getting the shit kicked out of him by one of his foster brothers."

Hollis blinks a couple of times, thinking about it. He's not stupid, this one.

"They're not testing us to judge our abilities. They brought us here to break us down. To turn us on each other. Got me?"

"No."

"I can get into people, right? You say you change perception, okay? And she's a stonechucker. Can't fly, can't move stuff too heavy. Why are we all in the same room?"

"To learn to work together as a team?"

"Bullshit. Maybe if this was in the comics or a movie. No, they want us to rip each other apart. It's survival of the fittest. And I'm not playing anymore." I look at Galine. Her eyes are wide. Her mouth is covered with blood.

I did that to her. I am becoming a monster. They're making me into one. I'm a block of wood to be whittled down. A mound of clay to be formed. And when they're through, I won't look like me anymore. Not even to myself.

You'll be able to look yourself in the mirror.

I close my eyes, go into the ether, cloudlike and furious. I expand to take in the immediate surroundings in the space/ not space, the beyond. There's a Helmholtz field nearby, a very small but very powerful one, and it hisses and skitters like water dropped on a cast-iron skillet. That's where they'll be, inside that field. The force of its thrumming makes my spirit cringe and wither, but the anger is upon me. I withstand it, though not without pain. Within the field, even at its hideous strength, I find three flames above us, behind the mirrors. There's Ruark, some other woman, and a man watching us. I circle them, swimming in the ether like a shark, mouth full of jagged teeth.

It's the man I want. The man, I'm sure of it.

There's a moment's resistance, and then I'm inside, blinking, looking out of his eyes at the video monitors that show us in what I can only assume is thermal mode. The room looks like the control center in a spaceship: computer screens, microphones, flashing lights. There's some sort of graph that indicates power levels and percentiles, but it's not marked.

His name is Bill Holden. Everyday average name, and I don't really care anything about the man except for what he can do, the special gift that keeps him incarcerado here. Because everyone is incarcerado here. Maybe even Quincrux himself.

I'm a bull now, a snorting, charging bull in his mental china shop, and I could give one shit about anything except finding his talent.

A buzzer sounds, and the dim awareness of it filters through his consciousness to me.

Ruark says, "Cannon's temperature is up again, so he's active. Inconclusive if he's using Galine again."

The woman next to her, dressed in the ubiquitous black fatigues, says, "I don't think so."

"What?"

"He's in Bill."

My nose and face are crimson. I'm bleeding copious amounts of blood, just gouts of the salty, sticky stuff. Gonna have to leave Billy-Boy a few pints low after these shenanigans.

In and down. Burrowing, diving into his memories until I find the last time he used his talent.

Another brute, this one. But more than a stonechucker.

I have it all in a moment.

I step around the banks of computers to the one-way mirrored windows that look down on the gymnasium. I reach out my hand and, in my mind's eye, grasp the cold metal of the bell.

I squeeze.

It's not like crushing a can; it's more like crushing the distance between atoms. Even here, behind the window, I can hear the metal of the bell screaming, shrieking, and with a great dreamlike detachment note that Galine and Hollis are covering their ears, mouths open in screams.

I clutch the bell. I crush it. It warps and distends.

It is enough.

Ruark screams, "Up the field, up the field! Get Negata in there!" while her companion punches buttons and turns knobs on the machines. I smile at them with Billy-Boy's face, showing his teeth, red and covered in blood.

"Afternoon, ladies," I say and vacate the premises.

I'm back in my body, and my ears are ringing, but not enough to stop me from walking forward, dropping down, and reaching my hand underneath the bent and distorted lip of the bell and snatching the slip of paper.

"Come on," I say. I remember Casey—the girl with one arm—helping me. It's the least I can do. Galine and Hollis follow.

At the door, I tap the code into the keypad; the door buzzes and clicks. It swings open.

I step into the hall, that clean antiseptic expanse of tile and fluorescent light, only to find Mr. Negata.

He is not smiling.

And he holds a Taser.

TWENTY-EIGHT

They've taken Billy-Boy to the infirmary—they couldn't get his nose to stop bleeding—and now it's finger-wagging time. They've got me in another small room, probably the same one I was in earlier this morning.

Negata watches me implacably.

"How did you get through the Helmholtz field, Mr. Cannon?"

"What field? Did you check your devices? Maybe they weren't running."

Ruark shakes her head, looks to her female companion, whose name tag reads Tanzer. Tanzer peers at her tablet computer, taps the screen, bites her lip. Eventually she says, "No, looks like it was running at ninety percent power, as instructed."

Ruark turns back to me. "So how did you get through the Helmholtz field, Mr. Cannon?"

I shrug. Might as well tell them. "I just gritted my teeth and bullied through it."

"No," she says. "I don't believe you."

"Huh. Yeah, it hurts, but you know—" Hard to figure why I can endure it and they can't. "Some folks take to suffering."

"You some kind of masochist?"

Now, there's an idea. Maybe I am. But hurting Galine felt too good. They're making me into their own monster.

So I say, "Is that a proposition?"

She blanches, disgusted.

"Hey, you're the ones holding my brother hostage."

Now she looks uncomfortable. Tanzer glances at Ruark.

Ruark shakes it off. "So you're saying that you just endure the pain of the field—"

"Yeah."

Ruark looks from me to Tanzer to Negata as if taking a silent vote.

"All right, Mr. Cannon. And since you brought it up, I'll restate now that, yes, we do have your brother. Remember that."

"Gotcha. I'd like to advise you to not put me in a position where I'll have to do something about it."

She smirks. "It might be time for you to have a visit with the director."

"The big guns, huh? Send me to the principal's office? Won't that show, uh, I don't know, that you can't handle me yourself?"

She ignores that, but her ears have turned bright red.

"You are dismissed, Mr. Cannon." She turns and nods to Tanzer, who taps more on the tablet. The plasma screen comes to life, showing the center of the gymnasium where both Galine and Hollis lean against the warped curvature of the bell.

"Miss Galine and Mr. Hollis, this concludes the testing. An employee will be there to collect you in a moment." She turns to the door, where Davies and Negata wait. "Remove him." She jerks a thumb at me.

...

No MRE awaits me, so I look under the mattress for my pack of matches, but they've been removed during the testing.

I lie on the bed and wait. I sleep, eventually.

•••

The lights flicker on. I can't tell what time it is or how long I've been sleeping. The door opens to reveal Davies and Quincrux.

Davies waits at the door, rifle pointed at me, and Quincrux limps over, sits on my stool. He crosses his hands over the handle of his cane and peers at me.

"So," is all he says.

"So what?"

"We have come to this. There will be no more testing. I have doubts that you could bear more anyway."

He's probably right.

He looks at me. Not smiling, not frowning. No indication of how he feels at all. "Do you wish to remain here, below, in the dark? Or would you rise above, to the world of men?"

I feel hollow. Reamed out. "I'm kinda liking it down here. Easy to sleep late with it so dark." Because his words make me so glad. I can leave here and never come back. I can feel sunlight on my skin. Wind.

He blinks. "The infrared video indicates to me you are lying. Our technicians have tallied the hours you've spent screaming into the darkness. The total is considerable."

What? I remember screaming the first night, but not since. "Well, anything to pass the time."

"My recalcitrant boy." He sounds almost fond of me. "Will you never relent?"

"No."

"You will never obey my commands?"

"Never."

"You would balk even when your brother is at risk? When Mr. Graves is?" He stares unblinking. "What must I do to compel you? Our goals are not so different. We both want an end to the entity in the East. But I must be able to trust you'll be safe among the rest of the members of our society. And they will be safe from you."

Silence. I bow my head.

Once, I made a mistake. I stole a truck. I took something that didn't belong to me, and so they locked me away from my brother. Because I was selfish. Because I was a slave to my desires. Because I wanted to escape from my shabby prison of a life.

"I offer you one last chance. Will you come with me? Will you obey?"

Vig is strong. He's tough like me. But in the end, the world is tougher. We're born into pain. And Jack is here. Him, I can help.

"Yes."

"You will obey?"

"Yes."

"That is good." He stands. "Mr. Davies, you may lower your weapon and turn off that infernal Helmholtz."

He extends his hand. I take it. And rise.

"Welcome to the Society of Extranaturals, Mr. Cannon. Mr. Davies will escort you to the surface."

PART FIVE:
THE CONFORMITY

TWENTY-NINE

In the motor pool, the blast doors slowly roll back to reveal the mountainside, burning with afternoon light—I've lost all track of time in the hole.

The world's a riot of colors and smells.

I fall to my knees. It is almost too much to bear, this earth of ours.

Davies grabs my arm and begins to tug me upright, but Quincrux says, "No. Let him weep."

They watch me as I sob. As I rediscover what it means to be human.

Two Jeeps wait with soldiers at the wheels. Quincrux gets in one, holding his cane, and looks back at me, saying, "Remember."

I don't need to be told what. I'm placed in the other Jeep, and we drive down the mountain.

●●●

We pass through a wooded area, the air rich and refulgent and full of the tang of birch and pine, the hint of rot. The air warms now as the gravel road levels and the land opens up. There's the river passing through like a mist-wreathed ribbon of hammer-worn metal threading its way off to the southeast.

On the inside, I feel like I'm expanding and contracting all at once. A grub that has finally emerged into the upper world. The world of men.

We pass over a bridge and continue on the other side of the river, rising now, passing into the shafts of sunlight, passing through the dappled shadows of trees. Ahead rise steaming buildings, thick and squat and officious looking. I'm reminded of Casimir and its dull brickwork, of Tulaville Psych with its outdated crenellations and rarefied heights. These were someone's idea of what the future must look like, all sleek lines with rounded edges. But the sight of them takes me to a level of elation bordering on mania. It's like a cocktail of all the drugs in the world, just for me. It's like being born again.

A few people walk the grounds, which are manicured in places, in others left to grow wild with flowers and grass. I marvel at that for a while, *people walking free*. That takes some getting used to.

There are bulls—army soldiers here—sitting in a guardhouse as we drive through. At the rear of the house sits another Helmholtz box, and when our Jeep's field passes through its field, the poison in the ether skitters into near-unbearable ranges, like a radioactive sound.

We whip by something that looks like a large apartment building, past a couple of adults in what look like lab coats discussing something near the front doors. One of them gesticulates with a fistful of papers. Then a parking lot full of golf carts and ATVs. It seems cars and trucks—other than the military stripe—are verboten here.

We roll through a massive copse of aspens, tall and willowy, and then up a rise and among more of the campus. All of the buildings look the same: tan quarried stone, large dimpled-glass windows, archaic lighting.

The few people walking stare at us passing, some in lab coats, some in exercise gear, some in fatigues. I feel another mind touching mine through the ether with butterfly wings, but after a moment the sensation subsides. The guardhouse bulls look at us blankly, and there's a still, morose air about the place. The eastern rim of the valley looks as though it is on fire, the hillside streaked with orange and red and the fierce colors of trees.

Eventually, the Jeep stops in front of a large, blocklike building with many stone steps rising toward antique-looking wooden doors fitted with thick, dimpled glass. A mixed group of teens sit on the front steps, smoking and drinking what look like sodas. Despite the bulls, and the employees scurrying about, it seems that Quincrux and the Society give the kids some slack on the leash.

Davies says, "Get out. This is the boys' dorm."

I throw a leg over the back and hop out.

I walk up the front steps while the kids stand around, watching me.

They make catcalls and kissing sounds as I take the steps. In juvie they call the new kids "fish." This isn't too different. I keep my head high, shoulders straight. I've done this walk before; it seems like too many times. I meet their gazes head-on. Some faces seem familiar. Maybe some of them are part of the team that nabbed me on the East River in Manhattan. So long ago.

Again I feel the sensation of insect wings battering at my mind like a moth to an outdoor light. Light and distracting, but not an attack. Not aggressive.

Maybe it's the girl again. The girl I swatted.

The ether thrums and vibrates. I'm entering another Helmholtz field.

The doors are a deep stained wood, and when Davies pulls one open, the hinges creak. A long tiled hallway is revealed, full of echoes. To our right is a sliding glass window like you might find in an old-school pharmacy. I flash back to trigger-happy Steve-O and his Taser. But the guy sitting framed in the open window is in his midthirties, wearing black fatigues. He looks up as we approach.

Davies signs a clipboard, looks at me up and down, and sniffs.

"It's been fun," I say.

"Yeah. Maybe in a few days your voice will come back." He sniffs. "Good luck, kid."

"Thanks. But you're not shut of me yet."

He looks puzzled.

I knock at his mind, once. Twice. "You still have something to do for me."

He nods, slowly.

"I've got this," the man says to Davies. Davies wastes no time turning on his heels and walking stiffly back out of the building.

"Okay, boy. Not too complicated around here. I'm Roberto." The guy behind the glass picks up his own clipboard and peers at it like it's some magical incantation. "Shreve Cannon. Inductee."

I've been an inmate, a patient, and a ward of the state. But whatever you call us, it amounts to the same thing. Incarcerado.

"When I came in, they called us initiates, but that smacked

of religion, and many of the brainiacs didn't want us to sound like a cult. That was before the government got so involved."

"So the army hasn't always been involved . . ."

He laughs, stands, and exits the small office via a heavy wooden door. "No, the government got involved when they realized that the Society could provide them with talent that they couldn't get elsewhere, right? Bugfucks. Flyers. Jocks and hotheads and various other post-humans."

"Ruark used that phrase. Post-human."

"Yeah, it's kinda a catchphrase around here." He points at a framed poster on the wall. It's been there since the seventies, judging by the fonts and weathering. It reads:

POST-HUMANS
DO NOT USE YOUR ABILITIES IN THE DORMS.
REMEMBER, WE'RE ALL ON THE SAME SIDE.

A smiley face glares at us from the poster's center. Taped beside it is a white sheet of paper, reading: COURTESY OF HEINRICH HELMHOLTZ. YOU'RE WELCOME, MUTANTS.

Someone has scrawled *asshole* and an arrow pointing toward Helmholtz.

Roberto leads me to another set of steps. "No elevators in the dorm. And you're on the fourth. Top floor." His breath starts coming in heaves as we take the stairs. "Here's the rules: No girls in the dorm after ten pm, and I'll know if there's one here." He waggles his fingers at me like he's performing magic. "That's my talent. It's territorial in nature. I know everyone within my domain, and this building is mine." He shrugs. "So no girls. If you're into dudes, there's not much we can do about that."

"But how will you know? About the girls, I mean? I can feel the Helmholtz field."

"It switches off and on, irregularly. The fields draw a lot of power, so they can't run continually."

"That's interesting."

"Don't get any ideas, kid."

"I'm not. Just curious. Seems like with the army involved they'd have engineers or something—"

"*Right.* The army?" He chuckles. "The admin and lab coats come up with the theory, but we put it into practice. And there's just no way to run a Helmholtz twenty-four seven." We've reached the next floor. Boys come from their rooms, some of them in various states of undress. Wrestling, catcalling. Full of horseplay and happiness. But it's quieter than Casimir and less desperate and sad than Tulaville Psych.

"How long have you been here, Roberto?" I ask, looking about. Some of the boys aren't laughing and horsing around. They're staring at me with bald and frank gazes, uncaring and unfriendly.

"Fifteen years since I became an employee. Tried to find a way for my talent to work in the field, but it seems my lot is a bit more domestic." He gestures at the walls of the boys' dorm. "Because of my ability, this is my home. I'm the nurse, the maintenance man, and the night guard. Other folks go on missions. I live here. So, I've got that going for me. Chalk one up to the crapshoot of genetics."

"Other employees, what do they do?"

He looks at me sharply. "You probably already know the answer to that. We do what we're told."

"And you're told what to do by Quincrux."

He looks at me like I'm an idiot. "Yeah, kid. He's the director."

"Like what?"

"Whatdya mean, like what?"

"Like what does he tell employees to do?"

"Use your imagination. I don't know. Army stuff. To go nab potential inductees, monitor the radar, make assignments, do scheduling and administration, man the bunkers and laboratories." He looks at me closely. "What do you think?"

I remain silent, but I think we're his weapon. The soldiers aren't here to make sure we don't go crazy and hurt folks. They're here to make sure we can't be used against the American government.

We take another set of stairs up. No talking now. It's a long haul to the next floor, and when we get there we immediately take another flight.

Seriously winded at the top floor, Roberto gasps, "This way," and leads us to a room at the far end of the hall. The door stands open and there's a kid, a very tall kid, standing framed in it.

It's Jack.

THIRTY

I didn't know what to expect. It's been a year, and suddenly my friend, my brother in all but name, looms above me.

He comes forward and grabs me in a fierce bear hug and lifts me off the floor. "Shreve!"

"Hold on, bro," I say. I've never really been too comfortable with hugs, honestly.

Jack tosses me around a bit—*holy crap, he's gigantic now*—and finally, after mashing the air from my lungs, sets me down on the ground. He's six foot five. Six foot six? And gangly. A field of angry zits covers his face like a chinstrap, running from under his ear, across his jaw, to his other ear. Puberty is a bitch.

He's still got all twelve fingers, though.

"Holy smokes, Jack. You're *humongous*."

At first he smiles. Then the smile fades, and we're just left there looking at each other.

From the room behind Jack, Hollis says, "Hey, Shreve. Remember me?" His black eye has faded, and his lips look almost normal now.

"Hey, man. Good to see you're still here."

"Haven't washed out yet."

Another kid lies on his bed. He's short and squat and thick with muscles. He glances at me and says, "What's up?" and turns back to the comic he's reading.

"That's Tap. They've paired him with Hollis."

"Paired?"

"Jocks and bugfucks, right?" At my blank look, "Telepath paired with a telekinetic. You know, brains and brawn?"

It makes sense.

I take a look at the room. It's a large space with two bunk beds. The corners are slanted with the shape of the roof—we're on the top corner of the building, with a view of the mountains and river out two big casement windows set inside dormers, each with its own hand crank to open it wide. It's hot, but there's an oscillating fan in the corner that stirs the air some. It hums and rattles.

Jack's watching me closely. And there's a suspicious little frown tugging at his lips. Not five minutes together and he's already distrustful. Welcome home, Shreve buddy.

"Come on. Let me show you the roof," Jack says.

"Uh, roofs aren't my favorite."

"Don't be chicken."

Hollis looks like he's going to join us, but Jack shakes his head and I say, "Hey, I'll catch up with you later, okay?"

Jack cranks the casement window open. He steps up on the sill, stoops and turns his body at an uncomfortable angle, and climbs outside. After a moment, his head peeks back in and he says, "You coming?"

I work my way through the window out onto a three-foot-wide ledge that looks like it circumnavigates the entirety of the building. The air stills with coming night, and I'm thankful there's no wind to screw with my balance. A vertiginous drop stretches before me, and the few small lights of the buildings of the Extranatural Society's Montana Campus twinkle below.

I shimmy around the side of the dormer and discover what looks like a small, handcrafted wooden ladder leading up. It doesn't look too sturdy. But I spy Jack's sneakered foot disappearing over the stone lip of the roof.

Damn, I'm not going to let Jack be taller *and* braver than me.

I climb up and over. There's a little tarred-in square of roof with nylon folding chairs like people bring to football games. Jack's sitting in one of them, his hair a shaggy snarl around his head, his long legs stretched out. He waits until I sit down to fish out a pack of cigarettes and light one. The square looks tiny in his over-fingered hand. He looks like the stretched-out carnival mirror image of a boy playing at being a man.

I look up at the sky and the stars beginning to prick the heavens with light. It's as rosy as a vodka and pink grapefruit in the western sky and the silhouette of the mountains just a jagged line across it. Big sky. A brilliant spray of stars. Then blackness. Maybe that's just an imitation of life.

"So," I say, smelling the tobacco. "You're all grown up now, huh?"

Jack looks at me, but it's dark enough that I can't puzzle out his expression.

"Believe it or not," he says, and again I'm struck at how deep his voice is, "I knew you were going to say that."

"Those cancer sticks make you feel good?"

He brings the cigarette to his mouth and draws the smoke deep into his lungs and expels it. Trying to act cool, like what I'm saying isn't getting to him. But it is.

"Yeah, they do."

I stay quiet for a bit. "You drinking now, too? They got booze here? Weed?"

"There's no candy dealers, Shreve. But I'm sure you can figure some scam."

Boom. Nice one.

"Thanks for sending the letters, bro. I especially liked the picture of you and that girl. She had a bunch of fingers, too."

He takes the smoke from his lips. Stays silent.

"What was her name? Your girlfriend?"

"Ember."

"Amber? That her name?"

"Ember. Like a smoldering bit of charcoal. An ember."

"Ah. Ember. She still your girl?"

"Yeah."

"Congrats."

"How'd they get you?" Jack says. "I heard you killed the Witch."

"What are we talking 'bout here? You and your girlfriend or the Witch?"

"The Witch."

"They sicced her on me. And . . ." How far back do I go? "It's been a hard year, Jack. Shit got real for a minute. You got huge and started smoking. But I grew, too. Maybe even more than you did."

"You still look the same to me. Maybe a little thinner."

"I'm not getting any taller, that's for sure." I laugh a little, but it hurts some. My throat is still raw. "But I *have* gotten bigger."

"That doesn't make any sense."

"Okay. Give me your hands."

"What?"

"Give me your hands."

"That's gay."

"It's not gay. I'm not gonna do anything. I just want to see your hands."

"No."

"So, you're still ashamed of them, even now? When you're surrounded by folks just like you?"

He huffs and sighs and then sits forward and sticks out his mitts in my direction. I take them in mine.

"You remember when we were on the run from Quincrux? Before the Dubrovniks?"

He's hesitant, but he says, "Yeah. I remember."

"And you didn't believe me, right? You couldn't believe that someone would do that, or thought that I might be making it all up, or even that the Dubrovnik asshole was just having fantasies he couldn't tell from real life. You remember?"

"Yes." It's grudging, but he says it.

"Remember how I made you see? How I went in and forced you to walk down into that pit in that freak's mind?"

Silence.

I grip his hands tight, until he starts trying to pull them away.

"While you've been up here eating corn on the cob and mooseburgers and whatever else they've been spoon-feeding you up here, I've had to make space on the *inside*. You understand?"

He jerks his hands away. Not quite the reunion he imagined, I'll wager. Not really how I pictured it either.

He shakes out another cigarette. Fumbles because his fingers are too big and too many to get it right. I snatch the pack from him, hold out my hand until he puts the blue Bic lighter in it, and light the cigarette, drawing on it only enough to get a cherry going and then handing it back to him. I've had lots of practice lighting cigarettes for children. And pouring drinks.

I take a deep breath and tell him what's happened to me. Most of it, anyway.

THIRTY-ONE

I gloss over the testing. Not much to say about being in the nut-hatch, and I strategically omit all mention of both Rollie and my conversations with the Riders. Rollie, because it's too painful and I feel full of guilt, and the Riders because, even though Jack is a knucklehead, Quincrux could probably penetrate him like popping a balloon. There's the possibility that Quincrux will read him, or anyone that I speak with here. I don't want him passing along everything I know.

I told Quincrux I would obey. I didn't say I'd be his bitch. He kept me in the dark. I can keep him there too.

"So, your girlfriend."

"Shut up, man."

"She was on the team who nabbed me."

He grins. "She told me that. Said you bolted. Running and running."

"Hey, it's what we're good at."

He chuckles but doesn't respond. Maybe he's not much of a runner anymore. Maybe he never was.

"She's a lot older than you."

"Three years. But—"

"Yeah, you both got the fingers."

"Not that. We were the same in more ways than that. Her parents—"

Oh. "Well, she nabbed me."

He nods in the gloom. "She's really good."

"At the flying and the jumping." Sheesh, I sound like Jerry. "At everything."

There's the silence I was looking for.

"So what's your fundamental dysfunction, Jack? Your letter sounded desperate, and Quincrux said you're not doing well. They're worried you're gonna wash out. He wants me to be your handler. Guess that's why we're paired."

He smokes his cigarette. However big he's gotten, he still has the awkwardness of a kid.

"Hey, just because your balls have dropped doesn't mean I'm not interested."

"I don't need you to ride in and rescue me."

"You wrote the letters asking me to come. And who's talking about rescuing? And you're the one who was always rescuing me, remember?"

"You know what I'm talking about."

"We used to make a great team."

"Yeah, but you bugged the shit out of me, constantly."

"My one talent is abrasiveness, it's true."

He laughs, this time fully and without reservation. "Damn straight," he says.

I go on the attack. "So, what's the problem? You still flying sloppy? Can't lift stuff when they want you to?"

He ignores that. I can tell I'm getting under his skin. Jack puffs on his square a little. Then says, "Tell me what happened to the Witch."

"They caught me in New York. East River. They were all floating and jumping about. They put the whole park asleep except for me and a guy with a Rider—"

"They're still out there?"

"You think they'd just go away? Yeah, man. People can't sleep, the world's shot to hell."

"It's just—" He waves his hand, and I get a good gander at all those fingers. "It's just hard to believe when I can't sense them myself."

It's true. In the past, he's taken so much on faith. He believed me when most people would have just written it off.

"They were just hanging in the air, the bunch of them—"

"Red Team."

"Red Team?"

"There's a pecking order here, you know. There's the employees—extranaturals who've pretty much grown up here and work for the Society—people like Roberto and Tanzer. There's the army guys, who just point guns at us to make sure we do as they say. Then there's the teams."

"And the Red Team was the one that nabbed me."

"Yeah. There's Orange Team; they're the top dogs, mostly tactical stuff, antiterrorism. You won't see them; they're in the field almost all the time. When they're here, they keep to their bunker."

I think about that for a while. How close I came to being stuffed down a hole.

"Most of us." He waves me to the edge of the building. "See those lights over there? Right on the skirt of that mountain, that's a residential section for the older Society members. The scientists."

"I passed an apartment complex on the way in. Golf carts in the parking lot."

"Yeah, no cars here. No vehicles except for the army's."

"They don't want them to leave."

"Not without some reason to make them return."

"That's the way it is? Incarcerado?"

"Of course. But it's not that bad here, anyway."

"So, it's a nice cage. You'd rather be here than anywhere else?"

"Where else would I go, Shreve?" He holds up his hands, fanning them. Good point. Where else could he go? "And, I can fly. If I want to leave, I can leave. But I won't."

I think about that for a while. Jack is unencumbered by the baggage of family. He doesn't have parents, or siblings, or anything to tether him to the outside world.

In the end, I'm his only baggage.

"So, what about the other teams?"

"The Greens, they're next in line—less tactical and more surveillance, I think, but it's hard to know exactly."

"Because it's all hush-hush."

"Right. Need-to-know basis. If you start asking questions, you'll be detained by the director."

"And the Red Team?"

"They're the backup to the Orange Team, or at least that's what Ember tells me."

"I got nabbed by the junior varsity team. Perfect."

Jack chuckles; then it dies and he says, "And their coach. What happened to her? Him?"

"Back to the Witch. I got in her head, Jack. I ate her memories. All of them. She's in me now."

He's quiet for a long while.

"That's what you meant about making space on the inside," he whispers.

I nod. It's all I can do. She's in me, under my skin. Like a hunger. Like desperation.

I don't know what he's thinking now; we've grown so apart and changed so much. But we never needed to fill the silences with chatter, and that remains the same. He flicks his cigarette over the lip of the roof, and it makes a cherry-tracer as it falls, burning out in its arcing trajectory. It's chilly now, and off in the distance I hear a scream like a half-bird, half-woman having an angry orgasm. Everything goes quiet once more, and the Helmholtz field picks up in intensity, thrumming, and I can feel it percolating through the mesh and foam of my flesh. The stars are blazing in the heavens in their multitudes.

The scream comes again, urgent and alien.

"What the hell is that? Someone messing with us?"

Jack says, "Mountain lions. They come down at night, prowl the campus. They have to fatten up for winter."

"That's kinda messed up. Why don't the soldiers shoot them?"

"They do, sometimes. But if it's not the lions, it's the wolves, Shreve." I can't see him shrug, but I still know him well enough to sense it when he does. "They're just doing what's in their nature, and I think Quincrux likes the idea of them prowling around. For most of the jocks, it wouldn't be a problem. The bugfucks, well, it might be dicey."

"I'm sure a mauled kid would give Quincrux a hard-on."

"Probably two." He grins. "There's a couple dudes here with diphallia. It ain't pretty."

"You've seen it? I mean them?"

"Community showers, man. Roberto says that back in the thirties, when this place was built, men didn't care if they saw each other naked. Each floor has a communal shower."

Silence.

"The world is full of wolves and lions, man. But so far, none in the showers."

That's good news.

The ether thrums, angry. It's like I'm becoming attuned to the fluctuations of the Helmholtz field without even being conscious of it. The field increases, and then suddenly it's gone so quickly it's like someone has flipped a switch. Maybe they have.

"Did you feel that?"

"What?"

"The dampening field?"

"A little. I usually only know it's on when I try to do something and I can't. That was scary, the first time. I thought it had gone away."

"I can imagine." He's not sensitive to it, but he's a telekinetic. That's something to know.

There's a rustling of clothing from above and a whoosh of furious wind and for an instant I think of raven's wings, some great bird descending upon us.

Suddenly, the girl is there, crouching on the roof with us. She stands, smiles at Jack.

"Hey, you," she says, and takes his hand. She wears a denim jacket, open wide to show her Black Flag T-shirt. They hug and then, despite me standing there, kiss. It's not quite an adult kiss. It's kittenish. It's lovey-dovey. Sweet.

She digs in her jacket and withdraws a pack of Marlboros. She has no trouble popping a square out of the pack, putting it to her blushing lips and snapping a Zippo underneath it, once, twice, like lightning flashes, until it's smoldering and filling the air with the cheap stinking smell of mass-produced, chemical-infused tobacco. What every growing girl needs.

"Ah. Now I see. You're the good influence."

"Shreve . . ." Jack says, holding up a hand.

"I don't promote, and I don't offer. He's a big boy," she says and then grins, winking at Jack.

"Shreve, don't be a prick."

I glance back at her. "He's just a kid. You're what, eighteen? I don't even know if you two are legal."

She puffs her cigarette, wreathing her head in blue smoke. "So what are you, his guardian angel?"

Both of them stare at me, locked together arm in arm. Look at me with a shared knowledge, a shared bond. One that I'm not a part of.

"I guess not." It's harder than I thought, letting go. "Sorry."

"It's okay, man," Jack says.

I extend my hand to Ember. "I'm Shreve," I say. "We met only briefly. Before."

She snorts, and Jack laughs. "Yeah, you were a jackrabbit." She giggles and moves her arms in a mincing, small gesture, like a rodent on a wheel. "*Running, running.*"

"I stopped running, eventually."

Her smile dies on her face, curdling. "Yeah, you did. Jack called him 'the Witch.'"

"He wasn't always a man. But she was always evil."

I don't know her very well, so the expression on her face is unreadable to me, but if I was going to take a wild swing at what she was feeling, I'd say horror. Disgust.

"How did you do it?" Ember asks. She really is pretty. I can see it now even in the low light.

I open my mouth, pause, and then clack my teeth together, a parody of hunger. Yeah, a pure bit of bravado, but I don't like her taunting me. "I've got a question that you might be able to answer."

She looks at me warily. I hold up my hands, placating. "Just a question."

"Okay," she says slowly. "Shoot."

"I thought you could be a jock, or you could be a—" I pause here, thinking about how distasteful the word I'm about to say is. "A bugfuck. But you can fly *and* you tried to get inside my head. How does that work?"

Ember touches her nose with the back of her hand, gingerly, as if remembering. "Yeah, my nose bled for hours after that."

I nod and it's hard, but I keep my face muscles from delivering the smile that really, really wants to come out. "You seem to be both jock *and* bugfuck. That happen often?"

"Some," she says, looking relieved. Like she thought I was going to ask if they'd done it yet. I can tell just by looking at them, they haven't. "They say it happens in girls occasionally. When I asked, they said it has never occurred in a boy."

"Never? Who's they?"

"Employees. Mr. Michaels, our continuing ed teacher. Other post-humans. Members of the Society."

"You ask them all?"

"I've been here a while."

"That's interesting."

"If you say so."

Jack looks uncomfortable. "You want to get some dinner at the canteen?" he asks.

For a moment I sit there, thinking of all the times I've been in cafeterias and community food dispensaries. I think about Ox and Fishkill and Mr. Fingernails and Rollie and all the hard looks and stares and the hungry boys looking to ease their boredom of life by causing pain in the crucible of the incarcerated.

Jack stands waiting, shoulder to shoulder with Ember, leaning into each other.

"I'm not hungry."

"You sure?"

I raise the hem of my shirt, showing my stomach. "Ever since the Dubrovnik woman stuck me, I just don't have much of an appetite."

Pain crosses his face. I don't know if it's the memory of what happened in that house or it's the sight of my scars that causes it.

"Well, I'm in," Jack says, disengaging his gigantic frame from the girl. I'm sure he has to eat quite often. Looking at his elongated bones makes my legs hurt. I can't imagine the night pains he's endured with his body distorting itself like that. "You able to get down on your own, Shreve?"

The girl gives a toothy grin. Look at the feeble bugfuck. He can't fly.

"Yeah, sure. Might hang out up here for a bit."

"Okay," he says. "I'll bring you something back."

I nod. "Thanks. You know, I thought I was gonna bust you out of here. But now I'm here, I think this is where I'm supposed to be. I just wish it had been my choice."

"I'm glad you're here, man," he says, and then they both crouch and launch themselves into the air in a flutter of clothes and rippling wind. It's hard keeping track of them. I have an instant of worry that the Helmholtz will kick on and they'll go plummeting to the earth. But it's not really my place to worry about Jack anymore.

I sit down and lean back in the folding chair and look at the sky again. When I close my eyes, I feel a panic, as though they've stuffed me back underground. A panic because I'm on a roof in a strange place. In the dark.

And there's still the thing sleeping in the East.

I might not have to worry about Jack. But there's Vig. And Jerry and Booth. And everyone else. The world is full of them.

I cast out my awareness, out over the space/not space, searching for those minds that haven't been awakened enough to stop the sleepless emanations coming from Maryland. The only thing I can do here is to shore up the unsuspecting folk who'll be subsumed by the sea of sleeplessness. It's not as bad, this far west. But I burn through the populace as quickly as I can, a forest fire of the mind.

...

I do it for as long as I can until I start feeling the cohesive fatigue that comes from touching the minds of so many souls. Moving through them like wind over a billion heads of wheat swaying in the fields, I flicker, each one taking something out of me. My strength dims. I become diffuse smoke and as massive as the sky. I work through Bozeman, Butte, Great Falls. Thousands and thousands of people I visit. I'm like an invisible Santa Claus you never knew gave you a gift, slipping inside the chimneys of the mind.

I have no sense of time, out in the ether—it could be moments and it could be hours. But finally, I pull back the loosely tethered awareness from the black plains and open my eyes.

Always, in the East, I feel the slumbering beast. It stirs and shifts, massive and invisible. There might be other eyes upon it in these etheric heights, but I cannot sense them, or they me.

It stirs.

THIRTY-TWO

It's cold now as I climb down. If I fall, I'll hit the earth with a soft explosion of dust and ash, to be blown to the four corners by frigid wind. Getting back into the dorm room is more difficult than leaving it, and there's one instant of terror when I lose my balance, teeter.

Hollis is in the room when I come through the window. Tap, our other roommate, is absent.

"Hey."

"'Sup," Hollis says. Still trying to be tough.

I move to my bunk—the one above Jack's, just like back at Casimir—and climb up. Cradle my head.

"So, how'd they get you?" I ask, glancing at his still-bruised face.

"On the way to the gym."

"They got a gym here?"

"Sure. It's Montana. It gets cold in the winter, I hear."

"Where you from?"

"San Bernardino."

"That in California?"

"Yeah."

"How old are you?"

"Fifteen. You?"

"Seventeen. Almost." I think a bit. "Who did that to you?"

"I don't know who they were. Couple of guys and a girl."

"You don't know why?"

"Jack says they do it to all the noobs. Keep them in line. See what kind of power they got. Might be because of Tap. He doesn't like me much. He's a competent flyer, but they paired him with me. I'm having trouble with training. Like Jack."

"So both you and Jack are having trouble? Like, how?"

"Tap doesn't listen to me when I try to help him. He can't lift me or doesn't want to. Jack doesn't even try."

"They had you paired with both of them?"

"Yeah. For just a little while. Neither of them wants to be handcuffed to a bugfuck."

"That's right. You said you could influence time."

"Sorta. The perception of it."

"Do it to me."

"What? Right now?"

"Sure."

"It's better when it's outside."

"Why?"

"Easier to notice the change."

"Show me."

He gets out of bed, takes off his watch, and hands it to me. "What time is it?"

I look at the watch. "Little after six."

He smiles and pauses. "You sure about that?"

"Yeah. See?" I hold up the watch, notice the face now reads after eight.

His hair's wet now, and he's changed into warm-ups. Like

he's ready for bed in a blink of an eye. But *oof*, my body aches. I've been still too long.

"That's a neat trick."

"Thanks. Probably can't do it again to you. It's especially hard to affect other telepaths."

That makes me think about time. "How long have you been here?"

"Two weeks."

"So, when we met in the testing, you were fresh off the boat."

"Pretty much."

"That was two weeks ago?"

"Almost. You said in the testing that they had you in a bunker. What was that like?"

"Dark. And now it seems like it was longer than I thought."

"You lost track of time." He laughs. Hollis does a good job covering up his fear and nervousness. Where Jack used to go all still, Hollis gets loose. Familiar. But he's scared. Doesn't take a mind reader to see that. Suddenly, the laughter dies. "They want us scared," he whispers.

"Yes."

"They're doing something to keep us from sleeping."

"You can't sleep?"

"I can sleep, but it's not restful, if that makes any sense."

"They're not doing that."

"Then who is?"

"Something else." I wave my invisible antennae in the air. No Helmholtz. I slip out and settle on Hollis like a vapor. No Rider, and his consciousness is as tremulous and wavering as a flower blooming in the snow.

I slip behind his eyes and light the match head of his consciousness. He blinks.

You should be able to sleep now, **I say inside his mind.**

How did you do that?

I waggle my fingers at him. *Magic.*

He smiles, but it only lasts a moment. Emotions stall out on his face. He frowns, puzzling things out. Then, kind of sheepishly, he smiles, a bewildered yet elated look.

Holy crap! I'm talking to you with my mind? Does this happen all the time?

I laugh. No, you're the first. But you shouldn't have any trouble sleeping now.

So, everything that's happened recently?

What's happened? They've had me incommunicado.

"War. Terrorism. Mass murders. You name it." Hollis looks surprised at the sound of his own voice.

What's causing this?

It's something sleeping in the East. An entity. Alien.

"Get out of here. Like from outer space? Area 51?"

"More like the darkness between stars. Bodiless." How do I tell him it's the mythical dragon? That it doesn't require form to exist?

He stands and winces a little. His wounds are still sore.

"They must've really worked you over."

"I think I broke a rib."

Wordlessly, we've agreed to stick with our normal voices, incarcerado within convention.

"You want to go get something to eat?"

"Not hungry."

"Okay." He sits down and then stretches out on his bunk. "I'll just hang here with you."

Hands cradled behind my head, staring up at the ceiling, I drift off for a moment. I don't want to close my eyes, but it's been a big day.

He's reading a paperback when I come out of my doze. The ether is still open, quiescent, and I when I ask Hollis where the restroom is, he tells me, stifling a yawn.

I trudge down the empty hall, stretching, and enter the communal bathroom.

I never even sense them until they spill out of the stalls.

My body compresses as if clutched in a great fist, bones creaking and stressing, my air gone. A wolfish dark boy darts forward and cracks me in the eye, rocking my head back and sending bright stars and imaginary tweety birds whistling in circles around my head.

When I regain my senses—still can't breathe—I see the other wee brutes stepping forward from stalls. It's my old friend Solomon Blackwell—the guy I bum-rushed in New York as he sat behind the wheel of a van—and he's got his hand up and out in a grasping pose, as if clutching a torch. Our gazes meet and he twists his hand and I feel my body twist in response.

Neat trick.

A battered metal trash can whips across the bathroom with a motion from a dark-complexioned boy. It makes a dull hollow *bong* as it caroms off my skull.

Blackwell is kind enough to let me fall with the blow. I do so with all the grace of a drunken, poleaxed steer.

When I can get my mouth working, I say, "You must be the ladies of the Welcome Wagon. Not really in the market for any Tupperware." My face hurts pretty good. The warm red sticky stuff courses down from my forehead and makes my left eye, the outraged blooming one, hard to open.

These idiots stare at me like I'm speaking Mandarin. Hell, maybe I am. Blackwell chucks his head like a horse tossing against the reins, and I fly up and smack the ceiling with an *ooof*. Come flapping back to the ground, an overcooked steak dropped from a skillet to splat on the floor.

"Payback's a bitch, ain't it?" he says, like he's the star of some crap B movie.

It sounds like a rhetorical question so I don't bother answering. My mouth is full of blood anyway.

I can't see very well, or at all really, so the shuffling and slapping sound I hear must be these assholes standing over me and performing ritual hand gestures. High fives all around.

One of them kicks me so hard in my crotch I can taste my own dick.

"And that's for Glouster. You *do not* mess with Red Team." Glouster must be the poor sap whose testicles I punted in the elevator while fleeing Jerry's. Hard to believe Glouster would hold such a grudge, that was so long ago. I've been to the underworld and back since then.

I try to get out into the ether to stop them, take one of them over and flail into the others, turning their bodies traitorous. But everything spins, pitching and yawing. Blood fills my eyehole, pools in my ear. Drips across the bridge of my nose and onto the tile floor of the bathroom.

The last thing I hear before everything goes dark is "Look! He's pissed himself!" Followed by cheery laughter.

Hell, yeah, I pissed myself. That's what I came to the bathroom to do, anyway.

THIRTY-THREE

I wash out my clothes in the sink, scrub the blood off my face, and hobble back to the room, prickled with goose bumps and buck naked. Hollis snores lightly. Tap has returned from eating and lies on his bed, headphones blaring music directly into his head. He glances at me, snorts, and then pulls a comic from under his pillow and begins reading.

Jack is nowhere to be seen.

I climb into bed, painfully, my testicles screaming outrage.

···

When I wake, the room's flooded with light. Jack stands above me with a surprised look on his face.

"Holy crap, man, you look like ground beef. They messed you up for real."

"You should see the other guys."

I begin pushing myself up from the bed. What sleep I did get was full of throbbing. Painful throbbing, which is not my favorite kind.

"Assembly in ten minutes, bro. Up and at 'em."

"Assembly?"

"Yeah. This ain't summer camp." He walks over to where Hollis snores and kicks the leg of the bed. "Yo, man. Assembly."

Hollis raises a tousled head from the pillow, glances at the window. "It's not even daylight yet."

"That's right. Assembly comes early."

Tap rolls out of bed and tugs up his trousers and pulls on some combat boots, an old campaigner.

"Did you even sleep here last night?" I ask Jack.

He shrugs. "Some."

"Thought there was no fraternization in dorms?"

"Ember's Red Team. And her room has roof access."

"Nice. Never realized how handy your powers were, did ya, till you got a girlfriend?"

He ignores this and digs a clean, white T-shirt out of his trunk and tosses it to me. "You might want to clean yourself up. They love weakness."

"Who?"

"The other kids. Ruark. The bulls." He shakes his head. "Hell, everybody."

"Who's weak?"

"It doesn't matter if you can lift a car, Shreve, you *look* totally spent." He pokes me in my ribs. "Damn, bro, you look like a little old man."

Standing, I hobble over to the chair and begin painfully shrugging on clothes.

I look down at my chest, my ribs, the purple-black fields of bruising. The scar in my gut given to me by the psychotic Dubrovnik woman. The gunshot wound on my shoulder. I look like a prisoner of war. And maybe that's what I am, a soldier in an invisible war.

I turn seventeen in a couple of months.

I almost scream pulling my jeans up and over ye olde testicles. They're a little testy.

We trudge down the stairs into the still-dark morning air. It's not freezing, but the breeze is brisk, and once the cold settles in, I'd maim someone for an overshirt. I have trouble keeping up with the other boys. The nuts are a problem, and my side is seriously tender. Blackwell and his cronies might have cracked a rib. Might be a little score to settle there.

Gravel crunching under our feet, Jack and Tap lead us down a path and through a lovely little copse of aspens standing like sentinels as a group. Other inductees and extranaturals migrate down the path, some chatting, some carrying flashlights, beams swinging wildly. On the paths, employees, men and women— some in lab coats, some in overalls, some in jackets and ties and business casual—breathe into steaming coffee mugs and make their way toward their duly appointed tasks, whatever those are. Auditing expenses, brewing up mutant superpowers, tightening up bolts on the rocket launchers.

You know, everyday, normal stuff.

Once we're through the copse of trees, the land opens up to a large, grassy field ringed in small outbuildings—maintenance and storage, I figure. Halfway up the steep slope of the far side of the narrow valley is a great behemoth of a building. It's got a massive front porch with benches, three stories of plate glass framed out like for some rich guy's hunting lodge. A paved road passes the field and runs up to its front door.

"That's Admin," Jack says, a little ominously. "Where Quincrux has his office."

"Ah. How much do you see of him?"

"Not much at all. It's not the director you have to watch out for, it's Ruark. She's a real bitch."

I've discovered that on my own.

A hopped-up golf cart with knobby tires buzzes down the road from the Admin building and slews to a stop on the assembly field in front of us. In a gaggle of young folks—most of them wearing red, I see—stands Blackwell. He grins at me and nudges Ember. As a group, they turn to look at me. I'm glad I can't hear what they're saying.

"I don't think your girlfriend likes me too much, Jack."

"Nah, man. She likes you just fine."

"You don't seem too broken up at my injuries."

Jack narrows his eyes as he looks at me. "Listen, it's different here. The teams are real . . . I don't know. They're like gangs, right? They show their colors at all times and watch each other's backs."

"Sure. I get it. There's no I in team."

"And there's no *you*. So don't get your panties in a bunch. They *had* to do that to you, Shreve."

"What do you mean?"

"You wiped the Witch. You cleaned the clocks of two team members. It was a point of honor. You're lucky they didn't kill you."

"They wouldn't have."

"Kids go missing around here. When I first got here, a strong mechanic—"

"Mechanic?"

"A tinkerer. One of us with a weird blend of telekinetic and telepathic power that can manipulate objects. Anyway, she disappeared, but all Ruark would tell us was that she washed out. Like that means anything."

"And you think she got sideways with one of the teams?"

"Maybe. I think it's possible. You're not anything if you're not on a team. You're about to find out."

Wait a second.

"Did you know they were gonna do that to me last night?"

Jack looks surprised. "No, not really."

"You know I can just bust down your door and see if you're lying, don't you?"

His expression sours. I can't tell if it's because he feels guilty or because of my threat. I'm mad enough; I don't really care.

He's saved by Ruark unlimbering herself from the cart and stomping toward where we wait. Negata is with her, moving like a dancer. He keeps his eyes on me as he walks forward, and when she stops, he stops. It's a moment pregnant with inaction, the time between graceful and possibly violent ministrations.

Today Ruark's dressed business casual—slacks, men's shirt, and tie. Hiking boots are her only concession to the environment. Once in an optimal position, she bellows, "Listen up, exnats! We've got a new fish in our midst!" She points to where I stand with Jack, Hollis, and Tap. Giving my face a once-over, she smiles a bland smile. "I can see some of you have already given him a *warm* welcome," she says to general chuckles and guffaws. Ruark glances toward the waiting golf cart and motions with one hand.

Roberto scurries forward. It seems everyone defers to Ruark.

"Absent?" Ruark asks.

Roberto places his index fingers at his temple, and his usually genial face takes on a constipated expression. "Matthis, Klein, Arundhai, Johnson are absent."

Ruark inclines her head at the soldiers, and two peel off from the others.

"Daily assignments follow—" Ruark removes a slip of paper from her blazer and reads, "Red Team maneuvers, lower airfield, morning. Afternoon, communications. Green Team, morning: maneuvers, upper airfield, tactical range. Afternoon, CE." A groan passes through the crowd.

"What's CE stand for?" I say.

"Continuing education," Jack says out of the side of his mouth. "It freakin' sucks, man."

"Orange Team, morning: communications training. Afternoon, upper airfield, tactical maneuvers."

There's a pause, and I look at the crowd. They're waiting for something. Blackwell and Ember and the rest of their crew watch Ruark with avid stares.

Ruark sniffs, places her hands on her hips, and says, "Orange Team, dismissed."

There's a great displacement of air as a passel of orange-clad young men and women launch into the air whooping, calling insults down below. "See ya, punks!" one girl screeches. A young man howls like a wolf as he swings high into the lightening mountain air, but the call diminishes and grows faint as they streak off back toward the dorms and other buildings.

Heads turn back toward Ruark, like dogs waiting for treats.

"Green Team, dismissed."

Another eruption of flyers, hooting.

"Watch out. Some of them spit," Hollis says, wiping at his eye.

"Red Team, dismissed."

Blackwell, Ember, and the rest of Red Team launch themselves into the sky, not as assured as the others but leaving no one behind. They make a circle over the field, dark shapes silhouetted by the sky. Ember blows Jack a kiss as she passes. He watches them far after they've disappeared from view.

Ruark turns her face away from the sky and looks sourly at those of us remaining on the ground. There are three girls and ten boys left. I know my roommates and no one else.

"And now we're left with you, the dregs of our little Society. You sad excuses for extranaturals." She rattles off a string of names, assigning half to groundskeeping and the other half to laundry. When she dismisses them, a couple fly off clumsily, and the others trot back toward the dorms.

Ruark waits until the field is clear and it's just us standing there, Negata and Roberto watching on, faces neutral.

"Cannon, Graves, Hollis, Tappan. You're assigned sanitation. The perfect job for such a motley crew and a wonderful way for you to get to know the pecking order of our little Society."

Tappan blows air through his nose, loudly, like a horse expressing its displeasure.

"Something the matter, Mr. Tappan?" Ruark says.

"It's Thursday."

"Thank you for stating the obvious, Mr. Tappan."

"Thursdays are bathrooms."

Ruark grins again. She's really getting into this evil sergeant role. "Oh, that's right. Start with Administration and work through the rest of the buildings. If you finish before sundown, you may use the lower airfield. Lakeside, of course, since none of you can fly tandem yet."

Tap's shoulders set in an angry pose, and Hollis looks defeated.

Jack glances at me and says, "I'll save you some."

"What?"

"Breakfast."

"What—"

"You are dismissed."

Jack and Tap both crouch, hands out, and then leap up into the sky, tracing irregular arcs in the now light morning.

Ruark turns toward the golf cart, Negata and Roberto in tow.

"Come on, Shreve," Hollis says. "We better get going if we want anything more than toast."

...

At some point during the march back up the mountainside to campus buildings, I say, "Hollis, go on without me. My nuts are killing me."

Taking small steps help. It's hard to get a full breath.

"It's not that far, man." He steps closer to me and grabs my forearm, as though to escort me.

I shake my arm away. "Get off me, dude. I'll be fine."

"Your face is white. You should go see the nurse."

"They've got a nurse here?"

"Yeah, Roberto."

I laugh, and it only hurts a little bit. "Nah, I'll be fine. I've had worse."

Technically that's true. A gunshot and stab wound. At least in *my* memories. I don't know if I'm gonna be able to have kids anymore.

By the time we reach the canteen, it's already half-empty, with the exception of the Red Team laughing and munching what look like breakfast sandwiches and slurping up pitchers of orange and tomato juice.

They turn to look at us as we enter.

"How they hangin', newb?"

"It's the pissboy! Hey, pissboy, don't fill your shoes."

I stop. Look around the canteen. There's a bank of buffet trays filled with what looks like powdered eggs, biscuits, and thick white gravy. My stomach gives a little growl of protest at what I'm about to do.

Jack sits with Tap at the table nearest to the Red Team, so he can chat with Ember. When he sees me, an alarmed expression passes over his features.

He knows me too well.

I've done this many times before. There's only one way to play it when you're incarcerado and everyone is against you. You walk up to the biggest, meanest bastard in the general pop and you fight.

I mosey over to the Red Team table, ignoring the frantic gestures from Jack.

Seeing me approach, Blackwell stands with a couple of other brutes. I notice an old friend I hadn't seen since the testing—young miss Cynthia Galine, stonechucker, poltergeist. I meet her gaze.

"Guys, uh, I wouldn't do anything right now—" Galine says, a slight waver to her voice. "He's really—" She stops, as if at a loss for words. But she's not.

I stopped her.

I raise my hands, palms faceup as if testing for rain.

"Hey, you feel that?" I ask, as casually as possible.

"Feel what?" Blackwell says.

"No Helmholtz," I say. No sooner than the sound is out of my mouth, I'm into the ether, inside Galine, and I have her shibboleth in control. It's a shuddering, electric merging, our two gifts combining to one.

I am you and you are me.

The tricky part is doing two things as once. MeShreve drops to his knees and bows his head. MeGaline, in a fraction of a second, scoops up all the eggs, gravy, biscuits, grits, grime, and grease and collects it all into a hovering gelatinous glob that MeGaline launches with violent force at the Red Team.

When the floating wall of grease and fat hit them it's moving at nearly five hundred miles an hour with the force of a point-blank shotgun blast.

One of them, a slight boy with glasses, is knocked off his feet. The others remain standing. Spattered but standing.

Blackwell splutters and tries to wipe the grime from his eyes. Galine blisters the air with curses. Ember laughs, a bright pealing sound.

"Hey, man! Friendly fire!" Jack yells, outraged, trying to get the slime off his shirt. A globule of white peppered gravy hangs from his nose. "Uncool."

He scoops up a handful of white stuff from his plate and chucks it at me.

Blackwell steps from around the table, coated with gunk and grease. He really is a hoss. Nostrils flared, he approaches me, his fists in hard knots.

Here's the deal in any incarcerado alpha dog situation: You have to be willing to fight, even if you're going to lose. If they think you're meat, you're meat. And earlier, Jack said I looked weak.

I am not weak.

"You just don't get the picture, do you, pissboy?" Blackwell says, coming close enough for me to smell the oil on him. "You do *not* fuck with Red Team. We will bury you."

There's a time for words and a time for action. I give him a little of both.

Over at the other table, Galine stiffens again as I slip behind the wheel, tears beading at the corners of her eyes and mouth caught in a smile.

"You can try," I say, my voice pitched low. Speaking when I'm in the ether—it's a delicate act while holding Galine immobile. She's my gun. "But you'll regret it. I can wear you like a suit." I move in closer, lowering my voice. "I have before. Remember?" That's technically not true, but I hope he remembers it that way. "You don't remember?" I lower my eyes so that when I step into his personal space, his brute lizard brain doesn't think it's threatening or amorous. My voice is a whisper. I'm way too close to him, kissing distance. "You got me in the bathroom. Head-to-head, I can blow out your mind like a candle, but I'll humiliate you first. Remember the Witch?"

"The Witch?"

"Norman. Er, Ilsa."

He remains silent, but his eyes shift in their sockets. He's remembering. As he does, I reach out with the invisible hand— thanks to Galine—and give his body a squeeze, like it was a tube of toothpaste.

I should be pleased at the expression on his face, but it just makes me feel horrible. His expression is one of pure terror, where your instincts kick in and all pretense of toughness or intellect is gone, and it's just unadulterated fight-or-flight reaction at the sudden awareness of a large predator. He'd run away or swing at me if I wasn't holding him in my invisible fist. And maybe I have Casey—that beautiful one-armed extranatural—to thank for that idea.

And then the moment is gone; I've released him. Ember and Jack stare at me. Galine and other Red Team members watch on, expecting a fight, either extranatural or just plain old flying fists.

"I'm giving you a gift," I whisper, so only he can hear. "You can walk away with your dignity intact. You understand?"

He blinks. He opens his mouth, shuts it.

"Consider it a truce. I won't mess with you, you don't mess with me or my friends. Not Hollis, not Jack. Not Tap or anyone else. Otherwise . . ."

This time I knock at the door of his mind. Hard.

He steps back. It's got the barest whiff of a stagger. He nods. A small inclination of his head. And that's not enough for me. I put out my hand, to shake.

He looks at it, realizes what it means. Shaking is capitulation. I've forced him into a truce. Isn't that how all wars end? Or is it how they start?

His face curls into a small whimper of disgust, at me, at the situation, at himself, I can't tell. It's not enough that I've threatened him, that I've scared him. The thing that smarts is that I'm letting him go without the spanking he deserves. He knows it, I know it.

The world makes monsters of us all. All it takes is a handshake.

He turns to go back to his cadre, the Red Team, and I can feel their gazes on me, and I don't care one damned bit what they think. This is war. They can whisper, they can fear me, I don't care.

I don't care.

...

After breakfast, we start the long swirl down the toilet. Each building has a closet marked SANITATION, full of spray bottles and scrub brushes and towels and rags. I'm familiar with the routine, thanks to my stint at Casimir.

The boys' dorm is the repository for all the pubescent pubic hair in America, scattered about in artful piles in the corners of stalls and the tiled corners of urinals. It takes some sort of caustic lye to remove the skid marks on the toilet's gutters.

In Admin, thank God, it's merely a mop and a wipe down. The adults—Quincrux, Ruark, Holden, Tanzer, et al.—they manage to get their piss and pubes in the acceptable receptacles. It might be the Society of Extranaturals, but their detritus is remarkably natural.

We walk through the Admin lobby, my nuts merely howling with pain instead of screaming, under the watchful eyes of the admissions secretary—even without peeking her, I suspect she's a bugfuck—and a metal bust of a man shoved in the corner, half-obscured by a large, bushy plant.

He's a proud-looking man, young and angular, cast in bronze and staring wistfully out the big plate windows at the mountains. He's got a slightly crooked nose, sensual expressive lips, pork chop sideburns, and thick, wavy hair done in a style from yesteryear. There's something antique about the statue's hollow gaze, but I can't tell what it is making it seem out of place in this office. Something about the stare feels familiar to me. As if I've met this man, and we've spoken and not all of it was pleasant. While the statue is bronze, burnished, there's black grime in the creases and craggy lines of its form— almost like the thing has been plucked from a fire.

The placard beneath the bust reads *Dr. Armstead Lucius Priest, Founder of the Society for Extranaturals.*

I feel like I should know that name. It has the ring of familiarity, yet I can't place it. I look at the statue again, and Armstead and I lock gazes once more. Huh. I hightail it out of there.

THIRTY-FOUR

Morning comes early, and Jack's kicking my bed again. Tap groans, and Hollis silently tugs on clothes.

On the field, Ruark ignores everything but assignments—Green to the upper airfield, Red Team to CE (groans), and the Orange Team to assemble on the lower airfield for transport, 0700 hours. Jack turns to look at me with raised eyebrows.

"What's that mean?" I whisper.

"They've got a mission."

The teams launch themselves into the air, but today with a lack of whoops or catcalls. I don't even think I feel too much spit raining down.

"What's the mission?" I ask Jack.

"How should I know?"

Clearly preoccupied, Ruark yells, "Morning: Tap, Cannon, Graves—sanitation." She clears her throat and shifts in her faux uniform. "Afternoon: Perdie, Holden, Cannon, Princent, Klein, Tappan, Graves . . . " She rattles off six or seven more names. "Lower airfield."

"What about me?" Hollis asks.

"You're to report to Admin for further testing." Ruark turns on her heel and saunters back to the golf cart.

There's a collective gasp from the remaining students, and Hollis begins to shiver.

"What's the deal?" I say out of the side of my mouth to Jack and Tap. Hollis looks terrified.

Jack shakes his head slowly. "Most kids who wash out . . . it starts with them going through testing again."

...

Our merry trio is assigned to sanitation for the morning. It's a messy job, gathering all the trash from the dorms and Admin and hauling it to a massive Dumpster. Messy, but relatively easy. The absence of Hollis seems to me like a missing tooth. I keep probing at it and noting its loss.

"You think he's gonna be okay?"

Jack shrugs. "No idea. You learn real quick around here not to think you have it all figured out."

"I got that. But he's a *good* kid." I chew my lip. "I just want to know what it means, washing out."

After lunch, we hightail it up to the lower airfield, which is ours for the afternoon with the exception of two guards near the Quonset hut housing the Society's jet. They pay us very little attention as Jack and Tap enter the hut to wheel out three massive reflective-silver balloons.

"So what's all this?"

"Obstacle course."

Each balloon is tethered to a large cement block by thick nylon rope. Each block is on a rubber-wheeled cart. I move to help Tap and Jack. The carts are heavy and slow to roll.

Once out of the hut and on the field, I spy a small gang of girls approaching. They're all in their mid to late teens, I think, standing with a group of boys also in their teens. More non-team members, it seems.

After flashing his pearly whites and gesticulating at one of the prettier girls in the gaggle, Tap pushes one of the weather balloons downrange and lets it rise. The balloon shoots two hundred feet into the air. Jack does the same with his as I struggle to get mine into position and released. Afterward, we walk over to the folks who've just arrived.

Introductions are made, we all shake, and a girl named Danielle says, "Someone called you the Little Devil in the girl's dorm. Is that your handle?" She's what they'd call ethnically ambiguous and absolutely stunning. Dark, mocha skin, long jet-black hair that makes me think she might be part Asian, possibly, but full lips and an athletic build.

"Yeah, I've heard they call me that."

"Why do they?" Danielle's voice is even. It's not prying or aggressive, just curious.

"I can get in people's heads."

"That's what I do," a boy says. "I can infect you with a rhythm."

"I can infect you with *me*. Possess you—like the devil, I guess."

The boy whistles and extends his hand to shake. "They call me Kicks, but my name's Bernard Perdie. Back home they called me 'Purdy.' They don't call me that here." His face falls a little, like he's sad that part of him was left behind. "I'm paired up with that super-duper over there. Ignatius. Iggy for short."

"Super-duper?"

"Nobody broke it down for you?"

I glance at Jack, who's coming back from positioning the weather balloon. "No, I guess not."

"Far as jocks go, you got your jumpers, your floaters, and

your super-dupers—they're regular old flyers who usually can't even tie their own shoes when on the ground but are pure magic once they get in the air." Perdie smiles, and I realize I like this guy, right off the bat. Some folks you just take to, I guess. He begins ticking off all the different flavors of extranatural on his fingers. "There's your detonators—your boy Jack is one—your poltergeists, your firestarters, your chilly-willies. Though I've never seen one of them in action. You got your choke-a-bitches, your bleeders, lockpickers, spoonbenders, and your crush-ya-heads."

"And your devils."

"That's what it looks like, man-child."

Jack trots up, slightly winded from the run. "It cool if we get started, Kicks?"

"Might as well. You two up to tandem?"

Jack scowls and ignores the question. He launches himself into the air, and Tap quickly follows suit, trailed by three girls. The landbound extranaturals gather below, like parents at a soccer match.

"With us bugfucks, it's different, you know?" Bernard says. "For every human emotion, there's some kid who can jigger it. You got your mentalists, your psychic cowboys, the brainiacs and mesmerists—"

I watch Jack wheel and streak across the vault of sky. He's better than he was when we were on the lam, it's true. It's hard to even tell that he's making the little invisible explosions that keep him afloat.

He's gotten better. But not *much* better.

Jack lances through the sky like an arrow, wheels around the first weather balloon, lightly touching it with his right hand as he banks around it, extending his other hand out to focus his energies on the microbursts directing his turns. The harder the turn, the more bursts, and Jack seems to shudder in a zigzagging pattern that's hard for him to recover from. He manages, barely, and drops in altitude very, very slowly toward the next balloon. After executing that turn smoothly, he arcs upward in a larger blast, losing some balance, and flips head over foot three times before he can steady himself in the air, all the while rocketing past the remaining obstacle balloon. He takes the return, reverse course with the limping caution of somebody just wanting to get through the rest of his miserable day. I can see it in the cant of his shoulders.

But Bernard's still speaking. "You've got your snoops. You've got your warm fuzzies and touchy-feelies. And then you've got the merchants of gloom, the emo motherfuckers that can swing your mood one way or another." He puts his hands on his hips. "And then there's me, Mister Shreve. Bernard Perdie, number one hitmaker, and the only rhythmatist in this whole round world."

"Uh, can't any DJ or drummer infect someone with a rhythm?"

"You're new here, so I'm not gonna take offense at your dumb ass, but in a word . . . *hell naw*."

"That's two words," I say.

Bernard laughs. "Taking it from all sides from the peanut gallery. But all I got to say to your boneheaded stuff is, go ask somebody 'bout those red shoes. I can make you dance till your heart gives out."

"I'll take your word for it."

"You do that."

Tap takes the obstacle course like an airborne rhino, bullying through the turns with bursts of linear speed. What he lacks in style, he makes up for in fierce, masculine force.

One of the girls—Danielle—whips through the course like a flying snake, fluid, electric, aggressive, her body twisting and turning with each change in direction, her long hair whipping behind her like an ink stroke. When she lands next to another girl—like some gazelle ending a leap on the soft turf of the veld—she walks over to a nearby girl, hair flying around her in a wild, beautiful mess, and they immediately put their heads together and begin to exchange notes on her flight. Looking at Danielle's companion, I realize it's Casey, the one-armed girl from the testing. I wave and smile at her, and she waves back. With her visible arm. She smiles.

"So, we're like flying coaches, even though we can't fly?" I ask as Jack lands and walks over to where we stand, his arms crossed and head down. Brooding.

"That's right. Because, at some point, our asses will be up there with them. They pair us up so that, once we're on a team, we'll already know how to rely on somebody else."

Watching Jack wallow about in the sky makes me terrified of flying tandem. He's lifted me once, but we were in dire straits. Watching him now, I know there's no way in hell he'll be able to pick me up.

"You gettin' scared, aren't you?" Bernard grins wide.

I just nod.

"Just you wait till you get to the lake and they let you fall."

"Huh?"

"You'll see."

Jack looks at me, eyebrows raised. "So?"

"Yeah. Um. You're flying better than I've ever seen you."

"Screw you, Shreve," he says. "I hate it when you do that."

"Do what?"

"Say the opposite of what you mean."

"Well, yeah, okay, that sucked. Pretty hard. When you were making that turn—"

"You mean screwing the pooch."

"No, listen. You *are* flying better than I've ever seen you. But back then, you were the only kid I'd ever seen fly, right?"

He remains silent, but I can tell he's listening to me.

"I don't know much, but I do know that you can't fly me around up there with you if you're not rock solid. True?"

He nods. Grudging.

"It's when you've got to make the harder turns that it throws you off-kilter, right? That's because when you bank, you're pushing yourself one way with pulses," I clap my hands together, *clap clap clap clap clap*. "Like that. But the pulses need to be less strong, but faster, got me? Otherwise, you'll get off-balance."

His eyes widen, and he nods.

"Hey, Bernard, can you pick up Jack's rhythm?"

"Who're you talking to?" He turns to Jack. "Listen to me. Eyes right here." He jabs two fingers at Jack's eyes and then at his own. The universal gesture for "keep looking at me."

"Sure," Jacks says, grinning now. It seems Bernard has that effect on people.

Bernard starts making sounds with his mouth, rhythmic plosives, bass expulsions of air, hisses. It comes out fast. Beatboxing. Like a drummer doing a sixteenth beat on a hi-hat and snare.

Jack at first seems amused, but something in Bernard solidifies, some unquantifiable something, and Jack's smile disappears, his pupils dilate, and his breath quickens.

"There you go, man," Bernard says, snapping his fingers.

"You mind if he goes again?"

"Nah, Iggy's toast for the day. But Jack's not gonna be able to keep that up forever. He'll need to find his own rhythm."

"I got you. Thanks."

"No problem. We're all freaks here." He winks at me. "Some of us, *superfreaks*." He saunters off toward the Quonset hut.

"You ready?"

Jack, bopping his head with the internal rhythm, says, "Hell yeah."

This time, he launches, banks smoothly around the first balloon, seems like he's going to lose balance but doesn't and sticks the rest of the course like a champ. When he touches down, he's grinning. Bernard, Iggy, Danielle, and some of the others give a smattering of applause.

"I think we're done here for the day," I say.

Jack shakes his head. "I should go a couple more times. Muscle memory."

"Sure." I look around to see if there's anything else I can do. In the jet's shadow, near the guards, stands a darker shadow. Negata watches me, silent and motionless.

I give the airfield another, closer examination. At least four cameras are trained on us.

Negata makes a small and curious inclination of his head, his gaze never wavering. If I didn't know better, I'd think he was saying hello.

Jack leaps into the air again, rocketing through the course, faltering only with his descent.

When he lands, I say, "Hey, nice one. But you're stumbling on the third balloon."

"Can't you give me one second of feeling good about myself?"

"Not really. Don't be a titty-baby about it."

"Screw you, man." He's thrumming, bobbing his head a little. Patting his thigh. Bernard's magic holding sway.

"No, this is good. You nailed the banking, right?"

"Yeah."

"So that let me see what else you're screwing up."

"Ass."

"So, when you're descending, what are you doing?"

"Falling. I'm always falling."

"Yeah, but when you have to lose altitude, you do what?"

"Allow myself to fall."

"Right. You're just letting gravity take over. And it's not doing it fast enough. You've still got some forward momentum."

He nods.

"So to drop fast enough to make the lower balloon, you're going to have to give a pulse upward. Push yourself toward the ground."

He doesn't like the sound of that. I can tell from his expression.

"I know it goes against probably every instinct of self-preservation you have, but hell, man, if you listened to your self-preservation instincts, would you be flying to begin with?"

We laugh. "Okay, I'll try it. That doesn't mean you're not a jackass."

"That I am, broseph. That I am."

He nails it this time. Perfectly.

I don't tell him so, though. I complain some more, just to aggravate him.

"Better, man. You have the grace of a whale caught in a fishing net."

He punches me in the shoulder. It's quite a blow. He meant some of it.

Good. I can still get under his skin. All of Shreve hasn't been burned away in the dark.

■ ■ ■

We watch the others finish their maneuvers until the sun passes beyond the mountain rim and casts the valley into blue-gray shadow. Strange expressions pass over the features of our group, girls and boys alike, as they come out of the golden rays of sun to land, back on Earth once more, in the shadow of mountains. They look haggard, wan. Even jovial Bernard, in this half-light, looks sallow, with deep bags under his eyes. His smile has disappeared, and I have one of those moments of clarity in which everything comes into focus and everything around me seems to go still and be revealed for what it truly is—beautiful or horrific, base or sublime.

These kids are scared.

"Something wrong?" I ask Danielle.

"No," she says, her face a mask. "It's just . . ."

"Night, Mr. Shreve. Hope they turn on that buzzer for a long time."

"That buzzer?"

"Yeah. What keeps the insomnia out."

"The Helmholz."

"That's right. The buzzer."

"So you can't sleep without the Helmholtz?"

"Ain't you listening, man?"

Danielle puts her hand on Bernard's arm to quiet him and says, "It's bad now, Shreve. At first, it was just on the radio. We'd hear about it in passing. We'd see it on the television in recreation. The news. But it's here now. And we can't sleep without the Helmholtz."

I don't know of any way to say it but just to say it. "I can help you."

"What you talking about, man? You can't help none—"

But I'm out, beyond my body in the nonspace between souls. Between stars.

I perceive each one of them, each one of them like an ember, slumbering, unrealized. Waiting to burst into flame. The match heads of their minds.

I burn through them, every one, and where I pass, their minds burn bright.

"What the fu—" Bernard looks stunned. "What did you just do, boss?"

Danielle sinks to the ground, legs crossing under her. She puts her hand to her mouth. "Oh my god."

Casey tugs at her bottom lip with the trembling fingers of her only hand. Bernard just stares at me silently, listening to the drumbeat of his heart. The dusk settles around us like a cloud, and there are desperate and uneasy echoes of what I've done in the ether. Something has changed.

Something has changed in us all.

Danielle looks at me and without her mouth she says, What have you done?

Brother, you're one infectious bugfuck, Bernard says into my mind.

I can hear you! **Casey says.** But you're not speaking!

I turn to look at Jack, and he's standing poleaxed in the half-light of evening.

I don't want this, **he says.** I never wanted any of this.

Neither did I. But something is coming. And we might need it.

I never asked for it!

"We have to keep this secret," Tap mutters. "Nobody can know."

I want one of you to try to get in my head. Can you do that?

I'm scared. Have I given them this terrible gift, or are we just bound together by some invisible tether?

Someone scratches at the back door of my mind, but that's it. Nothing more.

Casey says, If you can do this, what else can you do, Shreve?

THIRTY-FIVE

The five of us—Jack, Tap, Danielle, Casey, and little ole me—huddle together as the other kids walk past us, down the mountainside. We stand, looking at each other, whispering inside one another's minds.

It's like each of you has a different taste, **Danielle says.**

I bet I taste like chocolate, **Perdie says**.

More like a baguette.

With butter?

Would you two shut up? **Jack says**. It's hard to hear myself think with all this radio chatter.

Jack's tastes like lemonade, almost too sour, **Danielle says**. And Shreve, Shreve . . .

"Hey, look at that," Casey says, pointing into the sky.

There's a diminution from the Montana sky. I feel smaller, dwarfed by the landscape and the sky and Jack so much taller than me now. Dwarfed by the weight of the lives behind me, inside me. Dwarfed by my own fear of what is coming. Dwarfed by the gift I've given us all.

Tap looks toward the sky. "You guys hear that?"

The high-pitched whine tears a strip from the sky. It's hard to pinpoint its location.

And then the plane streaks across the vault of heaven,

screaming and trailing a tail of noxious black smoke and pitching terribly. It's not the deadly wedge of a fighter jet or the tinny buzz of a single prop airplane, no. It's long, tubular. It's a passenger jet. In seconds it passes beyond the rim of mountains in the east and disappears.

I hold my breath, waiting for the *boom* of an explosion, but it doesn't come.

"Did you see that?" Jack asks.

I'm in the ether, floating on a mountaintop, looking across the vast, soundless landscapes to the east, where the plane went. There's such a stir in the etheric heights, like ash from some psychic volcano. I can hear screaming, the echoes of terror and desperation. And beyond that? Beyond the plane coming down somewhere east of us in the wavefront of oncoming night? There's a blackness churning there, churning and fretting at the boundaries of sleep. Like some quiescent dynamo only just beginning to turn. A black thing stirring. A quick glimpse of horror in a bright, sun-kissed day.

"Yeah. The plane," I say.

"You think it crashed," Bernard says. He *is* a little yeasty.

"I don't know." I say. I shake my head. "Yeah, it crashed."

"Should I go see?" Jack asks.

"Yes," Danielle says. "Of course *we* should."

"What if you hit a Helmholtz? You'll crash too," Casey says, her voice hushed.

"Not if I get high enough and then head east. Even if I hit a Helmholtz, I'll have enough momentum to push through it."

"I'll go to Admin, let them know what happened," Tap says.

"That's a good idea," Jack says, taking a few quick steps away and crouching.

"Aren't they tracking us all with radar or something? There's that thing on top of the hangar. And the dishes behind it?"

"Does it matter?" Danielle's face is tense. "We have to *do something*."

"Screw it. I'm going," Jack says. Tap launches himself into the air, flying low, toward Administration. It's an incredibly dangerous maneuver—the chances of encountering a Helmholtz far greater that way than toward the airplane.

"Jack—"

"No time. They could be hurt." He crouches and leaps. He launches up, peeling away from the earth in an absolute defiance of the suck of gravity, a bullet shot straight into the bosom of heaven. I try to follow him in the darkening air, and he burns bright for a moment when he rises into the last light of the setting sun. But then I lose him. He's so high and small in the sky, and it's only when he makes his move to the east— above the effects of Helmholtz fields—that I am able to pick him up again.

Danielle leaps upward too, her hair whipping in a wild fin behind her. I get the quick impression of tears streaming away from her eyes as she rises, following Jack.

Hurry, I tell them. Hurry.

■ ■ ■

It's close to full dark, a wild spray of stars wheeling in the heavens, when Jack and Danielle land. It's clear she's been crying. It's hard to tell with Jack. His jaw is locked, the muscles of his cheek popping and shifting as if he's grinding his teeth.

Their lips are blue. Jack hugs his body, rubbing his arms. Bernard gives Danielle his jacket.

"You're frozen, Jack," I say. "Let's get you back to the dorm."

He sits down on a rock, holds his head in his hands. Stays that way for a long while. There's always these moments when you don't know what to do. There was a kid at Casimir, his dad died in a meth lab fire and when Booth came to tell him, he just nodded his head, kept nodding, like he'd gotten the information yet wasn't able to process it yet and Booth stood there balling and unballing his fists because he didn't know anything else to do with his body. Only when I'm touching someone's mind—when I'm invested in that violation—is there any closeness of understanding anyone else. We're born into pain and live our whole lives in it, isolated from everyone else by the gulf of flesh and space. Each one of us alone, to deal with our grief and love and loss in our own way.

Danielle sobs, covering her face in her hands and shivering in Bernard's jacket.

Jack's not crying when he says, "Saw the smoke reflecting the sunset. Black smoke. The wreckage. There were . . ." He stops, swallows. "There were pieces of them. An arm. A leg. Some body part I couldn't even recognize. And luggage and smoking clothing."

"Any response? Cops or anything?"

He laughs, a hard bitter sound, like I'm an idiot. "Out here? We're miles and miles from the nearest road. They were probably trying to land at our airfield."

"The world's ending out there, Shreve. Beyond these mountains. Everything's falling apart. And we're just sitting here, playing at being superheroes," Jack says.

Some poor soul, maybe a pilot, maybe an airplane technician, hasn't slept for days. Missed something on the job.

All because of the thing sleeping in Maryland. The dragon stirring. Causing this insomnia. All those people died.

"Is there anything we can do?" I ask, helpless.

"Hope the mountain lions don't get indigestion," he says, and I have a sinking feeling in my stomach. He's right.

"The director will do something about it," Danielle says, knowing it's not true. They're all dead. The world is collapsing around us. Why bother?

Bernard puts his arm around Danielle. Jack stands there, fuming, furious. At me, maybe, for infecting him with something he didn't want. With the world for being stubborn and full of destruction.

Finally, when we all realize Quincrux or Ruark aren't going to come and do something, we slowly walk back up to campus, heads down.

I feel something press against my palm and realize Casey holds my hand in hers. Her secret hand. Her invisible one. I let it stay.

Silent.

THIRTY-SIX

Strange, the body still has wants even when the mind is clouded. My stomach rumbles unmercifully. My nuts throb.

Ember's sitting on the steps of the canteen when we arrive. Walking through the trees back from the airfield, I thought I heard something rustling in the undergrowth, but I remained calm and walked steadily away just as the sodium lights kicked on. Along with the Helmholtz. They're pouring on the juice, but what they need to do is shoot some mountain lions. My swollen nutsack's beginning to crawl. Something watched me.

"Where's the little dude?" Ember asks, moving to put her arm possessively around Jack's waist.

"He got called to Admin this morning," Jack says, rubbing her shoulder.

"Oh, that's terrible."

"You don't know the half of it," he says.

Don't tell her about the plane—or this change, I say.

Why not?

The plane? Because why depress her with a freakin' tragedy none of us can do anything about. And this because it's not entirely yours to tell.

If you can help people here, you should! She's a bugfuck herself. Does she sleep well?

Yeah, but . . .

But nothing.

I pass the guards, recognizing a not-so-friendly face. Davies. He's at ease with all the jocks and bugfucks, but there's something about him that reminds me of Negata. A waiting readiness. And he doesn't like me. He has cause not to.

Inside the canteen, the big chalkboard menu to the right announces it's Eye-talian night—with a large, unappetizing bloodshot eye drawn in loving detail—with lasagna and pasta with meatballs on the menu. I take the lasagna and sit down at a table with Bernard, Danielle, and Casey.

I'm ravenous. I tear into the ovoid block of "garlic" bread and fork a big mouthful of vinaigrette-drenched salad into my maw.

"So, the Bomb, man-child?" Bernie says. "She sock it to you in testing?"

Danielle and Casey smile and look at me. Everybody's so curious about the Montgomery girl. Anything to take their minds off the plane crash. "Yeah," I say around my food. "My dick got harder than Chinese arithmetic."

It's easier to be crass. It's a wall. I can't just say, yeah, she turned my body traitor and I would've killed you all, laughed doing it, if only to have sex with her. I would've sold my soul. Plucked out my eyes. Destroyed myself and lit the whole world on fire and watched it burn just to screw a girl. How do you say that?

So I go crass and stupid. It's easier.

But Casey's eyes are bright. "It got to you, didn't it? Not her, but the power they're playing with?"

I nod. She knows. It's like they're playing with both the raw energies of the universe on the physical side and the tidal forces of the human heart. It's just too much.

Ember and Jack join us, sitting next to each other, hip to hip. He won't meet my eye, so I know he's told her.

> Couldn't help yourself, could you?
> What?
> Nothing.

We finish our food. Extranaturals wander in and out of the canteen, placing orders. Davies and his companion watch us, sleepy, bored, but never setting down their automatic weapons. US Army all the way, baby. At least they're not in full battle rattle.

Another soldier appears in the open door, shambling forward. He seems to be disoriented and unarmed. He's looking around the canteen.

Jack begins to stand. "Who's that guy? He's new aroun—"

The soldier's arm pops up, finger out, and like a compass point, he wavers and then settles on true north—my chest. His eyes roll back in his head. He screams, "It stirs! It rises in the East! The elder awakens!"

Everything seems to happen simultaneously. Jack's hand pops up, all six fingers splayed, as if he plans to blast the soldier back out the doors. Next to him, Ember dodges to one side, and Bernard, Danielle, and Casey follow suit seconds behind her—just in case the soldier has a gun. Davies hops up, unslinging his weapon. The other soldier looks to Davies.

The canteen crowd parts like the Red Sea, dashing away from the pointing soldier. One employee levitates crazily and goes crashing into chairs and a table, unable to hold his concentration in the Helmholtz haze.

I slip out of my flesh and go tap-tap-tapping at the soldier's noggin. It's steel; it's titanium. Now I know that all knuckleheads can be broken, it's even more jarring, the strength of the Riders.

And that's what that poor sod has got, a Rider.

The possessed man screams, "It stirs! It wakens! You must stop it!"

I snap back in my body. "Me? Why me?" It's a question I always ask.

"Enduring pain. The conformity will take us all!" the man says.

Davies raises his weapon. The other soldier withdraws a Taser and raises it like a pistol. Delicately, they move to each side of Rider-possessed man. The soldier keeps the Taser on target yet reaches for his tac-comm receiver and lifts it to his ear. With the clatter of canteen chairs and tables, the words he murmurs into it are inaudible.

"Doesn't sound like a winning combo to me," I say, pitching my voice loud enough to carry over the terrified din of the room.

"You will be consumed!"

The man contorts, twisting like someone's stuck a frog gig into the small of his back and given it a good twist. Then he drops to the ground, first on his knees and then bowing over for his face to hit the concrete with a meaty *SLAP!* Davies lets his weapon swing loose on its strap, and he jumps forward, placing his knee in the small of the Rider-possessed man's back, careful not to touch skin, while his Taser-wielding compadre continues to give juice to the guy. The air is full of the *pop pop pop pop pop* of the electrical charge being pumped into the man's body, and in my mind, that sound blends with the buzzing and crackling of the ether.

Between the two, they yank the man's arms behind his back, snap handcuffs on him, lift him up, and move toward the front entrance with practiced speed. They bust out of the canteen's double-barred doors and into the night air. The doors slowly swing shut behind them.

"I think it might be time to go back to the dorm," Jack says.

Out the doors and into the rapidly cooling night. Davies and company stand near the guard shack, smoking cigarettes. There's a Jeep rumbling in the drive at the base of the stairs with more army guys, plus the one possessed by the Rider. His head swivels on a greased neck, like a turret, to focus on me as the Jeep pulls away. But he doesn't scream or yell again. His gaze bores into me as long as the angle of the car and the limitation of vertebrae and sinew allow him to. When they're gone, red taillights disappearing around a curve, the two guards say good-bye to their cohort in the guard shack and leave him standing outside, smoking and cracking his back.

Jack and Perdie are saying good night to the girls and turning to walk back to the dorm. I holler, "Hey, I'll catch up with you," and ignore Jack's puzzled look.

"What about the mountain lions?"

"It's not that far, and there's guards."

"What are you up to, man?"

"You wouldn't approve."

He narrows his eyes but lets me go.

I hobble over to near where Davies grips a cigarette in his teeth and looks at me warily.

"Excuse me," I say, going into the ether even as I speak.

It's almost like I'm calving off part of myself, a huge shelf of ice shuddering free of an iceberg and plummeting into the sea, but more deliberate. "Can I have a word with you?"

"No fraternization with the inductees. Move along."

The Helmholtz is kicking, but I bully through it. The shibboleth is so strong, the limiting field is just a minor irritation now.

I take a few steps away from the guard shack and the canteen and make Davies follow.

"How're you sleeping, hoss?" I ask.

"Fine."

"That's good. So you've done as I've..." *Ordered? Commanded?* "Instructed."

He nods, but it's reluctant.

"Did Booth respond?"

"I am coming."

Suddenly I'm afraid. A chill settles upon me, the chill of the thing sleeping in Maryland, the dragon in the East. I may have just jeopardized someone I care about. But things are moving now, and I cannot stop them.

"Okay. You may go. You will remember nothing of this."

I turn to go back to the dorm. Davies shuffles back to the canteen, content to drink coffee and eat power bars and ignore the violation that just occurred. Somewhere in his hindbrain a rat on a spinning wheel has my name tattooed onto its tail.

I'm tired, but not too tired to realize I'm not above acting just like it.

My body is heavy, each step is a labor. I pass beyond the canteen and guard shack's Helmholtz field and into a moment's silence in the ether. It's as if there's been a month of rain and finally the clouds pass over in the night and you realize the heavens are strewn now with a billion stars, each one indifferent to your plight, but still wheeling in their massive and glacial course across the sky. With each step my side twinges, my balls throb.

I walk, limping. Past the girls' dorm the ether becomes clouded again with Helmholtz interference, and then it lightens and disappears to nothing in my course across campus. It's cold again, and my breath comes in plumes, frozen water vapor hanging in front of my face before being snatched away by wind.

I think back to earlier today when the doomed airplane screamed across the sky. I think back to when the Liar convinced me I was going to die, and I wept for myself like a titty-baby. The shame burns in my throat. Before I looked like an old man, I thought. But now I am one, trapped in this hurt and exhausted boy's body.

I'm climbing now, rising up the mountainside and crossing the quad where Jack and Ember had their images stolen at Quincrux's behest. I stop, look at the tree, the vacant and empty tableau where they held hands.

I turn away from the tree and the bench and the building I once scrutinized so closely in photograph form, and there in a shadow cast by high, yellow-tinted sodium bulbs, I see the mountain lion crouching. It's there, off the path between buildings, arrested in its movement, watching me with eyes burning bright in the jungles of the night.

And this seems perfect. I am too tired even to be alarmed. The ether is quiet, but I can still hear the purr and thrum of the big cat's throat, spotting its prey. Maybe it sees I'm wounded. Maybe it sees I'm in pain.

Our gazes lock. It takes a quick three steps forward—*whisk whisk whisk*—and pauses once more, lowering its long, tan-sleek body down to the mulched, manicured campus grounds.

I am going to die.

Screw it. I can't even bring myself to care anymore. I've become what I never wanted to be. I've become what I hate. If this animal, this careless, remorseless spark in massive feline form is my doom, then let it be.

But there's a hard, unyielding bit of me that balks. The argumentative, petty, spiteful part of me rebels against the idea that this meatsuit I was born in, that I've inhabited for seventeen years, will become cat poop. No, I can't have that. I won't end up in a litter box.

The ether is clean. If there's even a whiff of Helmholtz, I can't sense it.

I'll not be trapped in this body when I die! I'll be like the Witch! I'll take over someone else. SOMETHING ELSE.

The thought is strange after it occurs to me. But I am beyond understanding by human means now. Post-human, they call it. I am a cloud, I am a mote. I am the water vapor on the breath of the mountains, I am the twitch in a lion's tail.

It creeps forward. Its tail thrashes back and forth and then stills. I can sense if not see the claws extending and retracting from its front paws as it prepares itself to strike.

I am huge and tiny all at once. I am breath and stillness. I settle upon the creature like some fog in a miasmic Arkansas jungle, the jungle that I come from. I settle like a thought, an instinct.

I seat myself in the flesh. I seat myself in the throne of savagery, red in tooth and claw.

I leap.

THIRTY-SEVEN

They come to get me out of bed, Negata and Ruark, standing over me with a flashlight. Jack's digital alarm clock reads 3:43. Hollis has returned from wherever he's been and doesn't even raise his head.

Negata positions himself back and to the right, his hands free and ready for anything. I have a sharp memory of the mountain lion crouching in front of me. Extending claws.

If only I could *find* Negata, I'd take him like I took the lion.

"Get up, Shreve. The director wants to speak with you," Ruark says, kicking the leg of my bed like Jack does. Maybe she's where he got the bright idea. The ether buzzes, thrums with Helmholtz. She's come loaded for bear. Or mountain lion.

I blink and try to hide how much it hurts. My chest is sore now where the lion slammed into my torso in its mad, self-destructive leap. I had only enough time to retract the claws and clamp shut the slavering mouth. Inside the beast, I padded around my small, pathetic body, sniffing the crotch, the ass. I smelled my own blood and for a moment, a single instant, I felt the irresistible desire to devour myself, to sink my teeth into that bit of flesh and destroy my birth body forever.

Afterward, I ran. I hunted. I stalked the forest and the mountainside, shibboleth forgotten. Everything forgotten other than slaking my hunger.

I stalked the campus. In the tall grasses by the lower airfield, where the creek runs, I caught a doe as its hooves slipped on a stream-slicked stone and it fell. Its blood stayed in the fur of my muzzle, and its meat made my belly pendulous, my blood slow.

A thing of pure spirit and burning flesh. I feel tired and ashamed of all the memories I took and used up in Casimir like some junkie. The whole time there was *this*, the pure rush and joy of the carnal. The pleasure of the flesh of the predator, yowling and screeching and looking for a female to top and sire cubs upon.

When I came back to my body—to my humanity—I was wracked with shivers, my skin rippling with goose bumps. I stumbled back to the dorm, passing Roberto at the front door. He looked surprised at my appearance. Up the stairs slowly and into the creaky dorm bed. Hollis wasn't in our room.

Now Ruark stands above me. Would that I was a cat, stalking on padded feet.

"We brought you some fresh clothes, Cannon. The director wants you presentable." Ruark tosses a short stack of folded white and tan clothes on my feet at the end of my bed. "Get up, get dressed. The director is waiting."

From the light of the hallway, I see Jack stir in his bed. I make a patting gesture with my hand, letting him know to stay still. I don't have to worry about Hollis jumping in. Tap snores.

"Okay, mister," I say.

She doesn't leave as I strip off my soiled undergarments and examine the stiff, scratchy clothes she's provided. Everything looks a little too big for me. Naked, I hold the pants, not even trying to cover my junk. I'm too tired and hurt for any modesty. It's just the meatsuit she sees. Not the real me.

"You could use some fattening up. I'll tell Cindy at the canteen to double up on the sausage and cinnamon rolls for you."

"Laissez-moi tranquille! Il ya faims et il ya d'autres faims." That just pops out there. There are hungers and there are other hungers.

I tug the pants over my swollen nuts and wince. I studiously *do not* look at her face then, so as not to see her smile. She refrains from commenting any more as I tug on the clean white T-shirt, slip on my Chuck Taylors.

Everything's jumbled in my head as they march me downstairs and out the front doors. A golf cart waits, Negata directly behind me. I've become Public Enemy #1.

We buzz through the early morning air, through the campus. Somewhere, out there, beyond the campus buildings, there's a mountain lion slumbering meat-heavy and whiskered with blood.

At Admin, they escort me up the steps, past the blankly staring statue of Armstead Lucius Priest, and through a warren of small, overlit yet bland offices. There's no Helmholtz field.

We stop in front of a large wooden door. Ruark goes to an empty desk and presses a button on an intercom device that squelches. She says, "We've got him here, Director."

Quincrux's voice responds, "Wonderful. Do come in." And the door opens.

It's the office I popped into when I hijacked Quincrux. It stinks of cigarettes and coffee. I have the brief sense-memory of Moms and the trailer we lived in for so many years.

Tanzer, a short-haired woman with boyish features and lively expressions animating her face, stands nearby holding a clipboard and scratches at it with a pencil. Quincrux, sitting behind his desk, gestures to a chair in front of him. Ruark settles herself in a small, nearby desk covered with monitors and computer screens, and places a headset over her short-cropped blonde hair. I take the seat. Negata silently positions himself in the corner of the room, hands loose and free. Quite a party.

"I'm sorry to have to wake you this early in the morning, Mr. Cannon," Quincrux starts. He's not, truly. He knows it; I know it. "I only just arrived back on campus, and my lieutenant"—Quincrux nods toward Ruark—"informs me we've had an impenetrable appear on the grounds. Imagine my surprise when she showed me the video, and it had some dialogue with you."

He rummages in a drawer, pulls out a small crystal ashtray and a package of Peter Stuyvesants. He shucks the package a couple of times, gets a square, and pops it in his mouth. The room is still and quiet, and I can hear the tobacco and paper crackle when he lights it and draws the smoke into his lungs. I guess guys like him—and guys like me—don't have to worry about lung cancer: we can just boost someone else's body if the big *C* comes a-calling.

I wait. He's going to do this at his own pace.

"I am disappointed in you, Mr. Cannon. I thought we made clear to you your position here. Yet you withheld information regarding the impenetrables. The Riders, as you call them."

"Not really."

"You didn't withhold information?"

I shrug. "Possibly. I can't really recall if you asked me about the Riders before or after threatening my little brother. Or holding me in the dark."

"So, you meant to keep us in the dark as payback?" He takes another drag on his cigarette, holds it a long while as if considering blowing the smoke into my face, expels it toward the ceiling. He sets the cigarette down in the ashtray and takes a dainty sip of coffee. Somewhere, overhead, a vent kicks on and I can feel the air stir in the office and the smoke whisk away. "It is unfortunate that the situation has to be this way."

"Yep, it sure is."

"So, to preserve your brother's delicate state—it seems he's been having some trouble with a foster brother—why don't you tell me how much intercourse you've had with the Riders."

"We've moved past first base and are at the heavy petting stage of our relationship."

"How droll, Mr. Cannon. I am coming to the conclusion that we will need to have a contest of will for me to get to the truth."

This is the reason for the lack of Helmholtz.

"Okay, boss." I raise my hands in a helpless gesture. "We can do it that way, or I can just tell you."

"You've had opportunities to tell me before and haven't."

"True." *You kept me in a hole in the ground!* "I didn't feel like it then because you were being such a prick."

He blinks at my language.

I say, "How many people have you killed?"

"There are greater things at stake here than I can make you understand. I do not have to answer to you, regardless. Tell me what you know of the Riders."

"How 'bout a little tit for tat, huh? And I don't mean your

assistant." Ruark bristles, shifting in her chair. Somebody wants to Tase me.

He smokes and thinks. He has my brother. He could easily just force the issue. The fact that he's even considering it makes me think that he needs me. A little, at least.

"All right. You begin, and I will determine if what you tell me has any bearing."

I tell him about the boy in Casimir, how the Rider told me to leave before the "elder" awakened.

His eyes remain locked on mine. When I'm through talking, he looks at Ruark, who glances at me and then says, "He's not lying. He rarely lies, but he's definitely not now."

Quincrux nods and turns back to me, stubbing out his cigarette in the crystal ashtray. "What would you ask me?"

"The 'elder.' What is it?"

He shakes his head. "We don't know entirely. It is alien."

"Like from outer space?"

He looks at me for a long while. "Possibly. It is absolutely foreign to the experience and knowledge of humankind because it is perceptible to very few. Myself. You. A few others. Did it come from outer space in a spaceship? No. Most definitely not. But it is *la grande outre*."

A big other. Other, as in, from elsewhere. From beyond. The veil of night, maybe. Beyond darkness itself.

"Some kid went crazy talking about the 'dragon in the East.' This what he was talking about?"

"I think it is your turn to answer questions."

Shrugs all around. "All right. Can I get some ibuprofen or something? I was attacked by a mountain lion earlier. And my nuts are the size of grapefruits."

He glances at Ruark. She only nods, indicating I'm telling the truth.

"Will you, please, Amy?"

I refrain from messing with her about her name. But the urge is worse than giving a monkey a handful of poo. It just *wants* to be flung.

She leaves the office and returns with two pills and a plastic bottle of Ozarka water.

"Okay," I say after downing the pills. "Shoot."

"How many conversations have you had with the impenetrable entity?"

"Three." A nod from Ruark confirms my statement.

"What occurred in the second conversation? I know the events of the third," he says, tapping his computer monitor.

"That was when you had the goon squad chasing me."

He remains silent. Staring at me, humorless as an inquisitor.

I run over the event: getting out of my car, dashing across the parkway and into the East River Park. "He—*it*—said that I 'must away' to Maryland to face the 'elder.' I hate it when folks talk all *Lord of the Rings* and shit." I meet his gaze steadily. He's got gray eyes and a calm demeanor. Hard to tell how old the body he inhabits is. Older than fifty, but somewhat youthful and unlined. "My turn. You once said that you were weakened by your encounter with the thing in Maryland. What happened?"

He rubs his chin, passing the back of his hand across his mouth. Thinking for a long time.

"That is hard to describe, and painful to recall. But in the spirit of our conversation, maybe I shouldn't tell you. Maybe I should *show* you."

"No, I—"

"Yes, Mr. Cannon." He doesn't smile. "I think you need to see."

He reaches forward and touches my hand. And suddenly I see.

THIRTY-EIGHT

The report from Delacroix indicated that an inordinate number of people in the Maryland area are impenetrable, if not posing a definite and growing security risk to the Society and, consequently, the fabric of the American government. Through some sort of statistical or mathematical chicanery, Delacroix—an agent with a technician's demeanor, to be sure—gave his report using the word *algorithm* over fifteen times as he flipped through its PowerPoint slides and nervously directed a laser dot at the maps displayed on-screen. He had located, he assured us, what he thinks the epicenter of the impenetrable infection, a lower-middle-class neighborhood in Towson, Maryland. With Moteff in Lancashire tending to a new report of a strong adolescent extranatural, I venture there to canvass the area and sense what I can in the ether.

Coming off the flight at Baltimore International, I find the air uncommonly bright and humid. The hired car, low-slung, painted black with mirrored windows, whisks me away like some automotive thanatopsis, the interior cool and dark as a coffin, the air conditioning stripping the moisture from the air. The patches aren't working anymore, and I desperately want a cigarette.

The driver, a thickset and remarkably furry man dressed uncomfortably in a rumpled cheap black suit, asks me for directions. I hand him the packet Amy prepared, including a suggested route with maps, and say, "Feel free to take as much time as you need to get familiar with the material."

"What's all this?"

"Have we not acquired your services for the duration?"

"Sure, it's just that I usually pick up and drop off."

"Not today, I'm afraid. Mister?"

"Killette."

"Mr. Killette. Please become familiar with the material in that packet."

As he looks through the maps, face screwed into an interesting pretzel of concentration, I withdraw my laptop and attach the device Delacroix provided as cover. It would not do to have someone question my demeanor while probing the ether, and this gadget will camouflage my preoccupation with things undetectable to the human eye or senses.

When he puts down the packet and looks into the backseat, I have the gadget attached to my computer and I'm ready to proceed.

"What, are you like in the government or something?"

"Or something." I slip into the void and, as starlight, filter into his consciousness. He is a simple man, with simple tastes. He is uncompromised—our Chinese counterparts, the *mó fâ*, have not inhabited him, luckily—so as quietly as I entered, I leave him. No need to cause undue stress.

"Ah. Gotcha." He touches his index finger to his nose and winks at me, a curious gesture of bonhomie and overfamiliarity. But I'll allow him his presumption.

From Baltimore, we drive north. "Before we start on our appointed path, I would like to go to a certain address, if I may."

"Sure. You're the boss." Killette seems more comfortable with these sorts of instructions. A simple man, indeed.

"Sparrow's Point. Near the wharf and the rail yards. I'll give you more precise directions when we get nearer."

He nods, and the car begins to move. I spend my time rocking silently and looking out at the old whore of a city. The skyline lurches sluggishly across my view, and nothing stirs in me at its passing. The opposite of love is not hate. It is indifference.

Eventually, we pass by the huge squat warehouses and rumble over railroad tracks. While recognizable, the decayed landscape reminds me of some war-torn battlefield after the first great war, the one where Bryce and Haveford died in the Verdun mud. And I ceased for a time to care about my own life. For the final darkness will come for us all, and it matters not who is its agent. The Hun? Myself?

It matters not.

"Here. Wharf Lane. Turn here."

Driving quite aggressively for a hired man, Killette whips the car into the one area in this urban wasteland with trees, a secluded, trash-strewn bower with rubble and used prophylactics as flora and fauna. I step out and survey the lot.

It has been nearly forty-five years since I last saw Priest and he wooed—no, *compelled*—me to join the Society. This old body I wear now was young then.

I look at the shattered, weed-wracked space. A building stood here once. Stately and old and tall. Its deeply burnished wooden floors echoing the footfalls of countless extranaturals, its rooms full of comfort and understanding. So many people. All of them like me.

My body was young then, but me, my spirit, was aged, in my third incarnation. Yet I was different. Gentler, maybe. Lucius was more ancient still—I once heard him refer to Sulla, the Roman dictator, as a friend, and I realized how ancient he might truly be, and the possibilities of endless life yawed before me like an abyss. But despite Lucius's age, he was full of life, exuberant and spritely; he was possessed of that rare ability to spark inside me a wonder at our universe and hope for the human race. We believed we could escort humankind through its next step in evolution. We were gods among mortals, modern Prometheuses not bringing fire to humankind but lighting the fire within their minds. To this end I endeavored wholeheartedly.

Then there was the ruinous night. I had been away on assignment. A storm delayed my train. I arrived in the small hours of the morning, and when I returned, wanting nothing more than the comfort of bed, I found the old Society building an inferno. The few Society members left alive in the conflagration were gibbering and witless. Including poor Lucius. And it was then that the leadership of the Society of Extranaturals fell to me.

"The dragon . . ." Lucius whispered when I found him disheveled and soot-stained and bleeding in the hidden arbor behind the Society building. "The elder . . ."

My spirit detached from the sum of my parts and tried to settle upon him, to calm him and give his soul succor, but his spirit bucked and thrashed. I could no more calm him than a boat could moor in a storm-tossed sea. I felt massive forces warring within him, prodigious psychic energies shifting and settling like the tidal energies of stars. Looking at me, he blinked, and the thing that looked out of his eyes was no longer him, not anything I had ever sensed in my three lifetimes. I found myself shivering and cold at the darkness contained therein, and Lucius collapsed to a coma, never to regain any sort of measurable consciousness.

His body was very young too, at that time, though the personality that propelled it was not. When the ambulances came, and had I made sure that Lucius and the few other survivors were well taken care of, it was then time to deal with our shadow, the US government. I was closeted with them for weeks, it seems, and it was then we hashed out our current arrangement. Afterward, when I attempted to find the last members of the Society, though mad or comatose, I could not. The agents of this country, the noble United States of America, had obscured their whereabouts such that even I could not suss it out. And why? Secrecy becomes a habit and requires no more reason than "we have always done so." Yet I think worries over the ascendancy of the *mó fâ* spurred their actions.

But now, looking out at the deteriorating remains of such a beautiful old campus, I can almost taste the ashes in my mouth once more, smell the acrid and ruin-perfumed smoke. It is all just rubble; long ago scavengers picked over every bit of salvage there was to be had from the Society. Now there's a pile of tires lolling there, and the burnt-out husk of a car, surely torched in some spat of gangland warfare or exuberant youth.

I walk forward, into the tall, oily grasses that grow in clumps, snaring and snagging at my slacks. That once I called this spot home is unimaginable.

Behind me the car still rumbles.

I can remember his laugh. Despite changing bodies, always the same laugh. He was the best of us, and ever since then, we have fallen so low . . .

I turn away from the sight of all that once was, turn back to the car waiting for me.

Out of Sparrow's Point we drive, into the clutter and bustle of the withered city, and eventually, when I am composed enough to probe the ether, I send out that part of me that will never die, the incorruptible spirit, to sense what it can. To find the source of the impenetrables.

Killette makes sounds with his mouth, and in the ether, it is hard to assign meaning to any of his talk. I don't even try, and eventually, the man falls silent.

There is something here. It shivers in the invisible starlight of the void, and I can feel a tugging on the tendons and connective tissues of the ether. It's strange, but it feels as if I'm on a gentle slope and gravity pulls on me to go one way or, as the car turns, another. It leads me, inexorably, like the events in a dream. A nightmare in which I know all that is to happen, yet cannot change the outcome.

My gods, I need a cigarette. Bother this and all vibrations of the ether. I need a cigarette.

I withdraw from the void like a hasty lover withdrawing midstroke, and say, "Driver, do you smoke?"

"No, sir. Quit almost ten ye——"

"That is no matter to me. Take me to the nearest store."

It's only a few moments before he finds one. In the parking lot, I shuck my jacket and unbutton my shirt so that I might have access to the patch burning itself into my skin. I rip it away and rebutton my shirt. I buy two packs of Pall Malls. I will need to find a tobacco shop soon, to locate my old friend Peter Stuyvesant.

The hot, perfumed smoke fills my lungs even before reaching the idling hired car. Killette smiles at me with his window down.

"Sorry, the boss don't allow no smoking in the ride."

"Understandable," I say, taking the smoke into my lungs, so deep it feels like drowning. "Give me a moment," I say. "A few moments."

He nods and the sedan window rises, cutting him off from view.

I smoke and lean against the back wheel well of the car, looking at the lowering daylight filtering through the wires and packed-tight brownstones and cheap apartment complexes of Baltimore. There are thousands of souls here, living on top of one another. In some chamber of my mind, the reality of this future I never imagined or considered crashes in, cacophonous and frenetic. I was born so many years ago in the morning of the world; I see that now only in retrospect. When I was a boy, the forest in which I was born stretched from leafy New Haven to the far edges of Pennsylvania and beyond, though we didn't know it then. The world was flat, and I could test the unknown edges of it with this strange ability I had, ethereal and full of ghostlight. Now the sun-hammered world feels as old as I do, the surface of the earth spackled with concrete and tenements and desperate, near-illiterate serfs who don't even understand the depth of their own servitude.

I hesitate to touch the void. Something is amiss. It is a feeling I've had over and over again since I've touched down, but only now as I smoke and let the deleterious and woozy effect of the nicotine and tar swim in my bloodstream, only now when I'm sated and calm enough, can I recognize the feeling.

Something is wrong here.

Only after I've smoked three cigarettes, jump-starting each from the butt of the previous, am I ready to reenter the sedan and begin once more to probe the ruinous ether.

Killette drives slowly, allowing me to find my own bit of comfort in the rear seat as the tenements and strip malls pass us slowly by.

I am terrified. The dark gravity teases at my superattuned etheric sense. It's like the miniscule pitch and yaw of an airplane midflight—you're not consciously aware of it, but your body knows and reacts. It's the gravity well of a black hole, tugging with tidal forces.

We drive on interminably, hours pacing and stalking up and down streets full of cheap housing mashed together like blocks of clay, cars lining the streets. Whores and crackheads and dealers toddle about, desperately gesturing toward the sedan, and then we're out of that neighborhood and prowling through more industrial areas full of short, extruded-metal buildings and cinder-block reliquaries of the failing American business. The only balm is progress, for the wasted streets of America and for me. We are nearing our goal, unknown though it is.

Yet I know, feel in my bones, that it approaches.

I tell Killette to stop.

Outside I sniff, I probe at the ether, even while my hands work steadily to ferret the cigarette from the packet, bring it to my mouth, and light. The Kwik-E-Marts and mercados and Pep Boys seem beaten down in the vapored, humid air. The smoke is a noxious blossom, a cancerous flower blooming in the dark capillary dusk of my lungs, and its scent is heady and sweet and foul.

It is there. Just beyond that line of buildings. I know it.

After I smoke the cigarette, and then another, and then another, I get back in the car.

"Go over there," I say, leaning forward into the driver's area, pointing toward the source of my unease. "That's where we're going."

He muscles the sedan into traffic—which is, all things considered, quite light—and we find our way over two blocks to a row of antique-looking buildings.

A sign reads TOWSON VETERANS HOSPITAL. It's a massive, five-storied structure that looks as if it could fall at any moment, rain- and snow-streaked, paint scaling, beaten by the elements. It looks like it was built at the same time as our Society's Montana campus, a WPA project. But where the buildings in Montana are prime—preserved through a natural environmental blessing or the diligence of man—this hospital bears the brunt of the ruinous energies of entropy and decay. Annihilation always comes more slowly than we'd like, but faster than imaginable.

"Stop!" I'm nearly screaming. My composure is like a loose tooth, dangling on its last fiber.

He slides the car to a stop, and I lurch from its dark confines to stagger up the main steps of the Towson Veterans Hospital. At the dullard receptionist's alarmed look, I fumble at my pants and withdraw the NSA badge I'd been given for just these sorts of emergencies. And it does enough to preclude her from calling whatever negligent security this shabby hospital might have. None, I'm guessing.

In the elevator, I press all the buttons. As we rise, the doors open and shut. Fourth floor feels right.

I don't know what my body's doing. My avaricious desire for tobacco and nicotine is gone, and all I can do is keep my heart from going into tachycardia before reaching the end of this particular rabbit hole. I feel like a ship on the edge of the maelstrom, a satellite on the cusp of falling into the beginnings of a new star.

There are doors passing on my left and right. I pull one open to reveal a hollow-eyed man, a soldier most likely, with an obvious missing leg. He's emaciated and bruised.

I release the door and move onward, down the hall, until finally . . . *finally* . . . I stand in front of the entrance.

It is here. I feel it in all the ways I can feel. Beyond the capacity of my fellow man. In all my years. I feel it.

I push the door open. I move my body into the small, antiseptic-smelling room. There's the huff and hiss of a breathing apparatus, the soft dings of a pulse fed through a machine. I stand by the bed, looking down.

The ruin of years has not been kind to Lucius, languishing in this hospital. My old friend. He looks like a bundle of sticks with a white mop for a head. Wasted and liver-marked.

My mentor. Or what is left of him.

Or what is in him.

I feel something moving, something obscene stirring, coiling and uncoiling in its strength, hinting toward massiveness that makes it hard to comprehend.

Before me lies Armstead Lucius Priest, my old friend, and inside him now stirs all of our destruction. The dragon reborn into the world. The star-spanning darkness that will find us all.

Something in me, some receptive lone particle, quivers and thrums in the ether, and the dragon answers. The darkness swells.

And his eyes open.

He sees me.

It sees me.

It stirs, and I can feel the gaping maw of its awareness. The compulsion to throw myself into the abyss pricks itself up and into my consciousness, and most of it is not me. Most of it. The great necessity of death spreads itself like a lover beneath me.

I stumble out. I stumble away, heedless and sightless, like a beggar in a desert, blinded by the sight of a black sun.

I stumble. I fall.

Darkness covers me.

THIRTY-NINE

Quincrux removes his hand, withdraws his mind from my own. There was no fighting him, when it happened. With his touch—*his proximity*—he was inside me and moving. Showing me his own mind. It happened so fast. The clock says it's only been moments.

"So, it's . . ." I need to order my thoughts. "What? What is it?"

"You know as much as I. The insomnia, the dark emanations from the East . . . it is stirring."

"What happens if it wakes? That's what the Riders were warning me of. To rejoin Jack—and I guess you—before the 'elder awakens.'" That's a stinker of a thought, like a turd in the punch bowl. It has the whiff of prophecy. "But it seemed to me the Riders wanted me to go gallivanting off to face down the damned thing by myself."

Something clicks in my mind, my memory.

"What is it, Shreve?" Quincrux asks. Weird how we're just sitting here, chatting.

"It used the word *ember*. It said, 'These embers . . .'"

"And you are thinking it meant Ember Schultz?"

"Her name is Schultz? Who gives their kid the name Ember knowing it'll always be tagged with Schultz?"

"Dead parents," he says, humorlessly. He pushes back, away

from me. He takes another cigarette from the package of Peter Stuyvesants.

"All of my clothes, I mean, every piece of clothing I have, is gonna stink of that. I'm wearing everything I got."

"Amy, please requisition more clothing for Mr. Cannon. It seems he'll be staying with us for the duration."

"And the thing in the East?" I ask, glancing at Ruark. I'm still uncomfortable talking about it in front of people. "People are dying from lack of sleep. We've got to do something. We should do what the Riders say . . ." The thought terrifies me, but it seems like the only alternative. "Send me and Jack."

He shakes his head. "No. That is simply folly. You are so green as to be useless, and your partner Jack requires a burr under his saddle to function at levels becoming a member of our Society." He looks thoughtful. "And we already have plans in motion to neutralize the entity."

"How?"

"It is not a matter of concern for you."

"How you figure? That Rider didn't come looking for you. Doesn't this make you nervous?"

He places his cigarette in the ashtray and stares at me. "It makes me very nervous. As much as we've shared," he says meaningfully, "you are in a unique position to understand how seriously I take this threat. But it is only a matter of days before it will be resolved."

"Tell me."

"Suffice it to say, I am dispatching our Orange Team to deploy a new technology that will eliminate the threat."

"What technology?"

"A bioelectrical technology."

"That doesn't make any sense."

He obviously doesn't like being questioned. I wonder why he allows me to continue doing it.

"In the early eighties, we found a woman who could generate a stasis field. An absolutely impenetrable one. Anything inside the field was held inviolate and time did not pass. After billions of dollars of research, we've managed to duplicate that same effect through a combination of genome manipulation, biotechnology, and computers."

"You're gonna place the body of this Priest fellow in the field."

"Yes. And lock it away. Forever."

"You're gonna stick it in a dark hole, is that it? Didn't work too well with me."

"I allowed you to leave your confinement. The entity will not have the same fate as you."

"Hope that stasis thingy works better than your Helmholtz fields."

It doesn't faze him. "You would be amazed."

"You know, because I've been walking right through them."

"This is known." He inclines his head toward Negata, lurking silently in the corner. "It is good that Mr. Negata is with us to keep you company."

"And you've put the screws to my brother."

He ignores that. He probably doesn't like being reminded that he's an extortionist and kidnapper. Being a murderer is fine; it's so much cleaner, to deprive someone of life. But these lower crimes, these crimes of necessity, they besmirch his self-image.

But the implications of this technology, if true, are

staggering. No more wars. Colonizing other planets. Journeying to the stars. The mind boggles.

And they want to use it to lock away a dragon.

Oy gevalt, this guy.

"You gonna go with it? This stasis bomb?"

"No. My last encounter with the thing taxed me beyond all endurance. And I think whatever is left of Lucius in there, if there's any part of him that hasn't been replaced with the *other*, is sensitive to the presence of telepaths more than telekinetics."

"So you're just gonna send meatheads and jocks? Good plan." Both he and I know only a mind can contest another mind. And the dragon is one big throbbing, ugly awareness. A mind. "Send me."

"No."

"Send me. I can be your link to the mission. Your man on the inside." God help me for saying this. "You can sit in the backseat." I tap my temple.

"Quite a generous offer, Mr. Cannon, but no."

"Why not?"

"Two reasons." He raises a tobacco-stained finger. "You haven't proven yourself to me. You are obstinate. You aren't a team player."

True. But screw this guy. I can play well with others. The goddamned world is at stake. Maybe he didn't bring me here to make me his own toy soldier. Maybe he brought me here to take me off the battlefield.

"Two." He raises another finger. "The impenetrables seem to want you to come into *proximity*—" There's that word again. "With the entity in Maryland. Until I know the Riders' goals, I have no intention of doing what they want. So if they want you to encounter this *thing*, I will work to thwart that, if I can."

"I think you're making a mistake."

"It is within the realm of possibility."

"Everything is in the realm of possibility."

"Not everything."

"Name one thing. You've got a stasis field. Kids can fly. I can possess people and read minds. What is impossible?"

"You going to Maryland." He snuffs out his cigarette. "Thank you for your time and candor, Shreve. I think this is a good step forward for you." He turns to his laptop and pecks at the keyboard. "You are dismissed."

FORTY

On my way out of Admin, the statue of Armstead Lucius Priest stares blankly out the front bay window at the dark. Ruark is nowhere to be found. I was hoping for a ride in her golf cart.

I trudge up the slope on the northwestern path up to the male dorms, away from the manicured quad where I encountered the mountain lion. Nice night out, a bajillion stars illuminating the sky, a half-moon washing the valley in pale light.

Roberto greets me as I enter the dorms and begin to take the long stairs up to my room.

Ruark and Davies are there when I enter. Davies has his rifle up, pointed in the vicinity of the window, where both Jack and Tap stand, watching.

"What's going on here?"

I realize Ruark's tried to slip Hollis out while I was occupied with Quincrux. They all turn to look at me where I stand in the doorway. Hollis is halfway through packing his things in his bag. His expression is of pure terror.

"Hollis is going home," Ruark says. "The Society wasn't a right fit for him."

"What? Why isn't it?"

Hollis looks wrung out. "No, it's okay, Shreve," he says. "It's fine. I want to go home."

Something's not right here.

Hollis, it's going to be okay, **I send.**

I don't think so, Shreve.

What happened? **I ask.**

I've washed out.

How?

They kept trying to make me stop time.

Were you able to?

Yes. For a while. Then they took my blood. They made me—

What?

They took a semen sample.

Jesus.

So, what? **Tap sends.** You think they're just gonna send him home?

There's a long silence while Hollis stuffs clothes into his bag. Davies shifts his weight and readjusts his rifle. I don't know any way to say it and not have Hollis panic. If he panics, somebody's going to get shot.

I look around. Negata is nowhere about. The Helmholtz isn't running. Feigning indifference, I say, "Okay, Hollis." I lie down on my bed and cross my arms behind my head. "Sorry you're not gonna be around."

You're gonna be around. You ARE.

"Come on, Mr. Hollis, we don't have all night," Ruark says.

Hollis looks at me, stricken.

"Hollis," I say. "It's gonna be all right, man."

It is. I'm not gonna let anything happen to you.

We got your back, **Jack sends.**

I get up, stick out my hand. Hollis takes it, tentatively. "Nice to meet you, bud."

"Thanks, Shreve. Uh . . . thanks," he says, and then he hugs me.

Over his shoulder, I see Negata appear in the doorway. Ruark notices him too.

"Mr. Negata, while we're escorting Mr. Hollis to his—" She pauses. "His *exit interview*, I'd like you to remain here with Mr. Cannon. Just as a precautionary measure."

I sit back on my bed. "I'm going to sleep."

Negata looks at me, unblinking. He moves to the side and allows Ruark, Hollis, and Davies to leave.

"Don't let the door hit your ass on the way out," I say.

Ruark stops, gives me an *I'm-about-to-make-your-night* grin, and lifts her walkie-talkie. "Exchange, over. Exchange?"

The radio squelches something inaudible back.

"I'm going to need the boys' dorm Helmholtz field pushed to maximum. Divert power from elsewhere if you have to."

In seconds, I can feel the ether hissing and vibrating in the fillings of my teeth. It's the strongest I've ever encountered.

When they're gone, Negata silently steps backward, into the hall, and swings the door firmly shut.

The instant the latch closes, I hop up, move to the window.

"Jack, I'm gonna need your help."

"We can't do anything!" Jack says. He splays out his fingers at the wall, like he's going to give a small burst. Nothing happens. "We're stuck."

"Not quite, bro. Tap, watch the door."

Roger that, Tap sends.

Things have changed now one of us is in obvious jeopardy. He may not like us, but he is one of us. "Uh, what do I do if he comes in here?"

"He comes in, out the window as fast as you can and scream like the dickens."

"He's gonna eat me for breakfast."

"Just watch the damned door, will you? I have to hurry."

While I can't get out on the campus, I can get to the farthest edges of the field to try to do what I'm about to do. I shimmy out the window, climbing up to what I've come to think of as our patio. Jack's right behind me.

Once I'm there, I feel the ether, gauging the strength of that hideous field. Weaker, but still crackling like hot oil. Our patio is a five-by-five-foot area where the dormers and three planes of roofing meet in a flat area, but there are more areas to the roof. The angle up leads to some vents and beyond to the apex of the building.

With no time to waste, I scurry up, over the heavy slate tiles, higher and higher. The wind is fiercer now, colder, whipping down from those great heights, and it plays havoc with my balance. Jack seems to be having no problems. We keep moving up and up until we come to the peak where I had hoped there'd be a flat area. No dice. The roof immediately slants away in a tight angle, descending down to the rest of the building, the eastern side. From here, my body draped stomach-down on the peak of the building, pressed tight like some pathetic mountaineer, I see the valley spread out below me and illuminated by the moon. The lights on the buildings look small and pathetic underneath the canopy of stars and the brilliant lunatic sway of the half-orb hanging so low in the heavens.

I don't know if I can do this. Heights are not my favorite.

Don't sweat it, **Jack sends**. You've gotten off
of roofs before, haven't you?"

I smile. That's right. I did.

I touch the ether. It is weaker up here, the buzz and hiss and sandpaper scratch of the Helmholtz, yet it is still stronger than I've ever endured. There's nothing for it but to leap. I cannot fly, but the shibboleth is the common utterance of life. I can shuck this all off and find what I need out in the void.

"Hey, Jack?"

"Yeah?"

"Don't let me fall."

He grabs my shoulder. Squeezes. "Go."

I leave the meatsuit behind. The ether is like a firestorm and my spirit a piece of paper caught in an updraft of fire, rising yet burning away in the overwhelming heat. But our minds move with the currents of metaphor, and somewhere in me I remember the force of will it required for me to make that initial step out of my body, when the guard Tased me at Casimir.

I wasn't me; I was the electricity itself, and I traveled beyond my body.

There's a hardening in me, in my will. Not calcifying but tempering into something brilliant and diamond. An apotheosis of the indestructible. I am stronger than whatever they can pour on me, the hurt, the shame of physical injury, the heartache of mockery, the slow death of isolation. None of these things has killed me yet. None of them has ruined me.

Rising upon the invisible winds of the void like a thought, I am beyond influence of the Helmholtz field, and a small part of me realizes I was always beyond it. I just had to make the realization. Maybe all it ever took was a rooftop and the desperate need to escape.

I move into the space/not space. Where there once were billions of stars above, now there's only bright lights below. The individual flames of minds. I cannot see Negata—he is hidden from my gaze—but I see Hollis, wavering, and Ruark, burning brightly. Moving through real space. Invested in the physical. Rooted in flesh. And beyond them, out on the shoals of the sea of life and light, I see lesser flames, lesser minds. Finding the most suitable one for my needs—one that's fast and deadly—I settle upon it like the devil that I am.

The devil in the flesh.

...

It's a big male, and he fights me as hard as his limited bundle of awareness allows. Muscular and scarred. I chose a male because, in some ways, it might be easier for me, easier for him. The infestation needs familiarity. Like calls to like. I'm rougher than I should be, because I'm in haste. Inside him now, victorious, it's hard to concentrate, hard to pay attention to anything other than the hunt. No longer concerned with the rabbit warren or the coyote den or the burnt-bloody smell of man, I bound through the trees, heading west. Moving as fast as my meat-starved body will allow.

The softness of the forest floor, the rapturous celebration of the stretch and contraction of muscles—the rest of existence hangs like the fluff of cottonwoods suspended in the air as I move through it, the collective breath of the carnal instinct world. I am the arrow of God. I am the incarnation of Shreve.

When I catch the scent, I can't help but give vocalization to the pure joy of the hunt, my fur stiffening in the cooling night air. A scream. A howl. A *yaowl* of mastery of this form.

The stink of animal spoor and territorial urine markings. The noxious smell of asphalt and unnamable manmade scents as I sprint down the bank and swim the short shunt of stream between my quarry and me.

Up the bank into the brambles and shrubs, body moving fluidly over the ground, racing ever on. Toward Hollis.

And within sight of the lights. Lights hung on trees. Stone buildings flooded with the scent of man, the stink of humanity.

To the left and left and left more, rising again. Sprinting, pushing this body to its utmost speeds. I hear the buzz of the tires of a vehicle—my Shreve brain tells me—and I note it and follow. My vision is the vision of death, the vision of the dark and the hunt. It's easy to mark the people on the wheeled thing, the . . . *dimly, dimly it comes to me* . . . golf cart.

There's the plump woman, and a man, hard and muscular with the refulgent odor of oil and sweat coming from him in streamers, wafting behind in their forward movement. I keep pace, off to the side, moving through the trees and open spaces crouched low, each step masterful in its placement and silence.

Stalking.

And there's a boy. The smell of him is like a rabbit, freshly killed, full of fear and desperation and loneliness. To shred him, to devour his heart. Tug at his innards, spilling them on the ground.

No. No.

I wrestle again with the instinct of the beast I inhabit. I need the instincts, but only so far, and that is the problem.

Closer, I can see the woman gesturing to the man, the driver, to stop. The meat-redolent soldier. She raises something to her mouth. "Bunker F, entry requested. Ruark five three eight three nine alpha."

In the following silence I come forward, low, taking steps slowly, my breath featherlight. A moving shadow detaching itself from undergrowth.

A square of light appears in front of them, sliding open. Rumbling, squealing. Blast doors rolling back to expose the gullet of the mountain. More soldiers await within.

The guard takes the scrumptious boy inside. I creep forward, for the moment hidden by a sourbush. I stay still, stiffening with inaction.

From down the path, I hear the buzzing of another cart. Inside is another man. Reeking of tobacco.

Quincrux.

Ruark greets him.

MeShreve half wants there to be an embrace between the two. Because wouldn't that be fitting, if she loved him and he loved her and I could deprive them of that? But no. She stands almost at attention, big protrusions of delectable flesh sticking askew. Eating her would be like feasting on the fattest deer at summer's end, pregnant and spilling with extra flesh. The man, not so much. He's got a dry, burnt smell like a tree husked by lightning strike.

"This is unfortunate," Quincrux says.

Ruark dips her head in deference. "The talent itself has incredible potential. The boy, though, was—"

"Imperfect, yes. I know." He lights a burning stick and breathes in the fumes. "The hard ones, the hurt ones, always fare better. The orphans, the degenerates. Those of us who can live in a morally ambiguous reality—" He stops, looks about. His gaze passing over me and moving on. "It's a terrible thing we do, but we must do it. You understand this?"

"Of course. There's never been any doubt in my mind." Her voice is thick, and the Shreve part of me recognizes she's caught up in some fervor, possibly from Quincrux's power, possibly from her personal experience. It would take possessing her to know it all for sure.

"So, we harvest his talent tonight. When will the genetics team be able to start weaponizing it?"

"Not in time for the Maryland mission."

"Of course not. But beyond that, it will be needed, especially if this insomnia epidemic does not end with a successful completion of Orange Team's mission."

"A month? Two?"

He nods.

"Have you thought any more about the issue of the Cannon boy?"

"There's no way to weaponize his talents, I'm afraid. I've *worn* the boy. We are, essentially, the same in ability. We must focus on talents of *proximity*."

"He poses a serious threat to security. He should be harvested for safety's sake."

"No," he says, shaking his head. "No, I need him alive, for now at least. We expended too many resources capturing him and the Graves boy. I am not going to stomach that loss. I am surprised that you, with your—" He pauses, puffs on the cigarette. "Your accounting background, are not more cognizant of that fact. The Graves boy has been improving, correct? Have you reviewed the latest videos of his flight exercises?"

Reluctantly, she says, "Cannon has not had very much time with him, but there was a marked improvement their first session together . . ."

"This is good. We will need him to begin weapons training very soon, once his flying is up to Green Team levels and he can bear Mr. Cannon in tandem flight."

"Employ him?"

Quincrux drags hard on his smoke, expels the fumes into the night air. "What do you think is the purpose of all this? Relaxation? Juvenile rehabilitation? We are making the deadliest soldiers in the world."

"But . . ." Ruark looks over to where Hollis stands between three soldiers, waiting. "You will just accept the Cannon boy in our midst with open arms? He is . . ." Her eyes shift in the sockets, as if searching for something. Her breath quickens. "He is *treacherous*. Nothing you can do will change that. And no secret will be safe."

A long moment of silence between the two humans. I creep forward on padded feet.

"You are correct," Quincrux replies slowly. "The boy is feral. He will always be feral. But I need to make sure he is not out in the world, causing havoc. He is an uncoordinated motion, and I cannot have him affecting my plans. The situation in Maryland must be settled before we will have a resolution to the issue of the Cannon boy."

"Pardon, Director, but I still don't understand that."

"I have told you of Lucius? Our founder?"

"Of course."

"He left himself too open. Do you understand?"

"No, I—"

Quincrux stiffens in ways I'd never be able to see as a human. Heart rate up, temperature up. Thrumming with physical tension.

"Lucius was a mind. *A mind*. These children call us bugfucks. But we are antennae. We are the voice and emissaries of a species."

He takes a step toward her. She recoils, if only a little.

"We are pools of water spreading from an overturned glass." He curses then, in French. I can understand it even suited in this feline flesh. "There are awarenesses beyond ours, do you see? And when the glass is spilled, they will refill the glass. Do you see?"

"No, Director, I'm sorry—"

He passes a hand over his eyes, scouring his face. Exhausted.

"No matter. It is enough for you to know that while Lucius had vacated his body to places unknown, something else—the something in Maryland—inhabited it."

"Oh. My God."

"I think it is only like your god in that it is unknowable. And powerful."

"Director, I only meant—"

He waves his hand. "No matter. No matter. The Cannon boy, we *will* have to deal with him."

"Harvest his genome?"

"Yes. Perhaps one day."

Something in her body language changes. She seems more at ease. More relaxed. Easier prey.

"You are pleased?"

"*Yes*." It's a hiss.

"Still," Quincrux says, musing. Catlike himself. Playing with her. "The impenetrables are very interested in him, and I would be remiss if I didn't consider the implications of that."

"No, he should—"

"Amy. I *made* that boy. He is a wild, uncontrollable force, much like Mr. Negata. But for the moment, he is *my* uncontrollable force. Whatever sort of revenge scenario you have in mind, I require that you forget it. While I dislike probing my subordinates—"

"No! No. Of course you are correct, Director. The Cannon boy will remain at your discretion."

"At my discretion."

He moves away from her, back to the cart he arrived in.

"Meteorology reports a massive storm front moving in," she says. "Orange Team landed at Andrews early this afternoon. They're barracked and will be briefed at 0500 hours regarding the mission. I've sent the latest weather radar to your e-mail and tablet."

"The telecommunications link?"

"It's hot, though the storm front could cause some interference."

"I've just come from my office. I will go to Bunker A and brief the Orange Team." He coughs once and then spits delicately on the ground. "Rally the troops, as it were."

"May I accompany—"

"No. Please tend to the Hollis boy. He is an innocent. And at least we can dispose of him with the mercy he deserves."

I bound forward, fast and silent. There are instincts, and I let them have full sway, claws retracted no more. Red in tooth and claw.

Ruark screams, falling backward. Quincrux lurches sideways, digging inside his suit.

I snatch Ruark's leg, like hooking a trout from a stream, and feel the claws sink deep into flesh. *Deep.*

The blood-fury burbling inside me rises to match her screams. With two great heaves—she is *heavy*—I have her in the scrub brush at the side of the path, outside of the spill of light from the doorway where the soldiers have unslung their weapons and come running. Her wild fists batter my sleek, furred head.

I'm almost at her throat, jaws unhinged and snarling wide, when two sharp punctures of sound and light penetrate me from the side, where Quincrux lies recumbent. Legs spread, gun in hand.

I am stung, mortally. Blood spills out over my perfect killing fangs. I lurch away from the bloody screaming *thing* in the scrub and try to push myself up, but an absolute weakness falls upon me, and I feel tired, sleepy. Vast expanses of pain explode inside me.

I can stay here no more.

With the blood and the screams, I exit.

Rising again.

Into the ether.

FORTY-ONE

Rooftops aren't the best place for a nap. Somewhere, while I've been out in Big Cat World, my body has slumped down the side of the roof and lodged—*thank God!*—on the edge of a dormer. Jack's got both his hands gripped tight to my belt buckle. If it wasn't for Jack, the original packaging Shreve came in would be one big bloody egg frittata fifty feet below.

"What happened?"

The desolation of failure sweeps over me. My tears streak in the mountain air.

"I couldn't stop them. I hijacked a mountain lion . . ."

"You what?"

"I took over a puma, right? I needed to move fast. But I wasn't fast enough."

"You can do that?"

"Shut up. I followed them to the bunker. Bunker F."

"Inside the lion?"

"Yeah. Quincrux and Ruark were talking." My stomach twists, thinking about the reality of washing out. "There's no going home once you're here, Jack."

"What do you mean?"

"If you don't make it, they harvest your genome."

"What?" Outrage pours from him. His own personal Helmholtz. "What does that mean?"

"Quincrux said something about weaponizing our talents."

"You mean, like making a gun that . . . reads people's minds?"

"No." I have to think for a bit, replaying the conversation in my mind. "Quincrux said they couldn't weaponize my talent." Something clicks. A memory. "He said there was a woman twenty years ago who could create a stasis field. And I've heard them mention a few times a stasis bomb. So I think it's only some talents. Only some powers."

"Like Hollis's."

I think about his ability. To speed up the perception of time.

"Yeah. I think that's exactly what they want."

"He was never going to make it here, was he? They were always going to make him wash out."

"I don't know."

"So what now?"

Depression washes over me. The Helmholtz still buzzes. And I'm weak now. "He's gone."

"No. We can do something."

"I'm weak, man. They killed the cat I was in. I lost something when it died."

I feel too worn out to make another trip into the ether. For a while I sob, and it's hard to tell if my tears are for myself, at what I've lost, or if they're for Hollis. *I am you and you are me.* I told him it would be all right. That we would save him. And now he's gone.

Part of my strength is gone maybe. Forever, no, I don't think so. But I'll need time before I can hazard leaving my body again. This is what happened to Quincrux when he first encountered the dragon, I think. He was weakened.

I lever myself up, phantom afterimages of the muzzle fire from Quincrux's gun flashing in my mind's eye. The shots that killed me, taking parts of me with the cat.

"Mom. Vig. Rollie. And now Hollis. The list of people I've failed grows longer every day."

"Stop it!" Jack says. "We're in a goddamned war! People die."

"And we can't stop it."

Jack's face grows grim. His face becomes stern beneath the wild tangle of windblown hair. "They've lost any right to control us."

"They never had any."

The sky is wreathed now in clouds, the stars hidden, and the moon is just a lighter spot in the white blanket above. My fingers and toes are little blocks of ice. Jack guides me down, keeping his hand locked on my belt. It's a much darker journey back down to the patio where our folding chairs sit, and there's a moment, when my foot slips and I look down—see the edge and end of the roof—that my head swims with vertigo.

When I'm steady once more, I say, "It's more complicated than that, Jack. They're working to stop the thing in Maryland. They've sent the Orange Team to stop it."

He purses his lips, thinking. He runs his hand through wild hair.

"They said that?"

"Yes. Remember? They sent them on a mission."

"Yeah."

"They sent them to stop the entity. To stop the insomnia."

Jack begins cursing.

"They'll get what they deserve," I send. "But right now . . . "

"We have to wait."

...

We slip back through the window, into the warmth of the dorm.

"What happened?" Tap asks.

Jack just shakes his head. I'm too hollow to answer.

"You mean—"

"No one here gets out alive," Jack says. "You're in the army for the duration."

"Oh no. Oh shit no. Oh—"

"Shut up," Jack says. "This isn't going to stand." Such confidence from him. I can almost believe it.

The door swings open quickly, and Negata stands in the doorway, framed in light.

Maybe right now they're killing Hollis. Extracting his talent.

I move to stand directly in front of Negata, tears streaming down my cheeks. "You know what they do here, don't you?" I say. "I don't know what's going on in that head of yours, but at some point, they're gonna do something you don't like, maybe. Something in whatever shriveled part of you that cares about what's right and wrong. And when you refuse to do it? They'll harvest *you*. Whatever talent you have, invisibility, soullessness. Whatever. They'll take it for harvest. To *weaponize it*. Do you understand, Mr. Negata?"

I could give a damn if he's a ninja. He can Tase me if he wants.

My throat hurts from crying, stifling the sobs. My head pounds. I hear Jack and Tap breathing behind me. The wind outside whips over the dormers and ratchets into a howl.

Negata stands there for a long while, silhouetted by the lights beyond him in the hall. His hand rests lightly on the doorknob, and he looks like some father putting a child to bed.

"I do understand, Shreve," Negata says, very clearly, in a voice thick with an indefinable accent. "Go to bed. Things will look better in the morning."

FORTY-TWO

Cold rain runs in desultory rivulets down the window. A dark, mottled fog lies heavy on the valley, multiform and ever-shifting. Jack's awake now, sitting on his bed and staring into space, his long arms hanging loose between his legs. I dress. Tap's nowhere to be seen. Hollis is gone. Forever. Once again, it's just me and Jack.

As we make our way down the dorm stairs, I'm thinking about everything that has happened. I don't have a poncho, but Roberto lends me his umbrella on the way out. Jack's sunk deep into a hoodie, hands in his pockets. His face looks like grim murder.

Out and into the rain. It makes frying chicken sounds on the nylon fabric of my umbrella. The extranaturals—huddled under umbrellas and hunched in raincoats and ponchos—stand like muddy wraiths on the assembly field.

Ruark waits for us. She's supported by crutches, and her leg is wrapped in gauze. The pain is clearly etched across her features.

Glancing at Jack, I see a cruel smile growing on his face.

My old pal Davies stands with three more soldiers behind Ruark. Tanzer holds a clipboard, looking extra alert this morning.

No golf carts today, but there's a covered Jeep and three troop transports belching diesel fumes into the mountain air.

For an instant, I'm tempted to possess Davies, raise his rifle and mow down Ruark, Tanzer, and the other soldiers in a hail of furious gunfire. The only thing that stops me is the sight of Negata, staring at me with such intensity I feel frozen in place.

Negata spoke!

Ruark addresses us. "Today, the director wishes to share something with you. One and all." She hobbles forward. A ponchoed guard accompanies her, holding an umbrella over her head, "Red Team, transport one. Green Team, transport two. The rest of you, transport three."

Danielle, Bernard, and Casey stand huddled together, hunched in their rain jackets, hoodies drawn. They move to join us.

Casey looks at me closely. I feel her hand take mine, but when I look down, nothing is there. It's our secret, this invisible touch. There's mist caught in her eyelashes.

What's happened? **she sends.**

Hollis. They took him.

He washed out?

Bernard and Danielle are listening, I know. I gave them this gift. I know when they're dropping some eaves.

There is no washing out.

What do you mean, Shreve? **Bernard's mental voice is just as rich as his physical one.**

No one goes home from this place, **Jack sends.**

So what are these troop transports? **Danielle asks.**

She's scared now, and I don't blame her.

They going to stick us in a concentration camp? Shove us in an oven?

Maybe, **Jack says.**

Bullshit, **Tap sends.** That Ruark is a miser.
They've spent too much money on us just to throw
us away.

The Red Team clambers into the first transport. Ember keeps glancing at Jack, but he's not paying attention to her now. He's focused on us. On Ruark. On justice. Funny, but that's my middle name. But Jack's owning it right now.

Quickly, I tell them what happened last night, what happened to Hollis.

So, he's dead?

We don't know, **Jack responds.** But we're gonna find out.

How?

Casey's mental voice is calm, but I can detect a fury underneath. The outrage is infectious. She squeezes my hand, *hard.* Her invisible arm, it could be deadly, I realize now.

We are all weapons.

Before anyone can respond, Davies raises his rifle and belts out, "You. Stragglers! Get your asses in that transport!" The gun's not pointed directly at me. He's got his finger outside of the trigger guard. But the look on his face makes me think he's just desperate for a reason to shoot.

We climb in the back of the transport. Two rows of extranaturals sitting knee to knee. Davies hauls himself in after us, white-knuckling his rifle, while one of his compadres ties down the canvas opening to the rear of the vehicle. Some shouts and thumps sound from without, and then the rumbling diesel engine clatters and clanks into gear. We all shift and shudder with the movement.

Traveling blind.

When the transport rumbles to a stop, the familiar sound of a blast door opening filters through the canvas covering. A pause and then another short lurch.

They've taken us to a bunker, I send.

Down the length of the car, Bernard nods and glances at me.

That's right, Shreve. It's the bunker they test us in.

How do you know? Danielle asks.

Ladybird, open up your ears. I can hear the rhythm of the echoes. I know the space we're in.

The back flap opens to fluorescent brightness and the stink of exhaust and oil. Davies jumps out, whirls, gestures with the rifle barrel for us to get out as well. In Casey's, Tap's, Danielle's faces, I see the uncertainty and fear mount. Jack just looks furious. He'll go explodey soon, I think.

The soldier bulls fan out to the corners of the room. Ruark is nowhere to be seen, but Negata stands by the large, industrial elevator with Tanzer, who works the bio-scanner and keys in the code. We descend into the belly of the mountain in groups.

In the tight press of bodies, moving in, one of the bulls seems familiar to me, the slope of his shoulders, the shape of his head, but I only catch a glimpse before I'm beyond the motor pool and inside the elevator—featureless except for two posters: ALL POST-HUMANS WORK TOGETHER and a new one featuring a picture of a flyer, one arm out, rocketing through the air. SOAR, it says, and nothing else.

We move as segregated groups down a long, featureless hallway into the gymnasium-like room where, during the testing, Hollis, Galine, and I had to remove the key card from under the bell. The bell, I notice, is hanging high above on the metal ring that Hollis wanted us to use.

Smart kid. Was a smart kid.

Whatever they did to him, I hope it was painless.

On the room's far wall, underneath the high, mirrored windows that look down on the space—those same windows that looked down on Hollis and me during the testing, those same windows that I flew behind to possess Bill Holden and hijack his power—stands a sprawl of massive flat-panel monitors set in an semicircular array. Four technicians clack and peck at keyboards beneath the video-encrusted wall, nerd-chickens pecking at the ground in a high-tech barnyard. The screens remain dark, but in their centers spin luminescent wheels turning over the words *Acquiring Signal*.

And over it all, thrumming and skittering and juddering in the ether, is an immensely powerful Helmholtz field.

When we're all in the room, muttering, murmuring, a door opens and Quincrux enters, leaning slightly on his cane, trailed by Ruark on crutches.

> Don't they make a gimpy pair? **Jack sends.**
>
> I got a sneaky suspicion that you boys are responsible for that, aren't you? **Bernard asks.**
>
> For both, **Jack says.**

The crowd quiets, three hundred people, waiting, breathless. Soldier bulls watch the crowd from the corners of the room, automatic weapons slung over their shoulders, ready to be brought to bear. I feel like a prisoner in a World War II labor camp. But I have to wonder, if Quincrux or Ruark truly ordered them to fire, what would happen? The pure menagerie of genetics on display here, while hidden, could erupt into madness. Chaos. If shoved, these extranaturals will shove back with uncontrolled force.

In here, guns are an effective threat, but beyond that, they're just props. The real weapons are who and what the bulls are aiming at. Us.

And maybe some of the soldiers recognize that. I see fear on some of their faces. Scanning them, I catch the eye of one of the bulls and . . . *stop.*

It's Booth.

Looking older now. Grizzled. The hair at his temples has gone gray. But it is him, I'm sure of it.

He winks at me.

Jack! Booth is here! Booth!

Assistant Warden Horace Booth, esquire. At your service. Never been more glad to see his ugly mug.

How?

I sent a message to him.

How?

You don't want to know. And I don't want to tell.

No, dumbass, Jack sends. I'm sure you used some sort of bugfuckery. But how did he get in here? And as a guard?

I think awhile.

Quincrux infected me with this gift. Quincrux possessed Booth too. I think he's got the same abilities as I have.

So, he stole and lied and . . . And bugfucked his way in here? Jack asks.

Well, yeah.

Jack nods, thinking. He can see it now.

"Is there a problem, Mr. Cannon?" Quincrux's voice comes over the speakers, and he glares at me from where he stands. I have an instant of panic, thinking he's listened to our whole conversation. Thinking on it, I realize it's possible. He's like the father vampire—all of us spawned from him.

I wish now, when I was in the mountain lion, I'd ripped Quincrux to shreds instead of pouncing on Ruark.

I stop, turn toward the front of the room. "Sir, no, sir!" I yell in my best Army of One voice.

He ignores the interruption. The crowd shifts and tries to settle, but it's hard staring down the barrels of so many guns.

Quincrux limps to a center point, a few paces from the nearest extranatural. Away from the bulls and Negata. Away from Ruark. Behind him spans the wall of video screens, searching for the signal. They frame him perfectly.

He's a showman, he is, and wants center stage.

"Inductees, employees," he begins, leaning heavily on the cane. "In every one of your minds there is a question. Why are we here today?"

He lets that draw out. Working the crowd, the old huckster. He gestures at Ruark with the cane tip. Ruark motions to one of the technicians, who fiddles with a gadget that causes the screens to flicker and hiss into static.

"Many of you are aware of the crippling insomnia epidemic that has blighted our nation," he says, slowly walking forward, letting the crowd part a little. "Many of you, your friends and families, might have suffered from it."

The air smells of damp wool and ozone and deodorant. I look at the faces surrounding us. Ember glances from Jack to Quincrux, her eyes questioning, body held loose, at the ready.

Indeed, all of the Red Team seem at ease, yet ready to spring into action. Blackwell appears complacent, chuffing air through his nose. Looking at him, I realize my testicles haven't bothered me all day.

Roberto and Galine look on, faces placid, like still mountain pools. I spy other faces, some familiar, some unknown to me. All gazes are trained on Quincrux. I can't see Booth, but there's a cluster of extranaturals blocking my view of the wall. Many look confused.

How many of these people has Quincrux put the screws to?

Now, positioned directly in the center of the crowd, Quincrux turns around, arms out like some tent-revival preacher, trying to capture gazes in his own. I'd always thought of him as unassuming, but he's gathered to himself a gravitas that goes beyond his average stature and bland exterior. His eyes blaze with the fervor reserved for zealots. Or madmen.

"Today, I will show you your *own power!* I will show you the strength and will of this glorious Society that you've been called to join."

The plasma screens flash *Signal Acquired* and then flicker white, stabilizing.

The television displays thirty frames of video in a single second, maybe more with these plasma screens. Each image gets pushed out of the television screen and hits your eyes in a wave of phosphorescent light, incredibly fast, leaving tracers on your retinas. And there are hundreds of eyes, each one a moist, glistening surface covering an unimaginably greedy hole, desperate for understanding. We shiver with want and inaction.

In the left screen, the camera shows many soldiers with unfamiliar markings on their gear and armor. Full battle rattle. All carrying automatic weapons, at the ready. Except for two who hold a matte-black metal box between them. The box sprouts antennae. The camera wavers, twists to scan first the left and then the right sides of the lawn immediately outside a large gray building, and I realize the camera is mounted to a soldier's helmet. The view stabilizes, and the screen fills with the image of two grunts holding the box while an unencumbered man approaches it in the shadow of the gray building. The building I recognize now.

Scaling paint and streaked with water stains.

The Towson Veterans Hospital.

So the box must be . . . *the stasis bomb.*

In the center panel, an aerial view of Towson Veterans appears, from maybe three hundred meters of height. Too high to be another building. And that suspicion is confirmed when a figure—a flying figure—lances across the screen, bristling with weapons. I have a quick impression of orange, hunter orange. Nothing rhymes with it. Nothing matches it.

The crème de la crème. The Orange Team floats in the Maryland sky. As I watch, the cameraman of the Orange Team moves in relation to the hospital, and more floating members of the Society of Extranaturals hove into view.

I thought I knew what good flying looks like, but these guys are something else. There's two far-off blurs circling the area, four people hovering, laden with weapons and gear. Two more pairs circle each other in what looks to be a perfect, tight figure eight. Tandem fliers. Smooth and precise.

In the third screen there's a tarmac, a military airfield. The camera stares right down the throat of the runway. Support personnel and vehicles scurry about on obscure errands. A man in a gray poncho and navy baseball cap waves two hooded flashlights in semaphore. Looks like Orange Team has air support.

I glance over at Jack, but he's not looking at me; he's staring to his right. He catches my eye and points at Booth. When I pick him out—the crowd has shifted with Quincrux's theatrics—Booth's eyes are rolled back in his head, and he shudders once, body twitching. Closing his eyes.

When he opens them again, I don't need to surf the ether to know he's got a Rider.

> **Something's coming through, Jack!**
> **What?**
> **Booth has a Rider!**

Booth drops his gun with a dull plastic clatter, alerting the soldier next to him that something is up. He moves like a stone statue suddenly imbued with life, pushing the crowd apart. His gaze is fixed on Quincrux.

"Working with the US Armed Forces—and through the diligence of Amy Ruark and her team—we've been able to pinpoint the source of the insomnia epidemic." Quincrux points to one of the smaller flat panels, the one showing a green-yellow map threaded with red. "There, in Maryland! It is there our Orange Team will deal with the threat. Tactically. Watch and know that you too will one day be part of such a magnificent endeavor. This is the next stage for extranaturals. The next stage for humanity."

He pauses. Booth pushes his way closer, just two ranks of people away from Quincrux in the press of extranaturals. Something hangs over us all, a palpable miasma. The air is pregnant with tension, burning with ozone. The ether rasps and buzzes frenetically, painfully.

Quincrux turns to Ruark and says, "Tell them to begin."

Booth steps in front of Quincrux, arm out, pointing.

"Do not. *Do not!* You will wake the sleeper! Do not—" Booth stumbles, shudders, and shakes his head as if waking from some long nightmare. He raises his head, and in a voice more powerful he says, "Hiram, you must not do this."

Soldier bulls push in, rifles raised and aimed at Booth.

Quincrux's torso jerks as if receiving invisible blows. He waves a hand frantically at the bulls. "Lower your weapons!"

I shove my way forward, trying to get nearer. To get closer. To help Booth, maybe. To help the Rider. I don't know.

"Hiram, listen," Booth says in a voice not his own. "This is folly. I alone know what sleeps there. And *it will wake if you do this!*"

"Tase that man! Subdue him!" Ruark yells.

Negata stands still, locked in indecision or isolation, I can't tell.

"Lucius?" Quincrux asks. "Is that you?"

"Murder, Hiram? Harvesting these poor children's talents?" Booth inclines his head in a far more regal aspect than I would have thought possible. His expression is stern, but kind and infinitely sad. "I am so ashamed of you, my pupil—" He seems to be lost in thought. The crowd remains hushed, but I have a crawling sensation on my skin, as if something terrible is about to happen. "I was scattered, Hiram. And I found vessels to seat the shards of my spirit."

"But that is not possible. It's been years."

"Only now, when one of those bits of me came in proximity to you, was I able to center myself. To pour myself wholly into one vestment." Booth—or the spirit of Armstead Lucius

Priest—shakes his head. "To find you have fallen so low. There is much blood on your hands."

Quincrux shivers. A frown comes to his bloodless face. "I only meant to—"

"You have much to atone for."

Ruark barks "Orange Team, engage. I repeat, Orange Team engage!" into a headset she's holding in her hand.

On the screen, the teams begin to move. For a moment everything is still while we watch the Orange Team accompany the troops into the hospital. A young man, whose face I recognize yet can't put a name to, holds out his hand, and the matte-black stasis bomb floats in front of him as they run forward. It's like some macabre psychic game of football, and this is the offense pushing through the defensive line.

The reception area is deserted. They take the stairs up, quickly, each soldier moving as a cog in a greater machine, the stasis bomb floating silently over stairs and down halls.

In the center screen, the flyers of Orange Team come in closer to Towson Veterans Hospital, the building swelling into view. Two super-dupers hang in the air, holding what look like the long, deadly tubes. RPGs.

Another flyer has her hands out, head bowed as if she's sensing something. Abruptly, she spasms and drops from the sky. The crowd gasps. One of the other flyers darts like a bolt after her as she falls. Their bodies join and slow, but they both hit the ground.

"Oh no," someone cries from the audience. Other people moan. I see pained expressions on the other teams' faces—this is their worst fear, falling.

Yet the second camera zooms in closer on a wing of the

hospital even as the farthest right plasma screen displays the plane racing down the runway and lifting off.

Pushing through the crowd, I yell, "You have to call them off—"

Before anyone can stop her, Ruark pulls a firearm from her side and shoots the computer the headset is connected to.

The crowd jumps away from the sound of the shot as one. The faces of the employees, the inductees, show confusion, fear. At any moment, they'll become a mob.

Ruark whips around in a rage, facing Negata. "Restrain the Cannon boy."

Quincrux looks from his lieutenant to Booth and back. "Why did you destroy the transmitter?"

She smiles, fawning. "No recall, you said. Events set into permanent motion."

A terrible expression of confusion and loss illuminates his face, and for the first time, I think, Quincrux truly knows doubt. "Lucius, I—"

"Mr. Negata! Take this boy into custody!"

Negata glances at me and back to Ruark. For an instant I think he might speak—that he might speak and I'll know for sure I wasn't dreaming last night—but he simply shakes his head. Then he turns and, with the lightning grace he's always shown, exits through the door they entered from.

Moving fast, as if he was going for something.

"Negata!" Ruark screams, dropping one of her crutches. She limps after him. Then stops. Gun still in her free hand. She catches my eye, raises the pistol. She points it at me.

Quincrux is lost now, looking into Booth's face. "Lucius, I did what I thought best for the Society—"

"You were always power-mad, Hiram. And now it is your downfall. All of our downfalls. Look there." Booth extends his finger at the screen.

The stasis bomb team makes their way down a dim, tiled hall, past open doors and gurneys, down grimy tile corridors lit with lurid yellow lights. They slow, and two soldiers signal that the team is on target—a chopping motion of the hands. Soundlessly they bound into the hospital room.

The room I remember in my mind's eye.

He's still there, the emaciated bundle of bones wrapped in such paper-thin skin. His eyes are sunken, cheeks withdrawn, the shape of his skeleton easily visible underneath the ragged integument of flesh.

The man on the bed opens his eyes. And they are black—even in the HD video signal coming from the team member, they look as black as oil. Black and roving.

Full of darkness.

"It has awoken," Booth says.

The body of the wasted man—*Armstead Lucius Priest*—rises from his bed, arms cruciform, floating into the air, trailing an IV and tubes. My skin crawls with the sight. But it's more than that. Something is happening in the ether.

The Helmholtz field is gone.

Negata! He's disabled it!

On the screens, the soldiers in the room yell silently to one another, clutching their heads as if in agony. The flying team falls from the sky, the camera plummeting toward the ground and going to static.

In the hospital room, the cameraman drops to his knees and crawls to one of the bomb men. Hands scrabble at the fallen

Orange Team member. He grasps something and manipulates it. The screen goes to static.

"He's triggered the stasis bomb," Quincrux says. The crowd shifts and moans.

Ruark, looking from me to the screen, holsters her weapon and limps from the room, following Negata.

A signal is reestablished, and the aerial cameraman, obviously terribly wounded from his fall, musters the strength to raise his head. The hospital becomes visible once more. The building seems to give a silent shudder. Suddenly, the east end of the building sloughs off a shiver of dust, trembles, and cracks.

It implodes, leaving a perfectly black globe—a bubble— floating in the air, wreathed in smoke.

It rises.

High above, the black globe stops. Small figures rise up to meet it. At first they are indistinct, blurry particles rising from the earth to join with the black thing floating over the Maryland cityscape. Then more particles rise to meet it.

"Oh my God," a girl in the crowd murmurs. "Those are people."

And she's right. The motes are points of flesh, human beings snatched from their lives, their yards, their streets. Rising to meet the globe.

The cameraman isn't hurt so much that he can't bring himself into focus. He centers his gaze upon the globe. I can't imagine the strength he (or she, I don't know) must have. With a decided waver, he shoves off the ground and lifts into the air. Flying again.

There are cheers from the crowd. Until the view stabilizes.

Closer now. Hundreds of people rising to join the globe. Thousands of human bodies. The surface of the globe crawls with flesh, a jumbled collage of limbs, arms, legs, torsos, heads. And more flying to join it. It's a sun gathering star stuff to itself. It's a black hole that exerts its pull only on the flesh of human-kind. Thousands upon thousands of people rise to become one with the mass of flesh. They writhe. They squirm.

And in the ether, through it, I feel violent emanations rippling outward from the east.

And I know.

They are all alive. Each person. Man, woman, child. The thing inside the stasis field looks out upon our world with a hundred thousand eyes, each one sightless, each mouth howling in silent agony at the forced collective. It surges, this living star made from human flesh. It pulses. It throbs.

The visual on the screen wavers and then tumbles, falling into the terrible writhing flesh. Fluid and monstrous and reduced to some protoplasmic essence. The opposite of the ether. The ether of meat.

When the images stabilizes again, it shows only a seething mass of mindless, sightless body parts. A planetscape of agony.

I hear people retching in the crowd and smell their vomit. There's sobbing and dreadful screeching hysteria, but mostly stunned silence. The guards, many of them pale and watching the crowd nervously due to the emotions the telepaths broadcast, stagger toward the exits. Employees and inductees clutch each other, terrified by their own inaction in the face of such horror.

"Look!" Someone cries. And I realize it's Ember's voice. "The plane!"

On the last screen, the land races beneath the jet—it moves tremendously fast. A fighter jet, I'm sure now. Water, bays, neighborhoods, open expanses of bays again, all race beneath it.

The *thing*—the sun made from human misery and the flesh of humankind—hoves into view. But the plane, shuddering, lurches and suddenly tumbles. The screen shows earth, sky. Earth, sky, earth, sky, *earthskyearthskyearthsky*. Wheeling again and again. The screen goes dark.

Silence.

But in the ether, one trumpeting message howled from a thousand mouths comes through distinct and terrible: *Worship us, for we are made of your flesh. Worship us.*

"It has awoken," Booth says, shuddering, and he slumps to the ground.

Quincrux, crying, sags to the floor, holding Booth's head. "I'm sorry, Lucius. I'm sorry."

Ruark fled, Negata gone, Quincrux lost to remorse. Booth unconscious. There is no one left except me to say what needs to be said.

"Go, all of you. Go to your rooms. We will figure out what to do," I say.

They look at me with open hostility.

It's one thing to go out into the ether and settle upon the unaware, lighting the match flames of their minds, bringing sleep. It is a wholly different proposition doing that to a collective of extranaturals, some of them strong bugfucks. But they are alarmed and distracted, and I am stronger. I am large, I contain multitudes.

I settle on them like a mist, a thought. A single thought, to leave. To go back to where they feel safe and wait there.

Many shake their heads, blinking. Many nod and file out, slowly. It's hushed, the sound of them, just the swishing of damp clothing and the soft breathing of the stricken. In the end, they leave.

Jack and I are left alone with Quincrux and Booth.

FORTY-THREE

Quincrux's sobbing quiets. He's lost in his own realm of pain and remorse. I shouldn't feel this way—for everything he's done to me, for everyone he's killed—but I feel sadness for him. Before he was formidable. Now he has my pity.

Booth stirs.

"If there's one thing I know, Shreve," he says, lifting himself onto one arm, "you're gonna be the center of a shitload of trouble." And it's the old Booth. My Booth.

"You can't prove anything, *Assistant* Warden." I smile at him. "Do you even remember anything? How the hell did you get here?"

"I learned I could change my appearance."

"Your appearance was always important to you."

He smiles, but there's pain in it. "True. But after Quincrux—after you—that kinda turned inward, I think. And I discovered I could make myself appear as whatever I wanted. I think I went a little crazy, stopped going to work. They suspended me."

"No," I say. It's hard to believe that Booth won't be stomping the tiles at Casimir anymore.

"Yeah. And then, I got this phone call. Just a few days ago. A soldier. He didn't know why he was calling, but he was distressed. And he gave me your message."

"Is the Rider, uh, I mean is Lucius still in there with you?"

"Oh, yeah. He's here. Waiting. Watching."

"So he was the Riders? All of them?"

"Yes. Scattered among all of them. Until he came in contact with Quincrux. That shorted him out, I think. Collected him. Suddenly, it was like a flood in my mind," he taps his temple. "And I couldn't keep him out."

I nod, remembering fighting off the Witch. Fighting off Quincrux. "And now?"

"Now?"

"What do we do? That thing's killing people," Jack says, joining the conversation.

"I don't think it's killing them," he says, looking at Jack. Taking in Jack's height and the changes puberty has brought to his old ward. He nods, turns his gaze back to me. "I can feel it too, you know?"

"I thought you could, back at Casimir. I tried to talk to you about it."

"I remember that. My momma always said denial ain't just a river in Egypt."

I laugh, and he shifts his body, trying to rise. Jack moves to help him.

"So what do we do now? Everything's gone to hell."

From the door behind us I hear Ruark say, "I know what we're going to do."

Before I turn, I already know what I'm going to see. She's holding her gun in one steady hand. A cold fury making her face look immobile and waxen.

She's got the gun on me.

"We have a whole arsenal of weaponized talent. We have an

army. We will make war with that—that *thing*."

"Put down the gun, miss," Booth says, holding up his hands. "We aren't gonna hurt you."

She points the gun at Booth.

"Bullshit, I'm not," I say, but as I do, the gun swings back to me. Fast.

"I can shoot you, Cannon, before you can get to me. Before you can get in my head."

"Doubtful."

"Don't test me."

It comes down to this. To give up my body to save others. Now that the moment is on me, it seems like this is the movement my whole life has had, toward this choice.

I am about to slip into the ether—and maybe she can read it on my face. She takes two quick steps forward, but not toward me. Toward Booth.

"Maybe you don't care about yourself. You care about him," she says, pointing the pistol at Booth's chest, point-blank.

I freeze. I can still escape into the ether, but what happens next happens too fast for even me.

Quincrux, eyes streaming and face swollen, rises from where he'd lain, dissolute, on the floor. "You will not!" he cries, grappling for Ruark's arm.

The gun discharges, incredibly loud in the big, empty room without the baffling of bodies to absorb the sound.

"*You will not!*" Quincrux screams.

"Shreve! Get down!" Jack yells. We've done this dance before.

I drop to the ground—catching a glimpse of Jack with his hand outstretched and fingers splayed—and both Quincrux and Ruark are lifted off their feet to rocket away and hit the plasma screens with an explosive crunch and a flurry of sparks and billows of noxious smoke.

I scramble up and race to Booth. He's holding his chest.

"Damn," he says. "Damn, boy. Always in trouble, ain't you?"

"Booth—"

"Shut up, boy. *He wants to talk.*"

"Booth, don't die."

His eyes roll back in his head, but it isn't in death throes, not yet. When his eyes open again, someone else stares out.

"Shreveport," the voice says. "Justice."

"Yes. I'm here."

"Bring Hiram to me. Bring him to me. I must have the right . . . *proximity.*"

That word again. I nod, understanding. "Can you save Booth too?"

"No, he will be lost. I am sorry, child."

"Then no deal."

Booth's face looks confused. "You must. The evil we have loosed upon the world . . . it must be stopped."

"Not without Booth."

"You are strong, child. I have watched you of old," he says, and then he nods Booth's head in acquiescence. "I will save what of him I can. But you must hurry!"

I jump up. Jack is standing a few paces away, eyes wide, staring at Quincrux and Ruark and the ruined screens, looking amazed that the destruction came from him. Everything old becomes new again.

"Jack, help me get Quincrux over here."

I run to the wreckage. Quincrux bleeds from many gashes, and I feel his neck—strong pulse. Ruark is inert as a sack of flour.

We hook Quincrux under the arms and drag him to where Booth lies. As gently as we can, we place his body close enough for Booth to touch.

"That is well," Booth says and reaches out with a hand and brushes Quincrux's cheek.

It would be wholly unremarkable if I were watching it only with my eyes. But in the ether, that motion blooms with an eruption of color in the space/not space, like dye dropped into a vase of water. Blossoms of the shibboleth spill outward to coalesce and contract. And then it is gone.

Booth's body shudders and stills. He is dead.

Quincrux stirs.

I allow myself tears.

Tears for all of us.

FORTY-FOUR

In the morning, the rain has changed over to a hard, remorseless sleet. The fog twines and twists and roils about, wreathing the ground like a shroud. The campus takes on a muddy, treacherous demeanor, and from where we wait on the assembly field, I can make out many people slipping and falling on their way down the hill.

The man who once was Hiram Quincrux waits for them. He looks out on the gathered souls and says, "My name is Armstead Lucius Priest. I created this home, this *society*, for all of you."

He continues speaking. We will go to war with the entity. The collective flesh that wants only more flesh to join it. To conform to its design. We will take the fight to it. How? We'll learn that in the coming days. We are strong, and it has only just awoken.

Slowly, one by one, the crowd begins to cheer.

•••

I see someone standing off to the side, in the lee of a tree, shadowed and silent.

I leave Quincrux—it will take a long while for me to think of him as Priest—and push my way through the gathered crowd out into the sleet. Slipping, wheeling, I approach the man.

"Thank you, Mr. Negata."

He blinks and then raises his shoulders fractionally, lets them fall.

"I did nothing," he says. Each word separate, like bubbles rising in oil.

"Well, I appreciate what you didn't do. Namely, killing me."

He shakes his head. If I didn't know any better, I'd think he was frowning. "I do not kill."

"I'm glad of that." He remains silent, so I say, "Will you stay?"

"For the moment."

"We need you, I think."

He nods, noncommittal.

THE
TWELVE-
FINGERED
BOY
TRILOGY

THE TWELVE-FINGERED BOY
2013

THE SHIBBOLETH
2014

THE CONFORMITY
2015

ACKNOWLEDGMENTS

Once again, I'd like to thank the usual suspects: my wife for her constant support; my kids for their ceaseless queries as to when, exactly, will they be old enough to read the adventures of Shreve and Jack; my dogs for being cute and fluffy and always happy to see me; my agent for her diligence and patience with me; my editor Andrew Karre for having the sense to acquire *The Twelve-Fingered Boy* and then, when it turned out that my first title for this book—*Incarcerado*—would not work, providing me with the truly perfect title, the title it was meant to have, *The Shibboleth*.

I'd like to add someone to that list of regulars, Amy Fitzgerald, my copy editor at Carolrhoda Lab, who brought a level of fun to her insightful comments during the massaging and polishing of this manuscript for publication.

I'd like to thank all the folks at Lerner Publishing Group for their continued enthusiasm and support. Many thanks to Lindsay Matvick, a wonderful guide to publicity and tireless proponent of my work, and Laura Rinne, who designed both the cover for this book and the *The Twelve-Fingered Boy*. I can't wait to see what Laura's got planned for *The Conformity*.

Many thanks to Dr. Beth Storm Rule for providing me with information regarding the operation of mental wards and the treatment of the adolescent committed. When I described my plot, and the ubiquitous presence of Tasers, she told me that would never fly in a real ward. I responded by saying, "Luckily, my job entails lying for profit."

Any and all errors regarding the mental health system (or anything else) depicted in this book are solely my responsibility.

ABOUT THE AUTHOR

John Hornor Jacobs is the author of several novels, including *The Twelve-Fingered Boy*. He lives with his family in Arkansas. Visit him online at www.johnhornorjacobs.com.